SAVAGE SEDUCTION

The brilliant afternoon sunlight that illuminated the walls of the canyon was blocked by the brim of Luke's hat as he bent his head toward her. Her protests were muffled as his mouth captured hers. When at last he broke the kiss, Promise was breathless and furious, and she thrust him away with her small fists clenched, crying, "No!"

Her vehement tone amused him. "No? You seem to forget, we made a deal! My silence for your . . . company. Wasn't that the way it went?"

She gasped. "What kind of man are you to expect me to keep a promise like that?"

He gave her a long, enigmatic look. "The kind of man you shouldn't play games with, honey!" he muttered as he pressed her hungrily to him.

Despite her anger, despite all the bitter vows she had made, Promise felt her knees grow weak under the ardor of his lips and the caresses of his warm hands. As he lowered his head to kiss her throat, she realized dimly that there would be no stopping him, as there had been none last night. Luke Steele was a man who was used to having his own way in all things. If he wanted her, he would have her!

PASSION'S BETRAYAL

PENELOPE NERI

ZEBRA BOOKS
KENSINGTON PUBLISHING CORP.

ZEBRA BOOKS

are published by

Kensington Publishing Corp.
475 Park Avenue South
New York, NY 10016

First printing: May 1985

Printed in the United States of America

The desert wind sings a lonely song,
Of a hurtin' man whose woman's gone.
Too late, he learned
That he'd done her wrong,
And he rides the wind
To find her . . .

Chapter One

The lonely howl of a coyote's serenade to the silvery full moon sent shivers down Promise's spine. Way off in the timbered uplands of the mighty Rockies, another coyote answered.

The night wind rippled through the aspens and stirred the weighty boughs of the blue spruce. The leaves upon the bushes danced like—like feathers, she thought, wetting her dry lips with her tongue. Her heart began to throb like a small, insistent drum. Had it really been a coyote that she had heard, or was it Indians, signaling to each other? Pa had said once that they did such things, although Mama had scolded him and said that the mountain Utes were friendly folk, and that they wanted peace with the miners and settlers who had come into the Colorado territory in search of gold and new lives. But, she thought, biting her lower lip, you could never trust Indians, not really, whatever they said.

She cuddled closer into the lap of the burly man who sat cross-legged before the crackling campfire, curling herself into a tight ball against his chest.

"Scared, *mavourneen?*" he asked, his brogue thick and a little slurred from the liquor. "Ah, there's no need for ye t'be scared, baby girl. Your pa's here, he is, an' he'll

7

protect ye from the hounds o'Hell themselves if need be!" He bussed her fair head and hugged her more tightly.

"I know it, Pa," Promise murmured, fingering the seamed leather of her father's vest. Hadn't he always looked out for her? Beneath her head, she could hear the strong, steady beat of his heart. His broad chest was rock hard. His arms about her were strong and comforting. He'd take care of her, come what may, she thought happily.

Patrick O'Rourke chuckled. "Ah, d'ye hear that, Mary? She knows I'll take care o'her, th' little darlin'! The blind faith of a child—oh, 'tis a wondrous thing, a wondrous thing indeed!"

Mary O'Rourke snorted. "It is indeed—when it is not misplaced! Where were you until sundown, that's what I'd like to know? Where was your protection then? Leaving us alone here in the wilderness—why, anything could have happened! And for what? Gambling and liquor, that's what!" Her handsome face puckered up with distaste. "I'll be glad when we're over the Rockies and have left these mining camps behind. They're nothing but dirty tent cities filled with greedy, desperate men and—and loose women!"

"Psshaw! Enough of your blatherin', woman! When I tell ye what I was about, ye'll change your tune soon enough, and 'twill be a merry tune you'll be after singin', my lovely Mary!" He winked across the fire at his wife before returning his attention to his small daughter nestled in his lap. Though she'd said she knew he would take care of her, she still trembled ever so slightly in his arms, like a wee, frightened bird. A story would put a stop to her trembling, take her mind off her fears, Patrick

8

decided. She loved a story, did little Promise. He ignored the sour looks his wife was giving him and tilted Promise's face by the chin so that she looked up at him.

"Say, *mavourneen*, did I ever tell ye the story of Squire Harvey, and the fine dappled mare that I sold him back in Killarney?"

"No, Pa, you never did!" fibbed Promise. In truth, she had heard the tale perhaps twenty times in her short young life, but she wanted to hear it again.

"Well," her father began in the deep, bantering tone he reserved for his storytelling, "that mare was the prettiest little beast ye ever did see! She was as smart and dainty as yerself, Promise, me darlin', aye, smarter than any other four-footed creature that God ever put upon this earth—and a deal smarter than most of his two-footed ones!

"Squire Harvey was an Englishman with an eye for horseflesh, and he wanted that wee mare something terrible, he did. Now, me and me mother and father and all me little brothers and sisters had fallen on hard times, and there was only a wee bit o'food left in our cottage. The squire comes struttin' up to our place and he says t'me, 'Paddy,' he says, 'you'd best sell me the mare and be done with it. I'll give ye a fair price, and the money'll put food on your table.' Well, I didn't want t'sell my little Silky, but I didn't have much choice in the matter. I let her go with the squire and thanked him for his money. Little Silky bucked and tugged at her bridle, and her whinnyin' and carryin' on were tellin' me as plain as day that she didn't want to go. The sound of it fairly broke my heart in two! I went and hid until I was certain the squire had taken her away to his fine house, over ten miles away. Oh, it was a sad, sad day for your pa, believe me!"

"And then what happened?" Promise asked breathlessly.

"Well, the very next mornin' I went out t'the barn to milk our cow, and there was my Silky, prancin' about the meadow just as spry as you please, like she'd never left. Later that day the squire came back and, boyo, was the man like a cat with its tail tied! I swear, darlin', I was afraid he'd have himself a fit, I was, and drop down dead right there on the spot! 'Paddy,' he bellows at me, 'you stole that horse back from me, didn't ye?' O'course, I told him I'd done no such thing, and I caught Silky for him and watched while he took her away again. But do ye know what I saw the very next mornin'?"

"Silky'd come home again!" Promise supplied triumphantly.

"Ah, t'be sure, 'tis right you are, my clever chick!" Patrick O'Rourke agreed, letting out a rich, merry burst of laughter and hugging his daughter. "Now, I didn't dare let Squire Harvey find his mare back in our meadow again, so I took her down to our neighbor Liam's place and asked him t'hide her for me. He said that he would, and so we rubbed Silky's gray coat all over with boot blacking and kept her in Liam's stable. When Squire Harvey came thunderin' down to find his wee mare, he found only your humble father, milkin' our old cow! O'course, he came right out, blunt as ye please, an' accused me t'my face of stealin' her back from him. I told him he could go ahead and look for her, an' he did. But o'course, he didn't find my Silky, seein' as how she was at Liam's! He called the Irish no-good horse thieves, and more it wouldn't be nice t'mention before you and your mother, and rode off to look for her. As far as I know, he's still lookin'!

10

"Soon, the money the squire had paid us for the mare ran out, what with ten small mouths to feed. Me father told me I'd have t'get Silky back from Liam and take her t'the Horse Fair an' sell her again. So I did. The man that bought her lived fifteen miles away in the other direction from our little cottage, but do ye know what I found in our meadow the very next mornin'?"

"Silky?" Promise crowed, giggling.

"Aye, little Silky!" Patrick agreed, tousling her fair braids. "In all, I sold that clever beast seven times, and seven times she came back home t'me. Once, she'd been bred to a fine stallion before she ran away, and we got ourselves a handsome colt inter the bargain." He grinned. "A bit like interest on our investment, so t'speak!" He reached beside him and drew out a walking stick of polished wood. The handle was shaped like a horse's head, with a band of silver about the neck. "Ah, little Silky!" O'Rourke murmured. "She answered our problems more than once, she did." He eyed his daughter earnestly and tapped the walking stick handle with his finger. "Happen she'll do so again . . ." He hugged his daughter and laughed.

Mary O'Rourke clucked her disapproval. "Shame on you, Patrick, filling the girl's head with your wild stories! Why, what you did with that horse was stealing, whatever you may choose to call it! Promise, it's way past time you were in bed. Into the wagon with you, child!"

"Aw, but Ma—"

"No 'buts,' Promise. I said 'bed' and I meant it."

"Look! Will ye look up there, the two o'ye! Look, *mavourneen*!" Patrick suddenly exclaimed, pointing between the treetops high above them.

Promise looked up, her child's face rapt with delight, her wide green eyes shining as, through the ebony sky

11

above, a single bright star fell to earth. In its wake it trailed a blazing tail of silver fire. The night sky lightened momentarily with its passage to a deep blue, then became dark once more.

Patrick looked down into his daughter's face and saw that the magic of that fleeting moment was still with her. Her eyes were squeezed tightly shut now, and a smile teased the corners of her mouth as she silently mouthed something.

Patrick grinned and touched her freckled nose with his fingertip. "Well? Were ye in time, darlin'? Did ye make your wish before it fell?"

Eyes dancing with excitement, she confided breathlessly, "Aye, I did! I wished that—"

"Shush! Shush!" her father cautioned, laying a stubby finger across her little mouth. "If ye tell it," he warned in a low, conspiratorial tone, "it will never come true!"

"An' to make it come true, you must wish real, real hard, right Pa?"

"Aye, that's it, little darlin'!" her father agreed solemnly. He tugged one of her untidy braids. "Did ye wish *real* hard?"

She nodded. "Ever so!"

He cupped her face in his square hands and kissed her brow. "Then t'bed with ye, chick, as your mother said. God bless ye an' make all your wishes come true!"

She kissed his ruddy cheek, warm from the fire, then reluctantly scrambled off her father's lap. She went to give her mother a dutiful but loving peck on the cheek, hugging her briefly.

"Don't forget to say your prayers, honey," Mary O'Rourke cautioned as Promise, scuffing her boots in the dirt, made her way to the wagon beneath the trees. As she went, she heard her father ask, "Mary, me love, bring your husband the jug, will ye, lass?"

Mary O'Rourke's voice was shrill with her reply. "If it's more liquor you want, Patrick O'Rourke, you can fetch it for yourself! Whiskey and wild tales and wishing on falling stars—is that all you can think of? What about a new pair of boots for your daughter, and a decent dress for me? God knows, this one has seen its day! And what about a place for us all to live? I'm tired of calling that wagon a home! We're little better than—than gypsies, and I've had enough . . ."

The voices raised in anger continued, first one then the other. Mama's was shrill and worried sounding, Promise thought. Pa's was at first low and easy, his brogue slurred and softened with whiskey, but then his voice rose and grew louder, uglier, as his temper built.

Promise snuggled under a blanket in the rear of the painted wagon and covered her ears with her small hands to blot out the harsh sounds. She squeezed her eyes tightly shut. Nevertheless, tears somehow managed to leak out from under her trembling lashes and spill down her face. Fighting! It seemed they were always fighting these days, she thought, rubbing her knuckles in her eyes to staunch the flow of hot tears. Most of the time their quarrels were like this one, with Ma complaining about the money Pa spent on his rare jugs of whiskey, and about how she wanted to settle down. Other times, they were about something else, something Promise didn't understand but figured must have happened a long time ago, perhaps before she was born, since she was ten years old and didn't recall any of it. Something about Ma's father, and how marrying Pa had brought her "down in the world," whatever that meant . . .

Promise didn't much care what it was they fought about. She just wished they wouldn't! She loved them both, though in different ways, and it hurt—it hurt real bad to hear them say ugly, mean things to each other. She wished they were like the parents of the little girls Mama told her stories about: parents who never, ever argued; who lived in beautiful white houses with fine furniture and rode in shiny carriages drawn by spirited, blooded horses; who slept on silk sheets scented with lavender and went to church on Sunday mornings. Their little girls were dressed in lace and stiffly starched pinafores, and their mothers tied wide blue velvet ribbons in their golden curls . . .

As always when she was frightened or angry or upset, Promise escaped into her pretend world, peopled by the characters of Patrick O'Rourke's wild, Irish tales and her mother's rosy reminiscences. In her imagination, she wasn't really the daughter of Patrick O'Rourke, and her father didn't really travel from town to town in his painted wagon, selling bottles of "Wondrous O'Rourke's Indian Elixir—guaranteed to cure all ills that plague the common man." No, sir! She was really Princess Promise Katherine, a fair princess of Ireland, escaping the villainous Squire Harvey with her father, the noble king . . .

She sighed and wriggled her stockinged feet, withdrawing her big toe from the enormous hole that had sprouted in them earlier that day. She was aware now of the pressing need to relieve herself. That meant leaving the warmth and comfort of the wagon and going out again into the cold, spring night with the sound of those angry, raised voices. Perhaps the urge would pass, she decided hopefully, squeezing her little knees tightly together. But

14

it didn't. After a few minutes, she tossed aside the blanket and crawled out of the wagon.

It was cold outside, colder than she'd expected. She wished she'd waited and slipped on her faded calico dress again instead of coming back out here in only her flour sack petticoats. Starlight washed the clearing where they had made camp that night, the stars as frosty and bright as ice chips set in the deep indigo of the night sky. The breeze whispered amongst the cottonwoods and stirred the grass. Promise edged carefully around the shadows at the perimeter of light spilled by the fire, trying to block out the sounds of the furious argument in progress as she passed.

"Ye uppity baggage! Always did think yerself better than the likes o'Patrick O'Rourke, didn't ye? Aye, an' t'be sure, there's many that would agree with ye! But I know better, don't I, me darlin'? I know you weren't always as cold and haughty as you would have everyone believe, eh? O'Rourke were only yer father's hired hand, but he were good enough, even so, t'save ye from disgrace and give yer bastard child his name, weren't he now?"

"Stop it! I won't listen to you!"

"Then don't, Miss High-and-Mighty Haverleigh!" Patrick jeered, tilting his jug and drinking. Whiskey splashed down his vest and hung glistening from his chin. "But listen or not, in your heart you know that I'm right! I love the wee colleen as if she were me own flesh and blood, an' you know it, but—"

"Hush, you drunken fool! Can't you see she's right there!" Mary O'Rourke had swung about and caught sight of her daughter tiptoeing past. "And where are you off to, Miss?" she demanded.

Promise hopped from one foot to the other, a pained

expression on her face. "I got to go, Ma!" she insisted, jerking her head toward the bushes.

Her mother sighed. "Go on with you, then." As Promise disappeared between the bushes, she glowered at her husband. "We'll speak more of this later, Mister O'Rourke, when the child is sleeping."

"Pah!" He angrily waved her away. "Damn ye, woman, go t'bed yerself!" he growled.

They both looked toward the heavy shadows that ringed their camp as the faint jingle of a bit and the soft nicker of a horse carried on the night air. The horse's greeting was answered by their own sorry wagon horses, hobbled beneath the trees.

"Someone's coming!" Patrick hissed.

"I'm not deaf. I hear them," Mary muttered, still angry.

"Take the girl and get into the wagon—hurry now, Mary!" her husband ordered, instantly sobered. He'd be cautious until they found out just who it was riding into their camp. Could be it was another weary traveler, like themselves—and then again, it might be Indians! He reached for the rifle that lay beside him and smartly cracked the barrel as Mary ran toward the bushes in the direction Promise had taken.

In the act of lifting her petticoats, Promise quickly let them fall again as she, too, heard the approaching horse. She peered over the tops of the bushes and saw her mother hurrying toward her. Beyond, the silhouette of a lone rider was sharply etched against the white canvas of their wagon. He was dressed all in black, from the broad brim of the hat he wore pulled down low over his brow, to the pointed toes of his black boots. His silver spurs and the *conchos* that ornamented his vest winked in the light cast by the fire. The horse he rode was as dark as the

16

night that pressed close all around their camp. She saw that her mother had halted in her tracks to turn to look at the stranger. They both heard Patrick offer the man the hospitality of their fire and coffee to warm himself. They saw the stranger shove back the brim of his hat and slowly shake his head.

Patrick O'Rourke's gasp of shock sliced through the darkness like the crack of a whip. "*You!*"

The stranger smiled, and his dark eyes glittered in the firelight. "You seem surprised, O'Rourke? Did you think no one would suspect you? Is that it, you Irish rattlesnake?" he murmured, his voice doubly menacing because of its softness. "Where is it? Hand it over, and that'll be an end to it!"

Patrick wetted his lips. "I—I don't know what you're talkin' about, friend. I swear it on the Blessed Virgin herself!"

"Don't play me for a fool!" the stranger spat. "I want it, and I want it now, before Colter comes to and finds out it's gone. I didn't make the ride out here from Fairplay to go back empty handed!"

Both Promise and her mother heard the click as Patrick cocked the rifle, and gasped as he hurriedly raised it to his shoulder. He squeezed the trigger. There was a deafening explosion. Yellow spurts of fire blazed from the smoking barrel, echoed instantly by a matching burst of fire from the gun that had appeared like magic at the stranger's hip. As if motion were slowed, they saw Patrick torn from his seat and hurtled backward by the impact of the bullet as it tore into his chest. There was a single, short cry from his lips that ended in an awful gurgling sound. A spray of something dark and wet erupted from his vest-front like a miniature geyser. Birds screeched an alarm in their treetop roosts. A cloud of red

17

dust fountained briefly then drifted to the ground, like red smoke in the light of the fire.

Promise came to her senses first. *"Pa!"* she screamed, springing from cover a second too soon for her mother to pluck her back to safety. "Pa! Pa!"

She ran like a small, crazed thing to her father's side, blond pigtails flying, green eyes stunned with shock. Whimpering, she threw herself down beside his body and turned his face to hers.

Already the twinkling blue eyes were opaque and vacant in the flickering light. His expression was one of mild surprise at his own mortality, the eyebrows quirked up, the mouth slightly agape. One of Promise's hands had rested upon his chest as she turned him over. Now she drew that hand away, her mouth moving soundlessly as she began to wipe the bright, frothy, red bubbles of blood that smeared it on her petticoats.

"You'd best take her away from there, ma'am," the stranger, dismounting from his horse, told Mary O'Rourke. "I'm . . . sorry. I didn't mean for it to end this way. He left me no choice by firing first." He absently touched his temple. Blood trickled down from where Patrick O'Rourke's bullet had creased him.

"I know it," Mary whispered, her tone rustling and flat and emotionless. "I—I know it. Come away, Promise, my love," she urged, grasping the little girl by the shoulder. "Come on, honey!"

Promise looked up into the stranger's face. Beneath the shadow of his hat brim, glittering eyes as black as obsidian burned down into her own from the weathered tan of a cruelly handsome face—a face that was all angles and planes in the shadows—a face she would remember until her dying day!

Suddenly, she heard a high-pitched keening, a dreadful

wail of such abject grief and misery it made the hackles on her neck rise in terror. It was several moments before she recognized that the source of that unearthly, awful wailing was herself. As the realization swept through her, so did the sensation of warm liquid splashing down her legs—the final humiliation of a moment that was already indelibly etched upon her child's mind for all time . . .

Chapter Two

Promise stood looking at the wagon, memories of her childhood bombarding her as she ran her finger over the faded paint work on its sides.

How many miles they had traveled in this same wagon, she and her mother and father! How many little towns and settlements they had visited—so many, in fact, she had long since forgotten their names! If she cared to dwell on it hard enough and long enough, the harshness and uncertainty of her life then came back to her in painful clarity. But when she thought about it idly, casually, as she was doing at that moment, the past was gilded by the softening patina of time and the convenient forgetfulness of all childhood memories.

In moments such as this, she recalled only long, dusty trails from one fort to the next on the long road west of California, where Pa had dreamed of settling. She recalled endless miles of desert with the taste of sun and sand and wind burning her throat, and cactuses standing like tapering candles pointing upward to the vast, seemingly endless vault of blue sky above. They'd crossed the rolling prairies of amber grass that rippled like a golden sea, where herds of buffalo made a dark, moving blot of shaggy bodies and dust on the hazy blue of the distant horizon. In winter, they'd shivered through frozen canyons held fast in the fierce grip of Nature's cold fist, over rivers stilled by a crackling coating of ice, and seen the wagon horses straining through the drifts, their breath coming in great clouds of steamy vapor, their feathered hooves frosted with icicles.

With her mind's eye she could see Pa with a bottle of the black elixir in one of his meaty fists, his walking cane with the knobby horse-head carving in the other and hear the rich, rolling brogue of his voice as he extolled its praises. Blue eyes had twinkled merrily beneath a mop of jet black curls and a battered brown derby as he'd cried: "Roll up, roll up, folks, an' get your marvelous O'Rourke's Genuine Indian Elixir here! T'be sure, the recipe was given t'me by an' Indian *shaman* hisself, after yours truly saved his life from a herd of stampedin' buffalo back in '51. 'Twill cure whatever it is ailin' ye, an' that's a fact—be it the rheumatics creakin' yer bones or yer hair fallin' from yer head like a hound in the sheddin' season! How about you, my lovely lady, can I sell ye a pint o'this fine medicine? And what about you, young fellow-me-lad, can ye not see yer way t'takin' a bottle or two off me hands . . . ?"

A smile curved Promise's lips as she stood there, twining one finger in her fall of pump-water straight, cornsilk hair, her green eyes dreamy as she relived the past. The elixir had in truth been only snake oil, a concoction of diluted whiskey flavored with horse liniment and peppermint essence with liver salts thrown in for good measure, for Pa had understood human nature well enough to realize folks put no faith in medicines that tasted good. And as for the recipe being given him by an Indian *shaman*, why, the closest Pa had ever been to any Indians was when they'd stopped at

21

various forts on the way west, and they'd seen Indians and half-bloods and squaw men with their Indian women at the trading posts there. And even then, Pa had given them a wide berth!

But then, as always, another memory rose up before her like some horrible apparition come to haunt her, and she was a child again, staring wide-eyed up into the dark face with the burning dark eyes that belonged to her father's murderer and trying in vain to recall the features shadowed by the brim of a dark hat. She could not. Shock, mingled with grief and time, had in their own fashion been kind to her and had blurred her memories of that night, in part. Though she could recall the awful events of that spring night in the mountains six years ago as if it had happened only yesterday, the features of the stranger who had shot Pa were always veiled, shadowy. *Six years!* Where had they flown?

"Promise?" came a voice.

"Yes, Doctor?"

"Your mother's resting easy now, child. I thought that this might be a good time for us to talk."

"Yes, sir. Could I get you some coffee and a piece of cherry pie?"

"Indeed, coffee would be very welcome, Promise," the portly doctor accepted, following Promise from the rickety barn back to the cabin.

Their cabin consisted of only two rooms—the one in which they sat at a table while Promise poured them enameled tin mugs of steaming black coffee as a black stew kettle bubbled over the fire, and the second room, adjoining, where Promise slept and where her mother now lay sick. Despite the cabin's weathered exterior it was nonetheless cozy inside.

Braided rag rugs softened the rough-planked pine

22

floor, which was cleanly swept. Flour-bag curtains, fresh and starched and neatly pressed, fluttered at the rough-hewn windows like white flags to beckon the golden summer sunlight inside.

While Doctor Plimmer sipped the scalding coffee, he regarded Promise thoughtfully over the rim of the enamel mug, thinking as she moved gracefully about the kitchen that her fair, finely boned beauty was more what he would have expected from the daughter of Swedish immigrants, rather than from the wild, dark comeliness of an Irish colleen.

"What was it you wanted to talk with me about, sir?" she asked hesitantly, not wishing to intrude upon the doctor's thoughts but anxious to hear what he had to say about her mother. "Is Mama worse?"

Doctor Plimmer nodded gravely and set down the mug. He tugged at his drooping white mustache. "I'm afraid she is, child, and in a deal of pain to boot. I've increased the dosage of laudanum to ease it, but . . . it's just a matter of time now, I'm sorry to say. There's nothing more I can do for her, nothing at all." He reached out to steady Promise as she swayed, eyes closed, with the shock of his words. Filled with pity, he saw the sparkle of tears in her vivid green eyes when she finally opened them again.

"How—how much longer?" she finally managed, her voice husky with emotion.

"A few days. Maybe a week—perhaps even as long as a month. But I will not say 'If you're lucky.' It would be more of a blessing—the pain she's in—if it were to be as soon as possible," he said grimly. He'd learned long ago that it was far kinder to be honest than to try to give false hope where there was none to offer.

"I see," she said flatly. Her knuckles were bloodless

from her fierce grip upon the edges of the white wood table. "Thank you for being honest with me, sir."

He nodded, standing and pulling out a chair for her, firmly taking her arm and almost forcing her to sit on it. "Drink your coffee, child," he urged, spooning more sugar into the cup. Her stillness, her almost trancelike quality, concerned him. The news had been even harder on her than he'd expected.

"You've been a good daughter to Mary, Promise." He drew her slim, calloused hands between his own. "You have nothing to reproach yourself for, nothing at all. But it's time now, while your mother's still with you, to decide what you'll do when she has gone. Have you given it any thought?" She shook her head. "Then you should. Do you have any kin we might send word to—anyone at all?"

"Mama—Mama mentioned she had some folks back East, but I reckon there was bad blood between them, 'cos she didn't seem to want to talk about them." She sighed heavily. "No, no one at all. I guess I'll be alone when she's gone."

"And what about marriage for yourself? Have you given any thought to that? Is there any special young man that comes courting?"

She turned her head sharply to look at him, and with relief he saw that her dazed expression was gone. There was a glimmer of wry amusement in her unusual, slanted green eyes now. "Me—wed? No, sir! I don't have any plans in that direction!" she declared emphatically.

"I know it's hard, but give some thought to the future, my dear, won't you? It'll be easier if you have some definite plans," the doctor urged. "And remember, if there's anything I can do, be sure to let me know." He rose and retrieved his black bag from the floor, reaching for his hat on the peg as he left. Promise followed him out onto the rickety porch.

"Thanks for the coffee, Promise. I'll be by again tomorrow to see your Mama."

She nodded. "Thank you, Doctor. Good-bye!"

With a wave, he stepped from the porch and made his way past the pump and across the yard to where his shiny, leather-upholstered buggy waited, a glossy chestnut in the traces.

Through the tossing canopy of leaves and snowy, late apple blossoms that shaded the porch, Promise watched as he flicked the whip over the horse's rump and drove smartly away, leaving in his wake a cloud of dust churned up by the buggy's wheels.

No matter how deeply the doctor's words had affected her, there were still chores to be done after he left. Promise launched into them with almost vicious energy, seeking to smother her fears for her mother in hard work. She swung the wood axe with a will, and chips flew. The pile of kindling grew steadily until there was no wood left to chop. She stacked the firewood in the barn, where it would stay dry, then led Selfish, their milk cow, out into the meadow beyond the white rail fence where she could graze the sweet grass.

After checking to make sure her mother was asleep, Promise found hook and line, hoisted her pa's rifle over her shoulder, and went down to the creek to fish. She carried the rifle for her defense, for there had been several raids on settlers by the Indians in the Colorado Territory over the past few months. Hardly a week passed when there wasn't a report of a wagon train being attacked, or of stock being run off or stolen, and homesteads and ranchers burned out. Folks in Cherry Creek had implored her and her mother to come into town to live until things settled down some, but Mary O'Rourke had flatly refused, insisting that the good Lord would watch over them and see that they came to no harm. Promise knew that although her mother was a God-fearing woman this excuse was only partly true. She was also proud, and going into town would have meant accepting charity from someone, a circumstance more abhorrent to her than any threat of attack from painted savages could ever be.

Bees buzzed drowsily in the tall grass by the creek, and the blue jays chattered as the slender girl approached and rooted in the creek mud for worms to bait her hook. Finding some, she settled herself on a comfortably flat boulder and cast her line into the waters of the creek.

It was hardly more than a trickle now, Promise thought with disgust, unlike the swollen brown monster it had been in May when the creek had flooded farther up its course, close to Denver. The floods had been only the first of natural disasters that year. Weeks later, swarms of grasshoppers had swept across the territory like the Biblical plague of locusts, devastating crops in a green storm and leaving nothing untouched. For many farmers, this had been the final blow, and they had packed up their families and belongings and gone back East, where they had come from. Promise shuddered. For days, grasshoppers had been everywhere—in the milk pail, the laundry, the stew kettle, the butter churn—until it had seemed her flesh crawled even when there were no grasshoppers upon it!

She looked up, hearing the scream of a hawk far above in the bright blue sky, and shaded her eyes against the brilliant light that slanted through the cottonwoods and the willows. Beyond the hawk rose massive Pike's Peak, that mecca of prospectors in the earlier gold-rush days.

26

Mama had told her many times of the droves of people who had flocked to the Rockies, eager to make their fortunes in silver mining. People still came here in great numbers, but for different reasons: tuberculosis sufferers, seeking the crystal clarity of the mountain air in hopes of a cure; Englishmen wanting to pit their woodsmen's skills against the rugged terrain or to try breeding new, hardier strains of cattle. Whatever their original reasons for coming, Promise understood why it was they stayed on long after their initial purpose was accomplished. The beauty of the Rockies—the verdant upland meadows starred with wildflowers, rushing rivers and lofty pines—filled them—and her—with a deep sense of joy at living on the very pulsebeat of life. Here, one could breathe.

She tilted back her head and closed her eyes, feeling the warm sun upon her face. Her cornsilk hair fell in an unadorned golden curtain down her back. Its simple center-parting would have been too severe, perhaps, for many women, yet the simplicity of its natural style only focused attention on her eyes, remarkably beautiful eyes of a clear green hue, that were slightly slanted in shape and accented with curling, dark-gold lashes. Matching golden brows winged gracefully over her eyes, adding to the feline illusion of their unusual shape. High-set cheekbones, softened by golden, tanned flesh with the faint, golden fuzz of a fresh peach imparting a delightfully velvety texture to it, balanced a narrow little nose that seemed far too sophisticated for the girl she was, and the full, sensual mouth, naturally tinted a rosy pink, gave promise of the passionate woman she was yet to be.

As she lolled there, drinking the sunlight through her pores and waiting for the tug on the line that would signal

27

a bite, she thought over what Doc Plimmer had said about making plans for the future. She'd spoken honestly. There was no young man coming courting, though Todd Plimmer, the doctor's wild son, had been pestering her for as long as she could remember, sneaking up on her to steal a kiss or choosing a moment when she was alone to try to press his attentions on her. Her nose wrinkled up in distaste at the thought of Todd. He was as sly as a polecat and had always sniggered at her mother taking in laundry for a living, at their Irish background, and their rustic cabin. As the doctor's son, he considered himself far above the O'Rourkes in every way. He had ideas about the two of them all right, but she'd be willing to bet that marriage wasn't one of them!

After an hour, maybe more, she drew in her line, her face a study in disappointment. Beans, bacon, and stews could get mighty boring after endless weeks of one or the other. Her mouth had watered at the thought of a fresh trout rolled in cornmeal and crisp-fried for a change. But whether it was her mood, and the fished sensed her edginess, or whether they were just too lazy to bite on such a hot, summer's day, she left the creek empty handed and resigned to throwing something into the kettle over the fire yet again.

She was darning, sitting in the chair at her mother's bedside that afternoon, when Henry Crowley came by from the livery stables in town. She set aside her sewing and hurried from the cabin to meet him as he swung heavily down from his massive horse. Beneath the folds of her skirts, her fingers were crossed. Henry, dear Henry, with his ruddy face and whiskers and solid, sturdy build, could prove the answer to her and Mama's immediate problems, for all that he looked more like a Pennsylvania farmer than a knight in shining armor.

"Afternoon, Promise. Fine day, ain't it?" he greeted her.

"It sure is, Henry. I'm real glad you came. The wagon's in here, sir, if you'd care to see it now," she told him, leading the way across the yard to the barn with Henry lumbering along beside her.

"I sure would," Henry agreed, scratching his whiskers. "How's your mama? Sarah tells me she's grown no better these past weeks."

"She's real sick," Promise acknowledged, her eyes darkening to a murky green in her concern. "Doc Plimmer was here to see her earlier. He—he doesn't expect her to be—be with me much longer."

Henry's ruddy face grew solemn. He clicked his teeth in sympathy. "Heck, I'm real sorry to hear that, Promise," he said gravely.

"Thank you, Henry." Promise swung open the barn door and a scrawny chicken flew out, cackling noisily. "Here's Pa's old wagon. What do you think?"

Henry rubbed his whiskers again and circled the wagon, appraising it with knowledgeable eyes. At length, he straightened up, his expression guarded. "It's a mite more antiquated than I'd expected, t'tell the truth," he said finally. "Looks like it were one o'them travelin' wagons the medicine showmen use."

"It was," Promise told him. "My father, my mother, and I used to travel from town to town, selling Pa's elixir. Cured anything from people to chickens and hogs, and then some!" she said, smiling in a way that never touched her eyes and quickly fled her lips. "Is it worth anything to you?"

Henry eyed her doubtfully, opened his mouth to tell her the truth, then remembered what Sarah, his wife, had told him before he left that afternoon, and quickly closed it again. "Well, I reckon I could let you have a few dollars for it," he said hesitantly and named a sum. He winced as he saw the disappointment evident on her face. Her slender shoulders sagged, and she ran a weary hand through her straight, fair hair.

"Is that all?" she asked, trying to keep the desperation from her voice.

The livery owner shifted uncomfortably. He tucked a wisp of straw between his teeth and chewed on it thoughtfully. "We-ell, I could go a dollar or two higher, I reckon, seeing as how we're neighbors," he agreed. He hoped she'd accept his offer, since it was patently obvious she needed the money far more than he needed a rusted wagon with a broken rear axle.

She turned away, her fists clenched under the folds of her skirt. It wasn't nearly enough to pay the lease on the cabin! What, in God's name, was she to do? She had to keep a roof over their heads . . .

She looked at the dilapidated Conestoga basking in the bars of sunlight that fell through the barn door and, without allowing its appearance to be improved in her mind by the fondness of her childhood memories, realized for the first time the awful state it was in. With a sudden, tear-jerking pain, she realized that Henry was trying to be kind. He probably needed this rusty old wagon about as much as he needed a hole in his head. She decided then to accept his offer. After all, she really didn't have much choice.

"Then I guess you've bought yourself a wagon, Mister Crowley," she said lightly, turning to face him and blinking rapidly to avert the tears that threatened to fall. She tried to summon a smile to match the lightness of her words but failed miserably.

Henry cleared his throat, uncomfortable in the

presence of the young woman's obvious desperation. God knew, he'd have done more, if he could, then pay a few dollars over the going price on the broken wagon. But times were hard, and he had his woman, Sarah, and five young'uns to feed . . . He went across the gloomy barn to her side, drawing the silver dollars from the pocket of his shabby dungarees as he went. He pressed them into her palm, folding the cold, slender fingers over the coins. He squeezed her shoulder in a fatherly gesture meant to comfort. "I'll come by for the wagon in a day or two. Ain't no hurry," he muttered, his voice thick with pity. "You keep yer chin up, Miss Promise. Give my regrets to your ma," he added before he hurriedly left.

Promise stood there in the shadows for several minutes after he had gone, fighting to regain her composure. Finally, she held her head high and went back inside the cabin.

Her mother was awake, she saw. Mary O'Rourke's face was gaunt, with huge violet shadows circling her eyes above cheekbones grown overly prominent since the onset of her disease. Her hair had turned from gray-streaked brown to snow white over the past few months. There was little left of the weary but handsome woman she had been. Only the eyes seemed unchanged—large, beautiful eyes that were a mutable hazel color, like the creek water on a fine summer's day when it reflected the green of the trees that overhung its banks. And the hands. Oh, the hands! Promise thought, filled with a sudden hot rush of white anger at the cruelty and injustices of life. Before the sickness, Promise had bewailed the callouses that marred those same hands, and the rough, reddened areas and blisters on the long, elegant fingers caused by washing other people's clothes with so much strong lye soap and bleach day after day.

31

"You've got pretty hands, Mama, if it weren't for the callouses," she'd said one morning as Mary bent over the scrub board in the wash tub. "I'll reckon you could've played the piano, if'n you'd been taught."

Mary had smiled. "I was taught, child, a long, long time ago." She looked at her soapy, reddened hands and grimaced. "I could play a fair tune, too, though I say it myself. Oh, we had parties and balls then—such gay, lively times—with music and dancing and handsome men to whirl us about the floor . . . But that was then, and this is now. Thank the good Lord these two hands look the way they do, Promise. It means there's work coming in, and money, and that means food on the table. Now, enough daydreaming, child! Spit on that flatiron over there and see if it's hot enough yet. If it is, you can start helping your mama by pressing those shirts, if your lessons are all done. . . ."

Promise lifted one of her mother's smooth hands from where they rested slack upon the faded patchwork quilt. How soft they were now, how white—like the polished ivory statues the Chinamen sold in the railroading towns. The veins were pale blue threads, like the delicate veining in a fine piece of marble, and only the faintest pulsing at the wrist betrayed the life lingering within them. Not a callous—not a one! No rough, reddened spots or broken nails as evidence of hard work and proof of vigorous, undaunted life. They were the cool, unblemished hands of a statue. Right now, Promise would have given anything to see that vigor back in her mother.

"Honey—I asked you where you've been?" her mother repeated, a smile hovering about her pale lips.

Promise returned her smile. "I was out in the barn. Seems Henry is needing a wagon, and I thought I'd sell him ours, the rusted old thing. He paid me a fair price for

32

it, too," she added, dropping a kiss on her mother's brow.

"I thought I recognized Henry's horse. It always sounds short of breath." Her hazel eyes twinkled.

"Mama! Shame on you!" Promise scolded. "It isn't nice to tease so about poor Henry. He can't help if it he's—he's a mite on the heavy side." But her stern expression crumpled and she giggled along with her mother. "My, you must be feeling better today," she observed as she plumped her mother's pillows and straightened the bed covers. "Or else Doc Plimmer's been slipping you a jigger or two of whiskey along with the laudanum!"

"Oh, get along with you!" her mother retorted with an amused smile. Yet despite that smile, her hazel eyes held a deep weariness now, a nervous, apprehensive look that signaled the return of the gnawing pain that had been with her more and more often these past days.

Promise recognized the expression and automatically checked the scarred dresser to make sure Doc Plimmer had left a new corked brown bottle of laudanum there to replace the empty one. Relieved, she saw that he had, right next to a chipped jug holding wilted blue columbines that she'd gathered down by the creek for her mother earlier that day. She picked up the jug and carried it from the room with a cheerful, "I'll see to your supper, Mama, and then we'll get you your medicine."

As Promise ladled steaming beef broth into an earthenware bowl from the soup kettle that bubbled over the kitchen fire, she wondered for the hundredth time how she would come up with the money to pay Mister Hollander, the banker, the lease money on the cabin, not to mention the loan she'd made when her mama had first fallen sick. She'd been too busy then nursing her to keep up with the laundering—not that her mother knew about

33

that. Mary wasn't a woman who approved of loans, and so Promise had no intention of her ever finding out. Three days! Three days to come up with ten dollars. She'd never even seen so much money at one time in her life.

After supper, Promise measured out her mother's dosage of laudanum and sat with her after she had taken it, humming softly until Mary's eyelids drooped and the tenseness of her body eased as she drifted into pain-free slumber. It was almost dusk now, she saw, taking her shawl from the peg by the porch door and going outside.

She leaned against the railing, watching the crimson and flame colors of sundown gild the ragged peaks of the Rockies. The fiery hues faded gradually and were replaced by the misty lavenders, violets, and indigos of night. Stars came out one by one like naughty children stealing from their cots to peep at the still and sleeping world below. The crickets set up a reedy, trilling chorus in the tall grass by the gate. Promise smiled. They sure sounded as if they needed greasing tonight, like squeaky wheels. Soon the bullfrogs joined in from down by the creek, their deep notes booming alternately with the crickets' shriller notes. In the distance, closer to town, a dog barked. Promise pulled her shawl more tightly about her. For all that it was July, and the days sometimes hotter than Hades itself, the evenings were inclined to be cool, and the nights downright cold. Yet despite the cold and the lateness of the hour, she knew that even if she went to bed, she wouldn't be able to sleep. She was too filled with fears for their future in the long, lonely, dark hours. The cabin wasn't much, but Mama loved it. She just had to find a way to keep it.

After Pa's death that spring night six years ago, she had watched dry eyed while the stranger who had shot him dug his grave then piled rocks over it to keep the

34

coyotes and wolves away. It seemed only minutes later that there was nothing left of her father except for that tell-tale mound of rocks and a crooked cross of branches that Promise had fashioned herself. Her mother had read from the Bible, and that had been that. When Promise awoke the next morning, Mama had been driving the wagon back into the mining town of Fairplay which they had left the day before. The stranger had gone.

In town, Mama had sold their two wagon horses and most of Pa's belongings, which wasn't much, and excitedly told Promise that they would be taking the stage back east. "Going home," she'd called it. But that had been a dream. Even with the money from the sale of their horses and wagon and Pa's things, Mary learned they didn't have nearly enough to pay for the two of them to take the stagecoach. Her hopes crushed, Ma had bought back the wagon and Promise's favorite horse, Henrietta, from the miner they'd sold them to, harnessed her up once more, and driven them both eastward. They hadn't gone far, but far enough to leave behind the mining towns like Fairplay, with their greedy, desperate men and ugly tent cities. Mary, Promise recalled, had loathed mining towns with a vengeance. The morning they had rolled into Cherry Creek, about eighty miles southeast of Denver, Mary had hauled hard on Henrietta's reins and smiled down into Promise's dirt-streaked face.

"This is it, Promise, honey! Our new home!"

"Is this 'back east'?" Promise had asked, looking about her in disappointment. To her eyes, it hadn't looked much different from what they had passed through in the week's traveling they'd done since the night Pa had been killed.

Mary had thrown back her head and laughed like a

young girl. "No, it isn't back east, child, but it'll do. This is our new home. I'm certain."

"How do you know, Ma?" Promise had asked, screwing up her freckled snub nose. The little town had looked awfully quiet and sleepy, dozing in the sunshine. From the way Mama had been carrying on, she had half expected to see flags waving and bands marching down the main street any moment to welcome them.

"I just know, that's all," her mother had said firmly. "See—way up yonder on that rise? That's a schoolhouse, honey! You'll be able to learn your reading and writing and ciphering a whole lot better there than I've been able to teach you these past years." She ignored Promise's grimace and fierce scowl and carried on. "And do you hear that sound? Church bells ringing on a Sunday morning! Who'd have expected to ever hear that in this wilderness of mountains? I haven't heard bells like those for so long, I can't remember when . . . Straighten your shoulders, Promise Katherine O'Rourke. A lady doesn't hunch up that way. And wipe that dirt from your cheeks, child, do, and tie your bonnet strings. We want to make a good impression on our new neighbors, don't we? Smile, now, honey!"

"I reckon so," Promise had agreed doubtfully.

Her mother had smiled and tucked a stray strand of her daughter's fine, fair hair tidily inside the ugly, worn bonnet that framed her face. "I'd say we're settling down not a day too soon. You're starting to sound more like a frontiersman every day! 'Reckon so,' indeed! Get up there, Henrietta!"

And so it was that they had come to Cherry Creek, population seventy-four souls at that time, a town that the Colorado mining boom of '58 had given birth to, then left on the doorstep of the Rockies like a motherless

child, when the gravel beds of the creek had failed to
"raise color"—the color being the yellow gleam of gold.
Disappointed would-be miners, all eager participants in
the gold rush, whose wagons had optimistically borne the
legend "Pikes Peak or Bust!" on their journey west, had
left Cherry Creek and pushed on by the hundreds to the
overcrowded mining camps of Denver, formerly named
Auraria. The few that remained found the air in-
toxicatingly pure. The scenery—deeply wooded canyons, lush mountain meadows, soaring rock formations,
and virgin forests—was breathtaking and teeming with
game such as elk and deer. The mountain Utes were
friendly and their chiefs anxious to see that they
remained that way and kept peace with the settlers. The
newcomers sent for their wives and children, chopped
timber and built cabins of rough-hewn logs, raised first a
church and then a school, and took up the new threads of
their lives. Cherry Creek, the motherless child, had been
officially adopted.

Ma—or Mama, as Mary had insisted little Promise call
her after her pa's death—had taken in laundry from the
owner of the Cherry Creek boarding house and from any
single men that needed their wash done for them. It was
from the owner of the rooming house, Arthur Morgan,
that they'd heard of the two-room cabin a mile or so
outside of town. The lease had been more than Mary had
anticipated, and she'd grimly realized she'd have to wash
scores of shirts to keep her daughter and herself fed and
clothed and with a roof over their heads. Nevertheless,
they'd ridden out to look at the place, and Promise's
mother had decided it was worth breaking her back at a
scrubboard all day for them to have a home, a proper
home.

"Oh, honey," she'd exclaimed the day they had moved

their meager belongings in, "do you realize that this is the first home I've had, since I wed your father, that wasn't on wheels!"

"Don't you miss Pa, Mama?" Promise had asked suddenly, her own thoughts on a different track.

Mary had knelt down beside her. "Why, of course I do. He—he was a fine man in many ways, though maybe a bit wild in others. Sure, I miss him, child. I miss his great, rolling laughter, and his tall stories, and his grand, wild dreams—"

"Did you love him, Mama?"

"What a question!" Mary had exclaimed. "I married him, didn't I, so I must have, don't you think, Miss?"

Promise had shrugged. "I guess so." Whatever Mama said, she sure didn't seem to be hurting inside the way that Promise was hurting. Promise had shrugged off her concerns and turned her attention to the cabin.

The log walls had long since turned silvery gray with the weather and time. There was a narrow window in each of the two rooms, a porch with a railing, a barn off to one side, and a root cellar out back. An old apple tree grew by the porch steps, and Promise had figured the bottom branches would serve well to hold a rope for swinging. A rickety white rail fence enclosed the acre parcel of land, which was overgrown now but looked as if at one point it had been divided into vegetable patches. She left her mother exclaiming over wild berry bushes and wild onions and wild beans, and went exploring.

Beyond the fence stretched a grassy, rolling meadow dotted with wildflowers. Beyond that, cottonwoods and aspens and alders huddled close to the Cherry Creek that gave the township its name. To the west, beyond the foothills of the great Rocky Mountains, rose the jagged red teeth of the mountains themselves, still capped with snow in that month of April. Filled with awe, Promise had wondered that first day if sometime, when she wasn't looking very carefully, those mountains might just topple over and squash her and her mama and their little cabin flat. They hadn't, however, and as the years flew by, Promise had almost forgotten that she had ever childishly fancied they would . . .

It had grown cold now, and Promise left her spot at the porch railing and went inside the cabin. She undressed and slipped on a warm, flannel nightgown, blew out the candle, and quickly crawled into bed beside her mother.

"Good night, honey," Mary whispered, her voice slurred with sleep and laudanum.

"Good night, Mama. Sleep tight," Promise whispered back.

In the morning, she'd go into town and talk to Mister Hollander at the bank, she decided. He'd been very sympathetic the last time. There wasn't any reason he might be not be so again.

Chapter Three

It was a very jittery Promise O'Rourke who presented herself before the banker, Matt Hollander, the next morning.

In his office, she perched on the chair he offered her like a bird about to take flight, nervously toying with the worn strings on her bonnet or the knotted ends of her shawl, while the stocky man sat down on the opposite side of the desk and laboriously went through the ritual of lighting up a Spanish cigar. The tick of the clock on the wall and the puff and smack of Hollander's fleshy lips as he got the cigar started seemed overly loud, and Promise was filled with the wild urge to giggle, an urge which she rightly attributed to the shaky state of her nerves.

"Well, Miss O'Rourke—Promise—what can I do for you today?" Hollander asked at length. As he awaited her reply, he lolled back in his chair, watching with obvious satisfaction the spiral of fragrant blue smoke as it rose to the ceiling.

Promise moistened her lips with her tongue. "I've come about the lease money, Mister Hollander. You see, there isn't any way I can get the money by Friday," she said bluntly. There was no sense in trying to put it more delicately. Whichever way she chose to say it, the facts remained the same. She opened the drawstring of her small changepurse and emptied the contents onto the surface of the polished, cherry-wood desk. "That's all I've been able to come up with, sir. I—I was sort of hoping you could see your way to giving us another extension." She looked down at her lap, her face flaming. For all that she was poor, she was proud, too. It went against that proud grain to ask for charity.

A faint smile curled the banker's fleshy lips momentarily as he looked at her bowed, fair head, with its straight ribbons of corn-silk-fair hair escaping the ugly calico bonnet and streaming down past the soft swell of her ripe young breasts. A thick downsweep of dark-blond lashes hid her sassy green eyes. The innocence of her soft, pink mouth, tilted down now in an anxious pout, had never known a man's passionate kiss, he'd wager. He leaned back in his chair, stuck his cigar into the corner of his mouth, and brought his hands together on his ample belly, stubby fingertips touching.

"I'm real sorry to hear that, Promise," he said silkily. "I was hoping you'd come here to tell me that your mama was herself again. It's a shame, a real shame." He leaned forward and poked the small pile of silver coins on the desk top. "This the best you could do, you say?" he asked, his blue-eyed gaze feasting on her pale, finely boned face. "Seems to me a real clever young woman like yourself could have done better, what with an ailing mother and all . . . ?" His eyebrows rose inquiringly.

Promise's chin jerked up at the insinuation in his tone and his words. "Just exactly what do you mean by that, Mister Hollander?" she demanded.

"What I say, Promise. What I say," he said softly. He stood and came around the desk, sitting on it beside her. She could smell the cigar smoke on him and the oily

41

perfume of the grease he'd used to slick down his dark hair and mustache. "Pretty girl like you shouldn't have had too much trouble coming up with ten dollars," he continued. He chuckled. "I think you know real well what I mean!"

Heart thudding, Promise quickly looked down again to her lap. Her mouth felt suddenly parched, her tongue too big and clumsy to fit inside it. Where, she wondered, shocked, was the genial, sympathetic banker she'd spoken with only three months before? She felt bewildered by his sudden turnabout. Was he getting at what he seemed to be getting at, that slimy, no-good barrel of lard? Her fingers itched to slap his face, but right now she didn't dare. In Hollander's meaty paws lay the future of their cabin.

"Maybe I could have done better," she admitted, deliberately misunderstanding the not-too-subtle innuendo in his tone and words. "But my mama's real sick. I've been too busy nursing her to keep up with the laundering and such." She looked up into his face hopefully, her expression pleading. "If you could see your way to giving us an extension, I'd work real hard, honest I would! I'll—"

"Now, now," he cut in, leaning down and taking one of her slender, wash-roughened hands in his own, "that's not what I had in mind, Promise, and you know it. There ain't no need for you to break that pretty back over a washtub, not if you see things my way. I'm a generous man—a mite too generous for my own good, some folks say." He chuckled. "If you were to be sensible, as I think you are, you'd see what that generosity could do for that poor, sickly woman lying out there in that cabin. Money for food, blankets, a roof over her head—everything she's needing!" He smiled and pressed the fleshy ball of

42

his thumb suggestively into Promise's palm. "And all on account of you being a good daughter, being sensible and giving a man some . . . comfort from time to time." The sly smile that wreathed his face deepened to become a leer.

Promise's face had grown paler by the minute as he put her worst fears into words. Now two spots of vivid color flamed high on her cheekbones. Green fire flashed in the depths of her unusual, almond-shaped eyes. She snatched her hand from him as if she'd been snakebitten. "I may be dirt poor and desperate," she gritted through clenched teeth, "but for all that, I'm still particular!" She tossed her head contemptuously, gave him a withering look, jumped to her feet, and strode toward the door.

He barreled forward and gripped her arm in his meaty hand, spinning her around to face him. He shifted his grip from her upper arm to her chin, holding it so tightly she knew there would be bruises there in the morning. "Particular, are you, *Miss* Promise?" he jeered, breathing heavily. "Well, we'll see just how particular you can afford to be come Friday! If the money ain't here by eleven as due, you and that sickly ma of yours will be out of that cabin on your scrawny backsides, I guarantee it!" His lips curled back in a sneer, revealing teeth that were stained yellow with tobacco. "You'll be back—and begging for me to make you the same offer!"

"Take your filthy hands off my chin, *Mister* Hollander," Promise managed to grind out against the grip of his fingers. "Take 'em off me, or I'll sink my teeth in so deep you'll come up with only stumps instead of fingers, I swear it!"

Surprisingly, he released her. "Friday, girlie!" he said thickly. "Friday! I can hardly wait!"

"Oh, I won't forget," Promise assured him hotly, straightening her bonnet with furious, rigid fingers. "No more than I'll forget to tell Mrs. Hollander exactly what kind of interest you're charging in your bank. Should make for mighty juicy gossip at the next sewing circle meeting." With that, she swept out of his office and into the bank.

The pasty-faced bank clerk, perched on his high stool, looked up from his ledger as she stormed past, his eyes and mouth widening in amazement. Hollander, in the doorway to his office, wagged a finger in her direction and bellowed, "You wouldn't dare, you no-good little tramp!"

"Try me!" Promise flung over her shoulder without giving him the satisfaction of a backward glance.

The heels of her high-buttoned black boots tapped a furious tattoo on the wooden boardwalk that lined the storefronts as she flounced angrily down Cherry Creek's main street. She passed the General Store without even acknowledging old Olaf Erickson's cheerful good morning as she went.

What did he think she was, she wondered furiously as she stalked along. Some two-bit dance-hall girl from the Cantina del Sol on the other side of town? Some painted-up saloon girl with feathers and beads in her hair and rouge and powder on her face and more bosom showing than a decent woman showed her own husband? Oh, he was a snake, all right, that Hollander, with his poisonous, forked tongue and his slimy paws! She'd die before he laid one of those paws on her, yes sir!

Her anger vented somewhat by her rapid march down the street, Promise came suddenly to a halt, the full realization of her predicament hitting her like a slap in the face. With her hopes for more time to come up with the money soundly dashed with her rude awakening to the true nature of the banker's character, she was even worse off now than she'd been before.

She stared unseeing down the street, swaying a little as she stood there, fiercely clutching her empty drawstring purse, her neatly pressed but sadly faded blue calico gown even shabbier in the cruel brilliance of the sunlight. The same glaring light threw sharp shadows of the clapboard buildings across the hard-packed dirt street. Across from where she stood was Morgan's rooming house. Arthur Morgan had given Promise's mother laundering work in the past. On the opposite corner were the livery stables and smithy where Henry Crowley did business. The ring of a blacksmith's hammer carried on the air, and Promise glanced up.

The Crowley girls—Sue, Ann, and little Nancy—were sitting on the hitching post outside their father's stables, swinging their legs and giggling and arguing good-naturedly with two young cowboys. From the set of their shoulders and the rakish tilt of their Stetsons, Promise guessed that they'd just been paid from a cattle drive, and that the money was burning a hole in their pockets. Despite her despondent mood, Promise smiled. If their mother, Sarah, could see her daughters now, flirting with two range-crazy cowboys, she'd take a switch to their tails and no mistake. The girls were safe in their flirting for a while yet, though, since Promise had left Sarah Crowley sitting with her mama.

Reluctantly, Promise turned her attention back to the rooming house, giving the Crowley girls a wave as she crossed the street toward it. There was nothing for it but to see if Arthur Morgan had any boarders who needed their laundry done. She could never wash enough shirts in three days to make much difference, but they still had to eat.

Arthur was just on his way out of the rooming house.

45

He beamed on catching sight of her. "Promise! How are you, my dear?"

"Fine, thank you, sir," Promise returned with a smile.

"And—and Mary?" he asked hesitantly, concern in his eyes. "You don't know how I worry about you both."

"We're—we're managing, sir," Promise hedged.

"Are you being honest with me, Promise?" Arthur began. "You know you have only to ask and I'll—"

They both turned their heads sharply as a furiously driven stagecoach careened around the corner and hurtled down the main street, sending dogs and pedestrians scattering. It passed Promise and Arthur Morgan at reckless speed and finally shuddered to a dust-stirring halt in front of the sheriff's office. Excited yells and loud, angry, masculine shouts followed. In seconds, people had come from all directions to jostle about the stage. Promise and Arthur exchanged glances then hurried down the wooden boardwalk to join them.

The arrival of the stage usually created a stir but not this commotion, Promise thought as she lifted her skirts and hurried after Morgan down the street. On the fringes of the crowd, she stepped aside as Doctor Plimmer thrust his way through the people to reach the coach. As the crowd parted to allow him through, Promise glimpsed John Harding, the stagecoach driver, slumped on his high seat clutching his shoulder. Blood had seeped out from between his fingers and run down his arm. His son, "Little" John, had been riding shotgun and lay sprawled beside him, his hat tipped forward over his face. He was so still, he appeared dead. Promise gasped then, seeing the rusty, dark stain that had spread across his checkered shirt front and was even now drawing flies. He didn't only look dead, he was dead, she realized suddenly.

46

Sheriff Harding, John Harding's brother, came down the street at a run. The crowd parted to let him and his two young deputies through. The tall, bony lawman took a brief look at his nephew's body, cussed, and spat a thin brown stream of tobacco juice into the dust of the street.

"Goddamn it all, John, what in the hell happened?" he growled as Doc Plimmer cut the sleeve from John Harding's shirt to see to his bullet wound. Men came forward to lift Little John's body from the stage and carry it to the undertaker's. A curse that sounded more like a sob came from the boy's father as they carried the limp body away.

"It was Reynolds' Rebs, come up from Texas again, I'd bet on it!" he managed to grind out at length, his bearded jaw working furiously as he fought to control his emotions. "Those Confederate bastards jumped us as we were fording the river. They got Johnny straight off in the chest, then winged me in the shoulder before I could even squeeze off a shot at 'em. Took everything, they did. The passengers ain't hurt none, but they're pretty shook up. God, Roy, what am I to tell Joanna?"

Sheriff Harding clamped a heavy, comforting hand over his brother's shoulder as the man broke down and wept like a baby. "Easy there, John, easy," he urged gruffly. "We'll get 'em. Military's been after 'em for a while, now. They can't stay holed up forever. Steve, you and Frank go round up a posse. We're going after the Reynolds Gang—and we ain't coming back 'til we find 'em!"

A murmur of agreement rippled through the crowd, and several townsmen stepped forward to volunteer their services for the posse. The Reynolds Gang, led by Jim Reynolds, had come up into the Colorado Territory from Texas to recruit soldiers for the Confederate Army. Their

47

mission had developed into a number of robberies and
holdups. The rebels had sent the proceeds back down into
Texas, to aid the Southern cause. Stagecoaches had been
robbed throughout the territory, their occupants relieved of their gold dust, money, and personal effects, as
well as their weapons. It was little wonder that the temper
of the crowd had grown ugly. Women came forward to
offer their condolences to John Harding and their hopes
that the men who had killed his son would pay.

Promise had liked Little John. Feeling sickened by his
senseless death and moved almost to tears by his father's
grief, she turned away, colliding with a tall, dark man as
she flung about.

"Excuse me, ma'am," the man apologized, firmly
grasping her by the upper arms to steady her.

For a second, Promise was struck speechless as she
gaped up into his face, for his eyes were as black and
turbulent as a starless night in the shadow of his hat
brim, and as piercing as a hawk's beneath hooded black
brows. His complexion was burned copper-brown, the
skin stretched taut over high cheekbones that gave him
an arrogant, almost savage, cast. Only the tiny lines
crinkling the corners of his mouth and eyes, and a small,
silver scar at one temple, softened his chiseled features.
Belatedly, she realized that he was still holding her
firmly by the arms, and she blinked as if waking from a
spell as he drew his hands away. "No harm done," she
muttered in delayed response to his apology and saw a
fleeting glint of amusement dance in his black eyes. Lord,
when he looked at her that way it was like standing too
close to a blacksmith's furnace. Its heat left one scorched
and breathless! she thought dizzily, still staring at him.

Those smoldering dark eyes dropped their fiery gaze
from her flushed face and flickered down over her body.

It seemed he liked what he saw, for he was smiling a lazy smile when he looked her in the face again.

"No," he said softly, "no harm done that I can see. Everything looks just . . . fine."

He looked at her with an expression she couldn't fathom—long and hard and calculating—that made her feel peculiar inside in a way she couldn't describe, but she was darn certain she didn't like it! Despite the fluttering of her heart, despite the high color rising up her cheeks, she returned his look with a bold one of her own, her eyes meeting his unflinchingly, her small, stubborn chin rising obstinately. She had no intention of letting this arrogant, dark stranger see he'd unsettled her. "Then if you'll step aside, mister, I'll be on my way," she said coolly, half-wondering if he'd refuse.

To her relief, he stepped back and with an almost mocking flourish tipped his hat to her, showing straight, blue-black hair that brushed the collar of his pale blue shirt. She noticed now that there were silver *conchos* laced to the front of his black leather vest and that one tanned hand rested on the handle of a wicked-looking whip that dangled from a loop at his belt. It coiled like a snake against his thigh. A cattle-cutting whip, she realized absently.

"Don't let me keep you, ma'am," he drawled.

Her blush deepened. Flustered now, she tossed her head angrily and swept past him, heading toward Arthur Morgan without a backward glance in his direction.

Arthur was talking to his sister, Ginnie, who must have followed him from the rooming house. For a moment the pair didn't notice her, and she risked a curious glance over her shoulder in the direction of the fascinating, infuriating stranger. He had shouldered his way through the crowd and had offered his services to the posse now, she saw. Was he Mexican? His jet-black eyes and glossy black hair suggested that he was. Her curious expression turned to a frown as she heard the deputy's reply to the man's offer to join the posse.

"I reckon we've got just about all the help we'll be needin', Steele," the deputy said offhandedly. There was a jeering quality to his tone. "Seems to me it would be like settin' a coyote to watch the stock, were you to ride along, wouldn't you say?"

A shocked gasp rippled through the crowd as the dark stranger's fist suddenly snaked out and knotted in the deputy's shirt collar. "I sure hope you'll see your way to taking that back, Deputy," he threatened softly, menacingly, yet every word carried. "It'd be a real shame if Little John were to be having company to the undertaker's!"

The crowd held its breath to a man.

Beads of sweat erupted on the deputy's brow as the fist against his throat tightened its grip. "I—I reckon I take it back, Steele!" he rasped at length.

The man nodded coolly and released him, turning from him as if he'd ceased to exist. He tipped his hat to John Harding. "Your son was a fine boy, Harding. I hope you get them," he murmured before striding away through the crowd.

"Who was he?" Promise asked Arthur, who had caught the exchange. She was certain she'd never seen him in Cherry Creek before and, she thought with a little shiver, he was not the sort of man she'd be likely to forget if she had.

"Luke Steele's his name," Arthur supplied. "He owns the Shadow S ranch down by Santa Fe."

"Santa Fe!" Promise exclaimed.

Arthur nodded. "Yep. He comes all the way up here

50

'bout twice a year, God knows why. Stays for awhile and then he's gone again, just as sudden as he came. He keeps pretty much to himself while he's here. 'Ceptin' for me and Henry Crowley, he doesn't have much to do with the folks hereabouts. He took a room at my place a couple of days ago."

"How come Steve Carter said what he did?" she asked, thinking that Steve had come about a hair's-breadth away from getting himself killed.

Morgan shrugged. "Cherry Creek's a small town, and small towns breed small-minded people with long memories. Luke Steele did time in prison for robbing a prospector out by Fairplay back in '58. He got out two years back, and after old man Steele died, he took over the running of the ranch. I've never heard that he deals anything but a straight hand to those he does business with. But pitch has a way of sticking to what it touches, if you know what I mean. Folks around here don't have a good word to say about Luke Steele, or the Shadow S. They reckon he's proved his bad blood, and there's no way they'd see different if the truth were to slap 'em right in the face."

"Bad blood?" Promise queried, fair brows arched.

"Indian blood. Cheyenne, on his mother's side. Couple that with him having been in jail, and there's no way folks around here will believe anything but bad about him." Arthur mopped his face. "Lord, it sure is hot! Ginnie would be happy to fix you a glass of lemonade before you head home. How about it?"

"No, thank you kindly, sir, but Sarah Crowley's sitting with Mama and I should be getting home."

Arthur nodded. "I understand. You take care now, honey. I'll try to stop by and see your mama real soon."

"She'll be pleased to see you. So long for now." She

51

hurried off, knowing if she stayed Arthur would try to press a few dollars on her to help out—money he could ill afford, since the Cherry Creek Hotel had taken away most of his business this past year.

Arthur had been right, it sure was hot, she thought as she headed back down the main street toward home. It must have been close to high noon, for the sun was a spinning yellow disk directly above. Her blouse was sticking uncomfortably to her spine, and trickles of perspiration settled on her brow and upper lip and ran down the valley between her breasts. It was so hot the clapboard buildings at the end of the street shimmied and blurred in a heat haze, as if they were dancing.

As she passed the bank, she saw Hollander at the window, chewing on another cigar. He grinned as she passed by and nodded knowingly, and Promise felt an angry flush rising hotly up her throat at the gloating expression he'd worn, as if he knew something she didn't. She sure would like to wipe that cat-that-got-the-cream leer from his smug face. A sudden notion of how she could do just that came to mind, and she stopped dead and turned slowly around to look back at the bank. No, no, it was madness to even *think* such a thing, much less do it, she decided, turning back and continuing on her way. Yet the idea lingered in the back of her mind . . .

Ahead lay the Cantina del Sol, and beyond that only the road that led out to the creek and their cabin, shaded with cottonwoods and alders. She'd left a pitcher of lemonade cooling in the creek earlier that morning. It sure would taste good right about now, she thought, licking her dry lips and half-wishing she'd decided to accept Arthur Morgan's offer.

Her heart gave a sick little thud as she looked up and saw Todd Plimmer, the doctor's wild son, lounging up agaisnt the *cantina* wall with several of his pals. His checkered shirt was mussed and wrinkled as if he'd been drinking all night, and his cheeks had an unhealthy flush that confirmed her suspicions.

"Ooowhee! Just look at that little gal!" he jeered as she drew level with him. "T'look at her, you'd say butter wouldn't melt in her sassy lil' mouth, wouldn'tcha boys?"

The other men snickered and nudged each other in the ribs, winking slyly.

Promise shot them all a withering look and carried on, intending to ignore them.

"How come you're so darned high-and-mighty this mornin', Miss Promise?" Todd called. "Ain't we good enough for you, sugar?"

"Maybe Miss Promise done set her sights on a banker man!" Carl Lewers suggested, and the men held their sides laughing.

"Don't look so darned innocent, Promise, honey," Todd sneered. "You ain't foolin' us none. We know what you been up to, over yonder at the bank. Hollander was in here a while ago, and he told us all about it. Hell, our tongues were about hangin' down to the floor when he got through." He licked his lips. "How about you showin' us how sweet and willin' you can be, hmm, honey? Ain't nothin' old Hollander's got that we ain't got, 'ceptin' money, maybe." He nudged Carl, and they all roared with laughter.

Promise kept walking, though there was a tight ball of anger and misery bunched up in her belly. Let them talk, she told herself fiercely. She knew Hollander had lied. Whether Todd and his partners believed him or not didn't matter a darn. They were all no-goods anyhow.

Todd swaggered after her, yelling insults at her back as

53

she passed the *cantina*. "Hey, you hear me, gal? We're offerin' you our business, honey, 'stead of taking it down to Dirty Molly's place. You can take up where your mama left off when she got sick. Whole town knows Mary O'Rourke were takin' in more than launderin' these past years, yessir!" he crowed.

She felt the back of her neck grow tingly, and the hair stand right up on end. She whirled about to face him, green eyes flashing, lips thinned to a long, straight line, a cloud of red dust rising under her feet. She planted her fists on her hips and stalked back toward him. "You can think or say what you darn well please about me, Todd Plimmer, 'cos I don't give a plugged nickel what you pea-brained no-goods think about me. But you take back what you said about my mama, else I'll scratch your damned eyes out, see if I don't!" Trembling with fury, she glared at him. If he took so much as a step in her direction, she'd scratch his face to ribbons, she vowed hotly.

One of the men giggled drunkenly and whispered something to the man next to him. Both men laughed so hard then that they had to hold each other up. Todd glanced over his shoulder at them and grinned, tucked his thumbs in his belt, and swaggered toward her.

"Who in the hell you think you're talkin' to, gal?" he demanded. "Men don't take kindly to being ordered about by a woman!"

"You say so?" Promise drawled. "Well, heck, Todd, *honey*, I don't see no real men here, so I guess I can say what I darn well please!"

The two laughing let out a great hoot at this and slapped their thighs.

"Hell, Todd, she as good as told you she don't reckon you're a man! You gonna let her get away with that?" another man jeered.

54

"Hell, no!" Todd growled. His eyes filled with an excited glitter. He wiped his mouth on the back of his fist. "I've a mind to take her in back of the *cantina* and teach her her place. No two-bit tramp's gonna tell me I ain't a man, no sir! Come on over here to me, honey! We're gonna have us some fun! Carl, you take a hold of her arms—and hang on tight, partner! She's likely to buck like a bronco with a rope around its neck! I'll get them pretty lil' legs . . ."

"Don't you lay a hand on me, you yellow-bellied polecats!" Promise spat, fists balled at her sides. "I reckon I was right what I said the first time. No man worth the name would pick on a woman! Count yourself lucky I don't have my rifle, Todd Plimmer, or you'd be crawling away from here with a voice high enough to sing in the church choir, see if you wouldn't!"

Todd didn't laugh at her threat. He'd seen Promise win the sharp-shooting at the Independence Day picnics for too many years to laugh. "But you ain't got your little old gun, sugar pie," he mocked, "so it ain't gonna help you none, is it now?" His eyes flickered to something behind her.

Too late, Promise realized that as Todd spoke, Carl had been edging his way around to her back, blocking her escape.

The men watching leaned forward now, smiles gone, every one seeming suddenly to hold his breath, their eyes heated with lust as the two men circled the girl. The *cantina* girls had come out to watch the fracas and leaned eagerly against the hitching post, whooping encouragement to Promise and laughing and tossing their heads so that their golden earrings flashed in the sunlight. Behind them stood a tall, dark man, who had stepped from the shadowed *cantina* in their wake.

Todd suddenly lunged for Promise, whooping that he'd teach her a lesson she'd never forget as he reached for her skirt. But it was he who learned a lesson. His fingers barely brushed her when there was a loud crack on the air like a gunshot, and something long and dark snaked over their heads and coiled itself around Todd's wrist with a low hiss.

Todd let out a howl then grunted as he was jerked from his feet to land hard on his backside in the dirt, the lash wound tightly about him. His cocky stance had melted like snow in the spring thaw. Carl leaped away from Promise as if he'd touched a hot griddle, and he looked apprehensively over his shoulder.

The stranger shouldered his way between the Mexican girls and stood there silently. The black-snake, cattle-cutting whip dangled menacingly from his gloved fist. The broad brim of his gray Stetson shadowed his eyes, concealing his thoughts from the onlookers. His mouth and jaw were stern and set, as if they'd been carved from the rock of the mountains themselves. Not the twitch of a nerve in his cheek or the tautening of a muscle in his jaw gave clues to what his intent might be as he stepped into the dusty street, his stilt-heeled boots of Spanish leather soundless, stirring no dust as he walked. Twin six-shooters, both Colts with unusual carved ivory insets in the handles, rode low in the gunbelt across his lean hips.

"On your feet, Plimmer," Steele snapped. "It seems to me you owe the young lady an apology."

"We ain't got no quarrel with you, Steele. This here is Cherry Creek business," Todd insisted, wetting his dry lips nervously on his tongue.

"I'd say a couple of liquored-up yellow-bellies bothering a lady is every man's business. If he's a *real* man, that is." His tone said volumes.

Todd cursed and reached for his gun. Luke's hand flicked upward, and like lightning the lash came down again, and the forty-five flew from Todd's hand as the black leather coiled tight about him a second time. A vicious red weal, from which blood dripped, appeared like magic around Todd's wrist, and now there was a long rent in his checkered shirt. Steele jerked on the black-snake, and Todd lurched toward him. Reeling him in like a fish, Luke waited until Plimmer was within arm's reach, then grabbed him by the neck and hauled him over to kneel before Promise.

"Say it—and say it real nice!" Luke Steele gritted, his black eyes narrowed.

"The hell I'll—"

Before Todd could finish, Luke slammed him down to the ground, grinding his face into the dust with a well-placed boot across the back of his head. "You've got a dirty mouth, Plimmer," he drawled. "Didn't your mama teach you to mind your manners when there's a lady present?" The circle of men broke into nervous laughter. The *cantina* girls whooped their approval. He grasped Todd by the hair and jerked his head back. "I'll count to three, *amigo*. If you haven't apologized by then, you're going to wish you'd never been born! One—"

Todd Plimmer's expression was murderous, filled with hate. "I'm—I'm real sorry!" he blurted, spitting dirt.

Luke nodded and turned to Carl. "How about you, friend?"

"Heck, I'm even sorrier than Todd, Mister Steele!" Carl said quickly.

Luke nodded and turned to Promise. "Go on your way, ma'am. They won't be giving you any more trouble," he promised. And over Carl's shoulder, he gave her a solemn wink.

Promise smiled, taken aback. "I will," she murmured. "And—thank you."

He nodded. "Any time, ma'am."

All the way home, she half-expected Luke Steele to ride after her, but he didn't, and she reached the cabin without further incident.

Later, she went down to the creek for the lemonade she had placed in the water in a big old blue crock to keep cold. Water formed a pool about the bases of the rocks and her wavering reflection glimmered up at her when she looked down. Fair hair spilled untidily about her face, and her expression was meaner than the Devil himself. She shoved the mane of hair away from her eyes and stared long and hard at her reflection. Lord, she looked worn out from worrying, a younger, pale shadow of her mother . . . *Never*, she vowed silently. I'm not going to end up worn down and sick and old before my time from bending my back over a washtub, no sir!

She'd brought a clean cloth with her to wrap around the dripping crock, and on impulse she snatched it up and held it across the lower half of her face then dragged her hair back, away from her profile. A stranger stared back at her from the still water, and her heart skipped a beat. The idea she'd had earlier returned full force now, but the little voice that had urged her then to forget such a crazy scheme was ominously silent. Her heart thudded. The moment of reckoning seemed to hang suspended in time for endless moments as she weighed her chance for success, wavered momentarily, then made up her mind once and for all. There'd be no turning back. She'd do it, and Cherry Creek and all the Todd Plimmers and the Matt Hollanders could go hang—or she would, she thought grimly. That awful possibility just didn't seem to carry much weight any more, not since Hollander had seen to it that she lose the only thing she had left to her— her good name. Desperate times called for desperate deeds, and she was just about as desperate as she'd ever be. Desperate enough to try anything . . .

Back at the cabin, she checked to make sure Mama was sleeping then hurried to the trunk next to the stone hearth where she and her mother kept their clothes. She lifted the lid and took out the walking stick that lay upon the pile of garments and made to cast it aside. On second thought, she hesitated and clasped it to her breast. It had been her pa's, about the only thing she had left of him now, other than a few old clothes and his Stetson and guns. She ran her fingertip over the walking stick handle, carved cleverly with a horse's head correct in every detail right down to the flare of the nostrils and the fall of the mane. Little Silky, her pa had said it was. Her eyes brimmed with tears that trickled down her cheeks. "Oh, Pa, things would have been so different if you'd lived, I just know they would!" she muttered.

Furious at her weak moment, she angrily rubbed the tears away and set the walking stick aside. Rummaging amongst the clothes, she at last found what she'd been looking for—a man's shirt and some other items left behind when one of Arthur Morgan's guests had moved on, forgetting his laundry. She pulled the things to the top of the trunk and closed the lid, a deeply thoughtful expression on her face. All her life, things had happened *to* her, as if she were as much at the whim of Fate as the tumbleweeds that bowled hither and thither across the prairies, wherever the wind chose to send them. Well, all that was about to change. From now on, she'd make things happen the way *she* wanted them to!

Chapter Four

The dirt road into town had never seemed shorter than it did that Friday morning. It was fitting, Promise thought ruefully. When you wanted time to race by, it lagged. When you wanted a journey to be over quickly, it stretched out. When you wanted it to last forever and to postpone what would happen at the end of it, it had a way of becoming shorter than a frog's jump.

Cottonwoods and aspens bordered the narrow road, and the grass beneath was starred with blue and white columbines and polka-dotted with the pink and purple of wild asters. A light, warm breeze set the grass riffling like a small golden sea, and the leaves on the aspen quivered in its current. The sky was as blue as a bright-blue kerchief, and the Rockies seemed even redder, outlined against that blue. It sure was a pretty day, Promise thought. It didn't seem right that bad things should happen on such a pretty day. Bad things were for days when the sky was dark and lowering, with storm clouds swirling about the mountains' jagged peaks.

She brightened suddenly. Perhaps that was a sign—the pretty day—a sign that nothing bad would happen, at least not to her. The idea, though a fanciful one, was reassuring somehow.

She checked once again inside the basket slung over her arm, although she knew everything was still in there—the shirt, her pa's old Stetson, and his gunbelt and guns, both loaded. Under her skirts she wore a pair of men's pants and boots with stilt heels that pinched her toes a little as she walked. Satisfied all was in place, she continued on.

Minutes later, she was at the spot she had mentally set aside for changing her clothes. It would be easy to remember on the way back, when she'd be in something of a hurry—after robbing the Cherry Creek Bank! There were three blackened trees set very close together, their branches burned off from where they had been struck by lightning a few years before. Behind them was a clump of boulders. She stepped through the grass toward the boulders, unbuttoning her blouse as she went. Bare now from the waist up, she hurriedly drew the man's shirt from her basket and slipped it on, fingers trembling as she fastened it. She dropped her skirts next and bundled them into the basket after removing the hat and the gunbelt. She buckled the gunbelt across her slender hips, and jammed the dark-brown hat firmly on her head to cover her fair hair, which she had pinned close to her head before leaving the cabin.

She fumbled in the pocket of the tight-fitting pants and drew out a red bandanna, knotting it loosely in the open neck of the shirt. Feeling every inch the part of a desperado in the unaccustomed snug pants and the stiff, man's checkered shirt, she covered the basket with a linen cloth, placed it behind the boulders, then set off down the last half-mile to Cherry Creek, walking with what she hoped was a masculine gait.

Cherry Creek, Promise saw, was going about its usual

61

Friday morning business. She could hear the tinny plink of a piano from the Cantina del Sol as she passed by, and one of the *cantina* girls, lounging against the half doors of the saloon, gave her a sultry smile and pouted her rouged lips, murmuring, "*Buenos dias, caballero,*" as she drew alongside.

With a shock, it hit Promise suddenly that the girl had really mistaken her for a cowboy, and her spirits soared. She hunched her shoulders and stuck her thumbs in her belt as she sauntered past the *cantina*, murmuring gruffly, "*Hola, muchacha,*" as she passed, and winking broadly. The Mexican girl's throaty laughter followed her down the street.

So far, so good, Promise thought as she walked on. There weren't too many people in the street who might see through her disguise, and yet there were several horses tethered to the hitching post outside the storefronts. She'd need a fast horse to make good her getaway if all went well. Head down so that the brim of her hat hid her face, she ducked down the narrow alleyway that ran alongside the bank, leaned up against the clapboard wall, and pulled the bandanna up to cover her nose. Her palms were damp as they closed over the cold, heavy handles of the guns in her holsters, and she murmured a fervent prayer: "Lord, if you can hear me, I sure would like some help. That Hollander's a sinner if ever I saw one, but my mama's the closest thing you'll find to a saint on this earth. She needs that money a heap more than he does, Lord." So saying, she walked back down the alley, hugging the wall and drawing her guns as she went.

Four steps and she stood in the bank doorway, both weapons held hip-high and ready. Hollander and his clerk looked up to see her standing there, and both men's jaws dropping simultaneously. The two customers in the bank, a doddery old man and a frail woman who were obviously husband and wife, caught their expressions and turned around.

"Reach!" Promise growled. "Easy, now. I don't want no shooting, 'less I have to."

Obediently, all four people raised their hands above their heads. The woman was whimpering, her chin trembling uncontrollably, and Promise felt a momentary pang of pity in her breast which she instantly quelled.

"Okay, mister," she said, jerking her head at Hollander, "bring me that there bag of money—and no tricks, or I'll blow a hole in you so big you'll be turned inside out!"

Wetting his fleshy lips, Hollander swallowed nervously and hefted the money bag over the counter. He edged toward her as if he expected at any minute she'd make good her threat.

"Get a move on!" she snapped, her voice cutting through the deathly hush like the crack of a black-snake whip.

Hollander all but threw the bag at her feet, where it landed with a dull chink.

"Now, step back, easy now, t'where you was," Promise ordered.

He did as she had told him, and she nodded in satisfaction. "That's good. You folks have been real sensible," she growled, returning one gun to its holster as she bent to pick up the money sack, her eyes and her gun never wavering from the four before her. "If you gentlemen'll drop your pants, I'll be on my way."

"What!" Hollander exploded.

"Oh, Lord!" the white-faced clerk exclaimed, paling still more.

The old woman let out a small, horrified shriek, which her doddery husband silenced with a piercing glare.

"Drop 'em," Promise repeated, jerking the barrel of her gun in their direction in a threatening gesture.

With shaking hands, the clerk and the old man reached for their belts and suspenders. Hollander, his face working soundlessly, stood immobile, glaring at her.

"You, too, Slim," she menaced, taking a step toward him. "Last chance!"

Muttering an oath, Hollander reached for his belt.

In minutes, all three men stood there, looking ridiculous in their dark coats and long johns. Hollander's expression was murderous, Promise noted with enormous satisfaction. She began backing away, the bag still tucked under her arm. At the doorway she yelled, "*Adios*, friends!" and turned to run.

On the boardwalk outside, she barreled full tilt into Luke Steele, who had been about to enter the bank. Their eyes met for a fleeting second, and panic swept through her as she saw his eyes narrow and shift their black gaze to the gun in her hand. "Move aside," she threatened, jabbing the gun toward him. A smile tugged at the corner of his lips as he obediently did as she had ordered. She sprang past him down the steps to the street, leaped astride the first horse she came to, and tugged the reins free of the hitching post.

"Yah!" she screamed, kicking the horse in the flanks.

The chestnut whinnied in protest, then took the bit between its teeth and careened down Cherry Creek's main street, stirring a cloud of red dust beneath its flying hooves.

"The bank's been robbed!" she heard someone shout as she leaned forward over her horse's neck and raced out of town.

Hooves flying and eating up the dirt road beneath them, mane and tail streaming in the breeze, the stolen horse galloped as if a pack of horse-thieving Indians were on its trail. The hat had blown off Promise's head with the wildness of the ride, and it bounced on its cord over her shoulders as she steered the chestnut mare up to the spot where the three blackened trees marked the place. She slithered from the horse's back, dropping the money sack in her haste, dealt the mare a hefty slap across the hindquarters, and yelled to send it careening on its way once more. Then she grabbed the bag and raced toward the boulders where she had left her clothes and basket.

Less than five minutes later she stood by the side of the road once more, fair hair billowing about her shoulders, skirts fluttering in the warm breeze. In the basket slung across her arm were eighty shiny silver dollars covered with a white cloth. Behind her, hidden in back of the boulders beneath a pile of brush, were her pa's guns and belt, his old hat and the shirt, and, of course, the money sack. Stepping lightly, Promise again set out toward town, humming under her breath as she went. It had gone off smoother than she had dared to hope it would. Now came the real test. She intended to sashay coolly into Hollander's bank and pay him the rest of the ten dollars she and Mama owed him. She was certain no one would credit a bank robber with having the guts to return to the scene of his robbery minutes after it had taken place. At the very least her appearance would give her an alibi.

She hadn't gone far when she saw a party of men on horseback racing in her direction. In front was Henry Crowley. Other men from town made up the rest of the posse.

"Mornin', Promise," Henry greeted her, hurriedly tipping his hat as the others rode on past him, spurring their horses. "The bank in town's been robbed! See anyone ridin' this way?"

"Robbed!" Promise gasped, clutching her heart appropriately. "Dear Lord, yes, I did see a rider on a big chestnut horse. He forded the creek and lit out up yonder." She gestured vaguely toward the north. The vast Plains lay that way. They'd be chasing their bank robber until winter if they followed her directions.

Henry nodded. "Thanks. Geet up there." He rode off after the others, who were now splashing their horses across the ford.

Promise smiled. Poor Henry. By the time they all realized there were no tracks leading from the opposite bank of the creek, it would more than likely be dusk. The timing for her escapade had proved perfect, as she had hoped. Sheriff Harding was a shrewd man and good at his job as lawman. She'd have had a hard time pulling the wool over his eyes, whereas Henry Crowley was a kind, trusting soul who would never suspect that Promise was not as innocent as she appeared. But right now, thanks to the Reynolds' Rebels' attack on the stagecoach, the sheriff and his deputies were miles from Cherry Creek, and she stood a better than even chance of getting away with it.

Cherry Creek was in an uproar. Men were racing about, eager to exchange viewpoints on the identity of the bank robber. Women were gossiping in knots on every street corner. As Promise passed, she caught snatches of their conversation. According to what she overheard, the bank robber was a tall man of medium build, with one blue eye and one brown! He had multicolored hair ranging from blond to red to, some said, black. She muffled a giggle. It shouldn't be hard to find someone fitting their description—any circus freak show or traveling fair should have someone to fit the bill. Lord, she felt exhilarated by her brush with danger and the law! It was as if she had downed a whole jug of whiskey and was drunk on the contents. Her cheeks were flushed, she knew, and there was a fluttery feeling in the pit of her belly which made her want to laugh out loud, though, of course, she could not do that, not without drawing adverse attention to herself.

She continued down the street, strolling casually although she felt like running. Sarah Crowley and two of her pretty young daughters were standing on the corner by the bank. From their expressions it seemed they had been discussing the robbery.

"Mornin', Sarah, and to you, too, Nancy, Sue," she greeted the three brightly. "What's all the commotion going on here this morning? Haven't seen this much excitement in Cherry Creek since they tarred and feathered that man they caught cheating in the saloon!"

"Someone robbed Hollander's bank and got clean away!" Sarah supplied. "He's about fit to be tied, he's so mad." She grinned and nudged Promise in the ribs. "Serves him right. I never could take a liking to that man."

Sue, her pretty, red-headed, eldest daughter, nodded knowingly. "Me neither," she agreed. "Why, the way he looks at a girl, it's like he stripped her naked with his squinty little eyes." She shuddered.

Sarah swung about to face her, her expression horrified and the very picture of an outraged mama. "Susan Beth Crowley, you watch that mouth of yours! 'Stripped naked' indeed! I don't know where you get such ideas, I swear. I should wash your mouth with soap." She

67

clicked her teeth in disapproval while Sue turned away and hid a smile, winking at Promise. "Well, Promise, who's sitting with Mary this morning?"

Promise frowned. "No one, I'm sorry to say, Sarah. But there were a few things we were needing awful bad, so I had to leave her alone. If you'll excuse me now, I'd best be getting along. I'd like to be back home before she wakes up and finds me gone."

"You shouldn't have to leave her alone like that, child," Sarah said with a worried expression on her handsome face. "Why, anything could happen with her alone, especially with no-goods like the Reynolds Gang and that bank robber running around in broad daylight, stealing and shooting up the place. Not to mention Indians . . . Why, it's not even a month since those poor Hungate folks were attacked and killed!" She shuddered. "I was talking to a woman just yesterday who was in Denver when they brought their bodies into town. They'd all been scalped, and what those savages had done to their bodies after . . . If they can do that to an innocent man, his wife, and their poor little four-year-old daughter and baby, why, they wouldn't take pity on a sick woman like Mary, no, sir!"

"I know it," Promise agreed, her former elation mingled with guilt and apprehension now. "I'll be on my way. Be seeing you, Sarah, girls."

Sarah nodded. "I'll come by the cabin just as soon as I can."

"I'll look forward to it," Promise said warmly before turning into the bank doorway.

Hollander was there, pacing back and forth. The little old man and his wife were still there, too. One of the town's women was waving a burning feather under the woman's nose in an effort to bring her around from what appeared to be a fainting spell, though whether it had been brought on by the bank robbery itself or the sight of four grown men wearing only their long johns with their coats, Promise couldn't say. Hollander caught sight of her in the doorway and shot her a distracted look, running his stubby hand through his greasy hair.

"Good mornin', Mister Hollander," she said pleasantly, giving the banker a sweet-as-syrup smile. "It's almost eleven. I surely hope I haven't kept you waiting."

His eyebrows bunched together as he frowned. "Waiting? For what?" he snapped.

"The money me and my mama are owing you." She reached beneath the white linen cover over her basket and carefully drew out all but one of the silver dollars. "There's seven dollars here, sir. With the three I paid you the other day, I figure our debt to you is cleared until the lease money is due again next month."

He glanced at the small pile of coins she had placed on the bank counter, looking as if he'd seen something unpleasant and tasted something sour. "And where did you come up with that kind of money so darned fast?" he demanded suspiciously, his blue eyes narrowing.

"Well, I reckon you could say I took your good advice to heart the other day, sir," Promise told him sweetly. "You said you thought there were ways a pretty, clever girl like me could've done better than only coming up with three dollars, and I got to thinking that maybe you were right!" She gave him a grin and a sassy wink. "Seeing as how you were good enough to tell a whole string of lies about me and about how sweet and willing I was in your private office the other day, it didn't seem like I had anything to lose any more, since you'd already seen to it that I lost my good reputation." Her voice had risen at the latter, and she noticed that the heads of several of the bank customers had turned in their direction and that several pairs of eyes were watching the exchange curiously. "Heck, I reckon the next time I come in here, it'll be to make a deposit, sir, and it's all thanks to you!"

"Keep your damned voice down!" Hollander hissed.

"I'll do better than that," Promise told him cheerfully. "I'll leave—once you give me a receipt for what I paid you."

Hollander swallowed and nodded to the boggle-eyed young clerk to make out the receipt, but he signed it and thrust it into her hand himself. "Now, get out!" he ordered her, taking her by the elbow and hustling her to the door. "My bank was robbed this morning. I've enough trouble today without you hanging around and trying to cause more!"

Her fair eyebrows rose in mock surprise. Her green eyes widened. "Your bank was robbed? Well, I reckon I won't be making any deposits here after all, Mister Hollander, not if you can't take care of the money entrusted to you! Good day, sir." She stepped out of the bank and hurried down the wooden boardwalk before the laughter she had been holding back could escape and give her away.

She had not gone far when she was aware of steady footsteps behind her. Guilt had made her a trifle edgy by now, so she quickened her steps. Throat constricting, she realized that the footfalls behind her had increased their speed also. She was being followed, but by whom? A glance over her shoulder confirmed that someone's identity—it was the man Arthur Morgan had identified as Luke Steele, the owner of the Shadow S spread. She quickened her pace yet again, her pulse beginning to race erratically when he again quickened his to keep up.

Flustered thoroughly now, she decided to cross the street to evade him. Calm down, she told herself. You're like a cat with a stick of dynamite tied to its tail! She stepped off the wooden boardwalk and into the street, gasping in fright as a huge hand closed over her elbow and yanked her backward.

"Careful, *desperada*, or you'll get yourself run down," he cautioned, pulling her back just as a buckboard came barreling down the main street.

The blood drained from Promise's face. "What did you call me?" she asked, her knees feeling ready to buckle as she stared up into his deeply tanned face.

"You heard me," he said softly, taking her arm and forcing her to walk beside him.

"I don't know what you meant by that, but if you'll let go of me, I have to be getting home." She tried to pull free of his hand, but his fingers were curled so tightly about her upper arm that she could not shake them off.

He stopped suddenly in his tracks, spun her around to face him, and lifted his hand and held it before the lower half of her face. "You don't know what I meant by calling you *desperada*? Sure you do, honey," he insisted, smiling that faint, mocking smile of amusement he'd worn when she had collided with him after fleeing the bank. "Green eyes like yours aren't easy to forget—especially when they're set off by a red bandanna! What's in the basket, *desperada*? Biscuits? Eggs? Or . . . silver dollars, maybe?"

She whipped the linen cover from the basket and thrust it under his nose. "The basket's empty, mister! I really have to be going . . ."

She sped along the boardwalk, heart going like a crazed thing as she went. Lord, he *knew*! He had recognized her! What would he do? Still shaking like a leaf in fall, she

71

turned into Olaf Erickson's General Store. It was dark inside, and for some reason she felt safer in that gloom which smelled of flour and molasses, leather and grain.

While her eyes adjusted to the dimness of the store, she took several deep breaths and tried to calm herself, a feat that was next to impossible under the circumstances. Heat edged its way up her throat, prickling the back of her neck. Flustered, she rubbed at it, wondering if that was how it felt when they slipped a noose about the neck . . . Nervous, she wandered about the store, fingering bolts of pretty calico and silk and heavy flannel, picking up this and that and hurriedly putting it down again. Dear God, she couldn't even think straight! Would he dare to follow her into the store? Or would he be waiting for her when she left? Dare she hope he would say nothing, or was he the type of man who would bide his time and turn her over to Sheriff Harding when he returned from chasing after the Reynolds Gang? He had served time in prison himself, according to what Arthur Morgan had told her earlier that week. Could it be he just intended to frighten her but would say nothing? Oh, if only she knew! She couldn't stand *not* knowing!

"Good morning to you, Miss Promise. What can Erickson do for you today?"

It was some time before old Mister Erickson's singsong voice penetrated Promise's confused thoughts. When it did, she exclaimed, "Oh!" and dropped the last silver dollar on the sawdusted floorboards of the General Store. It rolled in a fascinating, ever-narrowing circle before it came to rest alongside a barrel of pickles. Promise watched it, then looked down at the slick palm she had been holding it in. A deep, red, circular mark had been left from gripping the coin so tightly when Steele had challenged her.

Mister Erickson bent stiffly to retrieve the coin and gravely held the shiny dollar out to her. "Money, it is hard to come by, *ja?*" he said, lake blue eyes twinkling in the gloom. "Hang onto it, young lady, hang onto it!"

Promise darted him an uncertain smile. "Thanks, Mister Erickson. I'm all thumbs today."

He nodded sagely. "So, and who isn't, what with der stagedriver's son being shot, poor fellow, and now der bank being robbed." He wagged a stern finger at her. "You be taking care walking home to your cabin, *ja?* It is not being safe anywhere these days." He shook his head morosely.

"I'll be careful, sir," Promise assured him. "I just came into town to fetch some things we're needing."

"And what are they?" Olaf Erickson inquired, peering at her.

She told him, then waited, fidgeting nervously while he wrapped the slab of bacon in clean, white paper and tucked the five-pound bags of flour and sugar and navy beans into the basket. It was heavy when she hefted it off the counter, and for a fleeting second she was reminded of the money sack she had left hidden just outside of town. She muttered her thanks to the old storekeeper and skittered toward the door like a nervous colt, her heart leaping as he called to her to wait.

"Your change, young lady, your change!" he scolded, coming after her.

She nodded and took it from him, wondering if he could see the color burning in her cheeks in this light. They certainly felt as if he must be able to, they were so hot. Guilt, she told herself. *Get a grip on yourself, girl!* Poking her head out of the storefront like a turtle from its shell, she looked both ways before she exited, to see if that half-breed, Luke Steele, was anywhere in sight. She

73

was relieved that he wasn't, and she set out down the main street of Cherry Creek at a spanking pace that caused heads to turn sharply in her direction before she realized that the attention she was drawing was dangerous, and she slowed down some.

At the turnoff in the road that led out to the cabin, she turned and looked back one last time over her shoulder. Her heart skipped a beat when she saw that Luke Steele was sitting his horse in the middle of the dirt road. Neither animal nor rider moved. Silhouetted against the lighter summer sky beyond, they seemed sculpted from blue-gray flint—dark and menacing. She walked slowly until she had turned the corner, but once she was out of sight of him, she picked up her skirts and ran like the wind past the trees where her things and the money sack were hidden and not stopping until she had flung herself, breathless, up the porch steps and into the little cabin.

Her breasts heaving with exertion, her face a brilliant crimson from running so hard, she hefted the basket onto the table and set about putting away the supplies. Her escapades had left her exhausted, drained, and shaky, and she still had to carry the basket back to the hiding place and get the money sack and her things. She straightened her shoulders resolutely. First, she must check on Mama, then she'd finish what had to be done. Luke Steele would be gone by then, she was certain.

Apprehension filled Promise as she stepped inside the cabin's second room. The narrow window let in little light, and her mother lay in half shadow. She appeared deathly pale and very still, and for a second it seemed Promise's heart stopped beating. She took two tottering steps across the plank floor and knelt at her mother's bedside, reaching with trembling fingers for her wrist to find the pulse there. Thank God, she was alive. Relief flooded through her. Tears suddenly filled her eyes. What have I done today, Mama? she asked silently as she wept. *Dear Lord, what have I done?* And what, came the even more pressing question, would happen to Mama if she were found out? It was a possibility she had not even considered before, she realized belatedly.

Later that day, still shaky and drained, but composed, she went back to the three burned trees to recover her things and the money. A glance told her everything. They were gone!

Chapter Five

Luke Steele lay on his bed in Morgan's rooming house, a slim Spanish cheroot jutting from the corner of his mouth, his arms folded beneath his head. Beside him on the nightstand stood a bottle of whiskey and two glasses. Beside him in the bed lay Rosalia, one of the prettiest girls from the Cantina del Sol across town.

"What is it you are thinking, señor Steele?" Rosalia purred, twining a slender olive arm about his neck to ruffle his blue-black hair.

He grinned, tossed the cheroot into the brass spittoon that stood in the corner, and rolled over to face her, leaning up on one elbow. "I'd say you know what I'm thinking, *gatita*!" he murmured, dark eyes flickering over her smooth, oval face. He cupped her chin in a large, tanned hand and covered her sultry red lips in a savage kiss. His fingers strayed to her temples, knotting in her black curls and arching her head back as he kissed her. One hand trailed down and began a lingering arousal of her slender body straining against his.

"*Por díos*! You are *el diablo* himself!" she cried breathlessly minutes later as he parted her thighs and eased himself between them, driving deeply into her moist heat as if he sought to exorcise some private demon

76

that possessed him. Rosalia cried out as she rapidly reached her release, her nails convulsively scoring long, red welts down the dark tan of Steele's smooth back. Her teeth closed on the muscled curve of his shoulder in the heat of her passion.

Minutes later he rolled from her with a groan of pleasure and fastened a towel around his waist. He leaned over and poured himself a shot of whiskey from the dark bottle on the nightstand.

"How about you, 'Lia?" he offered, gesturing with the bottle.

She turned her head in his direction, eyes heavy-lidded, her wide mouth reddened like the crushed petals of a scarlet rose.

"No, you bastard!" she refused, pouting sulkily. "You know it is not the liquor that I want from you, or the money! Tell me that you love me, Luke, *querído*! Tell me it is as good for you as it is for me when we make love. Please . . ." She scrambled to kneeling, and the bedding fell away from her nude body as she curled her arms about his shoulders and rested her cheek against his back. "Tell me that you'll take me back with you, this time, to your *ranchería*." She smiled eagerly. "Rosalia would be good for you. I would tend house for you, cook and clean—and keep you warm in your bed the long winter nights through," she giggled and drew circles on the flesh of his shoulder with a long fingernail. "Ah, *si*, so very warm. I would give you many strong, fine sons, *querído mío*, to run the *rancho* for you when you are an old, old man. You will take Rosalia with you this time, yes?" she repeated throatily.

"No, *muchacha*, no, on all counts," Steele said firmly.

He untangled her clinging arms and body from his, stood, and strode across the room to where his saddlebags hung across a chair back. Reaching inside, he withdrew a roll of bills, peeled off a couple of them, then added a third and tossed them onto the bed alongside the saloon girl.

"*Gracias*, 'Lia," he said casually. "*Hasta luego, entonces.*"

Her dark eyes were murderous. "Until the next time?" She bristled. Hurt welled inside her that he could toss her aside so casually, so cruelly. "No! There will be no next time!" she spat. "Always it is the same. I do not see you for many long months. My heart is heavy, for I am certain you are dead. But then, like the wind, you are here. A few days and then, poof!" She snapped her fingers. "You blow out of my life once again, *señor*. And each time, the hurt is worse than the time before. No more." She shuddered. "No more!"

As she spoke, she gathered up her embroidered *camisa* and her dark red skirt with the ruffles at the hem and put them on. Dressed now, she tossed her mane of dark curls over her shoulders, picked up the greenbacks, and spat on them before flinging the money at Steele. Then she stalked haughtily to the door and left, slamming it viciously with her exit.

For a second, Luke stood there. Then he shrugged, picked up the bills, and tucked them back into his saddlebags. He had made Rosalia no promises, had warned her more than once that she would get hurt if she let herself expect more from him than he was prepared to give. She had said at the beginning that she understood, but she had not. What she had wanted from him had been security, a future, *niños* tugging at her skirts, and a sole claim upon his heat, while what he wanted was . . . freedom. Marriage—loving one woman and one woman alone—would be only another form of imprisonment,

78

the walls as confining as those he had left behind him two years before.

He poured himself another drink and, as he sipped it, crossed the room and crouched down, picking up the worn brown Stetson lying there atop a pile of shabby men's clothing. In the sweat-stained, yellow silk hatband were the blurred inked initials P.M.O.—the same initials tooled into the leather of the gunbelt he had slung across his saddle in the corner earlier.

What must the girl have thought when she returned to find the things she had concealed so carefully gone? he wondered, a smile tugging at the corners of his mouth. Had those green eyes flared in anger—or darkened in fear that her secret would be revealed? The smile still lingered as he carried the glass back to the bed and lay down, one arm crooked beneath his head, long legs comfortably crossed. He was accustomed to women lowering their gaze when they looked into his eyes, afraid their interest in him, a half-breed, would show in their faces. But it had not been so with the one he had teasingly named *desperada*. She had matched his bold stare with an even bolder one of her own, the curiosity alive in her lovely face. His smile deepened. It had been many years since any woman had captured his interest. That this slender girl-woman had done so surprised and intrigued him. What had it been? he pondered. Her slanted, fascinating green eyes? The long sweep of cornsilk hair? The pretty mouth, too wide, too sensual, for the classically beautiful face? Or . . . something indefinable, some spark that had flared briefly as their eyes met, which made him potently aware of the woman within the slender, girlish body? Whatever, she did not belong here, in Cherry Creek. Of that much he was certain. Her loveliness and her proud manner set her apart from the settlers' daughters. She was a mountain rose in the midst of a bunch of wildflowers.

His chiseled features relaxed as he recalled how her eyes had widened above the red bandanna, resembling those of a wide-eyed kitten. He recalled her quick intake of breath and the rapid rise and fall of rounded, feminine breasts against the rough cloth of her man's shirt. Who was she, he wondered, and what in the hell had driven her to rob Hollander's bank? The mystery intrigued him and whetted his appetite to learn more of her. Somehow, he would find out, he vowed determinedly.

"*Salud, desperada!*" he murmured softly, raising the shot glass to the wan dawn light that filtered through the lace curtains. He downed the liquor in a single mouthful and lay back.

Already Rosalia had been forgotten.

Only half a bucket! Promise thought ruefully, shaking her head in disgust. The cow, lowing softly, turned her head to regard Promise from solemn brown eyes.

The cow was able to sense her agitation this morning, she realized. But after spending a restless night worrying about what that half-breed, Steele, would do with the knowledge that it had been she who robbed the bank, it was hard to be calm, and the cow was responding to her nervousness. Milk was one of the few things that her mama could stomach in her weakened condition, but their only cow needed to be freshened soon. She had to get a grip on herself and calm down, else there would be no milk today.

"When Mama named you Selfish, old gal, she sure knew what she was doing!" She laid her cheek flat against Selfish's warm side, humming as she pulled rhythmically on the cow's teats in an effort to extract the last drop of milk. The mother cat sat patiently in the shadows of the barn, licking her lips and cleaning her whiskers in readiness for the warm squirt that Promise sent her way each morning.

"Sorry, Jemima, I reckon you'll have to wait on your milk until we can get us a freshened cow. Selfish here's about dry."

As if the cat had understood every word she had said, she meowed plaintively and padded over to where Promise sat, looking up at her with her small, black head cocked to one side, and blinking her amber eyes solemnly. Promise laughed, reached down, and scratched Jemima's ears. "Okay, you win." She laughed. "Here it comes." She directed a large teat in Jemima's direction, smiling as the cat expertly opened her mouth to catch the warm milk that was her breakfast. Afterwards, her small pink tongue cleaned the last drops from her whiskers, then she arched once against Promise's legs and padded back to her little brood in the pile of hay.

Her back aching now, Promise straightened up from the three-legged milking stool and gave Selfish an affectionate slap on her bony rump. "Well, old gal, at least Jemima's babies will be happy, hmm?" She put a few handfuls of mash into Selfish's bucket, lifted the milk pail, and carried it from the barn across the yard to the cabin, stopping briefly before going inside to watch a hawk carving a dark arc from the charcoal sky. She hummed as she went. Her voice died away as she saw her mother there in the kitchen, leaning heavily against a chair back for support.

"Mama!" she cried, setting down the pail and hurrying to help her mother into the chair. "You shouldn't get out of bed. Whatever are you thinking of?"

Mary O'Rourke waved aside Promise's protests. "Stop fussing, do, honey! You're not a mother hen and I surely am not your chick, so just hush and sit down here beside me."

Promise obediently sat at her mother's feet, but not before she had taken the shawl from her own shoulders and placed it tenderly about her mother's. It was early yet and the morning air was cold.

Mary looked down into Promise's face and lovingly stroked her hair. "Promise, you've certainly grown into a lovely young woman. I can scarce believe you were once a skinny little girl, all legs and arms and freckles." She smiled. "You've grown up so fast, honey. Sixteen years—why, they've gone by like a puff of wood smoke in the breeze. I—I'd always hoped that I'd be around long enough to see you with children of your own, but I reckon I know now that what God feels is fitting and what Mary O'Rourke thinks would suit just aren't the same."

"Mama, please don't . . ." Promise implored her, her eyes brimming with tears.

"Hush, now, hush, it's taken me long enough to pluck up courage to tell you what I have to tell you. Please, honey, don't stop me now." There was a desperate light in Mary O'Rourke's eyes and Promise saw it and nodded.

"Okay, Mama," she whispered huskily.

Mary sighed. "Well, child. I've a feeling there's not much time left me now. Before I go, I want you to know about who you are, *really* are, so when you have children of your own, you'll be able to tell them.

"You see, my papa was a good man, he was, but a stern father," Mary O'Rourke began. "Back in New York where I was born, Papa was a lawyer. Some folks said they felt that one day he might even run for president. President Samuel T. Haverleigh—has a nice ring, doesn't it? Well, like I said, Papa had leanings toward becoming a politician and was forever being asked to give speeches and so on, and attending dinners and receptions and balls, and so your mama and your aunt Lucinda, my little sister, used to get to go with him and our mama. Oh, Promise, what times we had! We'd get all prettied up in our fanciest gowns with our fans and our shawls, and combs and feathers in our hair, and off we'd go. There'd be great crystal bowls of punch and all kinds of dainty tidbits to eat—and the people! The handsome young men came flocking around Cindy and me like bees to flowers, and every night our dance cards were filled before the balls had hardly gotten started."

Mary O'Rourke's tired face came alive as she recalled those times, and her hazel eyes took on a dreamy, far-away expression. "Then one night at one of these occasions, I met a young man. Lord, he was so handsome, Promise, with hair the color of a wheat field and eyes so green it was like someone had set emeralds in their place. He was so charming, I swear he could have danced with any young woman in the ballroom—or older woman, for that matter—but he chose me! He even filled out my dance card with his name in every space. 'Miz Haverleigh,' he told me, 'I've traveled here from the city of New Orleans, which boasts the prettiest belles on this entire earth. Yet if I might be bold enough to say so, I've never seen a young lady there whose beauty and grace could hold a candle to yours, no sir!' He took me in his arms and we danced the night away, and when I left him that evening, why, I think I was already half in love with him. He—he kissed me in the shadows while we were waiting for my cloak to be fetched, and when he did, it was like I was alive, *really* alive, for the first time ever!

"The next morning he came by our house and asked

Papa for his permission to pay court to me. I was listening outside the door, and I heard my papa tell him that there was no way on this earth that his daughter's name was going to be linked with that of the son of a cotton planter who made his living from the sweat of human misery and slaving. He told my Courtney to get out, and so he did. He was too much of a gentleman to argue with Papa in his own house, you see. That should have been the end of it, but it wasn't. Courtney sent me a note by one of our maids, begging me to meet him. I did, and that was the first secret meeting of many we had over the next few weeks. I—I am ashamed to say I used any deceit I could to slip away and meet him, and your aunt Lucinda helped me. Those times with Courtney were the happiest times of my life.

"Then Papa found out—how, I never knew, and the next thing I heard, Courtney's commanding officer had had him sent back down south. I—I never heard from him again. Honey, I thought I'd die of grief. I didn't care how Papa threatened and scolded and swore he'd send me away. It was like my heart was broken clean in two. But there was worse to come. You see, by then I'd realized that I must be carrying Courtney's child, and I was out of my mind with worry. I didn't dare tell Mama or Papa. The shame would have killed Mama, and Papa—why, he might have gone after Courtney and shot him! I didn't know what to do or where to turn for help. Keeping all this inside me got to be too much one day. Papa had a man that cared for our horses and carriages, a handsome Irish rogue. He was forever trying to flirt with me and pay me pretty compliments. Well, that day I just broke down and started crying and somehow, I don't recall quite how, I found myself crying on O'Rourke's shoulder and telling him everything about Courtney and me and even that I was carrying a child. He—he offered right there and then to marry me and give the child his name, if I would have him. He said he'd loved me ever since he first came to work for Papa, and that he'd take care of my child as if it were his own flesh and blood." Mary shrugged. "I—I guess the rest is easy for you to figure, Promise. We ran away the next morning and were married a few days later by a preacher who was so stand-up drunk he could scarce read the words over us. That's how I came to marry your pa, honey. I wanted you to know the truth before I die. You've good blood in you, child. Your—your *real* papa was a Fontaine, one of the finest, oldest families the South has ever produced."

Promise shook her head slightly. "No, Mama," she said gently. "My papa was a wild, Irish rascal who loved his whiskey and his horses and his grand dreams and stories as much if not more than he loved life itself. Your Courtney Fontaine might be my natural father, but it was Patrick O'Rourke who raised me. It was Patrick O'Rourke who gave me his name, who sat with me when I was ailing, and carried me when my legs ached and I couldn't walk any farther. Oh, I understand that he didn't always do well by you, Mama, truly I do, but he *was* my pa, and I loved him!" Her voice had died away to a whisper at the last and Mary looked down into her daughter's face, her hazel eyes swimming with tears.

"You knew, didn't you?" she asked huskily at length.

"Yes," Promise admitted, "or rather I guessed a long, long time ago. I remembered the fights you and Pa used to have, and the things you used to say. They didn't make much sense to me at the time, but I figured it out a while back and I knew Pa couldn't be my natural father."

"And—and now I suppose you think badly of me," Mary murmured, looking down at her hands clasped slackly in her lap. "Well, one day you'll understand, God willing, what it is to love a man so much you feel like you're only alive, truly alive, when he's there beside you, holding you . . . and die a little each day that you're apart."

Promise nodded mutely. There was nothing left to say, not really, except for maybe one thing. "I love you, Mama, I surely do love you," she whispered, holding Mary close and burying her face against her hair as she had when she was a little girl.

"I know it, I know it," Mary answered, "and I love you, honey, you've no idea just how much. You're what made life worth living after Courtney left all those years ago." She sniffed back a tear. "You know, I'd surely like to get myself all prettied up today and sit out on the front porch and watch the sun come up. Do you reckon you could help me, Promise?"

Promise nodded, smiling through the mist of tears that veiled her own eyes. "I reckon I could, Miz O'Rourke," she said brightly. "It sure looks to be a beautiful day for it!"

Promise helped her mother to dress in her prettiest gown—normally worn only to church—of deep blue calico sprigged all over with tiny flowers and trimmed with narrow bands of lace at the collar and cuffs. She fixed up the two rough-hewn chairs from the cabin to serve as a day bed and bolstered them with down pillows before assisting her mother slowly out onto the porch.

They watched the sun come up together, first as only a saffron and orange lightening of the sky in the east, then glorious golden light thrusting back the charcoal clouds and flooding the meadows and the plains beyond with its warm rays. It was a spectacular sunrise, vivid and breathtakingly beautiful, the clouds becoming a pale, creamy yellow edged with a glittering border of gold. Birds began singing in the apple tree that grew by the porch steps, and, while Mary watched them fluttering and hopping from twig to twig, Promise combed her mother's long, white hair and carefully braided it before coiling the braids about the crown of her head. Mary reached up to touch her hair and smiled.

"Why, you've done my hair like a young girl's instead of a tired old woman's! Whatever were you thinking of?" she chided, but her eyes twinkled.

"Well, I thought that seeing as how you were all prettied up today, you'd best have your hair fixed to match," Promise said firmly, tucking the last hairpin into place. "There. Now, you sit just where you are, and I'll be right back. I'm going to pick some flowers to put in your hair."

"Oh, Promise, what an idea! Come back here." Her mother laughed, watching as her young daughter sped across the yard and out into the tall, golden, meadow grass, cornsilk hair flying behind her.

The blue and white columbines and the yellow buttercups and the purple clover were just opening their petals to the sun's wakening warmth, and dew still clung to their leaves. Promise crouched down and picked and picked until her fists were filled to overflowing with the wildflowers. So happy was she that her mother felt well enough to get up, that she vowed she would tuck flowers in Mary's hair, her best dress, *everywhere*, until she was all decked out like the Queen of the May. Satisfied at last that she had picked enough, she sped back through the white rail fence to the cabin.

"Look at what I've brought you, Mama. Aren't they pretty?" she cried, flinging herself up the porch steps, breathless from running. "Mama? *Mama!*" There was no answer.

Mary O'Rourke was sitting as Promise had left her, the morning sunlight falling on her hair, her face turned to the vastness of the Plains beyond the horizon. Her hands were still clasped loosely in her lap.

The flowers tumbled from Promise's fingers, blue, white, yellow, and purple blossoms spilling about Mary O'Rourke's feet. Promise sank to her knees beside her mother, shaking her head in disbelief and denial. It didn't matter that she had expected it, known that any day her mother could die. Now that it had happened, the knife of grief in her breast was unbearable. She laid her cheek against her mother's cool, still hands, face working uncontrollably.

"Oh, Mama!" she whispered as the tears began to fall.

Chapter Six

Luke Steele picked up one of his blue roan's hoofs and inspected the new horseshoes Henry Crowley had just nailed in place. He nodded his approval. "Fine job, Henry," he acknowledged. "Isn't a man can match your blacksmithing from here to Santa Fe."

Henry grinned. "Let's hope not, Steele. I've a mind to make me some real money in the next few months, if things go the way I want 'em to."

"How's that, Henry?" Steele asked idly.

"Folks up in Denver and thereabouts seem to think we'll have a full-scale war with the Indians on our hands before summer's out. They reckon the Cheyenne and Arapahoe are going on the warpath, what with all the raidin' that's been going on around here since the spring. There's talk of raising another regiment, the Colorado Third, of hundred-days militia men. If they do, they'll be asking around for blacksmiths and horse traders to see them fitted out right. I aim to land me a fat contract with the government, yessir!" His eyes narrowed and he eyed Luke eagerly. "Heard anything about an Indian war in the wind?"

"No," Luke said. "Leastways, not the Cheyenne and the Arapahoe. Their chiefs seem keen to make peace, the way I see it. Black Kettle of the Cheyenne is willing to put his people under military protection according to Governor Evans's proclamation. Doesn't sound like there's a war brewing to me. Could be the Sioux and Comanche feel differently, though. When we came north, they'd closed the wagon trail west, down by Bent's Fort and the Cimarron Trail and beyond, on account of all the raids down that way." He frowned. "You've disappointed me, Henry. I wouldn't have taken you for a man keen to see a war started up."

Henry had the grace to look ashamed of himself. "Naw, Luke, it ain't that. There's enough fightin' going on amongst my own people, what with this darned civil war. But—but it sure would be nice to have a little extra money coming in come winter, say, instead of barely breaking even. I'd like to get some gee-gaws for Sarah and the girls, and lay in some tools and supplies from back east for the smithy. I wouldn't lift a finger to see a war started, nor do nothing to stretch it out once it did, but if there is war, I aim to make what I can off of it. You can't hold it against a man for turning the times to his advantage." He waggled the tongs he was holding at Steele. "Say, I reckon you could make a parcel, too, supplying the militia with fresh beef, if you've a mind to." He caught the expression in Luke's eyes and hurriedly amended, "We-ell, no, I guess not, seeing as how the Third would be fighting your mama's people. But after the war's over, meat'll be in short supply everywhere, what with ranchers and farmers throwing down their ploughs to take up arms. When that day comes, I'd say you'll be a rich man."

Steele gave him a slow smile. "Reckon I'd have to agree with you there, Henry," he drawled. "Reckon half of Texas would, too."

Henry nodded sagely. He mopped his ruddy, sweating face on a grimy handkerchief and bent to pump the bellows of his forge. Fire roared as the air rushed in. "Them boys of mine have a hankerin' t'be cowboys," he continued, rubbing his whiskered chin. "They reckon it's all fancy ridin' and struttin' around with a pair o' Spanish leather boots and a pretty ole saddle all fixed up with silver. I've tried my darnedest t'tell 'em different, but it's like they was deaf. They don't want to hear nuthin' about hard work, no, sir. They're a sight more interested in the figure they'll cut for the gals."

Steele grinned. "Any time you've a mind for them to learn different, I'll be glad to have them at the Shadow S."

Henry smiled warmly. "I appreciate the offer, Luke. Maybe I'll take you up on it, too. But if you happen to run into my Sarah, don't mention it. I don't reckon she'd be too fired up t'hear her boys have a hankerin' to be cowboys. She had her way, they'd be sent back east to study doctorin' an' such." He snorted. "Don't know as I could stand seein' those boys o' mine all slicked up in collar and tie and fancy coat and pants." He shuddered.

Luke nodded. He rubbed the white scar on his temple and frowned, the lines at the corners of his night-black eyes crinkling as he did so. "Say, I ran into a pretty little thing in town a day or so ago—green eyes and long, yellow hair. I reckon she must be new in town since I was here last. Know who I'm talking about?"

Henry gave one last resounding clang with his hammer against the horseshoe he was beating into shape on the anvil, picked it up with the long-handled tongs again, and dropped it into a shallow trough of cool water. He side-eyed Luke speculatively before answering, while the horseshoe steamed and sizzled.

"Yep, I reckon I know who you mean. I heard tell you helped her out when Todd Plimmer and his pals were giving her a hard time. That right?" Seeing Luke nod, he continued, "I'll tell you here and now, Luke, whatever you might have heard about her down at the *cantina* ain't true. She's a good little gal, best there is short of my own three."

"I reckon you know me better than to think I'd listen to gossip, Henry. I know what it can do to a man—or a woman—better than most hereabouts." A bitter smile deepened the furrows about his chiseled lips.

Henry had the grace to grin and look abashed. "We-ell, I reckon you do, at that." He eyed Luke slyly. "Wouldn't say that gossip's bothered you overmuch, though."

"Hell, no," Luke agreed, smiling himself now.

"I'm hoping Promise is the same way, but I reckon it's harder on a woman, having folks talkin' dirty about her." He shook his head. "Poor little gal. After all the misery she's had these past months, and now her Mama passing away, it don't seem right she has to put up with Hollander and the Plimmer boy making things harder." Grim faced, he took a sharp knife and pared some of the overgrown hoof away so that the shoe would fit well. As he hammered, his ruddy face grew ruddier still from the heat of his forge. Sweat rolled off him, soaking his shirt.

Luke waited for Henry to get to the point, fighting the urge to tell him to get on with it, for he was not a patient man by nature. He was used to doing things in his own way and in his own time. Since his life often depended on his ability to react with no more than a hair's-breadth hesitation, waiting on the slow-moving blacksmith didn't sit well with him. Nevertheless, he had determined to learn more of the lovely, green-eyed *desperada*, and if

Henry knew of her, he was willing to make an exception.

"Promise O'Rourke's the girl's name," Henry supplied at long last. "Her mama, Mary, passed away yesterday morning. Poor little gal's all alone in the world now. The burial's this morning, out at their cabin off the creek road." He jerked the tongue in Luke's direction and added sternly, "If you've a mind to go botherin' her, I'd think twice if I were you. If you're looking fer a woman to paint the town red with, I heard tell Rosalia down at the *cantina's* been lookin' all over fer you." He clicked his teeth and rolled his eyes. "Handsome woman, that Rosalia, yessir!"

Luke Steele wiped the grin from Henry's broad face with an expression that was colder, bleaker, than a Colorado winter. "*O'Rourke*, you said?" he gritted, as if he had heard nothing Henry had said after the girl's name. His body was no longer relaxed, but tensed as a bowstring. There was a savage, cruel light in his piercing black eyes now.

Henry grunted that he had.

"I . . . knew a fellow named O'Rourke a few years back," Luke said carefully. "He and his family had a traveling wagon and went from town to town selling snake oil, back in '58, that was."

"Yep. I reckon that'd be Promise's pa, all right," Henry agreed. "If you and he were friends, I reckon she'd be pleased for you to stop by and offer your condolences. There'll be few enough that will. The pious old hens we have here in Cherry Creek won't want nothin' to do with her, since that damned Hollander over yonder at the bank dirtied her name up. Shoot, I reckon there was more harm done in this world from a gossiping tongue than was ever done by any number of bullets. Promise'll be staying here, with us, until she decides what to do with herself.

93

You come on by when you're ready."

"I will," Luke said curtly. "Me and the boys'll come by later to load the supplies on the wagon. I'll be seeing you, Henry."

Luke left, the rhythmic clang of the smith's hammer ringing in his ears as he went. He turned onto the boardwalk and started down it on soundless boots. A small boy peered around a rain barrel at him, his eyes almost popping from his head.

"Hey, mister!" he piped, looking like a prairie dog poking its head from a hole.

Luke looked back over his shoulder, his hard features softening. "Yep?"

"My pa says you're a God-blamed redskin. Is that true, mister? Is it?"

Luke crouched down alongside the boy. "Hell, yes," he admitted. "My mother was a full-blooded Cheyenne woman. Her name was Singing Wind."

"Cheyenne! Oh, boy!" The boy's bright blue eyes grew rounder still, rounder than saucers beneath his uneven thatch of carrot-red hair. "Did—did you ever scalp anyone, mister?" he asked hopefully.

Luke eyed him at length. "Nope. I don't reckon I ever did. See, I have me a hankering to make the first time I take a scalp real special—you know what I mean? I figure the first one I lift has got to be from a redhead. Know anyone that might fit the bill?"

The boy's eyes looked about ready to fall into the dust of the street as they bugged out of his now-pale, freckled face. He jammed his hat down hard to hide his carroty thatch and gulped. "Nope!" he whispered, dry mouthed, as Luke uncoiled to standing. The boy gaped up at him then suddenly dived between his legs and lit out down the dusty main street as if a whole party of Indians on the warpath were after him, yelling, "Mama! Mama!" at the top of his lungs.

Luke smiled and continued on down the boardwalk to the rooming house. In his room at Morgan's, he washed up and changed into a dark shirt, the closest he could come to funeral wear on such short notice. Finally, he hefted his saddle and saddlebags over his shoulder and went back downstairs.

Half an hour later he was heading toward the O'Rourke cabin on his blue roan horse. He wasn't smiling any more.

Sarah Crowley put a motherly arm about Promise's shoulder, offering her support to the grief-stricken girl. Promise's eyes had been swollen from crying all night, but cold-tea compresses had done wonders. Now she was ashen faced but composed, looking even younger than her sixteen years in her mother's good black dress which was too large for her. She wore her pretty hair scraped severely back into a knot and had draped a black lace shawl over her head. Sarah sighed. Thank the Lord she had come by to visit early yesterday morning. There was no telling how long the girl might have stayed kneeling at her mother's feet if she hadn't.

In all, only a handful of people had shown up for the funeral—and even less for the burial beneath the apple tree—despite the many kindnesses Mary and her daughter had done for the townsfolk. Such small-mindedness on their parts made Sarah's blood fairly boil. Were they all so blind and stupid that they couldn't figure out Matt Hollander for what he really was—a loud-mouthed braggart and a liar into the bargain? Sarah pursed her lips grimly and looked across the grave to where the bank manager stood alongside his prissy wife, Mae-Ellen, and she snorted inwardly. It would do Hollander a power of good if she were to whisper a few timely words of warning in Mae's ears and put a stop to his tom-catting and mouthing-off once and for all. To look at him—hair slicked down, mustache newly waxed, pompous as a rooster in his dark frock-coat and tall hat— he seemed the veritable pillar of the community he wanted everybody to think he was, rather than a lecherous old bull who'd try to take advantage of an innocent, sweet child like Promise, and her hardships.

"Easy, darlin', we're almost through it," Sarah whispered. "You just be strong a while longer. You're mama's restin' easy now, honey. She ain't in no more pain." Sarah steadied Promise, squeezing her hands to comfort her. "After, you're coming home with me and Sue, to stay with us for a while, and I won't hear differ- ent. Reckon I could use another daughter, anyway—that Nancy's so darned idle."

Promise smiled wanly and gave a slight nod, wanting to show Sarah she appreciated all she had done. The rest of the funeral passed in a blur. She threw a handful of dirt in the grave at Sarah's urging, then the preacher droned on for a few more minutes and it was all over. The few folks who had made the ride out from Cherry Creek came and offered her their condolences, among them Arthur and Virginia Morgan, old Mister Erickson, Sheriff Harding and his wife, and portly Doctor Plimmer, who couldn't look Promise in the eye. She knew right then that he had heard the lies Hollander had spread, and believed them. She noticed that, behind his gold-rimmed spectacles, Arthur's eyes had been bloodshot from crying, and her heart ached. Poor Mama! Pa had loved her, and Arthur, too, and yet she had clung all her life to her memories of stolen kisses and Courtney Fontaine, instead of building herself a new life. Promise broke down and sobbed again, and Sarah thrust a handkerchief into her hands. Promise held the rough cotton square up to her face, trying to regain her former composure but failing miserably.

"What are you starin' at, Mister Hollander?" Sarah snapped, putting her arms protectively around Promise. "Hasn't the child gone through enough without you gapin' at her that way? Where's your sense of what's fittin' at a time like this?" She turned an angry blue eye on Mae-Ellen, Hollander's prissy, plump, blond wife. "As for you, Mae-Ellen, can't you keep that husband of yours to home, where he belongs, 'stead of lettin' him go about bad-mouthin' young girls and oglin' at 'em?"

Mae-Ellen opened her mouth to retort, her fair complexion reddening angrily. "Well, I never, Sarah Crowley! You'd—"

"Shut up, Mae-Ellen!" Hollander barked excitedly. "Roy," he said, pointing a shaking finger at Promise, "it was *her*! It was her that robbed my bank! D'you recall I told you the boy had green eyes? Hell, it just hit me right then where I'd seen them eyes before, when she held that handkerchief up to her face. I'm as certain as I'll ever be about anything!"

Promise paled still further and looked about her wildly, wanting to bolt like a frightened jack-rabbit but frozen in place by sheer terror. "I—I never—I . . ." Her voice trailed away.

"The hell you didn't!" Hollander exploded. "Sheriff, I'm demanding you take her in. The Reynolds Gang may have got away with what they did, but I'll be damned if that little tramp is going to!"

"Calm yerself, Hollander," Sheriff Roy Harding said,

holding the banker back by the arm. "I reckon feelin's are runnin' pretty wild today, so just get a hold of yerself, man. Maybe the fellow that robbed your bank did bear some likeness to Miss Promise, but that ain't no cause for you to go shootin' off your mouth again an' accusin' her. Hell, Hollander, it's her mama's funeral we've come here t'witness!" Harding shook his head in disgust.

"Weren't just resemblance to her, Roy, I'm telling you, it *was* her! She came sashaying into my bank only three days before the robbery and told me she didn't have the money that she and her mother were owing me, and no way t'come up with it." He sneered. "Don't it seem downright suspicious that the very same mornin' the bank was robbed, she shows up cool as you please with a fistful of silver dollars and pays off her debts? Ask her where she got the money, Roy, go on, ask her."

Roy sighed and walked across to where Promise and Sarah and Susan Crowley stood beneath the shade of the apple tree.

"Miss Promise," the sheriff said gently, "d'you reckon you could oblige me by telling me where you did get the money?"

Promise wet her lips, her green eyes traveling from Harding's weathered, travel-tired visage to Hollander's smug, fleshy face with its sheen of sweat, then she looked up into Sarah Crowley's handsome, motherly face as if imploring her to help.

"Go on, honey, tell him," Sarah urged "and then we can get your things and go."

Promise swayed a little, aware suddenly of how hot it was this morning and the way the sun was beating down. Mama's black dress stuck to her spine, and there were tiny beads of perspiration on her brow and upper lip, standing out against the ashen pallor of her face. She swallowed, her fingers plucking nervously at the trailing ends of the black lace shawl. Time seemed to hang suspended while everyone stared at her, awaiting her answer.

"I—I borrowed it," she whispered.

"You did, did you?" Hollander jeered, barreling forward to stand inches from Promise. The smell of his oily pomade made her feel like retching. "Who'd you borrow it from, *Miss* Promise?" he demanded. "Speak up, girl. We're all waitin' on you."

"She borrowed it from me, Hollander—not that it's any of your damned business," said a voice behind the knot of people.

They turned to look as one man, and even Sarah Crowley's eyes widened to see Luke Steele standing there. Promise swallowed a gasp of relief. She didn't know why Steele was doing what he was, but Lord, she was sure glad to see him!

"You?" Hollander snorted. "If you believe that, Roy, you'll believe any damned thing. Why'd a half-breed rancher lend money to a little tram—"

He never finished the sentence. Luke's fist cut him solidly under the chin, reeling him backward to the dust of the yard spitting blood and teeth. "It's about time someone shut you up," Luke said calmly. "I reckon I don't like you overmuch, Hollander, or the things you've been saying all over town about Promise." He turned to Roy Harding who was hiding a grin. "Man's got a right to put a stop to people bad-mouthing his intended, wouldn't you say, Sheriff?"

Roy Harding nodded. "I reckon I'd have to agree with

you, Steele. Hollander, you and Mae-Ellen had best get on back to town."

"You haven't heard the last of this, Promise O'Rourke, nor you, Steele!" Hollander threatened, lumbering to his feet and wiping the blood from his mouth with the back of his hand. Mae-Ellen fussed and clucked about him until he waved her angrily aside and stalked across the yard to where their buggy waited by the white-rail fence, his wife picking up her skirts and scurrying after him.

Sarah turned to Promise, her expression confused. "Your intended, Promise?" she asked. "But, you never—"

"We were waiting for the right time to tell everybody, weren't we, honey?" Luke Steele said, stepping alongside Promise and slipping his arm about her waist. Their eyes met—his, black and glittering beneath his hat brim and filled with the power he now held over her; hers, wide and startled and still shadowed by grief. His grip tightened about her waist.

"Ye-es, yes, that's right," she agreed in a small voice, looking quickly away.

Roy Harding extended his hand to Steele. "Then I guess congratulations are in order, Steele, Promise. It's nice t'think something good's comin' your way, Promise, after today." He tipped his hat. "Be seein' you folks. Good day Sarah, Miss Susan. C'mon, Mrs. Harding, let's be going." He took his wife's elbow and led her to their buckboard, leaving Sarah, her daughter, Promise, and Steele watching as he went.

"I don't know what to say, Promise," Sarah said after they'd driven off. "Why, I never even knew you two knew each other, let alone . . ." She shook her head while Sue muffled a giggle and side-eyed the handsome

Luke. "Will you still be coming to stay with us?"

Promise opened her mouth, but before she could speak Luke had answered for her.

"No, I'm taking Promise back to the Shadow S with me. Hollander's fixing to make more trouble—I'd stake my life on it—and I wouldn't want her mixed up in it. We'll ride into Santa Fe in a week or so and have the preacher there say the words over us." He smiled and his teeth showed white against the dark, weathered tan of his face. "Thanks for taking care of Promise, Sarah. Henry has himself a fine woman." He turned to Promise. "Is there anything here that needs taking care of before we leave, honey?"

"There's Selfish—our milk cow—but I'm not—"

"Can you have Henry come by for the cow?" Luke asked Sarah. She nodded. "Then I guess everything's taken care of. Promise, I'll see the ladies to their buckboard and leave you a few minutes to yourself," he added, nodding at her mother's grave. Promise stood there dazed as he took Sarah and Sue by the elbows and escorted them to the wagon. When they drove away minutes later, she was still standing there staring after them.

Luke strode across the yard back to her side, and she recovered enough to realize that she was alone with him. The thought made her throat constrict.

"I—I guess I have to thank you again," she murmured uncertainly. "That's twice you've helped me out, Mister Steele. I'm obliged to you. I'll be just fine now, if you want to be going . . ." Something in his expression silenced her. He stood there looking down at her, an unfathomable expression on his face. He reached out and cupped her chin in his hard hand, gently but firmly, then his hand slid downward and his fingers splayed lightly about her throat and stayed there. She closed her eyes, afraid of what he might do next, far more frightened than she had been the day Todd Plimmer had tried to force himself on her. The pulse in her throat fluttered against his fingers and she wondered, feeling weak at the knees, if he meant to choke her with those long, tanned fingers.

"I'm not going anywhere without you, *honey*," he said softly. "Get your things together and stack them on the porch. I'll have one of my boys come by for them later."

His fingers still rested lightly on her throat and she gulped, her mouth too dry for speech. "But . . . I don't want to go with you! I don't even know you!"

His fingers tightened slightly and he used the pressure to pull her closer, suddenly lowering his dark head and covering her lips with his own cruel mouth. His kiss stole the breath from her and sent shock waves ricocheting throughout her body. When he released her, there was a dazed look in the green pools of her eyes, and her lips were stained a deep coral from his kisses. The black lace shawl she wore over her head had fallen back, revealing her hair coming unpinned from the severe coil in which she had worn it. Cornsilk tumbled in an enchanting mass about her slender shoulders. His black eyes raked the pretty picture she made standing there, still stunned by his embraces as he towered over her, her hands fluttering to her breast to still the sudden tumult of her racing heart.

"You'll know me well enough real soon, *desperada*!" he promised harshly, surprised to find his own breathing as erratic as hers seemed to be. "Silence has its price, wouldn't you say?" His eyes left her in no doubt as to what that price would be. He returned his fingers to her throat and stroked it lightly, menacingly. "Which will it be, honey?" he breathed. "Will you be coming with me—or shall I tell Hollander that he was right, maybe even show Harding the clothes you wore to rob the bank?"

"You don't leave me much choice, do you, mister?" Promise replied, misery in her heart.

"No, I don't reckon I do," Steele agreed grimly.

Chapter Seven

By midafternoon, Cherry Creek was far behind them, nestled somewhere in the foothills of the mighty Rockies that rose like fresh-baked biscuits, golden topped in the afternoon sun. Ahead lay the barren plains which seemed a bolt of brown and amber calico cloth unrolled as far as the eye could see, with low hills rippling like folds in that cloth forming shallow valleys between them.

Tumbleweeds bowled past from time to time in the ever present wind, great balls of nothing, coming from nowhere and going the same place. Soapweed showed its straggly pink head, and spiny clumps of pointed sharp cactus known as Spanish dagger dotted the reddish earth. Sometimes Promise would look up from her seat on the supply wagon and spy jack rabbits bounding for cover, or look up to see the massive wingspread of a golden eagle etched against the vivid blue sky, or glimpse a gopher sneaking a look at them from its hole as they passed by. The few cottonwoods that grew here were warped into something misshapen and grotesque by the weather and the absence of a protecting gully or a shielding bluff to buffer them from the elements. Gnarled and stunted as they were, they reminded Promise of malevolent dwarves.

104

"How long will it take to get there, to Mister Steele's ranch?" Promise asked the driver beside her as she kneaded her fists into her aching back.

Black-Strap grinned, his teeth a startling white against the seamed ebony of his skin. Shoving back the brim of his floppy felt hat, he scratched his woolly gray head. "Ah reckon 'bout the same as it always does, Miz O'Rourke," he said, smiling. "Three weeks there an' three weeks back, if'n we're lucky."

"You mean we have to sleep out here in the open every night?" Promise asked, aghast at the thought.

"Yessir, missie, that's right. But you don't have to fret none. We got usselves plenty o' grub and bedrolls in back o' dis wagon. It'll be jest like you was to home, an' you'll sleep like a lil' baby." He grinned broadly.

Promise made no comment, not at all convinced by the wrangler's reassurances. Whatever words of comfort he might offer, she sorely doubted she would ever feel truly safe again; not for as long as she had traveling companions such as these—a Mexican, a Negro, and the menacing, dangerous, half-blooded Luke Steele.

After leaving the cabin, Steele had ridden back into Cherry Creek with Promise clinging tightly to his belt, behind him on the blue roan. He'd left her at the livery stable while he went in search of his hands, Black-Strap, his wrangler, and the Mexican cook he'd introduced casually as Joaquin. Henry Crowley had looked askance at Promise as she waited for Steele to conclude overseeing the loading of his supply wagon.

"Sarah tells me you and Luke Steele are fixing to get yourselves hitched. That so?" he had asked her, pulling on his red whiskers.

She couldn't meet his piercing look without flinching and turned away. "Reckon so," she murmured, coloring hotly.

"How long exactly have you known Steele?" Henry had asked, eyebrows arched.

Promise had turned to face him and looked him square in the eyes. "Altogether . . . maybe half an hour, Mister Crowley, sir," she murmured frankly.

Henry had nodded. "Reckon you know what you're doing, girl?" he had asked, and Promise had known by his lack of surprise at her announcement that even if she had chosen to lie, Henry already knew the truth.

"Yes, sir," she had answered. It was go with Steele or hang, she thought. She knew what she was doing, all right.

A grunt that could have meant plenty or nothing was Henry's response. "Good luck to you then, Promise," he had said gruffly. "I reckon you know there'll always be a place for you here with me and Sarah and our young'uns, should you ever be needin' it. Don't be a God-blamed fool and stay out at the Shadow S if it turns out you've made a mistake. Takes a smart man—or woman— to admit when he's licked and get hisself out from under. Only a fool or a weakling buries hisself in deeper, an' don't you forget it, y'hear?"

Promise nodded mutely, but her jaw had stiffened.

The stern expression had ebbed from Henry's broad face. He grinned suddenly. "Heck, girl, if you ain't a pair! Luke Steele and Promise O'Rourke. It just might work out at that. There's a stubborn streak running through you, girl, that I reckon will set ole Luke back on his heels once he runs up against it—and I'd stake my livery stables he will, yessir! I just wish t'God I could be there t'see it, an' that's a fact . . ."

Promise squinted against the sunlight as Steele rode back toward the wagon, the Mexican cook riding alongside him astride a mean-looking buckskin pony that was dwarfed by Steele's blue roan.

"We'll bed down for the night by the creek bed up yonder, Black-Strap," he announced.

"Yessir, boss," Black-Strap agreed, giving Promise an I-told-you-as-much look.

Minutes later, Black-Strap hauled on the reins and jumped spryly down from the wagon. Beyond lay the creek bed Steele had mentioned, overhung by scraggly willows and a few twisted cottonwoods. The wrangler came around the wagon and reached up to help Promise down. She put out her arms and smilingly accepted his offer.

"No need for that Black-Strap," Luke growled over his shoulder as he unbuckled his horse's girth. "Miss O'Rourke will have to look out for herself soon enough. Might as well start now. See to the horses."

Black-Strap looked from his boss to Promise and then back to Steele, who had returned to unsaddling his horse. He shrugged.

Promise glared at Steele's back, then smiled down at Black-Strap. "I can get down just fine by myself. You'd best get on."

Black-Strap nodded and went to unharness the team and lead them down to the creek for watering. Promise clambered down, stretching joints grown stiff over several miles of travel and the wagon's bone-jerking rhythm. She didn't recollect ever having an ache in her body no matter how many miles they had driven when she was a child.

She stood there uncertainly for a minute or two, wanting to ask the cook if he needed any help but reluctant to make such a move and risk Steele's disapproval or anger. Just as she had decided to offer anyway, Luke came striding toward her, his saddle hefted over his shoulder.

"If you're planning on joining the rest of us for chow tonight, you'd best make yourself useful. We've got a rule out at the Shadow S. A man don't pull his weight, he don't eat. That's it, pure and simple."

Despite her fatigue, Promise's green eyes took on a fiery emerald glint. She tossed her damp mane of fair hair over her shoulders and glared at him. "There was no need for you to tell me that, mister," she snapped. "Us O'Rourkes may have been poor, but we were never freeloaders!"

A mocking smile twisted Steele's lips. "How about liars and thieves?" he flung over his shoulder as he strode toward the campfire Joaquin had already started.

Promise stormed after him, crimson color riding high on her cheekbones. He sensed her at his back and spun to face her.

"Was it something I said, Miss O'Rourke?" he drawled.

Promise brought herself up short, fingers itching to slap his insolent face. Instead, she gritted between clenched teeth, "If I were a man, I'd make you eat those words, Steele."

His dark eyes raked her, lingering on her flushed face momentarily before they dropped to her breasts, which were heaving against the black cloth of her dress in her anger. Slowly his gaze returned to her eyes, slanted and bright as shards of green glass in the rapidly fading light. "If you were a man, honey," he said softly, "you'd be dead, coming up behind me like that." He turned his back on her again and picked a spot by the creek bank, dropping his saddle on that spot before sliding down to the water and cupping it in his hands to wash up.

His soft-spoken threat had taken the wind out of Promise's sails momentarily. She simply stared after him, hating him, furious to feel tears pricking her eyes. *I won't cry. I won't!* she vowed silently, but it was hard not to after all she had been through that day and the day before. It took several painful swallows before the dry lump of misery that choked the back of her throat eased enough that she could speak. She offered Joaquin her help and, although his expression indicated he resented her help in his domain, the camp kitchen, he had overheard the exchange between the two and grudgingly muttered, "*Sí*," delegating to Promise the task of making the biscuits.

The horses had been watered, hobbled, and staked out to graze when the four sat down for supper an hour later. There was coffee to drink, thick and black as paint, sweetened with even blacker molasses, and some sort of spicy stew of beef and tomatoes and beans spiced with green chilies that almost blew the roof off Promise's mouth when she unsuspectingly took a mouthful. She turned beet red and reached blindly for her mug of scalding coffee, tears streaming from her eyes, her tongue feeling as if it had been burned clear through.

Black-Strap and Joaquin burst into guffaws of laughter across the fire from her, unmoved by her painful coughing attack and making no move to help her in any way. When she finally recovered enough to open her eyes again, she saw that Luke Steele was also smiling faintly, mocking her distress. Resolve swept through her. Damn his hide! she seethed silently. No matter what it took, she determined, he'd never laugh at her again, no sir. Come what may, she'd smother any indignity, any hurt he sent her way, with a stoicism that would do credit to an—an Indian. The resolution to fight back was almost as exhilarating as the risk and danger involved in robbing Hollander's bank had proved. New energy coursed through her tired body and aching limbs like a fiery dose of spirits.

She casually took another spoonful of the beef and tomatoes—aware as she did so of the three pairs of eyes watching her expectantly—swallowed, then followed it down with a bite of biscuit and another swig of coffee. She looked up, smiling sweetly across at the Mexican cook. "Why, Mister Joaquin, that's mighty tasty once you get used to it some."

Joaquin's mouth dropped open. He grinned, brown eyes twinkling, and nodded vigorously, and Promise knew she had gained ground this time. "*Gracias, Señorita* Promise," Joaquin began enthusiastically. "Tomorrow, I show you how to make, *si?*" His smile dwindled as he caught his boss's eyes, and he hurriedly returned his attention to the contents of his own tin plate.

The moon rose while they were still eating, a thin, silvery sliver laid on its side like the curved spread of long horns atop a cow's head. The sun sank beyond the hazy rust blur of the distant mountains and for a few moments it was as if the horizon were afire with crimson, flame, and gold. Darkness settled over the shallow gully where they had made camp. Stars came out one by one to twinkle high above, bright and shiny as tiny silver spurs. In the distance the coyotes howled, while nearby the horses whickered or coughed in the shadows.

With nightfall, the men turned to swapping yarns and smoking. Promise felt her eyelids droop as weariness overcame her. She must have dozed off where she sat leaning against the rough trunk of a cottonwood tree, for she was jerked awake by a hand clamping over her

110

shoulder and shaking her, if not roughly then very firmly.

"Time to bed down, *desperada*," Steele murmured. "Come on."

"Wh—where?" Promise mumbled sleepily, dragging herself to her feet.

Luke thrust a bedroll into her arms and led her beneath a cottonwood that branched low over the creek, far from the cook and the wrangler. He set about building them another fire before jerking his head to where his own bedroll was spread, indicating he intended she should sleep alongside him.

Too tired to protest, Promise unrolled her blanket and spread it on the hard ground next to Luke's before tumbling wearily onto it and rolling the rough woolen blanket around her. She sensed Luke stretching himself out close by, and she drowsily muttered for him to go away as his arm coiled about her waist and drew her firmly against the length of his body. Some still-alert part of her mind registered that he was lying beside her and that she should demand he sleep somewhere else, but the greater part recognized only the warmth given off by his body, and accordingly she moved closer in search of that warmth. In seconds, she was too deeply asleep to care.

In the flickering firelight, Luke smiled mirthlessly. She had made little protest when he lay beside her. Rather, she had snuggled closer to him, fitting her slenderness to his hard male body. You were wrong, Henry, he thought, your innocent little girl is about as innocent as I am! I'd stake money on it . . .

He slid his hand up from where it had curled about her waist and cupped one of her small, firm breasts, feeling the heat of her body against his skin through her clothing. At the brush of his fingers, there was a subtle hardening as a pert nipple rose in response, and desire filled him, fired by his need for revenge. She murmured in her sleep and pressed backward against him, her derrière lodging snugly against his hard hips, and her long, silky hair tickling his nostrils. The feel of her warm female body so close to his—her fragrance so sweet and innocent as a wildflower filling his senses—aroused him as Rosalia and others like her had never done before. Why not? he thought, pulling her closer. Why not here, now? It was as good a time and place as any for what he had planned for Patrick O'Rourke's daughter . . .

He rolled her over onto her back and took her roughly in his arms, knowing how frightened she'd be to waken and find herself locked in his tight embrace. He wanted to see the fear fill her wide green eyes. *It's time for you to pay, desperada*, he said silently as he covered her soft mouth with his bruising lips.

For a second, she lay loose and relaxed in his arms, still deeply asleep. But as his fingers knotted in her hair and his kiss grew hungrier, she awakened, stiffened, began to struggle to free herself, her cries muffled by his mouth, her body writhing under his weight. She tried to flail her hands at him, to kick him, do anything to break his hold upon her.

"No, *desperada*, it's no use fighting me," he whispered huskily, gripping her chin firmly between his fingers. "We made a deal, you and I. I aim to see you keep your part of the bargain!"

The lust for revenge burned like wildfire through him, eroding his gentler side, blotting out all tenderness as he fondled her, feeling his hunger for her build and gather until it became a raging storm tide of fury. Deaf to her pleas, unmoved by the sheen of tears upon her cheeks in the starlight, he cruelly rent the black gown from her body. Her other garments followed. Her slender body lay bare in his arms, luminous as pearls in the moonlight.

"No!" she cried out, knotting her fingers in his hair and tearing it out by the fistful. "Dear God, no!" she sobbed. Panic swept through her as she realized his strength was too great for her to resist him. Nevertheless, she lashed furiously at his dark head, thrashing wildly with her legs. In desperation, she sank her teeth into his shoulder as he pinned her to the ground with his weight. Yet he seemed not to notice, holding her wrists above her head and parting her thighs with a roughly placed knee before kneeling arrogantly between them, breathing heavily.

Her cornsilk hair was a tangled river of silver where the moonlight glinted in its depths, and red-gold where it reflected the light of the fire. For a moment he looked down at her, stunned by her innocent loveliness, and their eyes met. He saw the tears shining in her frightened green pools, caught the tremulous quiver of her little mouth—now a dark rose from his cruel kisses—as she fought her sobs. "Please," she whispered, her voice husky, breaking at the end. "Please, don't do this . . ."

Her beseeching tone touched something deep inside him, something buried beneath his fierce hatred and need for revenge, and for a moment his resolve wavered. "I must," he growled at length, his night black eyes aglitter with desire. Yet he did not take her cruelly then, as he had intended. Instead, he dropped his dark head to her breasts, hating himself as the satin flesh shivered away from his lips in terror, then rose treacherously against his mouth. He heard her soft moan of despair and knew that despite her fear, against her fervent wishes to the contrary, something of his desire had aroused her. To

113

have her respond, to have her cry out in passion to him—
to *him*—yes, it would be payment enough for now, he
decided, and drew the vulnerable flesh deep into the heat
of his mouth, darting his tongue tip again and again
against the sweet warmth until she writhed beneath his
lips even while begging him to stop.

Promise gasped as his flaming mouth seared her body
with kisses and caresses, and his strong hand grazed down
over her rib cage and lower to explore and inflame the
intimate hollows of her woman's body that no man had
ever touched before. Shame burned through her as her
body responded to the gentleness of his inflaming caress.
She shivered. She wept. Yet she could not escape his
imprisoning arms any more than she could escape the
knowledge that his touch gave her perverse pleasure,
that her treacherous body was awakening uncontrollably
in response to the fierce, hard heat of his. *Lord, help me!*
she cried silently, filled with horror that this savage
stranger's cruel passion could wreak such havoc inside
her. She was no better than a saloon girl, or one of the
girls at Dirty Molly's place, to have surrendered herself
to him so easily. Why couldn't she have borne his cruelty
in silence, without pleading? She clenched her fists and
gritted her teeth, trying to remain unmoved by his ardent
assault as he touched and teased and moved his hot
mouth and maddening hands over her burning flesh. Oh,
she would have rather he had taken her roughly, against
her will, then bring about her willing surrender this way,
with calculated gentleness and sensual strokings. Damn
him. Her pulses were singing, and oh, the heat that his
touch sent raging through her, building, tingling . . .

In her innocence, she had no knowledge of how to
withstand the heady fires he created so masterfully inside
her, no means to hide her reluctant pleasure. When at

the last he loomed above her, muscled shoulders gleaming in the ruddy firelight, his black eyes lit from within by desire, his mouth ardent and hungry upon her own, she made no more than a token protest as he thrust strongly forward to bury himself inside her. There was a curious, shameful hunger inside her, too, that cried out to be satisfied. She felt an instant's searing pain that was soon replaced by a delicious sensation of fullness that she wanted to go on and on.

He lay quite still upon her suddenly, and she was certain that it was all over, and yet she felt no relief that it should be so, for the little aching deep in her belly was still there, still yearned for something more . . . Was there more? Or was that all there was? Was there to be no matching pleasure for her, no equal to the groan of delight that had been torn from him? She stared numbly up at the glittering, cruel stars, at the moon racing with the clouds, at the flocked boughs of the cottonwoods dancing in the night breeze, and hated herself as much as him.

Although it was only a short while, it seemed like forever that he lay still upon her, his weight pressing her heavily to the hard, stony ground, his rough chest crushing the softness of her breasts. But then she felt a stirring and his great hardness filled her again. She felt him begin to move once more. Gone was the fury now, but in its place was something better, something so exquisitely pleasurable that she held her breath as he moved rhythmically, deeply within her, unwilling to do anything to detract from the sensations sweeping through her.

The strange yearning built again. It became throbbing bubbles of pleasure everywhere inside her, in her tingling breasts, so full, so exquisitely sensitive now, and in that

secret, small place between her thighs that quivered on
the brink of bursting for endless moments before finally
exploding and filling her with breathless, sated rapture.
In the midst of her pleasure, she curled her arms about
his throat and kissed his dark, handsome face, whispering
her delight. But angrily he thrust her from him and
stood, shrugging on his pants. She watched silently as he
strode away, a lump welling up in her throat. Her joy of
scant seconds before was tarnished now, cheapened by
the knowledge that he had only used her. The desire she
thought she had glimpsed for a fleeting second in his eyes
had been only lust, nothing-more. "You won't use me
again, never again, Luke Steele!" she whispered bitterly
on the night air. Gritting her teeth to keep from crying,
she gathered her clothes about her. "I'll die before you
lay a hand on me again, mister!"

When she was dressed, she waited for him to come
back. When several minutes passed and he did not, her
hopes soared. The horses were hobbled beyond the
wagon in the opposite direction to the one he had taken.
She would run away, she vowed, run away before he
could touch her again.

Keeping low, she sprinted back toward the glow of the
other campfire, seeing Joaquin and Black-Strap rolled in
their blankets alongside it, their snores coming loud and
regular on the hush of night. She scampered around the
supply wagon and edged toward the horses, her palms
slick with fear. The horses nickered and shied away from
her outstretched hand, circling nervously at her un-
familiar scent. Belatedly, she realized that they wore no
bridles—not even a hackamore that she could hold
on to—and she had never ridden bareback. She had
really never ridden much at all. Tears of frustration filled
her eyes. She would have to go back to Cherry Creek on
foot.

116

She flung about and began running blind, not caring where she was headed, not even afraid of Hollander and his accusations any more, knowing only that she had to get away, *must* get away, from Luke Steele. The stony ground hurt her bare feet. Only a wall of blackness lay ahead, filled with dangers she could only guess at. The coyotes' eerie howls on some distant rise sent prickles of terror dancing down her spine. Still she ran, tripping, stumbling in and out of gopher holes, her breath rasping from her parted lips and a vicious cramp knotting her side, skirting boulders that loomed out of the patchy darkness like giant eggs. Sagebrush and thorn bushes reached out with cruel fingers to snag at her skirts, to tangle in her tumbled hair, to scratch her face. She tore herself free of their grasp and forged on, racing the moon and the scudding clouds that cast their fleet shadows on the ground ahead of her, always ahead of her. She heard the shrill cry of a nighthawk, the ghostly whisper of the wind, and . . . the furious drum of hoofbeats coming up fast behind her!

Where to run? Where to hide from him? There was nowhere, no sanctuary where he could not find her. She ran faster, sobbing now, every breath agony, and still the hoofbeats came closer, louder . . . and she knew in her heart that she could not hope to escape him.

She flung about as he caught up with her and reined in his horse. For a second or two neither of them spoke, horse and rider etched black against the sky, the woman straight, proud, only the glimmer of long, fair hair betraying her sex. He held out his hand to her. "Climb on up, *desperada*," he commanded, his voice stern. "You gave it your best shot, but there's no way you can escape me, not on foot."

"Come back with you, so you can do—do that again? Never, you—you savage!" she cried fiercely.

117

She broke away suddenly and began running again, but in only a few swift strides the horse was upon her, its breath hot against the back of her neck, and she felt herself snatched from the ground and lifted roughly before Steele upon its bare back. He fastened his arms tightly around her like manacles. She could feel her heartbeat throbbing against his hand as he swung the blue roan's head around in the direction they had come.

The campfire's light seemed such a puny little glow against that vast blackness all about them, and miserably she wondered that she could ever have thought she could escape on foot. Luke's bare chest was like a wall of oak against her back, his breath fanning her hair. She should have been afraid of the anger that crackled all about him, but she felt suddenly bone weary, too weary to care, to fight him any more, or even to stay upright before him should his arms loosen their tight grip about her. If he let go, she knew she would tumble from the horse's back. "You won't win," she mumbled tiredly, "you won't! You'll only make me hate you more and more each time. I'll keep on running away, again and again, until one day you won't be able to bring me back, because you won't be able to find me."

"I've already won, *desperada*," he said coldly. "And there's no place on this earth you can hide—not from me. Remember that." He kicked the roan into a swift gallop, carrying her back to the camp.

Luke lay on one elbow watching her sleep, moved despite himself by the pale lavender circles that ringed her eyes and by the exhausted but innocent loveliness of her face in slumber. Had she guessed, he wondered? Did she have any inkling of why he had left her in anger last night? His jaw tensed, his lips becoming thinned and cruel. He had wanted her to find only heartbreak and shame in his arms, but instead something had moved him to give her pleasure. The white blood of his father in his veins had weakened him, swayed him from his purpose as no true son of the People would ever permit himself to be swayed.

He reached roughly for her, intending to take her again and prove his mastery over her, but as his fingers curled about her shoulder, she murmured sleepily, "Mmm, Pa . . ." and snuggled closer against him, curling one slender arm about his neck.

He stiffened and drew back, filled with a rush of anger that rapidly eroded the desire he had felt seconds before. Fists clenched, he gritted his teeth and turned away from her. In sleep, she had murmured the one word that could have stopped him from what he intended to do. *Is this your doing, O'Rourke?* he asked silently. *Do you protect her even now, from beyond the grave?* He smiled mirthlessly. It wouldn't work. Her father couldn't help her now. She was his, until he chose to cast her aside.

"Rise and shine, *desperada*. The sun's coming up."

Her long, fine lashes fluttered as she turned sleepily to face him, for a moment at a loss as to where she was and with whom. Memory returned then, and with it grief as she recalled that her mother was dead, that she was here, with *him*. She groaned in disappointment. She had dreamed it was not so, that Mama and Pa and she were rolling along a dusty trail in the painted wagon, headed for a settlement just over the next rise. All night they had ridden without reaching it . . .

"Already?" she grumbled aloud, pulling the blanket up to her chin against the morning air, as well as to hide herself from his smoldering eyes. Summer or no summer, it was cold in the morning, she thought, snuggling into the blanket and watching Luke warily as he sat up.

It was still more dark than light, and in the flickering glow of the fire his face was even darker, more savage, than by day. The glittering black eyes were set deep beneath a broad forehead and offset by brows that were like black slashes against the deep bronze tan of his flesh. Tiny lines winged out from their outer edges, evidence of too many days spent outdoors, squinting against the dazzling light. His cheekbones were set high in his face, the skin stretched tautly across them. Tousled strands of thick, straight, blue-black hair disheveled by sleep fell about his brow and temples, where a small triangular-shaped scar on one side showed silver against the tan. His nose was aquiline, and his lips held a sensual, relaxed droop as he put on his boots.

A shiver ran down her spine as she recalled his brutal assault of the day before. For all that he spoke like other men, dressed like other men, she sensed the untamed dark natures of his savage blood smoldering beneath the white man's veneer and knew it would not take much to bring them exploding to the surface.

He jammed his gray Stetson on his head and looked down at her. His lips softened, parting in an amused smile. "Seen enough, *desperada*?"

She blushed, but thankfully she lay in his shadow and he could not see her heightened color. He laughed softly at her expression and reached for the gunbelt beside him, uncoiling to stand with the same mountain-lion grace with which he did everything and towering over her as he buckled it across his lean hips. Then he took out his six-guns one by one and checked them, sighting down the barrels before spinning them easily back into the holsters.

Other sounds reached Promise now: Joaquin's humming of a lilting Mexican ballad as he got breakfast started; Black-Strap's colorful cussing as he readied the horses for traveling. The fragrant aroma of coffee carried on the air and with it the fresh scent of earth yet damp with dew. Promise lay where she was, reluctant to get up, hoping in vain that if only she stayed still long enough and wished for it hard enough, reality would recede and she would be back in the cabin by Cherry Creek once more, and her mama would be alive . . . It was a sort of game she had played since childhood, using her wishes and her imagination to make things the way she wanted them to be. She supposed that, like the resilience of her young body to traveling many miles in a rolling wagon, she had lost the knack of making it work the way she wanted it to.

Luke Steele left her then, returning minutes later carrying a bundle in his arms. He let it fall at her side and she saw he had brought the clothes she had worn to rob the bank, right down to the red bandanna. There was no gunbelt, or either of the guns, however, or the money sack.

"Put those on," he ordered. "They'll be a damn sight more comfortable than that funeral dress." With that, he turned away and swung his leg over the back of the roan Black-Strap held waiting and rode off.

It was dawn before he returned, and the morning meal of cold biscuits, warmed-over stew and hot coffee was ready. Promise refused the spicy beef, eating instead only biscuits sweetened with a trickle of molasses and three cups of scalding dark coffee. As she ate, she looked up and caught the approval in Steele's eyes over her change of clothes and quickly looked away.

Let him think she had obeyed him if it lulled him into

121

believing she was some sissy that he could turn meek
with harsh words and a threat or two. She had seen for
herself the sense in what he had said, though, and it was
for that reason and that reason alone she had put on the
men's clothing. She smiled inwardly as she dabbed up a
trickle of molasses with a morsel of biscuit before
popping it into her mouth.

Joaquin's and Black-Strap's eyes had come close to
bugging clean out of their heads when she had stepped
out from the cover of the willows that bowed low over the
creek bed, dressed this way. The checkered, red and blue
shirt had been cut to fit a man's flat-chested shape, and it
swelled snugly about each of her breasts. The open neck
ended in a deep V at the start of the valley between them,
exposing several inches of pale gold throat. She had
knotted the red bandanna loosely about her neck and let
the ends trail down to cover that expanse partially, for
modesty's sake. Fair hair fell straight and silky to
midback, streaming down from under her pa's old brown
hat with the curled-up brim. The heavy dark blue, man's
work pants, worn tucked into the tops of the stilt-heeled,
too-tight boots, fit about her womanly bottom like a
second skin—maybe tighter. How the eyes of the old
biddies in Cherry Creek would pop if they could only see
her now. Why, "tramp" and "hussy" wouldn't probably
be words they would consider too good for her then.

Breakfast was a hurried affair, notable only for its
silence. Afterward, she and Joaquin carried the tin plates
and mugs down to the creek, scoured them clean with
sand, and rinsed them off before stacking everything
back into the wagon. After the fire had been stamped out
and covered over with dirt, they set out once again and
were rolling along before dawn's pink flush had fully
faded from the sky. Luke rode far ahead on his roan while

122

Black-Strap rode the mean-tempered buckskin and Joaquin handled the wagon.

The Mexican cook, who was younger than Black-Strap, proved a far more loquacious traveling companion than had the wrangler. He whistled as he drove or sang snatches of songs in mournful Spanish that Promise rightly guessed were love songs. Even better, he didn't seem to mind answering her questions or even volunteering information on his own.

"*Señor* Steele, he goes ahead to scout the trail, *no?*" he remarked, jerking his head toward the distant, dark speck that was his boss. "The Indians, they are *muy peligroso*, very much dangerous, you see. Many times this summer they raid, shoot, kill many settlers. The young warriors are angry because the old *jefes*, the chiefs, want to make peace with the white men. The warriors say that this can never be, that the white man does not keep the promises he makes and that many of their people starve on the Agency lands the Great White Father sends them to."

Promise frowned. "But *Señor* Steele's half-Indian himself. Surely he has nothing to fear from the Indians?"

Joaquin shrugged. "Times, they are hard, *señorita*, for all men. But for the Indian they are even harder. Soon the winter will be here. The hunter must find game now, so that his woman can dry the meat and make pemmican for the months when snow lies thick upon the ground and game is scarce. For the Indian, the buffalo is life, *señorita*. The skins they use to build warm lodges or for clothing; the meat is their food—even the bones and sinews are not wasted. They use everything. But the buffalo is harder to find now. No longer do the great herds roam the plains. The settlements of the white man have scared them away. Hunters with the new repeating rifles have killed many thousands for their skins. Without the buffalo, the

123

Indian warriors are afraid their women and children will starve. When there is great hunger, fear, mistrust, and despair, *all* men are enemies, *señorita*, even those who share your blood in part. Even *Señor* Steele.''

Promise murmured her understanding, yet Joaquin's words had filled her with unease. Somehow, she had believed that Steele's Indian blood would prove a measure of protection against them being attacked by savages, and that at least on that score, she could rest easy. Now it appeared they had no such guarantee. Sarah's description of the murder and mutilation of the Hungate family returned to her mind then, and it was several miles before she could put such terrifying thoughts aside and return her attention to Joaquin's cheerful ramblings.

At about noon—she judged by the sun's position directly above them in the sky—they halted to rest the horses in the sparse shade of a few gnarled cottonwoods. Jerked beef and canteen water were passed out, then Luke gave the order to move out yet again. Promise rose, fanning her hot face with her hat, and headed for the wagon.

"Done much riding?" Steele asked, walking after her.

"Enough," she answered pertly, dismissing him with a glance.

"Black-Strap, bring the buckskin," he ordered. "I reckon it's Miss Promise's turn at riding now." He gave her a long, cool stare as if expecting her to refuse or protest.

Instead, she nodded. Minutes later she was astride the buckskin pony, hoping she didn't look as scared as she felt. Luke couldn't know it, but apart from the getaway gallop from the bank, it had been years since she had sat a horse, and even then only Henrietta, their old wagon horse, or one of the ponies belonging to the girls at the schoolhouse, who let her ride on the way home from school. She'd be damned if she would admit that to Steele, though, she decided, gathering the reins in her hands and kneeing the cow pony to canter after his roan.

The buckskin had a bone-jarring gait, she soon found. Riding him was rather like she imagined being thrown up into the air thirty times a minute would be, and landing each time on a bed of rocks while someone wrung your arms clean off at the shoulders. But apart from the discomfort, she liked the feel of the wind streaming through her hair, the heady sensation of speed, and of riding free across the land.

She hauled hard on the reins as the buckskin drew alongside Steele's horse, feeling enormously pleased that she had managed to stay on and been able to make the pony halt when she wanted him to. She gave Luke Steele a defiant smile.

"Quit hauling on the reins before you saw his mouth clean off," Luke growled, bursting her bubble of pride with his eyes.

She dropped the reins as if they were red hot. Suddenly, the animal's head went down between its forelegs and she felt a shiver of bunched muscles ripple underneath her in the fleeting second before his rump shot up like a rocket on the Fourth of July. She had no time to grab for the saddle-horn before she went flying through the air to land ignominiously on her buttocks at Luke's horse's feet. The air slammed from her in a sickening rush as she hit the dirt, and her teeth snapped together like a beartrap. The jerked beef and water in her belly rose up to about the region of her throat.

She groaned and dragged herself to standing, rubbing her bruised flanks. Gritting her teeth resolutely, she retrieved her fallen hat, used it to dust off the seat of her pants, and headed grimly after the buckskin who was quietly grazing the scrub grass nearby, reins trailing.

Just as she reached out for the trailing reins, the pony—who'd been rolling a crafty eye in her direction all the while—shied away. It happened twice more before Promise realized she wasn't going to catch him so easily and decided to try to best him at his own game. She stuck her thumbs in her belt and made as if to march determinedly past his head, hoping he would think she had given up. Once past him, she spun about and grabbed for the reins, almost whooping in triumph as she held them fast in her fist. The pony whickered and backed off, but Promise held firm. She mounted up again and drew a deep breath before daring a glance at Steele.

For a fleeting second, she thought she saw a glint of grudging admiration in his dark eyes and was surprised by it, for she had expected a mocking smile or worse, outright laughter. But if the admiration had truly ever been there, it was swiftly masked by indifference.

They rode on alongside for a mile or so, Promise stealing glances at Luke from time to time and trying to imitate the easy, erect way he sat his horse, moving fluidly as if he and the blue roan were one. Before long, a wet trickle of sweat ran down her back and stuck her shirt to her spine. Her inner thighs ached from gripping the buckskin's sides. Her rear felt black and blue, and her palms were beginning to blister from the chafing of the reins. Despite the hat, her cheeks, nose, and chin were becoming redder and tighter by the minute from sun and windburn. She bitterly regretted not having argued with Steele when he had said it was her turn to ride, but it was too late for regrets. In comparison, her seat atop the supply wagon now seemed as cozy as a feather-bed. Still, she would ache in silence rather than admit it to Steele. Somehow, she would stick it out . . .

Ahead lay a vast canyon, strange formations of red rock rising from the flat plains like the flying buttresses of some transported medieval castle. Luke signaled for her to wait and went on ahead, returning minutes later and beckoning her on. The supply wagon was still only a dust cloud far behind them, a toy wagon pulled by wooden horses from this distance. She touched the buckskin's sides with her heels and cantered after Luke, down into the canyon.

A narrow trickle of water meandered through the floor of the canyon, no more than two feet across in most places, and perhaps a foot deep, though the stream bed showed evidence of a higher water line in wetter seasons. Walls of red rock, shaded with brown and muddy ochre, towered above them on either side. The canyon was eerily silent and shaded, no sign of life anywhere in any shape or form. Luke dismounted and led his horse to water, removing his bandanna and wetting it before wiping the dust and sweat from his face and neck. Promise slid down from the buckskin and led him alongside the roan, reaching for the knot of her own kerchief to do likewise.

To her surprise, Luke grasped her shoulder and turned her to face him. She held her breath, heart fluttering with fear, as he bathed her burning face with his freshly wetted bandanna. She gasped as the tepid water touched her sunburned skin, then sighed with the sweet relief that followed as the stinging, salty perspiration was washed away. "Thanks," she muttered, daring a wary glance at his face. Her eyelashes swept quickly back down to curtain her thoughts as she looked away. He took her firmly by the chin and tilted her face up to his, his dark

127

eyes grave as he squeezed something cool and sticky onto the burned areas of her cheeks and brow.

"Cactus pulp," he explained, smoothing the gel into her skin with a touch that was surprisingly gentle. "It'll take some of the bite out of the burn."

She stood quite still while he doctored her, very aware of his nearness. His male scent—of horses and sweat, leather and tobacco—was full and tantalizing in her nostrils and brought back sharply the night before. When he was done, she made to turn quickly away from him, afraid her nearness would remind him, too. He cast the cactus pulp quickly aside and spun her into his arms before she could escape.

The brilliant afternoon light that arrowed its way over the walls of the canyon was blocked by the brim of his hat as he bent his head to hers. Her protests were muffled as his mouth captured her own. When he at last broke the kiss, she was breathless and furious, and thrust him away with her small fists clenched, gasping, "No!"

Her vehement tone amused him. Laughter twinkled in his eyes and caught up the corners of his mouth. "No? You seem to forget, *desperada*, we made a deal."

Color stained her cheeks. Angrily, she tossed her head and glared at him, her eyes like shattered emeralds, fierce and brilliant. "*You* made the deal, Mister Steele. Not me."

His black brows quirked up. "Not you? I seem to recall different, honey," he insisted softly. "My silence for your . . . company. Wasn't that the way it went?" His long brown fingers splayed across the slender column of her throat in a gesture that was calculated to remind her of the agreement they had come to the day before. His fingertips drew lazy circles against the wild throbbing of the pulse in her throat.

She gulped. "That's not fair!" she protested, shrugging off his hands. "My—my mother had just been buried. What kind of man are you to expect me to keep a promise made at a time like that?"

He gave her a long, enigmatic look. "The kind of man it's dangerous to play games with, honey," he threatened. He grasped her suddenly and jerked her against his chest, wanting to hold her in his arms as he had held her the night before, relishing the feel of her slender body arching furiously against his. Gripping her chin, he held her head still and again parted her mouth beneath his own. His tongue surged between her lips, arrogant and demanding in its possession of her velvet recesses, his fingers tracing the delicate knobs of her spine through her shirt as he pressed her hungrily to him. He looked into her eyes as he kissed her and saw that her eyes were wide open, glittering with hatred—and, yes, he thought there was desire there, too. She knew it, and it filled her with fury.

Promise seethed as he kissed her, as much from the new and heady feeling the warmth of his lips imparted as from anger at him. His knowing touch upon her back sent tingles coursing through her. His lips robbed her of reason and thought. Oh, but it was wickedness to feel that way, to be so weak and spineless on account of this . . . stranger's touch! Where was the vow she had made last night? Never again, she had sworn, and now . . .

Despite her anger, despite all the bitter promises she had made, her knees grew weak under the ardor of his lips and the caress of his warm hands. Even when her hat fell off and hung by its cord across her back, he still continued to devour her soft mouth, his lips tantalizing, teasingly gentle one minute, and merciless as he took

129

what he wanted the next. As he lowered his head to kiss her throat, she realized dimly that there would be no stopping him, as there had been none last night. Luke Steele was a man used to having his own way in all things. If he wanted her, he would have her. She was powerless to withstand him, too physically weak to successfully fight his greater male strength. Her only hope lay in using her more subtle, feminine wiles . . .

Wild, fluttery sensations tickled in the pit of her belly as his hand traveled lingeringly up the narrow ridges of her spine over her damp shirt, while the other clung to her slender curves and traced their outline with his palm. His hand burrowed beneath the silky weight of her hair and teased the downy nape of her neck, eliciting hot stabs of excitement in her that made her peculiarly reluctant to fight him off. She stiffened as one hand moved caressingly down, across her hips, to mould the taut swell of her bottom, and from somewhere she managed to find the will to react and wrench free of his arms. Like lightning, his fingers came out and laced in her hair, tugging it painfully. Without thought for what his reaction might be, she instantly brought back her hand to strike him hard across the cheek, feminine wiles forgotten in her outrage, but he caught her wrist in midair and wrenched it up and behind her back. She yelped, tears of pain filling her eyes.

"I warned you not to fight me, baby," he breathed unsteadily as he dragged her relentlessly against his chest once more.

Where his fingers ended against her rib cage, she could feel his body heat through the cloth of her shirt, and her heart began a wild, erratic thump-thumping that she knew he must be able to feel, but she was helpless to control it. His fingers slid to the pearl buttons of her shirt, easily slipping them free of the buttonholes. The cloth seemed to fall away like melted butter on a hot griddle as his fingers reached inside, drawing a taut breast into their warm cage and lazily stroking. His mouth trailed fiery kisses to below her ear, and his heated breath sent gooseflesh rising all over her as he murmured Indian words against her hair, his voice strangely thick.

"It won't work, Luke," she gritted, damning the fiery tide sweeping through her. "I warned you last night. Each time I'll hate you more and more, I'll never—*never* give in to you! You'll have to stake me out to hold me still—but then, that shouldn't be too hard. Isn't that the way with you folks—raping women who can't defend themselves? Is that what you want? Is that the only way it's good for you?" A great sob of rage heaved itself up from her lungs, and she clawed her hand down his hard, tanned face, knotted her other fist, and struck out blindly for his cheek, loading the blow with all the force she could summon in her blind rage. Her knuckles rang with the pain. "Do what you want, mister!" she cried. "I don't care any more. I thought back in Cherry Creek the other day that you were better than Todd Plimmer or that Matt Hollander and the rest, but you're no different, no different at all. Do what you mean to do, but I'll fight you every step of the way, so help me God!"

His head had snapped sharply back with the violence of the blow, and strands of jet black hair fell forward across his brow. His features were tight, and a nerve pulsed at his temple. For a second he said nothing, and she was certain he intended to strike her back, but she braced herself for a blow that never came. Instead, he scowled, black eyes smoldering, and released her so suddenly and forcefully she lost her footing and sprawled on the ground. Blood oozed from where her nails had scored his cheek. A livid mark rode high on the other. He muttered a curse under his breath and stooped down to retrieve his hat from the ground where it had fallen in the scuffle. He stood and looked down at her, at the hellcat's fury blazing in her green eyes, at the tight, hard line of her mouth, at the rigid set of her body, breasts heaving against the cloth of her shirt, and knew she meant every word she had said. He might break her body, but she would die before she submitted her proud spirit to his will. Even as he watched, she spun around and ran to her horse, flung herself astride it, and dug in her heels, galloping the buckskin from the canyon.

Black eyes narrowed, he let her go, realizing belatedly that he had handled it wrong, all wrong. What triumph was there in forcing her to submit to him so long as her pride remained intact? None. None at all. He had rushed it, allowed his desire for her to take precedence over his revenge, and in so doing had gravely underestimated her spirit. She would use her hatred of him to fuel her courage, he knew. If he wanted to see this through, it called for different tactics . . .

A thin smile split his lips as he recalled the look that had been in her eyes for a fleeting second as he had kissed her, and the self-reproach in her expression as she had responded to his touch the night before. There. There was the answer! He would use the desires of her woman's body—desires he had awakened—against her. He would fan that fragile spark of attraction into a raging fire that she would be powerless to withstand. Sooner or later she would give herself to him willingly, hungrily, totally—and how much sweeter his vengeance would be then. With her proud spirit broken, he would have avenged himself on her damned father more completely than he had thought possible. Gentle caresses, tender kisses—

they would work better than any amount of force, he saw now. He would take her self-respect and her proud spirit, and grind them into the dust under the boot heel of his scorn and rejection, and laugh in her lovely face when she begged him to stop, to tell her it had all been some cruel game he played . . .

His night-black eyes smoldered like dark coals, and his hawk-like features tightened. Now he understood the revenge raids of his mother's people, the Cheyenne—the lust to draw blood, to inflict terrible pain on those who had betrayed or killed their loved ones. It consumed the soul, made all else pale in comparison to that single quest for vengeance. As Patrick O'Rourke had caused his freedom to be taken from him, so he would cause his daughter to suffer in return.

"Hiyaah!" he yelled and flung himself astride his horse, touching the roan's flanks to urge it into a swift gallop after the girl. He could see her now only as a swiftly moving cloud of red dust far ahead. He had to catch up with her before she decided to keep on riding clear back to Cherry Creek. He had no intention of losing her, not now . . .

Chapter Eight

Late afternoon of the third day, they camped alongside a river, known to the white man as the Arkansas, and to the Cheyenne, whose territory this was, as the Flint Arrowhead River.

It had been two days since Luke had ridden after Promise and forced her back to the wagon, but still she refused to speak with him, look at him, or acknowledge his existence in any way. When his back was to her, he could feel her eyes upon him with such fierce intensity that the hair at the back of his neck rose and prickled as if he were being stalked by a wild animal; yet when he swung around to face her, she was looking elsewhere! If she had her way, he'd be buried up to his neck under an ant hill—or worse, he thought ruefully, watching her through slitted eyes as he struck a lucifer match on his boot heel.

The girl was like a prickly burr lodged under his skin! Hardly a minute passed when he didn't find his eyes drawn to her, didn't catch himself watching her admiringly as she moved gracefully about the camp. At night, she pointedly dragged her blanket roll several feet apart from his, and he lay wakeful. Staring up at the glittering, dark sky spangled with tiny, hot stars, he knew that he wanted her, could not deny the hunger within him to hold her warm, slender body in his arms, to kiss her, caress her, take her. Knowing she was so near and yet so far away was a form of torture more subtle than he could ever have imagined, and one of his own devising, since he had determined to change his strategy.

In the past two days, he had learned to read her expressions, her little mannerisms, in much the same way he had learned to read the behavior of the pronghorn, or the otter and the beaver on those occasions when his father, Thomas Steele, a former trapper, had taken him hunting, or those other times when he had gone with his mother, Singing Wind, to learn the ways of her people, and he had hunted the hump-back, or buffalo, with the other young braves. "Breathin' spaces," his father had called those visits his bride made, knowing how Singing Wind had craved the freedom of her old, nomadic life. Right now, the wary expression in Promise's eyes signaled that she was aware he was watching her. The way she toyed nervously with her hair told him that knowing he was doing so set her on edge, and it gave him perverse pleasure to continue his scrutiny.

"The *señorita*, she is angry with you, no, *señor*?" Joaquin observed, hiding a grin as Promise glared at *el señor* and flounced away.

"The *señorita* is very angry with me, yes, *amigo*!" Luke rejoined, grinning, drawing a cheroot from the pocket of his checkered shirt.

"When the man is angry, he hurts only himself. When the *mujer* is angry, everybody suffers, eh, *señor*?"

"You're right there, Joe," Luke agreed with feeling. Their camps these past two nights had been crackling with hostility. "I reckon I'll be glad when we reach Bent's

135

Fort. Maybe all the coming and going there will snap her out of it." He shrugged doubtfully.

"Ah! Your grandfather, he will be there with the Cheyenne?"

Luke nodded. "I sure hope so. But . . . he's an old man, and last winter was long and rough." Apprehension darkened his eyes, and he drew deeply on the cheroot, exhaling the smoke in twin streams through his nostrils. "I guess I'll find out if he got through it in a day or two." Despite his words, his tone was uncertain. So many of the old ones were dying, he thought bitterly, their will to live gone now that their old hunting grounds had been lost under white settlements. Yellow Rock, the *shaman*, belonged to old Chief Black Kettle's Cheyenne, and was cared for in his old age by a nephew, Scarred Hand, and his wife. Yellow Rock and Scarred Hand, his uncle, Four Winds, and his wife were all the Cheyenne family left to him since the cholera epidemic back in '49.

"I hope so, *señor*," Joaquin said sympathetically.

Luke dropped the butt of his cheroot to the ground and crushed it beneath his boot heel before tossing the frayed tobacco wad into the campfire. Fire was a constant threat on the dry grasslands during the long, hot, summer months, and he would take no chances of starting one. Thumbs hooked into his belt, he strolled down to the creek where Promise was drawing water for coffee and stood there silently watching her for several minutes before she was aware of him.

When she turned and saw him, her green eyes darkened in anger. Did he have to sneak up on her so damned silently like that? Oh, how she wished she could get away from him, far, far away! The expression in his black eyes left her in no doubt as to what he was thinking, none at all, and the knowledge made her feel peculiar—

sort of breathless and skittish. *Fear*, she told herself firmly, hefting up the coffee pot in both hands and stalking past him, it was fear of him that made her react in that fashion, fear that he'd force himself on her again. But . . . did fear cause her breasts to tingle in that strange, exciting way when he looked at her? Was it fear of him that sent hot color flashing to her cheeks? Is that why her nipples grew swollen and sensitive as they brushed the cloth of her shirt? Was it fear alone that made her voice husky when she spoke and caused that— that strange heat to flood through her belly? She risked a backward glance over her shoulder in his direction and, as she confirmed her suspicions that he was indeed watching her again, she missed her footing, stumbled, and caused most of the water to slosh over the rim of the coffee pot. *That polecat! That darned sidewinder!* she fumed silently. She flung about and marched back toward the wagon, angry at herself and even more furious at him when his low, mocking laughter floated after her on the wind.

Joaquin gave the call to chow, and Luke took up his tin plate and held it out to Promise to fill with salted pork, beans, corn pones, and wild greens she had gathered earlier, down by the river. The look she gave him as she ladled the food onto his plate was a mixture of wariness and defiance. He grinned, his hand brushing hers as he accepted a spoon from her, a contact that made her flinch and filled her green eyes with confusion in the second before she hurriedly looked away.

"My thanks, Yellow-Haired-Woman," he murmured in Cheyenne.

She cocked her head to one side like an inquiring kitten, curious despite her anger. "What did you say?" she demanded.

Still grinning, he told her.

"Is that what the Cheyenne would call me? Yellow-Haired-Woman?"

"Maybe," he acknowledged, and winked. "If you'll bring your supper and sit next to me over by the fire, I'll tell you the legend of Yellow-Haired-Woman, and how the Cheyenne believe she brought the first buffalo to our people."

She glowered at him, and swept her hair angrily back, over her shoulders. "No thanks, Mister Steele. I'm not a child, to be won over by fairy tales!"

Shrugging, he moved easily toward the fire. "Suit yourself, *desperada*," he said casually, hunkering down across the campfire from Black-Strap. "Say, did you ever hear about Yellow-Haired-Woman?" he asked the black wrangler, knowing how the man loved a good yarn spun about the fire at night.

"No, boss, Ah don't reckon Ah did," Black-Strap said thoughtfully. He tucked a quid of chewing tobacco inside his cheek and sat back to listen, his eyes glinting with amusement as he caught the sly wink Luke threw his way.

"Well," Luke began, this is the story as it was told me by my mother, Singing Wind, daughter of Yellow Rock of the southern Cheyenne, the *Sowenia*.

"Many, many winters ago," Luke began, watching Promise from the corner of his eyes, "the People had no big game to hunt and store for food during the winter. They had only smaller animals such as the wild goose or fish, and the People were always hungry." Luke paused and waited for Joaquin to settle down alongside him, aware that Promise had carried her plate to a rock barely within earshot and was sitting there eating, pretending little interest in his tale. "One day," he continued, purposely lowering his voice, "they were so hungry that the chief sent two young hunters far from the camp in search of more game, with orders that they were not to come back until they had caught something.

"Now, the two young hunters were serious men and concerned for their people's welfare. They tracked and tracked for miles and miles in all directions, not stopping to eat or drink anything themselves, until they were exhausted from traveling so far and from lack of food or water. It seemed they would die without doing what their chief had ordered them to do. Ahead of them rose a mighty peak, towering against the sky. They decided that this would be their place to die." Luke paused, giving weight to the seriousness of the hunters' plight. He eyed Promise, noting that she had moved a little closer and was now just outside their circle around the fire. "Cold?" he asked her, knowing well that it was early yet and she was nothing of the sort.

"A little," she lied.

"Move over, Joaquin," he ordered, and Promise threw him a grateful smile as she took the place between Joaquin and Black-Strap, safely across the fire from him.

"Now," he continued the story, "as the two hunters were about to climb this mighty peak which would serve as the marking place for their bodies, they found that a stream lay across their path. They tried to cross, but, suddenly, out of the water came the biggest water snake ever seen! He took one of the hunters in his coils and held him fast. They both figured they were done for, when a medicine man dressed in the skin of a coyote dived into the water and chopped off the serpent's head with the large knife he carried. The old medicine man and his wife took the two hunters to the mighty peak, and when they reached it, the stone face opened before them like a door in the white man's wooden lodge. The old man and woman fed the hunters there until they were again strong and no longer tired from their travels. When they were ready to leave, the old man offered the hunters his beautiful daughter, Yellow-Haired-Woman, as a bride for one of them. For her dowry, he gave the lucky hunter who was to be her husband the secrets of the planting of corn and the use of the buffalo for food. Before they left the peak, the medicine man warned Yellow-Haired-Woman that she must never show pity for any animal to be killed for food, for if she did, the gift of buffalo would be taken away. All went well for some time, and the People had all the buffalo they needed for meat, for hides for their tipis, for fat—everything. But then, one day Yellow-Haired-Woman forgot the promise she had made her father. She saw some of the young boys from the camp dragging a calf by a rope about its neck and throwing dust in its eyes. Her gentle nature rebelled. She cried out in pity for the lowing calf, realizing too late that she had broken the taboo by her words. That day all the buffalo vanished, and the People went hungry again. Yellow-Haired-Woman returned to her parents, and with her went the two young hunters. They were never seen again, and it was many winters before the People were again given the sacred use of the buffalo for food."

Black-Strap snorted and spat into the short grass. "Now Ah'd say that's jest like a woman anywheres, wouldn't you, Mistah Steele? They doan nevah know jest when t'keep their pretty mouths shut, they doan'!"

Joaquin laughed and Luke smiled. Promise gave a snort of her own, set her plate aside, and walked away from the campfire, down to the river. Luke shrugged at Black-Strap and Joaquin and followed her. The two hands nudged each other and exchanged knowing glances.

Promise walked down the sloping banks to the river.

The cottonwoods were enormous here, their branches sighing in the night breeze above her. She stooped, picked up some small, round pebbles, and tossed them into the water angrily. *He never missed a chance, not once!* she thought irritably. She had a sneaking hunch he had known she would want to hear the story and had purposely kept his voice low so that she'd move closer to listen, knowing full well that at the end of the tale, Yellow-Haired-Woman—as he had called *her* earlier— would be shown up as a garrulous, too-soft female!

He came up behind her so silently he might have worn moccasins instead of boots, for he was only inches away when she became aware that he had followed her.

"Take no notice of Black-Strap," he said softly. "He didn't mean anything by it."

She snorted. "Black-Strap wasn't why I left the fire," she snapped.

"My story? It wasn't directed at you, *desperada*. I guess your hair put me in mind of it, that's all."

"Is that supposed to be an apology?"

"No. An explanation, I guess."

"Then you've explained! I came down here to be alone for a spell, Mister Steele. I'd count it a favor if you'd go on back the way you came." She turned her back on him, hugging herself about the arms.

"Henry said you nursed your mama on your own, put food on the table, and kept a roof over your heads. It must have been real hard, losing her," he said suddenly.

She whirled on him, tears springing into her eyes. "That's not fair!"

"What isn't?"

"Talking about my mother to force me to speak to you."

"I figured you needed to talk to someone. Keeping it

141

inside the way you're doing won't help any."

"Huh! And I suppose you're the perfect person for me to talk about it with!" she stormed. "You've got some nerve, Mister Steele, after what you did the other night!"

He ignored her outburst and crouched down, dropping pebbles one by one into the gleaming dark water, watching how the ripples grew outward in ever-widening circles and caught the silver of the moon. "I know what you're going through," he continued as if she hadn't spoken. "I lost my own mother when I was about your age. My father understood her real well. He knew she felt caged up at the *hacienda*, and that sometimes she needed to be set free, like a bird. She'd travel with her people, the Cheyenne, for a month or two, and then she'd come home. Those months without her were pure hell for him. He'd worry about her, get to missing her real bad. Each time she came home, it was like he came alive again. Until that last time, when she didn't come home." He stood, hurling a final pebble angrily into the water, seeing the spray thrown up like a shower of diamonds as it broke the surface. "Her village contracted cholera from some German traders, and it spread like wildfire. The Cheyenne have no resistance to it, you see, like other diseases the white men have brought west with them. I lost two of my aunts, my grandmother, an uncle, and my mother, Singing Wind, in less than two weeks. If I'd gone with her, as I did sometimes, I reckon I would have died, too. Only my grandfather, Yellow Rock, survived."

She had grown very still as he spoke, moved by his words and by the flat, guardedly emotionless tone in which he had said them. "I'm—I'm sorry," she murmured sincerely, for the moment forgetting her anger at him.

He nodded. "I think you are. I'm sorry, too. About

your mother. From all accounts, she was a fine woman."

"Yes!" she whispered, and he saw that her eyes were brimming with tears about to spill over. Embarrassed, she turned away. He reached out and grasped her gently by the shoulder, turning her to face him.

"Don't be ashamed," he said huskily. "Cry it out. Losing someone we love gives us the right to shed a few tears, I'd say."

Somehow, she found herself held in his arms, hot tears spilling onto his leather vest as she wept, her fingers clenched fiercely over his arms. He stayed quite still, stroking her hair while she unburdened herself, her slender shoulders heaving. After several minutes, she pulled away and stood there, the night wind riffling her long, straight hair, the moonlight catching the moist sheen of her eyes.

"Better?" he asked.

"Some," she admitted, venturing a smile. She laughed through the watery mist, a wry little laugh. "What a turnabout! I never expected to be crying on your shoulder, Mister Steele—not after the other night!"

He grinned. "It's Luke," he corrected. "And I'd be a liar if I said I came down here expecting you to cry on my shoulder!" His black eyes glimmered with amusement. "I half expected to find a knife between my ribs!"

Grimly, she smiled. "Believe me, I thought about it!" They both laughed, and the laughter eased the sudden tension that had risen between them. She leaned back against the trunk of a cottonwood, watching him. "Why did you come after me?" she asked hesitantly.

"I figured it was time for a peace talk," he said frankly. "And . . . I decided I owed you an apology. It wasn't an easy decision, believe me. Apologies don't come easy from me."

Surprised, she said nothing, only nodding.

He frowned. "I came to tell you you're free to go, if that's what you want. I won't try to stop you. I'll see you safely to Bent's Fort. I'll even give you enough money for the stage fare back to Cherry Creek, or someplace else. Just say the word." He waited, almost holding his breath. He was taking a gamble in offering her her freedom, but it was a risk he knew he had to take. "On the other hand, there's nothing for you back in Cherry Creek, and Hollander's not liable to keep his mouth shut about the bank hold-up. If you decide against going back, you're welcome to come to New Mexico with me. It's beautiful land down there, Promise, wild and free—a good place to start a new life."

"And you? What will you do if I decide to come with you?" she asked warily, the doubt and mistrust blatant in her eyes and in her tone.

He laughed softly, and the sensual quality to it sent her heart leaping in her breast. "I won't promise anything," he said huskily. "You're a beautiful woman, Promise. You make a man feel—and act—*loco*! I'd have to be made of stone not to want you." His dark eyes flickered boldly over her, sending heat to her cheeks. "But . . . I'll do my damnedest not to force you into anything again, my word on it. What do you say?"

She bit her lip and turned away from him, walking slowly down the river bank to the water. Could she trust him? He was so different tonight, seemed so sincere! She didn't know what to do . . .

He came after her and turned her to face him. His dark head dipped and he pressed his lips gently over hers, tasting the salt of her tears upon them. "Like I said," he whispered huskily, "I won't promise anything. I want to kiss you, Promise, honey, I want to hold you, and more, but the rest is up to you, baby . . ."

His warm mouth slanted across hers with a gentle ardor that stunned her. The icy wall built of anger and fear that she had erected around her heart melted away as he gathered her into his arms, and the full force of her attraction to him swept through her like a hot desert wind, carrying caution away. She relaxed in his embrace, enjoying the way his hands felt as he stroked her hair, the touch of his calloused fingers as they trailed along her throat to the nape of her neck with caresses as gentle as the brush of a butterfly's wings. His earthly male scent of tobacco and leather and clean, masculine flesh was warm and arousing. She looked up into his dark face, all planes and rugged angles in the moonlight that spilled through the cottonwoods and willows above them, and tingles prickled up and down her spine. Lord, he was handsome, for all his savage blood! she thought dizzily. When he finally let go of her, it was somehow difficult to breathe, as if the air were constricted in her throat.

"Well?" he asked, a smile curving his lips and crinkling the corners of his ebony eyes. He held her by only her fingertips as he awaited her answer, knowing by the look on her face, the slight trembling of her body, the effect his kisses had created in her. "Will you trust me? Will you come to New Mexico?"

She hesitated only briefly before nodding. "I—I guess so. Yes," she added more firmly, "yes, I'll come!"

"Good! Tomorrow's a new day, Promise." He reached out and caressed her flaming cheek with the back of his hand. "We'll take it as it comes—together." Guilt welled up inside him as he saw the way her eyes shone, eager and filled with hope. He finally quelled the pricks of his conscience. It was no more than O'Rourke's daughter deserved, he thought bitterly. "Do you remember you

145

asked me back at the camp if my mother's people would call you Yellow-Haired-Woman?" He saw her nod, fair brows drawing together quizzically. "I said they might, but I'd give you a different name."

"Oh?"

"I'd call you Mourning Dove."

She repeated the name softly, liking the way it sounded and felt on her tongue, lilting and gentle. "Why that name?" she asked shyly.

He traced the curve of her neck with his fingertip, ending at the moist line of her lips, now a slightly deeper pink from his kisses. "The mourning dove's voice is low and mournful, like a woman who weeps for her lost loved ones, as you do. She's soft and beautiful," he continued huskily, "and yet, despite her gentleness, there is strength in her, the ability to survive hardships that other, bigger creatures cannot. She is all that a woman should be."

She flushed, pleased by his choice of names for her and the reasoning behind that choice. "Thank you," she murmured. "Will—will you tell me your Cheyenne name?" she asked tentatively, uncertain as to whether he would wish to discuss his mother's people with her. Yet she was fascinated to learn more of a people she had hitherto considered murdering savages with little of beauty or love in their lives.

He nodded readily. "My uncle, Red Star, who has been dead many years now, named me Walks-in-Shadow at my birth. He was saddened that his sister, Singing Wind, had chosen a white-eyes above the men of her own people to be her mate. He said that the son of Singing Wind could never belong wholly to the People, nor to the world of the white man. Because of my mixed blood, I could only hope to walk in the shadow of both worlds, never truly belonging in either.

"I carried that name amongst the Cheyenne people until I became a man, and then I changed my name, as is our custom. From that time on, I made it known that I wished to be called by the name Tall Shadow, as a reminder to myself and all people that I would walk tall, first and foremost as a man—not as a white man or a red man. Just . . . a man."

Promise quietly murmured her understanding, looking up into Luke's face in the deepening shadows with new eyes. Could this sensitive, gentle man before her truly be the same man who had tried to force himself upon her two days ago? He had as many facets as the pretty cut-glass beads Mama had admired in Erickson's store, and each facet revealed a totally new aspect of this compelling, powerful, yet eloquent man. She wondered, with a peculiar, fluttery excitement deep within her, what facet he would reveal next.

He lifted her hands to his lips and kissed them. "Will you come back to the fire now, *desperada*?" he asked, his voice low and husky in the shadows.

"Soon," she promised. "After I've washed up."

"I'll wait for you, up there," he said gravely, nodding to the thicket of trees farther up the riverbank. "It wouldn't do for you to be so far from camp alone."

"I won't be long." As he left, she recalled the deputy's comment in Cherry Creek that morning the stagecoach was robbed, about how letting Luke Steele join the posse would be tantamount to letting a coyote guard the stock. Shouldn't she feel that way, with Luke up there on the low bluff that overhung the river, acting as lookout for would be assailants? Perhaps she should, she admitted as she peeled off her shirt. But somehow, she didn't.

She glanced over her shoulder up to where he stood,

his back to her, his lean body framed against the darkening amethyst sky beyond. The red tip of his cheroot glowed in the gloom, and the pleasant scent of tobacco carried to where she crouched. Face burning, she recalled his kisses, the way his warm, masculinely rough hands had felt against her skin, and she shivered as she unlaced her bodice and cast it aside. The cool night air fanned her body, which felt strangely flushed, but it wasn't the air that made her feel so strange, so light-headed and breathless. It was him!

An alarm bell jangled loudly in her mind when he'd urged her to trust him, yet its clamor had been ignored in the new and exciting sensations of his ardent kisses and tender embraces. Until now, no man had ever stirred such giddy feelings inside her. The few kisses she had experienced before seemed to have become pale, insipid, little-boy kisses by comparison. Luke had made her feel like a woman; desirable, beautiful, special . . . Yes, she must have misjudged him, she decided happily! He had not been able to help himself that time in the canyon, he had said, and she believed him. After all, it was harder for men to control their desires, and he had said—she recalled with a heartskipping thrill of pleasure—that she was so beautiful, she had made him crazy! He had wanted her from the first, else why would he have gone through that charade of blackmailing her into going with him?

She looked down into the water. The windblown ripples gleamed in the silvery moonlight in a way that was reminiscent of the way his night-black eyes had gleamed when he took her in his arms. She felt as if she trembled on the threshold of some great happening in her life, and her tomorrows seemed suddenly filled with the promise of excitement, adventure—perhaps even love! Yes, especially love. . . .

Suddenly, she saw a trail of light scoring the dark water and looked up to see a star falling from the night sky, its tail blazing silver fire. She closed her eyes tightly and wished very hard. When she opened her eyes again, the shooting star had gone.

"Good night, Tall Shadow," she murmured softly to the rustling breeze. There was a tender smile upon her lips. Papa had said that if you wished upon a falling star, your wish was sure to come true—if you wished hard enough.

Chapter Nine

At midmorning of the fourth day, Luke reined in his blue roan alongside the buckskin on which Promise was again mounted, and pointed up ahead.

She looked in the direction he was pointing and saw, through the willows and the cottonwoods that flanked the grassy flood plain on either side of the river, that the smoke of many fires was rising above the treetops. She could also see tall wooden poles crisscrossed between them, hear the barking of dogs and the cries and laughter of children at play.

"My mother's people," Luke said simply.

"How do you know?" Promise asked uneasily.

"It is their custom to set up camp by a river where there are trees for shelter from the wind and rain," Luke explained. "Other tribes will not camp in such a place in case of ambush. They prefer open spaces." He looked down at her, a challenge in his expression. "Will you come with me to meet my people?"

After a second's hesitation, she nodded. Luke gave orders to Black-Strap to drive the wagon on to Bent's Fort about two hours drive downstream, then he clicked to his roan and set off toward the Indian village with Promise following at a slower pace.

The poles she had spied above the trees, Promise soon saw were the lodge poles of many tipis. Dogs came out barking excitedly to worry their horses' heels as they rode into the village. Women looked up from their chores and examined Promise curiously, their dark eyes widening as they looked her up and down in her men's clothing. They exchanged whispers behind their hands and giggled, and Promise felt a hot flush rising to her face from her neck. The children were not so reticent to come forward. Chattering like magpies and jumping up and down, they poked at her horse, her saddle, anything they could reach until the mean-tempered buckskin bared his teeth and sent them running, naked, back to their mothers.

Promise looked about her, avidly curious. The tipis were arranged in a large circle, perhaps thirty of them in all, each easily twice the height of a tall man. The hides were a deep yellow, decorated with colorful circles and triangles in repeating patterns. Some bore pictures of men on horseback or of many horses and seemed to tell a story. Outside most of them, ponies were tethered to a stake in the ground or a dog scratched at its fleas. Women crouched industriously over gourds, pounding berries into pulp, while others stirred their cooking pots over the fire watching the newcomers covertly as they did so. Promise returned her attention to Luke as the flap of one of the tipis was lifted and a tall man with long, shiny black braids bound with some kind of fur ducked out from under the low opening. He was tall and copper skinned, his nose jutting proudly from the arrogant flat planes of his face. He wore only a long, painted breechclout and beaded moccasins on his deeply tanned, hard body. His only decoration was the eagle feather he wore hanging from his scalp lock.

"Welcome, Tall Shadow," the man greeted Luke. "It has been many moons since you have visited the lodges of Black Kettle's people."

"It has been long, Four Winds, my uncle," Luke agreed. "And the winter was a hard one. How is my grandfather, Yellow Rock?"

"He is an old man, indeed, but as strong as many of our young warriors. The moons of snow killed many of our people, yet Yellow Rock lives," Four Winds said solemnly. "He stays in the lodge of your cousin, Scarred Hand, and is well cared for in the manner of our people."

"I am happy to hear he yet lives," Luke replied.

Four Winds nodded. "Come, I will take you to him. The woman, she is your woman?"

Luke smiled, wondering what Promise's comment would have been had she understood the Cheyenne tongue and heard his answer. "Not yet, my uncle, but soon she will share my blankets. I have named her Mourning Dove."

Four Winds nodded and called to his wife to prepare food for the visitors. "I will take you to Yellow Rock," he told Luke, "and later, you will be welcome in my tipi to share our food."

Four Winds's wife, a plump woman dressed in a simple shift of bleached buckskin, fringed heavily at the elbow-length sleeves and hem and belted prettily with a beaded band, came forward to take their horses. She smiled shyly up at Promise as she held the cow pony for her to dismount, and she murmured something Promise could not understand.

"She is asking you how you are named," Luke translated, "and if you would honor her by visiting in her tipi while her husband and I go to my grandfather's lodge." He said something, and the Indian woman's smile broadened and she nodded eagerly. "I have told her that you would be pleased to visit, and that your name is Mourning Dove. She says that her name is Flattens-Grass."

Promise returned the woman's smile and dismounted, watching as Flattens-Grass tethered her pony alongside those of her husband outside their tipi. She went to the flap that was her lodge's doorway and beckoned Promise inside.

Luke, at Four Winds's side, grinned. "Go on, Mourning Dove. She doesn't look as if she has it in mind to lift your scalp! Sit to the left when you enter the tipi— I don't want her thinking I haven't taught you any manners, even if you are a white-eyes!" With that, he followed Four Winds along the circle of tipis, leaving her no choice but to accept Flattens-Grass's offer.

She did as he had said, turning to the left after ducking through the low door flap and sitting as Flattens-Grass gestured she should.

Inside, the tipi was far larger than it had seemed from the outside and remarkably cool despite the warm summer sun that beat against the hides used to make it. Sunlight filtering through the opaque walls gave a golden glow to the interior. Two low couches with backrests were placed opposite each other upon the walls. By the top of the tipi, where the poles crisscrossed and were lashed together with rawhide thongs, the buffalo skin was blackened by smoke and clear blue sky showed through the vent.

Flattens-Grass went to one of the pouches and withdrew something, returning to sit beside Promise with her legs modestly tucked to one side. She said something and held out a pair of moccasins to her. They were of soft, white hide, fringed at the opening and beaded with a scalloped design about the edges. Promise nodded and murmured some admiring words, thinking Flattens-Grass meant only to display her skill at moccasin making, but when she returned them to the Indian woman, Flattens-Grass pressed them back into her hands, and she knew they had been given as a gift. Touched, she smiled and thanked her warmly, gestures that needed no translation.

There were voices at the tipi flap then, and much giggling. Promise looked up as three other women entered, looking expectantly from Flattens-Grass to Promise. Flattens-Grass greeted them and gestured for them to be seated, smiling broadly.

The young women sat, and the one who seated herself next to Promise reached out to lightly touch her long, straight, fair hair. She made some comment, and the other women nodded agreement, pointing to the opening in the top of the tipi and the distant sun far above. Promise nodded to show that she had understood they were comparing her hair to the color of the sunlight and then repeated what they had said, finding the strange words clumsy on her tongue. Yet the gesture to use their language delighted the women, who beamed and patted her arms and shoulders to show their approval.

Flattens-Grass stood and went again to one of the pouches, or parfleches, that hung on the walls and withdrew a shiny button that appeared to have been taken from the uniform of a soldier. She held it up between her fingers and asked the other women a question. They nodded eagerly, dividing themselves into two teams, one on either side of the tipi. Flattens-Grass palmed the button, indicating that Promise should watch. She then hid her hands behind her and shuffled the button from one to another before extending both closed fists before her and letting the opposite team choose in which of them it was hidden. Squeals of laughter followed when a member of the opposite team chose the wrong one, and the woman pouted ruefully. It was Flattens-Grass's turn again. She moved closer to Promise, gesturing for her to put her hands behind her back as did she.

By now, Promise had realized that the game was one which she had played as a child, using a silver thimble instead of a button. Her face expressionless, she took the button from Flattens-Grass then smoothly palmed it back to her before both women held out their closed fists for the opposite team to guess which of them held it. The women whispered and argued good-naturedly amongst themselves, reaching out as if to touch first one of the fists then the other, watching Flattens-Grass's and Promise's faces for some reaction as they did so. When at last they chose Promise's left hand, she and Flattens-Grass laughed merrily, for they had chosen wrongly yet again. The game continued, although Flattens-Grass left the tipi from time to time to inspect the chunks of venison cooking on wooden skewers over her fire or to stir the savory stew of buffalo meat, prairie turnips, and wild greens that simmered in a cooking pouch heated with hot rocks and hung from a tripod of three tied sticks alongside the fire.

As the game began again, Promise wondered what Luke was doing, and if he had found his grandfather well. Flattens-Grass's voice, lightly chiding, brought her thoughts swiftly back to the game at hand. Several pairs of eyes twinkled with amusement as color suffused her face. Had they guessed her thoughts were of the one they called Tall Shadow, she wondered as she palmed the button again. Somehow, their expressions implied they had indeed!

Luke entered the tipi of his cousin, Scarred Hand, and raised his hand in greeting to his grandfather, Yellow Rock, who sat cross-legged before the fire. A light kindled in the old man's dark eyes as he looked up at the tall, straight man who was his grandson, and whose height and breadth seemed to fill the large tipi. He extended his bony arms, and Luke bent to embrace the *shaman*, satisfaction in his own eyes. As Four Winds had promised, Yellow Rock did indeed appear well, despite his years. His white hair hung down past his shoulders, contrasting sharply with the deep copper of his lined face. Though his once-hawklike features were softened now with the years, his eyes were as bright and clever as the all-seeing eyes of the mighty eagle, his gnarled hands without tremor as he clasped Luke's hands.

"My heart leaps with pleasure to see you are well, Grandfather," he said, his voice husky with emotion.

"As does mine, my grandson," Yellow Rock replied, his voice cracking. This one, the son of his beloved daughter, Singing Wind, ever held a warm place in his heart, for all that he was sired by a white man. Many moons had passed since Tall Shadow had come to his mother's people. He had feared that perhaps his grandson had turned his back on his Cheyenne family. But no, the wind had told him that he would come, and the wind told no lies . . . He touched the powerful medicine bundle on a rawhide thong around his neck and said a silent prayer of thanks.

"It has come to me that you did not come here to the lodges of Black Kettle alone," he said at length, a smile tugging at the corners of his mouth and deepening the furrows alongside it. "It is said that you have brought a woman with you—a white woman with hair the color of the sun. Is she then your woman?"

A sheepish grin creased Luke's face as he took a seat opposite his grandfather. "Your years rest lightly upon your shoulders, Grandfather! It seems time does little to dull the sharpness of your eyes or the keenness of your ears. It is so. The woman waits for me in the lodge of Four Winds."

Yellow Rock snorted. "You have learned to speak after the manner of your father's people, my grandson— saying many words that tell nothing! I ask again—is this woman with the yellow hair your woman? And if this is so, why did you not bring her here to meet with me?" Luke dropped his gaze, unable to meet the piercing look the old *shaman* gave him. "Ah!" Yellow Rock exclaimed softly. "There is shame in your face, Tall Shadow, written there for all to read! Will you share the burden of your shame with me, or must I only guess at its cause, as a blind warrior guesses the course of his arrows?"

Luke sighed heavily. "No, Grandfather. I will tell you. The woman is the daughter of he who wronged me many years ago." His eyes burned. "Through her, I shall revenge myself on him!"

"Such a course does you no honor, my grandson," Yellow Rock said gravely. "Such a young woman could have been only a little maiden at the time her father wronged you. It is not fitting that the son of Singing Wind should hold her accountable for the actions of her father, of which she had no part. My grandson's bitterness is like a wound filled with poison. It is time now to cleanse that wound and let it heal."

Luke's jaw tightened. "My grandfather mellows with the years," he said tersely. "He forgets that which was

157

done to me—but I do not!"

"To become mellow with age is no fault, Tall Shadow. When the hot blood of youth that blinds the eyes and hardens the heart is cooled, then wisdom takes its place and the eyes see more clearly, the heart feels more truly. This you will learn, too, in time."

The angry scowl which contorted Luke's features was not displaced by his grandfather's words.

"A vision came to me three suns past. I stood upon the top of a tall mountain and looked down upon the earth even as the Great Wise One Above looks down on His creations. I saw a mighty hawk in the blue of the sky, and below, flying crookedly as if its wings were damaged, a little dove. As I watched, I saw the hawk swoop down upon the dove, its prey, and heard the rush of the wind as it dropped to clasp it in it talons. The dove was silent, unmoving, and it was my thought that the hawk had taken its life. But then, I saw the dove flutter free, and the hawk was lying still upon the ground where before the dove had lain."

"Will you explain your vision to me, Grandfather?" Luke asked, his countenance taking on a more puzzled expression.

Yellow Rock shook his grizzled head. "No, my grandson, I will not. I will only caution you to search your heart for the meaning of what I have said. Therein lies the answer."

The hackles on Luke's neck rose. He nodded, for once uncertain of what to say to the old man. Yellow Rock smiled and looked up as a young woman ducked under the tipi flap, her belly rounded with child beneath her creamy shift of fringed buckskin. "The wife of your cousin, Scarred Hand, comes. She is called Red Leaf. Her child will be born in the moon of the first snows."

158

"Where is my cousin?" Luke asked after offering shy Red Leaf his greeting.

"He has gone with others to hunt for the buffalo," Yellow Rock said. "Tell me of your life these past moons since last we were together."

Relaxed now that the disquieting subject of Promise O'Rourke had been dealt with, Luke leaned back upon the day bed and began to talk.

Luke had been gone for almost two hours, Promise guessed, when Four Winds entered the tipi with Luke in his wake. The Cheyenne women moved respectfully aside to give the men the most comfortable seats upon the buffalo-hide-covered rests, and Promise did likewise. The three female visitors made their excuses and departed, leaving Four Winds and Flattens-Grass to entertain their guests in privacy.

Flattens-Grass served the men their midday meal first, then she and Promise had their turn to eat. After the savory meal, Four Winds left his seat in search of his pipe, the everyday pipe he smoked in the company of his close friends or relatives. It was carved from the wood of the willow tree, and the pipestem had been burned with a pattern of birds' feet. The bowl was made of reddish stone carved into the shape of a buffalo's massive head, and Four Winds filled it with *kinnikinnick*, a mixture of fragrant herbs, and lit it with a glowing stick from the fire. He held the pipe out to Luke first, as a sign of courtesy, and he puffed deeply for several moments before passing the pipe back to Four Winds. Blue-gray smoke and the woodsy scent of sumac, willow bark, and other herbs rose through the hole above them and was wafted away on the summer breeze. As they smoked, they talked seriously, and Promise wondered what it was they discussed that produced such solemn expressions to them.

"Where is your chief, Black Kettle?" Luke asked.

"He has gone to the fort with others of our people to trade. He is an old man, and his body feels the cold even in the summer months after moonrise. He and his woman go to trade for the warm, red blankets of the white-eyes, so that when winter comes again, he will not feel the cold."

"And does Black Kettle still parley for peace with the bluecoat chiefs?"

Four Winds nodded. "He does. Many of our warriors are angered by this. They say he is old and no longer fit to lead his tribe—that he has grown too used to the white man's sweet powder and whis-kee, his warm blankets and his coffee, and that he has forgotten that the People were meant to be free, to roam Earth Mother and share the gifts she gives us. He speaks of going to the white-eyes' wooden village, the place they call Den-vah, with other of our chiefs who feel as he does. There he will make peace treaties with the one called Evans and the bluecoat war chief, Chiving-ton, who it is said have the ear of the Great White Father in the East."

"And what does Four Winds, my uncle, say to this?"

Four Winds shrugged. "I am of two minds, nephew. My heart says do not listen to the white-eyes. It says that he cares nothing for those he calls his red brothers, and that he does not keep the promises he makes. It says he is only greedy for the land, the Earth Mother of our People, though she can be owned by no man.

"And yet, I have heard stories of chiefs from other tribes who have journeyed far into the land of the rising sun and have seen the wooden villages of the white men that stretch many days of riding in all directions. I have heard of iron horses that breathe smoke and have seen the singing wires that speak the white-man's tongue, and my reason asks me if we, the People, can defend our Earth Mother against these men? They are soft and weak in battle unless they have guns with which to fight, and yet they have knowledge of things which we have not yet dreamed of. They breed like the rabbit in its warren, while our children are killed by the evil spirits of the sickenesses they have brought to our land. They plant fields and feed upon the fruits of the Earth Mother, even as our people cry in hunger for the buffalo, which they have killed by the thousands for their robes, leaving the meat to rot upon the plains. The answer I hear is that perhaps we would be wiser to make treaties with the white-eyes, since we cannot rid our Earth Mother of the white grubs that infest her body. They are as countless as the grasses that cover the prairies! Perhaps we should seek peace, before the People are no more."

Luke nodded. Their conversation had ended on a bleak note, and he could offer no words of comfort to Four Winds. It was his opinion that many, many more of the People would walk the Trail of Tears to the white-man's Indian reservations before this was done; that the white-man's superior knowledge, his greed for the land, and his vast numbers would, in the end, prove devastating to the People. His chiseled face was grave as he rose from his place in the tipi.

"I must leave now, my uncle," he said. "We go to Bent's Fort. May the Wise One Above watch over you and your village until we meet again."

"And over you, my nephew," Four Winds answered.

Luke beckoned to Promise to follow him, and she ducked under the opened flap of the lodge in his wake.

Flattens-Grass brought their horses, bidding Promise a smiling farewell and chattering on in a friendly fashion in the Cheyenne tongue as she pointed to the beaded and fringed moccasins Promise held tight in her hands.

"Flattens-Grass says she hopes that the moccasins will carry you swiftly and silently for many miles in comfort, and that one day you will return to play the button game with her and the other women of the village," Luke translated.

"Please give her my thanks and say that I would be honored to come back one day," Promise replied, smiling down at Flattens-Grass.

They rode from the Cheyenne village to the accompaniment of the barking dogs and the screaming, playing children just as they had arrived. The trail that followed the river to Bent's trading house grew more barren as they rode nearer. Trees had been felled to provide timber for the fort's many buildings, Luke explained, and vast numbers of forlorn stumps bore out his words. Many Indian encampments around the fort had eroded the grass over the years and left the earth bare save for a powdery layer of gray-brown dust that rose in clouds beneath their horses' hooves.

As they drew nearer, they passed many Indian families traveling in the same direction, some with dressed buffalo pelts lashed onto wooden travois behind their ponies, pelts they would trade for the fine pots and colorful blankets of the southern Navajo tribes or for glass beads, needles and thread, blankets, shirts, or iron kettles, which were highly prized among them.

The Cheyenne men wore fringed shirts of soft, creamy buckskin, and the numerous metal cones that dangled from the hems of these shirts set up a merry jingling as they rode. Instead of only breechclouts and moccasins on their lower bodies, they also sported fringed leggings. Their magnificently feathered war-bonnets sat upon heads held high as they rode their finest painted ponies. Their women were also splendidly dressed, perched high in their wood-framed, leather saddles. From some of these hung cradle boards with dark-eyed babies gazing out at the world. The noisy cavalcade had something of a festive atmosphere about it. The excited chattering and laughing of the women and the hearty greetings some of the braves called out to Luke heightened the festive spirit.

"Best enjoy it while you can, Mourning Dove," Luke said with a grin. "After today, it's keep-your-eyes-peeled time! We'll be traveling deep into Comanche country. There's nothing they like better lately than raiding a supply wagon."

Promise swallowed, her mouth suddenly dry. In her pleasure over the morning she had spent in the company of Flattens-Grass, she had all but forgotten that there was another side to the Indian—a bloodthirsty, cruel side that showed no mercy to the hated white-eyes and took delight in the torture and killing of men, women, and even little children. Her heart gave a frightened flutter, and a small, crampy knot of fear bunched up in the pit of her stomach. Her expression must have betrayed her anxiety, because Luke reached down from his horse and tugged playfully at a streamer of her fair hair in an attempt to bring the sunny smile back to her face.

"Loosen up, *desperada*," he urged her softly. "Chances are the Comanches will be too busy hunting the buffalo to bother with us."

She forced a wan smile, but it was a fleeting, false thing, and he could have kicked himself for speaking so rashly and scaring her.

They rode through the vast, wooden gates in the sandstone walls of Bent's New Fort about an hour later. Spiny cactuses topped the massive walls, an effective means of deterring would-be attackers from that direction. As a further deterrent, the shiny black snouts of four howitzers gleamed in the sunshine from the towers at each of the four corners of the fort.

Inside the fort's walls was a scene which could have been recreated from Promise's childhood travels. Gray-brown dust and the pungent odor of horse droppings hung in the air. Wagons drawn by teams of oxen were pulled up to some of the log buildings that lined the walls, waiting to be loaded with barrels, sacks of provisions, or small household items. Blue-uniformed cavalry officers strode impatiently back and forth, intent on the business of equipping their men and beasts. Would-be settlers, destined for the far west via the Cimarron Crossing, sat disconsolately upon their wagons and, as they passed them by, Promise and Luke overheard the reason for their long faces: it seemed the overland trails had been temporarily closed due to the hostilities of the Indians against wagon trains in past months. The pioneer women appeared sickly and dispirited, and they watched wearily while their skinny, tow-headed offspring chased each other and some of the Indian children through knots of blanket-wrapped half-bloods squatting on the ground with the sons of William Bent, who were smoking, dicing, and drinking. Traders were much in evidence, as were trappers. The latter were bearded mountain men in fringed buckskins, whose faces were as hard and seamed as the wild terrain in which they set their traps for the weasel, ermine, and beaver. Prospectors were busily lashing gold pans and shovels onto already overburdened mules or donkeys, and their braying added to the cacophony already filling the enclosure.

Indian women were jostling for first place to enter through the door of the trading house itself, brandishing finely crafted moccasins or proudly lifting folded buffalo pelts adorned with colorful, dyed quills or tinkling dangles for William Bent's inspection, calling in high-pitched, excited voices for him or one of the other traders to survey their wares. The general din was increased by the clucks and squawks of numerous, scrawny hens flapping about, pursued by an amorous rooster, and the squealing of a penful of Berkshire hogs, rolling in the muddy wallow they had made in one corner of their pen.

Luke and Promise spied their wagon and headed across the compound toward it. Black-Strap and Joaquin, who had been idly lounging against it watching the ever-changing scene, strolled across to meet them.

"We's jest about done, Boss," Black-Strap announced, grinning up at Steele. "Ah done loaded th'ammunition, an' Joe done got th' new pots he's been needin'—though I don't reckon they'll help his cookin' none! Ah reckon we's about fixed t'head fo' home, yessir!"

Luke nodded and swung down from his horse, holding the buckskin's head while Promise did likewise. "Be with you soon, boys," he told the hands. "First, me and Miss Promise here're going to take ourselves a look around the trading house and have a word with Will Bent."

"You jest go right 'head, Boss," Black-Strap urged, giving his boss a sly wink. "Me and Joe was fixin' to wet our whistles some, anyhow's, seeing as how you keep a dry trail."

"Do that," Luke said amiably. "But I want you both back here, ready to roll and sober enough to drive a wagon, in an hour." He eyed them sternly. "*Comprende, amigos?*" He took Promise's elbow and steered her toward the trading house.

It was no Ali Baba's jeweled cave inside the dark confines of the log-walled trading house, but by western standards Promise imagined it came pretty close. The walls were festooned with goods, everything from wood axes to tobacco twists, scarlet Hudson Bay blankets, kegs of rum, flour, and molasses. Wooden gun cases were stacked on shelves, as were leather sheaths with wicked-bladed hunting knives, boots and belts, saddles and harnesses. Heaped to one side were the Indian goods brought to exchange for these marvels of the white man. There were stacks of beaver, weasel, and ermine pelts, heaps of plain or ornamented buffalo robes, the moccasins that many trappers wore in preference to shoes or boots.

Promise watched the haggling going on all about her while Luke prowled the shelves of guns and rifles. It appeared the most sought-after commodities among the Cheyenne women were sugar and flour, although beads and looking glasses, tweezers, gallon black-iron kettles, and yard goods seemed a close second. For the most part, the yard goods consisted of bolts of red, blue, or black flannel with a few of pretty calico mixed in. She squirmed her way between two plump women, her eyes falling on a bolt of pretty green and white gingham that took her fancy.

As she was about to pick it up to feel the quality of the cloth, one of the Indian women snatched it from her and said something in a loud, angry tone. The other women grabbed the other end and a fierce tug of war ensued between the two, with Promise caught helplessly in the middle.

Luke heard the ruckus and came across. He said something in a sharp tone and the two women dropped the cloth as if it were red-hot. Luke bent and retrieved it, holding it out to Promise.

"Here. I reckon they gave up. Do you want it?"

"Yes—no, I don't have anything to trade for it with."

"Will, add this on to the rest and tally it up," Luke told William Bent, who was a slightly built man with shrewd, sad eyes.

"Surely will, Steele," Bent agreed. "This your woman?"

Promise flushed and Luke laughed deeply. "Nope. This here's my new hand, Promise O'Rourke. She's a—a mite trigger-happy, so we just call her *desperada!*"

Bent nodded, eyes twinkling. "Pleased ter meet you, ma'am. Anything else you'll be needin' along with the cloth—a paper of pins, maybe, or needles and thread?"

Promise looked up into Luke's face, not knowing what his ranch might or might not have in the way of sewing supplies.

"I reckon we'll have everything the lady'll be needing out at the ranch," Luke said. "Margita's pretty handy with a needle. She'll have thread and such. Say, you can give me one of those fancy looking glasses, though!"

Bent nodded and added it to the pile. "Which way're you headed, Luke? Raton Pass?"

Luke shook his head. "No, Will, not with the wagon and the girl."

"You'll go around then." He shook his head and clicked his teeth. "Can't say I envy you none. The Comanche are mighty fractious lately, an' even some of Black Kettle's braves have been raiding anyone that they come across. I reckon you're in for a wild and woolly time of it, Luke!"

Luke's lips split in a cruel grin. He tapped one of the wooden gun cases. "I reckon I'm ready for it, Will Bent!"

PENELOPE NERI

Bent smiled. "Anyone else said that, I'd say he was a darned fool. But I reckon you know what you're doing."

"I sure hope so!" Luke agreed. He touched his hat and bade Bent a good day.

He joined Promise minutes later with the bolt of cloth tucked under one arm and the long box of rifles hefted on his shoulder.

"Thanks," she told him shyly, nodding toward the gingham cloth. "I don't know how I'll be able to pay you back."

"We'll think of something," Luke said speculatively and grinned as he saw crimson color fill her cheeks.

"How did you get those women to give it up?" she asked, steering their conversation back to safer ground.

"I told them it was bad medicine," he said solemnly as he strode beside her to the wagon. "I said you were a mighty medicine woman amongst the white-eyes, and that you'd work a powerful curse on them if they didn't let you have the cloth. One peek into those green eyes, *desperada*, and they believed me!" He reached inside his shirt and drew out the looking glass he had bought from Bent, handing it to her.

The mirror was oval, inlaid in German silver with flowers etched into the metal frame and twining about the handle. Promise peered into it, astonished by her appearance. The fierce sunshine of the treeless plains had deepened her complexion to a burnished gold and bleached her lashes, brows, and her flowing mane of cornsilk hair from pale gold to almost white-blond. In the midst of that golden face, her eyes were greener than grass, green as emeralds glittering against the tan, their slanted shape adding to the illusion that they were the eyes of a tawny-pelted mountain lioness.

"See what I mean?" Luke asked huskily. "Those eyes

168

would frighten any woman into running home to her tipi!"

"Am I so ugly?" Promise retorted.

"No, *desperada*—you're too damned beautiful for your own good!" Luke murmured looking down at her as they crossed the compound with desire burning in his lustrous black eyes.

The look made her heart race.

Chapter Ten

They traveled the Santa Fe trail from Bent's Fort for the remainder of that day, taking the branch of the Cimarron Trace in a southwesterly direction that led into New Mexico. Spanish dagger and sagebrush and boulders littered the trail through this arid region, and once in a while they came across the bleached bones of a pack animal or a wagon team that had succumbed from lack of water. The air was crystal clear, although distant rock formations shimmered in the heat. Far beyond, against the horizon, they could see the outline of the Rabbit Ears mountain range, hazy blue in the distance.

"There it is, that ole Rabbit Ears!" Black-Strap said with a whoop of sheer happiness. "Ah reckon we're homeward bound, all right!"

They traveled onward through the rest of that day, following the track rutted by the wheels of countless wagons through canyons and across endless plains that seemed a motionless ocean of rust and ochre. As the day grew older, the sky changed from a vaulting blue canopy to one of glorious, blushing pink streaked with subtle hues of peach and gold and shading into a breathtaking vermilion upon the horizon itself. The mountain ranges became sleeping giants painted in indigo and amethyst.

Then the moon rose, full and silvery, and surveyed the gaudy sun's triumphant descent with a peerless, ethereal beauty of her own, dappling the mesa with gray, shifting shadows as she raced the evening clouds.

Black-Strap drove the wagon up a gradual incline and hauled on the reins. In the gully below, Promise saw numerous white cones, like mushrooms against the hard, dark earth, and she heard the silvery notes of a bugle on the cool night air.

"Sibley tents, *desperada*," Luke answered her unspoken question. "Must be soldiers from Fort Union, southeast of here." He decided to ride on ahead, to see if their commanding officer would have any objections to sharing the bivouac in the gully with them. Several times that day he had noticed the tracks of unshod hooves on the trail, marks left by Indian ponies only recently, for the dew of that morning would have hardened the imprints had they been older. There was safety in numbers, and the amount of Comanche "sign" he had spotted—especially over the last few miles they had traveled—had made him uneasy. Once, he had glimpsed smoke rising from the distance and had seen the signal answered by yet another column of smoke at their backs. He said nothing of this to Promise, reluctant to scare her further, though he confided his suspicions to Black-Strap and Joaquin, and the three men agreed that bedding down alongside the cavalry detachment seemed the best course.

Captain Hughes was a melancholy fellow, yet he was quite willing to have them join him and his men for the night. He introduced himself and confided to Luke and Promise that he was sick and tired of fighting Indians against whom no proper military attack could be waged, seeing as they had no constant home to surround and

171

conquer but were nomadic, capable of being in one spot one minute and miles away the next. He expressed a wistful desire to be summoned to join the rest of the Union fighting the Confederate Army as so many troops from the region had already been summoned. "They," he said earnestly, "at least know him to conduct a proper war."

By means of sign language, Luke conversed with Hughes's fierce Apache scouts, and they confirmed his suspicions that there was a Comanche war party in the vicinity. They invited him to join their fire and share their rations but Luke declined, knowing full well the Apaches' volatile temperament. A wrong word, an innocent look, and they could turn on you and cut you to ribbons. He had no liking for them, even though they were of the Indian race, for the Apaches had long been enemies of the *Tsis-tsis-tas*, the "slashed people," as the Cheyenne called themselves, and he knew their friendly smiles for what they were—the hungry eyes of tigers waiting for the moment to spring upon their prey. They were not to be trusted. Promise shied away from them, too, uncomfortable to feel their expressionless black eyes appraising her. They had none of the colorful appeal of the Cheyenne she had met that morning but appeared somehow like scavengers, dressed in faded shirts of cotton which they belted with strips of cloth. Similar cloth strips were knotted in bands about their heads over thick, raven-black hair that flowed unhampered past their shoulders. When coupled with their dark blue military trousers and high-legged moccasins, the incongruities of their attire were frightening.

With relief, she heard Luke refuse their offer to share their fire and was grateful when Captain Hughes invited them to his tent for supper. She followed Luke and the captain down the neat rows of white tents, conscious of the soldiers' admiring glances as she passed and blushing to her hair roots as she realized that every feminine curve she possessed must be accentuated by her snug men's clothes. Black-Strap and Joaquin unharnessed the wagon team and turned them out with the army beasts which looked exhausted and dispirited for the greater part. The travel-worn appearance of the animals and the majority of the soldiers was explained by Captain Hughes as they sat at supper, meager fare of crackers and jerked beef, washed down with weak coffee.

"We left fort Union two days ago at dawn, tracking a war party of Comanche who had attacked three wagons headed west—which, I might add, had left despite my orders to the contrary in light of the recent hostilities in this area. They were set upon three days ago. All were slain or taken captive save for one old man who escaped and rode back to the fort for help. What we found when we got there was like something from a nightmare! The wagons had been torched and stripped of every scrap of metal they contained. Personal belongings were strewn all about, and had been trampled in the dust. Not a horse or an ox remained of the livestock. But far worse than this were the bodies; murdered men, women, and older children, all mutilated beyond easy recognition! It appeared the females had each been violated several times—excuse me, ma'am—prior to being killed. Three small children had been carried off, from what we could determine from the old man who was half out of his mind from the shock of it all." Captain Hughes shook his head and took a hefty swig of his coffee, grimacing. "We've been tracking those red devils for two days now, as I said, and haven't come closer than four miles of them." His young-old face was haggard. "My troops are exhausted.

173

The beasts are little better, what with the shortage of grazing and water in these parts. And, tonight is a full moon! Any man who travels the plains knows what that means!" He sighed heavily. "Comanche moon, the Spanish called it, and with reason. It's fortunate you and Miss O'Rourke and your men happened upon us, Steele. I wouldn't have given much for your chances if they'd come upon you alone, though I suppose your Indian blood might have afforded you an edge."

Luke shook his head. "Not with the Comanche, Captain. My mother was a Cheyenne woman. The Comanches and the Cheyenne have not been on friendly terms for many years."

"Hmm. I would have thought it would benefit the Indian people to band together against the whites," Hughes commented.

"It would, indeed," Luke agreed. "But old enmities die hard. I doubt any of the tribes will ever band together as allies with other tribes they've raided and fought for decades. That, sir, will be their downfall."

Hughes nodded. "Well, Miss O'Rourke, Steele, I'll say good night to you now. I've seen that a tent is prepared for you, ma'am. If you'll excuse me, I have to see to the posting of extra lookouts tonight. I wish that I could offer you some reassurance that your safety with us is guaranteed, but I regret I cannot. We can only hope that there will be no attack tonight and put our faith in God to see us through it if there is."

Luke walked with Hughes a short distance away, where Promise could not hear what he had to say. "Captain, are you aware that the Comanche are behind us now?"

Hughes nodded. "So my scouts have informed me, Steele. I did not wish to alarm Miss O'Rourke further by mentioning it in her presence."

A supply clerk came to escort Promise to the tent the Captain had mentioned. She went with him, a bleak expression in her eyes. Hughes's parting words had filled her with unease. Faith in God seemed a mighty fragile thread to cling to under the circumstances, and Luke's grim expression as he accompanied the captain had done little to allay her fears.

Sleep would not come despite her exhaustion some while later as she stretched out inside a Sibley tent on a canvas ground cover. Visions of whooping, painted savages—feathers fluttering from their hair and lances, and brandishing tomahawks—filled her mind and sent drowsiness scattering like a leaf in an autumn wind. She figured about two sleepless hours had gone by when she heard a low voice calling her name at the tent flap and lifted it to see Luke crouching there.

"I figured you'd still be awake, *desperada*," he whispered.

She nodded and held aside the flap so that he could enter. "I guess I'm too jittery to sleep," she said wearily, sighing as he crawled inside the tent to sit beside her. "I know what the captain says, but do you think we'll be attacked tonight?" The expression on his face answered her question without the need for words. "Oh, my God," she whispered, pressing her fist to her mouth to staunch a sob, "what can we do?"

"Fight them, and win!" Luke said firmly. "There's a score or more of trained men out there. We've a good chance of running off any but a very large war party. Heh, *desperada*, where's the courage you found to rob the bank?" he teased, chucking her beneath the chin. "The *desperada* I knew could have gotten through this on sheer guts alone!"

She smiled wanly through her tears. "I think I left her

back in Cherry Creek!" she whispered.

"No, you didn't. She'll come back when she's needed, you'll see. Fear does funny things to people. It turns strong men into sniveling cowards, and quiet ones into heroes. My Mourning Dove is gentle, but she's also strong. Remember that."

"I'll try to."

He nodded, reached out, and stroked her hair. Even in the shadows it gleamed like gold dust. "Would you feel better if I stayed here with you for a while, until you settle down?"

"Yes. Oh, yes!" she admitted fervently, a shiver running down her spine.

"I brought you your guns," Luke said, pressing something cold and heavy into her hands. "I figured you'd feel better if you could protect yourself."

"Thank you. You—you've been very kind, Luke."

Her voice was little more than a whisper, and for a second he was plagued with guilt. He should have left her safe in Cherry Creek, a small, nagging voice insisted, and he knew that the voice was right. Yet still, revenge won out in the form of memories—of an airless cell from which the sky could be seen as a thin, bright-blue strip where he had lain prostrated with heat during the summers and half-frozen with cold during the winters, and he hardened his heart to the nagging voice of his conscience. She was afraid. She was alone. Both factors would drive her into his arms as surely as a robe flapped behind a horse would drive it onward. He slipped his arms about her shoulders and pulled her against him.

"Oh, Luke!" she whispered, burrowing her face against him and clinging to him desperately. "I'm so afraid!"

He murmured endearments against her hair, his strong

hands stroking her back soothingly through the cloth of her shirt while she wept against his chest, the sobs racking her slender body.

"Sssh," he whispered. "It'll be all right, *desperada*, you'll see." He tilted her face up to his and placed his lips gently over hers.

"Hold me, hold me tight," she implored him, and he did so, crushing her against him and kissing her again.

Her breasts were flattened by his broad chest as she clung to him, and his lips were hungry, hard against her soft mouth, blotting out her fears with their fierce pressure. His tongue surged between her lips, exploring the velvet recesses of her mouth in a way that sent her pulse racing and filled her with warmth and a strange, tingling excitement in the pit of her belly. His mouth left her lips and trailed down the soft column of her throat, kissing her gently, oh, so gently! Shivers ran up and down her spine and his dark eyes glittered in the shadows as he smiled.

"I want you, *desperada*," he murmured, his voice soft as the night wind in the darkness. He dipped his head again, lips branding their fiery mark on the golden-tanned V above the fastenings to her shirt. His hands toyed with streamers of her fair hair as he kissed her, interspersing each kiss with love words in his Cheyenne tongue. It seemed as if fire kindled where his lips touched her flesh so sensually, and she sighed deeply as her own fingers laced in his thick, black hair. How different it was to be made love to like this, instead of with the bruising ardor he had attempted before! She felt as if she were melting, dissolving, right here as she lay in his arms . . .

His fingers glided tentatively across her shoulders, grazing her breast momentarily as they traveled to the buttons of her shirt. He felt an answering hardness to his fleeting touch and smiled. Whether she knew it or not, she wanted him, too, if only to make her forget her fears. Her skin felt like velvet under his touch as he slipped his hand inside her shirt and caught the soft weight of her breast in the warm cup of his palm. The nipples rose at the teasing touch of his fingertips, surging upward to become a rigid little peak that demanded his caresses, and he was surprised to feel a hardening in his loins and a feverish urgency to have her that had little to do with his desire for revenge, but with desire of a different sort.

Luke covered her aching breast with his mouth, tenderly devouring the tumescent crest, swirling the hot length of his maddening tongue about it until Promise felt she would go crazy if he did not somehow put an end to the building sensation of excitement within her. He moved his lips to her other breast and caressed it in the same way, sometimes grazing the exquisitely sensitive flesh with his teeth or drawing it between his lips in such a way that the blood sang in her ears and her fingers knotted tightly in his hair, and she moaned—though for what, she was still uncertain. She knew, in some still-unmoved part of her mind, that she should not be here like this with Luke Steele, bare-breasted in his arms, that good girls did not let men take such liberties with their bodies, and especially a man who was little more than a stranger, and a half-breed at that! If her mama could see her now, she'd be horrified! Then again, she thought dreamily, aware of Luke's tanned fingers gently circling the hardened peak of her breast, maybe she wouldn't . . . Hadn't Mama felt just this way in Courtney Fontaine's embraces, and hadn't she, Promise, been the result of the passion they'd shared. Hadn't she—hadn't she . . . ? Cherry Creek moralities just didn't seem to count here, not any more, when their very lives were being threatened, and he was doing what he was doing and making her feel this wonderful, light-headed way.

He kissed her full upon the lips again, kissed her until she felt like a thirsty man in the desert who has found water and can never get enough! He stroked the slender curves of her buttocks and thighs beneath the heavy men's pants she wore, and the sensation of his touch, so close to her flesh but so achingly far away, made her tremble with desires she could not come close to explaining, for she had not experienced this longing when first he had taken her. His urgent fingers trailed upward to unbuckle her belt, and she sucked in a shivery gasp and closed her eyes tightly at the brush of his fingers against her belly.

Soon, she would be his, Luke thought, his breathing growing husky as she yielded eagerly to his embraces, his kisses and caresses. He had captured her innocence, but when he claimed her this time she would share equally in their passion, powerless to deny its strength. After tonight, when she gave herself freely as a woman with her woman's needs and desires awakened by him . . .

He broke their kiss and leaned up, his head cocked to one side, his body tense as he listened to the silence beyond the tent. There! Again he heard what had alerted him seconds before; the distant howl of a coyote. Prickles ran the length of his spine, for he knew that despite all sounds to the contrary, it was no real coyote that had howled. He leaned back and gently wrapped Promise's unfastened shirt about her, then reached out to lightly touch the curve of her cheek with a caress. "It's coming, *desperada*," he whispered, his tone filled with regret. "The Comanche are getting ready to attack! Don't move, don't leave here, until I come for you, understand?"

He crawled toward the tent flap, not waiting for her

179

answer. The light pressure of her fingertips against his hand had been enough.

Luke quickly saw that he was not the only one who had recognized the coyote howls for what they really were. Soldiers were moving about purposefully in the gray patches of moonlight that dappled the shallow gully, keeping low as they scurried to the positions assigned them, their rifles in hand. The horses had been herded into one wide circle, and they tossed their heads nervously as they smelled the excitement in the air. Luke found Black-Strap and Joaquin already in position, lying under the wagon, and he cursed the lust and the hunger for revenge that had slowed his reflexes and delayed his awareness of the impending attack. Captain Hughes sighted him and strode swiftly to where he stood.

"Steele, keep your people with you," he ordered. "We'll have no chance to keep an eye on them once this begins. Do you have ammunition?"

"We do," Luke confirmed. He spun about on his heel and headed for the herd of horses.

"Where are you going?" Hughes's voice barked.

"I am to see how many of them we're up against, Captain—unless your scouts have already determined that?" It was obvious from Hughes's expression that they hadn't. He nodded and started after his blue roan, who came at his low whistle like a dark shadow, separating itself from the rest. He grasped the horse's mane and swung himself astride it, bareback, before cantering from the camp.

Fights-Wolf crouched in the shadows on a nearby low hill, watching the camp of the white-eyes with a cruel smile on his red-painted face. Very soon, he, Fights-

Wolf, war chief of the Comanches, would swoop down upon their camp like the golden eagle from its mountain aerie, to bring death to them all! Soon, fresh scalps would dangle from the points of their lances, along with the many scalps they had taken three suns before. They would return to the camp of the People with captives, with the white man's strange and wonderful possessions, and best of all, with his guns, riding the zigzag path of victory and whooping their triumph! The eyes of the women would glow like dark stars when they saw the fine picture he made upon his coal-black pony, and one woman in particular, Little Otter, who was as sleek and lovely as the creature for which she had been named, would look upon him with new eyes. She would see now that he was a worthy mate for her and not spurn him as she had done before; nor would she reject the many horses he would pay her father as her bride price.

He touched the medicine bundle that hung about his neck on a rawhide thong and felt its power go coursing through him, hot and swift as the lightning-water of the white men. He stood erect on the crest of the hill in the moonlight, threw back his head, and bayed at the moon, the chilling howl of a coyote's lament. His white teeth flashed in the handsome, copper planes of his face as his call was answered from across the gully by Nine-Toes, his younger brother. All was ready. The thrill of danger filled him with a rising tide of excitement that he could scarcely contain. Striding swiftly, silently, he gestured to the warriors with him to mount up. Like shadows, they grasped their ponies' braided mane loops and swung astride them, their faces painted in fierce reds or black, feathers hanging from their scalp locks as proof of the *coups* they had counted in battles gone by.

Astride his coal-black pony, Fights-Wolf sat erect. He

raised his bow and brandished it aloft, emitting high-pitched, yipping war whoops as he called to the others to attack.

"Shall we ride, my brothers?" he asked, eyes glittering through the vermilion paint on his face.

"We shall!" came their instant response.

"It is a good day to die!" cried Fights-Wolf and kneed his pony forward, down the sloping hillside.

Behind him surged more ponies: buckskins and paints, roans and grays, coyote-yellows and whites. On their backs rode Death, with twenty different faces.

Promise strained her eyes to see through the gray shadows painted by the moonlight, and saw Luke come careening back into the camp. He sprang down from his roan and went straight to Captain Hughes, and she watched their earnest conversation.

Despite Luke's orders to stay put, she had left the tent and now lay on her belly under the wagon alongside his men. She had determined that if they were to be attacked, she would not lie helpless in a canvas cocoon and play the victim but meet the attack head on and add her guns to those of the cavalry and infantrymen all around her! She had scorned Black-Strap and Joaquin's protest that women weren't supposed to fight and showed them the guns Luke had returned to her. Muttering their objections, they had handed her a rifle and cartridges to go with it.

Captain Hughes's men were positioned in a wide circle around the herd of horses, the supply wagons, and Luke's wagon, which had been drawn up in a line. They had utilized clumps of cactus and rocks for cover and shouldered their weapons, ready to fire the instant

Hughes gave the order to do so. Promise listened to their low voices wagering how many redskins each would kill that night, laying bets on the outcome, and swapping lurid tales about past forays with the savages. She wondered how they could all appear so calm when she could feel fear rising up through her chest until it seemed to fill her lungs and jeopardize her breathing. Dear God, let her shots count! she prayed. This was surely a very different prospect from target-shooting at the Independence Day picnic!

Luke slipped to the ground alongside her. One glance at her face, waxy-pale in the moonlight, betrayed her fear; yet she had disobeyed his orders to remain in the tent and had come here nonetheless. Grudging admiration filled him. It had taken guts to leave the tent's false sense of security, and he could not help but gain respect for her as a consequence. He grinned fleetingly. She'd braided her hair in two long braids in the Indian fashion to keep it out of her eyes and set her worn, brown hat atop them. Lying on her belly, her rifle braced against her shoulder, she looked as if she knew what she were doing, too, and he wondered if she'd ever held a rifle before, let alone fired one.

A ripple of excitement coursed through the waiting men.

"Here they come!" Luke whispered.

Promise looked to the ridge beyond and her heart skipped a beat as she saw the Comanches, silhouetted briefly against the indigo sky before pouring over the hill in a rolling charge that seemed would surely sweep clear over the camp and surge on in an unstoppable tide. But at the last moment, the leader wheeled his pony and the tide swept around them in a wide arc, the shrill whooping of the Indian warriors interspersed now with the sharp cracking of the soldiers' guns, seen as spurts of yellow fire all about her. There were screams of agony as soldiers fell back, impaled by the shower of arrows that rained like hail from the savages' bows as they wheeled past, and she saw some of the Comanches throw up their arms and topple from their ponies' backs as bullets caught them in the chest.

She sighted down the barrel of her rifle, sweat greasing her palms. Dear God, how did one shoot an enemy who was moving so swiftly and hanging down under his pony's neck to hide from your bullets? She squeezed back on the trigger and seconds later, a brave spun from his mount's back, bounced once on the hard ground, rolled over, and lay still. There was no time to congratulate herself, for even as she raised her weapon to fire yet again, a second party of Comanches was pouring down from the slope at their backs to join the first. At her side, Luke was calmly reloading. He saw her glance across at him, and he grinned.

"Nice shooting, *desperada*!" he murmured.

She nodded and fired again, dimly aware of the rest of the battle being waged all about. Aim, squeeze, fire! Aim, squeeze, fire! She silently repeated the words in her mind until they became a litany, her actions a reflex. To stop, to think, she was certain, would mean death!

As Luke had warned Captain Hughes before the onset of the Comanche attack, the second party swept down the sides of the gully, bent on stampeding the horses and stealing guns. Accordingly, Hughes had divided his forces into two parts, one to guard their rear and the herd, the rest to meet the war chief's frontal attack. Chaos reigned as Fights-Wolf leaped from his coal-black pony into the thick of the soldiers ranged on the ground, brandishing his tomahawk in his fist. His eagle feather fluttered as he raised the axe above his head and brought it down against the chest of the bluecoat beneath him, kicking him aside with his moccasin before spinning to attack another of the hated white-eyes. Around him, his braves followed suit, for their quivers had long since been emptied of arrows, and there were few among them that possessed guns. Cries rent the night air. Blood spattered the leggings of the Comanche warriors now. Their whoops of triumph struck terror into the hearts of the less-seasoned soldiers. One tow-headed corporal looked down in horror at the place where his hand had been only seconds before and began to laugh, hysteria and shock blotting out all pain for the moment. Another soldier plunged backward, a knife piercing his lungs, his dying curses mingled with the froth of pink blood staining his lips, while the Comanche who had killed him tugged the knife from his chest and reached to take his scalp.

Hughes's men fought bravely, yet even the six-shooters each carried were no match for the frenzied savagery of the Comanche war party. Luke realized that the battle was going against them and hurriedly slithered from his place beneath the wagon to aid the men pinned down. Fights-Wolf spun from the body of a fallen soldier to meet him, a fresh scalp dangling from his rawhide belt, his hands stained dark with blood. His lips curled back from his teeth in a grimace as he saw the half-breed poised before him.

"Ah! A half-breed dog! Will you fight, son of a Cheyenne whore who would spread her thighs for a white-eyes?"

Though his words were in the Comanche tongue, they needed no translation. Luke nodded, eyes fastened on the eyes of the Comanche, for in them would be his decision to attack. "I will fight," he murmured softly. "And win!"

For a fleeting second, Fights-Wolf's eyes flared, fire within their dark depths, and Luke nimbly stepped aside. The Comanche checked his lunge in the nick of time, knife upraised. He twisted his body and lunged again at Luke, and Luke felt the draft of air as it whistled past his cheek. He reached out and clamped his fist around the Comanche's wrist, squeezing and forcing his arm down, down until his grip relaxed and the knife toppled to the dirt. He brought up his clenched fist and struck the war chief a savage blow across the throat, sending him reeling backward where he lay, dazed. Another brave leaped upon Luke's back, fastening his fingers around his throat and wringing the breath from him. There was a loud crack, and Luke felt the brave atop him go limp and fall, a bullet in his spine. Luke flung around to see Captain Hughes standing there, gun in hand. He nodded his thanks and whirled to defend himself yet again . . .

Promise's hands shook as she reloaded the rifle for what seemed like the hundredth time. She heard Joaquin's soft grunt of satisfaction beside her as his shot found its target, then looked up to see a brave take aim from under his pony's neck, sending an arrow directly for him. Her sharp, warning cry came too late. Joaquin gasped as a feathered shaft whirred home, embedding itself in the soft tissue between his neck and shoulder.

"No!" Promise gasped, turning to help him. Black-Strap heard her cry and crawled across to her. Together they were able to tug Joaquin under the wagon.

Promise set her rifle down and shook her head in horror. Never had she seen a wound like this before. She didn't know where to start!

"Ain't as bad as it looks, Missie," Black-Strap rasped. "Pull it out and stop the bleedin'. That'll hold him 'til

186

we's rid o'these red devils!''

She nodded as the black wrangler quickly scurried back to his position. She'd do her best.

She ripped a piece of her shirt free, wadded it about the shaft of the arrow for purchase, and pulled hard. With a dragging sensation, the arrow pulled free, leaving a jagged, gaping wound that bled copiously. Stop the bleeding, Black-Strap had said. She wadded the cloth into a pad and pressed it hard against the wound. Joaquin's eyes fluttered open as he regained consciousness. He grimaced in pain, then managed to smile wanly. *"Gracias, Señorita Promesa.* You save my life!''

"De nada, caballero!" she answered, managing to smile back at him but dreadfully afraid she had done nothing of the sort.

The cloth she had used for a pad was soaked now and useless. Dear Lord, his life was draining away with that red flood! She cast about her for something else with which to fashion a pad but found nothing. Instead, she decided to use Joaquin's own shirt. She tore his shirttails free and tugged, but the heavy cloth resisted her hands. Damn! Damn! She darted a furtive, frightened look over her shoulder. Many of the Comanches had had their ponies shot out from beneath them now and were fighting on foot. The moonlight glinted off the blades of their knives, and in the moonlit gully the faces of Captain Hughes's men were pale as ghosts. Horrified, she saw just a few yards from where they huddled under the wagon, a savage crouched over the sprawled, lifeless body of a soldier, his tomahawk raised, the soldier's hair bunched in his other fist. Involuntarily, she screamed.

"No! *Por Dios!*" Joaquin moaned, struggling to sit up.

The savage straightened and swung about, teeth splitting in a cruel smile as he saw the woman crouched by the wagon. He left the body of the bluecoat and padded quickly toward her. Fights-Wolf, his brother, would be pleased to take such a captive, with her long yellow hair, he thought as he neared her, his eyes fixed on her pale, terrified face.

Promise blanched as the Comanche moved toward her, paralyzed by fear as she realized his intent, and by the terrifying sight his red-painted face presented. She crouched stock-still, like a small, frightened animal frozen by the eyes of its predator, unable to look away, to act, to do anything but cower there, looking up at him.

"*Señorita*, the gun!" Joaquin moaned. His cry brought her partially to her senses. She opened her mouth to scream as the brave raised his fist above his head to strike her senseless, and somehow she found the rifle in her hands. Her finger jerked convulsively on the trigger and she fired at the same instant she angled the barrel upward, to point straight into his grinning face.

Nine-Toes flew backward under the impact, tissue and brains spurting from the gaping hole between his eyes even as he slammed, dead, to the dirt. His body continued to jerk as his nerves twitched uncontrollably, and for endless seconds he still seemed alive, doing some ghastly puppet's dance on the ground. Promise fired again and again at the lifeless body, until the trigger clicked hollowly under her frantic fingers and she dimly realized that the rifle was empty. It fell from her suddenly numb fingers and she covered her face with her hands, great tremors shaking her body.

Luke crawled under the wagon to her side and saw Fights-Wolf, again astride his coal-black pony, riding toward them, intent on recovering the fallen brave's body. He fired, and the brave ducked down, the bullet whistling harmlessly over his head. He kneed his pony away from the camp, yipping to his comrades to retreat.

"Easy," Luke urged Promise, shaking her slightly. "They're running, *desperada*, easy now, easy baby, they're leaving. It's all over." She nodded, then clung to him as if she would never let him go.

Dawn's lemon-colored sky found the soldiers tending their wounded and burying their dead. Casualties had been heavy, as had the loss of lives, and Captain Hughes was stony faced and grim as he gave the Apache scouts permission to do what they would with the bodies of their enemies, the fallen Comanches.

"Goddamned savages!" he cursed, kicking out at his campstool in his anger. But they'd learn that Captain Roger Hughes was not a foe to be scorned . . . He knew full well that the Apaches would mutilate the bodies of the Comanches, so that their damned heathen spirits would never find peace in their heathen hereafter. It was for this reason that all tribes tried so desperately to recover the bodies of their fallen comrades. A warrior's death in battle was considered a glorious death, but the mutilation of his body was to rob its spirit of all glory, to condemn it to walk the earth through eternity in torment and in shame and never join its loved ones on the star road in the sky. He laughed bitterly. Maybe they'd think twice about coming back and risking their savage souls!

Luke found Promise helping to bandage the wounded who were laying in rows alongside the supply wagons. Her face was still pale and her eyes ringed with violet shadows. He took her by the arm and drew her away.

"Time to sleep," he insisted. "We've a long way to go today, and you look about ready to drop. Come on, *desperada*, back to the tent with you."

"No, I can't," she argued, shrugging off his hands. There was a wildness to her green eyes that he knew was

189

the result of shock from the Comanche attack. "Joe's dressing needs to be changed, and there's—"

"No. Enough's enough, Promise," Luke cut in sternly. His tone brooked no refusal. "Joe's going to be fine. You've done all you can here." Before she could protest further, he swung her up into his arms and carried her down the rows of tents to the one put aside for her use, apart from those of the men. Once there, he set her down. "Get some sleep," he urged. "I'll wake you when we're ready to roll."

"I won't be able to sleep, I know it," she said with certainty. She shivered. "I—I keep seeing that Indian's face, all red with paint, like—like blood! He was coming for me, looking at me—and I knew what he'd do, but I just couldn't move . . . !" A strangled sob came from her, and she clamped her fist over her mouth to contain it.

Luke nodded, concern in his face as he looked down at her. There were smudges of dirt on her cheeks, dirt mingled with tears. He drew her to him and brushed them away with the balls of his thumbs. "I know, honey, but it was kill or be killed. You didn't have a choice." He held her trembling body close to his, folding her tightly in his strong arms, moved to comfort her despite himself. She burrowed her tear-streaked face against his chest as he stroked her braids, her fingers clamping tightly to his arms in her fear of being alone.

After a few minutes, Luke held her at arm's length and gave her a little nudge in the direction of her tent. There was a turbulent look in his black eyes, for the protective feelings she stirred in him warred violently with the cold-hearted resolve he had made. He cursed under his breath and turned to leave, but she caught him about the wrist, her nails digging into the tanned flesh in her desperation.

"Stay with me, please, Luke!" she implored him

huskily, her expression pleading as she looked up into his handsome face. "Please don't leave me now. I couldn't bear to be alone . . . !"

The nerve at his temple twitched, and the silver, arrow-shaped scar there throbbed. He turned slowly to face her, and as his glittering black eyes swept over her pale face—beautiful even in her fear with the sheen of tears in those lustrous green eyes, her vulnerable, pink little mouth aquiver—he knew that he was lost. The rising sun touched the glinting cornsilk of her hair with saffron rays, and he gave in, letting the yearning to comfort her flood through him and carry him away. Silently, he nodded.

Within the tent, lying at her side, he cradled her against his chest, soothing her with silly, gentle words and little kisses as if she were a child. As he spoke, his hands moved over her, gently stroking, insistently but surely easing the tension of her body with his touch. Under his caresses, she at last grew warm and relaxed. Her breathing became even again, without the tremor that fear induced. Still his hands smoothed lazy, warm circles over her body, until her languor changed subtly, and a rosy flush spread through her as if she had sat too long before a fire.

A long, drawn-out sigh escaped her lips as he dipped his head to kiss the corner of her mouth. She laced her fingers in the thick, black hair at the nape of his neck, drawing his head down that he might kiss her again. Her lips blossomed under the unhurried, sensual heat of his, becoming swollen with desire and incredibly sensitive. She moaned deep in her throat as the fiery arrowhead of his tongue delved between them to explore the sweet, silken recesses of her mouth. His broad chest crushed her soft breasts as he kissed her, arousing fierce stabs of longing in the center of her loins that pulsed with a beat as wild and throbbing as the racing of her heart.

Without haste, he removed her clothing and unbuttoned and drew off his shirt, folding it to make a pillow to cushion her head. With eyes grown smoky with desire, lips parted, she lay back and watched as he slipped from his pants, gasping at the sheer magnificence of his body. Coppery flesh glowed as if oiled in the hazy golden light diffused through the canvas walls of the tent. The play of muscle and sinew under his taut flesh made the breath constrict in her throat as he leaned down to gather her into his arms. They kissed again and again, each kiss growing deeper, more ardent, building the fever that leaped and danced like fire throughout them.

When he finally released her, he lifted her braids to his lips and kissed each one, then unbound them and spilled the cornsilk curtain like a cascade of water through his fingers. He buried his face in the shiny mass and inhaled deeply of the sweet, meadow-grass scent of it, of her. How sleek and golden and soft her skin was, entangled with the hardness and copper of his! Her small, high breasts, each crowned by a swollen, dark-rose nipple, seemed to demand his caresses and kisses, seemed fashioned perfectly to fill his hands. His lips blazed a fiery trail to these enticing peaks, and he covered them one by one with his hungry mouth, his expression that of a man about to taste some rare, delicious fruit. A low, sensual growl from far back in his throat confirmed that they were ambrosial indeed. His hand followed the sleek curves of her body down to the soft pelt at the joining of her thighs. While he feasted on her breasts, he slid his hand possessively between them and readied her with delicate strokes for his throbbing manhood, even now straining against the curve of her flanks. Small gasps came from her at the touch of his hand upon the very center of the inferno raging throughout her, and she clasped his head between her palms, fingers knotting in his hair's glossy blackness with wild abandon as his caresses increased in fervor.

Their eyes met, locked gazes, and held as he eased himself upon her. She took him eagerly, joyfully, deep within her, curling her slender arms about his neck as he arched forward and filled her with his hardness. For a second, perhaps two, he lay quite still, then he leaned up and began to love her very slowly, surging full length into her, then withdrawing, only to plunge forward once again in a way that sent her senses reeling. As he loved her, he caressed her swollen breasts, tenderly fondled and drew circles about each nipple, stroked her velvet body even as he thrust, until with a great cry she flung back her head and arched upward, taking him even deeper into herself as rapture claimed her. He crushed his lips to the exposed angle of her throat and cried her name against the pulsing hollow there as he joined her in her ecstasy. Together, they soared to the heights, bodies joined, arms entwined, lost for that moment suspended in time to anything but the glory of their union. In the blissful peace that followed the storm tide, they still clung to each other, lips meeting in a kiss of tenderness that spoke of the great pleasure they had shared.

Much later, when they lay quietly side by side, she looked up from where her head had rested upon his chest and brushed her lips against the dark furring there. She was flushed in the afterglow of their passion, her eyes dreamy and heavy lidded in the lemon sunshine that streamed like lantern light through the white canvas enclosing them. "Thank you," she whispered. "Thank you, my dearest Luke, for making that—that nightmare—go away!" Her lashes trembled fleetingly against her rosy cheeks and she sighed as she drifted into exhausted sleep, her limbs, thrown carelessly across his, loose and relaxed now.

His jaw tightened. A muscle worked violently in his cheek. God, her eyes had been trusting, so *damned* trusting, as she looked up at him! At every turn, she made him feel things he didn't want to feel for her, O'Rourke's daughter—had sworn he would never feel again! He should have been elated that he had done what he had set out to do. She had given herself to him readily, without restraint or protest, the offer of her body implicit in her pleas for him to stay with her. But instead he felt only hollowness where triumph should have been and a bitter taste in his mouth that was like gall.

Fights-Wolf slithered from his lathered pony's back and gave voice to a wailing cry. With one swift, savage move, he wrenched his knife from its sheath and hacked off the long black braids that had been his pride. Two more sweeping arcs with the wicked-bladed knife, and he had carved two long, bloody troughs in the copper plane of his chest that flowed unchecked. Yet the pain inflicted upon himself did nothing to lessen the agony in his heart. *Nine-Toes, small brother!* he cried silently. *Where are you now?*

There was no answer, and Fights-Wolf had expected none. He knew only too well where the spirit of his younger brother must be. He had watched from the hillside and seen the Apache scouts of the white-eyes drag his brother's body away behind their ponies, knew what they would do to it. *Dogs! Offal!* he cursed. Scalped and mutilated, his brother's ghost would walk the stony *mesas* and the endless plains forever, disfigured and in terrible torment, his soul unable to take the star path to the Great Hunting Ground in the sky . . .

Others of the war party reached him at the rendezvous then, some of them also mourning loved ones they had lost in the fierce battle with the white-eyes. All hung their heads in shame. Their losses had been great, and in the way of their people, there could be no victory if braves were lost. There would be no triumphant ride back to the village. When dark fell, it would be the keening and lamenting of the women that fell upon their ears, not the yee-yeeing of the victory song. Little Otter would eye him with scorn, scorn for the war chief who had boasted much of what he would do this day but had left the place of battle with many men lost and without even the body of his fallen brother. He looked across to where their captives huddled, three small children taken from the wagons they had raided four days before. The two small girls and the boy stared vacantly into space, too exhausted from the long days of riding with little water and less food to show emotion. His lips curled back from his teeth in a rictus of hatred. He jerked his head toward the three. "Kill them!" he ordered softly and strode away.

He squatted down on his haunches, unfeeling and deaf to the screams that carried from the tangle of thorny bushes behind him. What had he done wrong to cause such a disaster to befall them? Had he not fasted and prayed for victory the night before they had left the village? Had he not painted himself and his pony with the magic symbols that would ensure the counting of many *coups* and the invincibility of himself and his men? Had his power been weakened in some way? His eyes were distant as he recalled Nine-Toes's death and the white

woman who had killed him. She had fought like a
Comanche woman, unlike any white woman he had ever
seen before! Her eyes had blazed with green fire in the
shadows. Was this, then, the secret of her courage? Was
the grass color of her eyes some strange and powerful
medicine he did not understand, a power possessed by the
whites? Her face remained imprinted on his mind and
swam now in a blood-red haze of hatred before his eyes.
He imagined that pale face contorted with agony as she
writhed under his knife, dying slowly, inch by inch, in a
hundred ways. At the last, he would pluck out those eyes,
so that her ghost would be forever blind and without
power! Somehow, he vowed, he would find her.
Someday, she would be his captive. And when she was,
she would pay for the life of his brother!

Chapter Eleven

"Pa! Pa!" A child's terrified screams rose higher and higher, penetrating even the depths of sleep to which Promise had descended. She fought her way to waking, realizing as she did so that the screams had been her own, and the child, herself as she had been.

A nightmare; it had been another nightmare, that was all, she thought, sinking back onto her bedroll, weak with relief. Her heart's rapid fluttering ebbed to a steady thud as the minutes passed, and her breathing gradually grew regular once more.

Dear Lord, it must be five, maybe six, years since she'd last had that same nightmare! She'd thought that time had laid to rest the horror of that long-ago spring night her father had been gunned down by the dark stranger who had ridden into their camp. The Comanche attack ten days ago must have resurrected it. Every night since then she had awakened to the same dream, drenched with perspiration and trembling with terror. She had begun to fear the setting of the sun each day and to dread sleep as an enemy to be feared, rather than a welcome friend—an enemy she could not escape. Ten days of hard riding across arid wastes with little water to spare had left her exhausted, with eyelids drooping before she even

tumbled wearily from her horse's back. There was no way
to avoid sleep, or the terrors that it brought.

Luke rose up on one elbow on the rumpled blankets
beneath them and picked up a strand of her cornsilk hair.
He rubbed its softness between his fingers. "Same bad
dream, *desperada*?" he asked her. She nodded and he
dipped his head and kissed her gently upon the lips. Her
body was soft and warm against his in the coolness of
early morning. "Do you want to talk about it? Maybe it
will go away if you do."

She shook her head, reached up, and curled a slender,
bare arm about his neck. She drew his dark head down to
hers. "Uh, uh. I'd sooner forget about it. Kiss me, Luke!"
she whispered, and her lips parted sweetly beneath his,
drawing him deeper into their velvet trap.

His jaw hardened. For a fleeting second, he was
tempted to move away, to deny her his kisses. Yet as she
pressed herself against him, he felt himself grow hungry
with desire, could not resist the seductiveness of her
breasts rubbing sensuously against his chest like a kitten
begging to be stroked.

He caught her fair mane in his fingers and kissed her
lingeringly. "God, *desperada*, you're so damned beautiful!" he groaned against her hair. His hand sought and
found the curve of her breast and molded it to fill the cup
of his palm, feeling the nipple honeycomb under his
touch to press against his hand like a small, demanding
peak.

She laced her fingers in his blue-black hair, gazing at
him momentarily before he buried his lips in the cornsilk
tide of her hair. His eyes alone held the power to send
prickles of excitement radiating outward from the pit of
her belly, those dark, magnificent eyes with the lambent
fire of jet in their depths. His mouth, that chiseled,

sometimes cruel mouth, could leave her spent and yielding with silken kisses or fiery caresses that robbed her of reason and breath. Since that awful dawn with Captain Hughes's men lying wounded all around them, when he had tenderly made love to her in that glorious, unselfish way, answering her need to be held, to feel safe and protected, they had made love several times, and each time had seemed more wonderful than the last. What was he thinking? she wondered. Did his thoughts and feelings in any way parallel her growing need for him? She shivered as he trailed his lips down her throat to linger in the valley between her breasts and moaned softly as the rosy flush of desire swept through her. Lord, how she quivered, how she ached to feel him buried deep inside her!

He teased the velvety, flat plane of her belly with his tongue tip, holding her still as she trembled under the teasing torment of his caress. When he released her, her hand moved tentatively to the buckle of his belt and closed over it, and her eyes told him in the morning light that she wanted him, wanted him desperately, more than words could ever say.

"Slow down, *desperada*," he breathed, nuzzling the downy, pale gold of her skin before him. "There's time, honey, and plenty of it . . ." His dark head moved lower and she gasped as he parted her thighs and grazed his lips across their silky inner skin, moving irrevocably upward until he was poised between them. His tongue darted fire against the very source of the bitter-sweet longing flooding through her.

She closed her eyes, glorious sensation spinning her around and around as if whirling on a carrousel until she was dizzied by the sheer momentum and felt as if she would surely fly free into the air. "Oh, oh, Lord,

Luke . . . Luke!" she sobbed aloud as she soared weight-lessly into ecstasy, waves of rapture pulsating through her body.

"'Oh, Lord, Luke' what?" he murmured teasingly, looming above her and entering her in one lithe move. He caught her limp body up into his arms and drew back before burying himself deep within her liquid heat once more. Over and over he drove deeply into her, riding her strongly, swiftly, then slowly, sensuously until she was spinning once more.

"Oh, Lord, Luke, I think I love you!" she finished for him, feverishly kissing his rough cheek, teasing the corner of his mouth with the tip of her tongue until he growled deep in his throat and worried her lower lip with his teeth in mock retaliation.

All teasing ended as he crushed her mouth beneath his, kissing her hungrily until she was breathless. Suddenly, his body went quite still. A shudder rippled through him and he groaned aloud as she responded a second time to the shattering release that exploded like a storm within him. She arched upward to meet his fierce thrusts, drawing him hungrily into herself until he finally relaxed, his dark head pillowed on her breasts.

"Dearest Luke!" she whispered, stroking his thick, black hair. "My dearest, dearest Luke!"

They lay there for several minutes in the drowsy afterglow of their lovemaking, with the dawn chorus of the birds filling the dewy air all about them. He seemed as loath to destroy the lazy intimacy of the moment as she, but then he suddenly rolled from her side and sat up, raking his fingers through his tousled hair. He glanced sideways at her and grinned slyly.

"Too tired for a swim, *desperada*?" he challenged, reaching out and tugging a stray streamer of her fair hair.

She batted his hand away, squirming as he quickly changed his attack to tickling her in the ribs until she giggled helplessly.

"Enough! Stop it! I'll go swimming with you, you beast!" she promised, cornsilk hair tumbling about her, green eyes sparkling.

He nodded in satisfaction and released her. Before he could react, she was up and scampering through the pearly yellow dawn light, down to the silvery Pecos below. "Last one in is a skunk!" she called over her shoulder, shrieking in mock fright as he leaped to his feet and charged down the river bank toward her.

Side by side they plunged into the chilly water, gasping as they resurfaced. Luke clasped her about the waist and pressed a light kiss to her wet nose. "Who's a skunk now?" he asked breathlessly, water streaming down from his plastered black hair giving him the look of a sleek, dark otter.

She smiled and escaped his arms, swimming lazily away.

Cottonwoods graced the river banks, and beyond, the snowcapped magnificence of the Sangre de Cristo mountain range reared its beautiful, forested silhouette against the rose and saffron sunrise. The moon still lingered above, a foamy, pale circle against the sky, attended by a single bright sister star. It was a magic morning! she thought dreamily. Her body felt sleek and content as she moved easily through the water, the result of Luke's wonderful lovemaking. Her heart felt filled to bursting with her love for him. Even when she was old and wrinkled, she'd still remember the smell of fresh dew clinging to the grass, the pearly light, and Luke's eyes looking down at her as she lay in his arms. Oh, she felt like doing something wild and reckless with this heady feeling inside her! Was that what Mama had meant about the way she'd felt about her Courtney? She felt as if she would surely die a little each day if they were separated. The thought was a sobering one. What if something happened, and she'd never once told him how she felt? She arched forward to bring herself alongside him, wrapping her arms around his neck and gently brushing her moist lips against his mouth.

"I—I think I meant it—what I said back there," she confessed, suddenly shy. "I really think I love you, Luke!" Her heart was in her eyes. There was wonder in her expression.

But a shadow seemed to fall across his face. He untangled her arms and pulled away. "Don't," he said harshly. "Don't say it, don't think it, don't feel it! Nothing but hurt will come your way if you let yourself get tangled up with me."

Disbelief filled her expression. "No, no, that's not true!" she denied. She hesitated. "Is—is it because you're half Indian, because if it is, I don't care, Luke! It's you I love—*who* you are, not *what* you are!"

His jaw hardened. "That's not what I meant, baby," he growled. "See, it's not the same for a man as it is for a woman. That back there wasn't love. All those nights on the trail weren't love either. They were *need*, same as breathing or eating or drinking. If you've convinced yourself otherwise, then maybe you're still just a little girl. Maybe you're not ready to be a woman and accept that." Even as he said the words, her lovely face paled and her lower lip quivered with hurt. Peculiarly, the disillusionment in her eyes cut him to the quick. He ached to hold her in his arm and tell her he didn't mean it. Damn! he cursed himself. Wasn't that what he'd wanted her to say, that she loved him? Hadn't he set out to make her feel just that? Then what in the hell was he doing now, trying to talk her out of it? Everything he'd done, said, since they had left Cherry Creek had been with that one object in mind, so what in the hell had made him urge her to forget such feelings?

Her expression was crestfallen. Tears glimmered in her beautiful, slanted green eyes. "No," she whispered. "It may have been only need for you, but it was far more than that for me!" She swam away from him, cleaving the water swiftly, angrily, to put as much distance between them as she possibly could. She wished he'd swim after her, say he was sorry, say something to take the sting out of his cold words. But he didn't. After a while, she gave up hoping that he would and clambered up the rocks to dry off in the cool, sweet, morning air. She perched there on a smooth boulder, watching Luke as he swam. His arms cut through the water with vicious skill, and she knew that her confession had made him very angry for some reason. Some of his anger rubbed off on her, and she was pouting and tight lipped when he stalked from the river, his deeply bronzed body dewed with water that sparkled like diamonds in the sun.

They dressed in silence, clothes clinging to their still damp bodies, then Luke said curtly, "I want an early start today. Go see if Joaquin needs a hand with breakfast." He strode up toward the wagon without a backward glance.

Promise marched after him, inwardly furious. He hadn't needed to tell her that! Hadn't she been doing her share ever since they left Cherry Creek? She joined Joaquin at the fire and began banging pots and pans about, stirring pancake batter with a violence that caused Joaquin, testy on account of his wounding, to tug the bowl and spoon from her hands and finish the mixing himself. "I can make, *Señorita Promesa*," he insisted. "If you angry, the pancakes, they are no good, *comprende*?"

"*Si*," she acknowledged angrily and flounced off.

Joaquin shrugged and turned back to his cooking.

Black-Strap was slapping salve on the raw, chafed area on one of the wagon horse's backs when she stormed past him. Her angry movements startled the beast and he shied nervously away from her, almost stepping on the wrangler's foot in the process.

"Whoa, there, Billy boy," Black-Strap soothed, fixing angry eyes on Promise. "Well, missie, Ah reckon if you're all in a tizzy 'bout somethin', you'd best keep it t'yourself an' not come around botherin' the hosses!"

Promise grinned sheepishly. "Heck, I'm sorry, Black-Strap! Is there anything you want me to do?" She grimaced. "Mister Steele seems to think I'm not pulling my weight, and Joaquin says he doesn't need any help—well, sort of," she amended.

Black-Strap's eyebrows arched. "Ah don't reckon you're in any frame o'mind t'help with the hosses, missie. They needs a gentle hand and a calm voice, and Ah don't reckon as how you've got either today! Boss done got you mad?" he asked, lowering his voice.

She shrugged and sighed. "Reckon so. One minute everything is fine. Next thing I know, he's glowering at me and acting like he's got a burr under his saddle."

"Ah reckon he does," Black-Strap said, giving her a sly look. "But don't ask ole Black-Strap just 'zacly what that burr is, 'cos Ah don't know! Ever since Ah done started working for Mistah Steele, Ah've seen these moods come on him. It's like somethin's eatin' away at him, but Ah'll be darned if Ah know what it is. Th' boss, he keeps his self to his self, see?"

Promise nodded. Black-Strap gave the horse an affectionate slap across its broad rump, corked the bottle of salve, and gave Promise a wink. "Reckon breakfast is ready, missie. You plannin' on riding today, or taking it easy on the wagon?"

She grinned impishly, green eyes sparkling. "I guess I'll ride. A few miles on that ornery buckskin broncho would snap the vinegar out of anyone!"

Black-Strap chuckled and together they walked back toward the wagon.

They ended their long, grueling journey late that afternoon.

The terrain across which they traveled the latter part of that day was breathtakingly beautiful yet rugged and stark all at once. The grasslands were starred with red and blue wildflowers and an occasional cactus. Canyons and buttes seemed carved with a blunt knife into weird and wonderful configurations, then colored with the bold, brash strokes of a mad painter's brush in savage earth tones—ochre, rust, brown—that somehow seemed perfectly appropriate and left Promise feeling strangely awed. Mexico, it seemed, was an enchanted land where the exotic was the norm, and normal things took on exotic aspects. Santa Fe was no exception.

As they climbed higher, the sun set and the adobe walls of the buildings far above seemed dipped in molten copper and gold in the dying rays. There was an aura of tranquility, a calm about the town that was elusive, the effect of mellow light on rose-tinted walls where vines trailed and countered the warm tones with cool splashes of green or the vibrant red of strings of drying chili peppers. From the mission of San Miguel came the sweet tolling of the vespers' bell. Dogs lolling in the shadows stirred themselves, wagged their tails, and ambled off to the *cantinas* in search of tidbits for their evening meals. Small *carretas* drawn by donkeys rumbled homeward through the narrow streets, and the dark-eyed, black-haired children saw the gathering dusk and left their play, trailing bare feet in the dust as they meandered to their *jacales* for supper. The aroma of cooking wafted everywhere in the almost-deserted streets and made Promise's mouth water.

They made their way to the central *plaza*, fronted with still more adobe buildings and protruding wooden beams and rustling cottonwoods, over which the impressive arched facade of the Palace of the Governors brooded like a protective *patron* over his people. The faint strains of guitar music drifted tantalizingly on the air, promising *mariachi* bands hidden somewhere within the maze of narrow, winding streets and perhaps, a *fiesta*.

Luke ordered Joaquin to see to the wagon and Black-Strap to the horses, then lifted Promise down, taking her elbow and leading her to a small adobe hotel where, he said, the lodgings were clean and comfortable. She nodded coolly, still simmering with a mixture of hurt and anger over his heartless words that morning.

The room that Señora Diego led them into was cool and spacious and very clean, though sparsely furnished. There were Navajo pots of colorful clay, in which they might wash themselves, set on a heavy, dark-wood dresser. Brightly patterned blankets crafted by the same Indians were spread across the heavy, Spanish-looking bed that dominated the room, and still more warmed the bare floors. A narrow window grilled with wrought-iron bars overlooked the *plaza* they had just seen.

Promise looked about her, reluctant to show Luke her pleasure at the almost luxurious nature of their lodgings. Nevertheless, she was pleased by them. There was a brass spittoon in one corner and a crucifix of carved dark wood with a rosary looped about it hanging on one wall, but it was the enormous bed that pleased her most of all. It was all Promise could do to keep from jumping right onto it and reveling in its softness! After those endless days in the saddle or perched on the bone-shaking wagon, she knew she had callouses in places where decent women didn't even know they had places! Despite herself, that thought made her smile, and Señora Diego nodded and beamed in satisfaction.

"Ah, good, the *señorita* approves of the room, *si*?" She headed for the door. "Come, *Señor* Steele, this way, *por favor.* I will show you your room, yes?"

"It's right here, Señora Diego," Luke growled, scowling.

Señora Diego looked aghast. Her hands flew to her breast. "Oh, no, *señor,* is *impossible*! It would not be proper for you and the *señorita* to share this room. She is not your wife, is she, *señor*?" she asked doubtfully, dark eyes searching Luke's face.

Before Luke could reply, Promise said quickly, "Oh, no, *señora*! *Señor* Steele and I are hardly more than acquaintances!"

She grinned as the *señora* firmly led Luke from the room, muttering under her breath in rapid Spanish about the decline in morals amongst young men as she went. Promise half-expected Luke to protest heatedly, but all he did was dart her a withering, furious look over his shoulder as he left, which Promise returned with an innocent smile and a wave of farewell.

After the door had closed in their wake, Promise stretched out on the inviting bed. It was every bit as soft and comfortable as she had imagined, and in minutes she had fallen into a deep, dreamless sleep. Her last thought before she drifted off was that a few nights of sleeping alone would surely sweeten Luke up! She didn't have to be an expert where men were concerned to recognize the look that came so frequently into his eyes for what it was. . . .

When she awoke, shadows stretched themselves like long, gray cats across the walls of her room. The air was cool. From below she could hear the strumming of guitars and the sawing of a squeaky fiddle, coupled with voices raised in singing.

She swung off the bed and hurried to her window. The *plaza* had been almost deserted when they arrived, but now it was filled with people: Mexican men, women, and children; settlers from Missouri, stopping here on the long journey west; mountain men clothed in strange assortments of rags; shaggy-bearded and shaggy-haired, ferocious-looking fellows whose trade was trapping; Anglo cattle ranchers with broad-brimmed Stetsons. A small area in the center of the *plaza* had been cleared, and it was here that the musicians had taken up their places while the young people danced. Promise looked down at the scene below wistfully. Oh, how she would love to run down there and join in the merrymaking! It seemed as if the music called to her, beckoned, and bade her hurry, before it was too late!

She flew to the wash basin and quickly bathed herself in tepid water, donned the fresh blouse and skirt she had brought up from her battered trunk in the wagon, and smoothed down her hair. Feeling refreshed and more than a little excited and reckless, she hurried down to the *plaza* below.

Her petticoats and skirts felt alien about her bare legs

as she stepped out into the square. She had grown used to the snug fit of her pants, she realized ruefully. Darting a wary look over her shoulder to make sure that Señor Steele was nowhere in sight, she squirmed between the throngs of people to the area set aside for dancing.

The musicians, she soon saw, were Mexican *vaqueros*, cowboys still clad in their working clothes of goat-skin chaps and braid-trimmed hats and vests. They laughed and yip-yipped and flirted with the dark-eyed *señoritas* who flocked around them as they played; and in the flaring light of the torches that lit the *plaza*, there was the roguish look of the *bandito* about their handsome, mustached faces. Many people were already dancing, the women's colorful skirts flying, their petticoats swirling, the men drumming their stilt-heeled, silver-stamped boots arrogantly in the dust and clapping their hands to the rich chords of the many guitars. The lively music stirred Promise's blood, made her feel wild and restless in some strange way, and the rapid rhythm seemed to pulse in time with the beat of her racing heart.

"*Señorita Promesa*, would you like to *bailar*, to dance with me?" asked an uncertain voice at her side.

She spun about to see Joaquin standing there, looking bashful. He held a silver-trimmed hat in his hands that she had never seen before, and he wore a short, dark jacket with matching, tight-fitting pants that she had also never seen. His boots were as elegant as those of the guitar players.

"I'd be pleased to!" she accepted eagerly, inclining her head. With a relieved and pleased smile, Joaquin led her to join the other dancers.

Holding her by her fingertips, Joaquin demonstrated the steps of the *cuadrilla* and Promise quickly adapted her steps to his. Minutes later, she was twirling with the others, laughter bubbling up from somewhere deep inside her as little Joaquin nodded and adopted the arrogant stance of the Spanish male dancer and haughtily turned his back on her, hands clapping a staccato rhythm that was echoed by the furious drum of his heels in the dust beneath them.

Promise tossed back her mane of fair hair and planted her small fists on her hips. She began to circle Joaquin with a seductive arrogance that rivaled his own, lips pouted sultrily, eyes half closed. The music quickened. She brought her hands up high, above her head, and snapped her fingers, while all about her the women played their castanets. She took her skirts in her hands and showed her petticoats as she had seen the others do, swirling about the *plaza*, stamping and clapping until she felt drunk on the music, the scented night air, the dance's blood-stirring movements. Oh, how gloriously alive she felt, tingling in every part of her! If only it were Luke she were dancing with—Luke, whose dark eyes she was gazing up into . . . She shrugged and laughed, discarding such thoughts. For the first time, she was aware of Joaquin as a man, and she was startled to realize that he was very handsome too, in his own way. His curly black hair offset his gentle brown eyes, thickly fringed with long, black lashes, and his mouth was sensual with none of the cruel twists that Luke's mouth was wont to have . . .

The music wailed to a sudden stop, the last note of the fiddle yowling like a scalded cat on the hush. For a beat or two more, Promise continued to dance, lost in the sound. She realized only belatedly that Joaquin was still, his eyes and those of all the others riveted on something—or someone—behind her. She swung slowly about, coming face to face with Luke.

His black eyes glittered in the torch light. His expression was one of coldly restrained fury as he strode toward her. He had seen the look that passed between her and Joaquin, and a stab of something peculiarly akin to jealousy had pricked him. He eyed her face, flushed in the flaring light, her breasts still heaving against the thin white cloth of her blouse with the exertion of her dancing. Roughly he reached out and placed his hands on her hips, tossing his hat to the dust.

"If you dance, *desperada*," he said harshly, "it will be with me. No one else. *Comprende?*"

Her heart fluttered. She swallowed and nodded, unable to tear her gaze from the black depths of his eyes. He glanced at the musicians and they began to play once more, a slow, lilting melody this time. Still gazing down into her flushed face, he began to sway, and after a few moments' hesitation, she managed to stir herself enough from the daze his arrival had created to follow his lead.

It was not like dancing at all, she thought with a delicious quiver as she swung her hips to and fro, very aware of the weight of his hands resting upon them. Dear Lord, no, it was as if the two of them were making wild, passionate love here in the *plaza publica*, with countless jealous eyes upon them! He moved fluidly, gracefully, like a sleek male panther, his body exuding a potent animal magnetism that drew and held her powerless in its force. She felt as if she were drowning in the fiery black sea of his eyes that never lifted their smoldering gaze from her face. Her breathing quickened, grew husky, as she swirled about him, and despite her former anger, nothing could hide the arousal she felt as he caught her into his arms and the hard peaks of her breasts brushed his chest. The breath hissed from between his lips as he held her tightly against the swaying, long, lean line of his body. Pressed against his hips, she knew without a doubt that he wanted her as badly as she wanted him. As other couples joined them in the dance, he knotted his hands in her hair and arched her head back, raining kisses upon the exposed angle of her throat, her lips, until she was weak and trembling in the circle of his strong arms.

Somehow, he led her from the *plaza* and into the deep shadows of an arched portal. Pressing her back against the adobe wall, he kissed her again, his hand covering her breast in a possessive caress as he did so.

"No, not here!" she managed to protest, staying his hand as it traveled the sleek, flat plateau of her belly.

"Why not here, *desperada*?" he breathed hotly against her ear. "You drive me to madness, dancing in the *plaza* with another man like a little *puta* from the *cantinas*." His hot breath sent shivers of excitement up and down the length of her spine. "Tell me why I shouldn't take you here, my lovely witch, just as you are, in the shadows with your skirts thrust up?" Moonlight glinted in his dark eyes as he reached for the hem of her skirt.

Heat flooded her face. "I'm—I'm not a *puta*!" she protested indignantly. "Besides, what do you care where or with whom I dance? Maybe I just wanted to take care of those—those *needs* you were talking about this morning!" Her eyes blazed defiantly into his, like a cat's in the gloom.

He laughed mirthlessly. "Any *needs* you have, Promise, I'll take care of," he threatened, grasping her by the chin. "Understand?" She nodded. He kissed her again, his tongue and his lips arrogant in their possession of her, surging over her like a searing brand to mark her, claim her for his own. His kisses left her clinging helplessly to him, longing for far more than kisses.

Silently he stepped from the archway, taking her by

the elbow and pulling her roughly after him. In minutes, they were in her room at the *posada* and he was looking at her, leaning against the door. Dark eyes raked her from head to foot, and as his black gaze swept over her body, it was as if tongues of flame seared the clothing from her and left her bare in the wake of their wildfire. In two swift strides, he crossed the small chamber and struck a match against his boot heel to light the candle upon the scarred dresser. In another stride, he was beside her, towering over her. Still holding her captive in his dark gaze, he unknotted his bandanna and cast it aside. He shrugged off his leather vest, then unbuttoned his shirt, dragging it from his arms and tossing it from him without shifting his eyes from the green of her own.

Barechested now, candlelight gleaming on the play of muscle and sinew and blue-black hair, he took her in his arms and undressed her, slowly, lingeringly, toying with tiny buttons and fastenings until she was filled with reckless impatience and desire. She ached to thrust his hands away and tear her garments from her body to stand proudly naked before him.

When she was finally unclothed, she stood quite still and let him feast his eyes on her bared beauty. The candle flame writhed in the cool draft, touching her pale flesh with light, then shadow. Soon his slim, tanned fingers reached out to press and caress her skin, stroking the full curve of her uptilted breasts, teasingly circling the dusky-rose crests that trembled and grew achingly rigid with his touch. The candlelight also glinted in the gold of her hair, and the tiny beads of moisture upon her upper lip and in the valley between her breasts caught the light and held it like pearly drops of dew. His lips parted as he knelt at her feet and captured a breast in their warm, moist trap, and she shuddered and arched back her head as his maddening mouth drew the vulnerable flesh deeply into it. His tongue flicked against the exquisitely sensitive tip and sent gooseflesh rising along her arms. Her knees threatened to buckle. She clutched at his broad shoulders and moaned softly as his hands cupped her sleek buttocks and drew her still closer to him, the better to ply her with kisses. At length, he drew her to the bed and stretched out beside her, unbuckling his pants and drawing them off so that he was as naked as she. He caught her to him in a fierce embrace, his lips slanting across hers, then rained kisses across her cheeks, her throat, the lovely curves of her bare shoulders that gleamed like satin in the moonlight which spilled through the grilled window. His questing hand delved between her thighs and stroked her delicately, yet he found her already moist and eager for his loving. His lips captured hers yet again as he plied her with rhythmic caresses. Her nails dug desperately into the smooth flesh of his back and her slender body arched upward to mold its soft curves to the strength and hardness of his in an effort to assuage some of the aching of her desire for him.

Damn, damn, Promise thought, her mind in chaos. Had she not one ounce of pride, that she could want him so very much while knowing it was not love he offered her, but merely an easing and pleasure of his touch and his body? Oh, despite his motives she wanted him, wanted him so! She cried out as he loomed above her, broad shoulders blocking out the candle's wavering light, dark hair shining with a deep blue luster as he arched forward and drove strongly between her thighs. "Luke, oh, Luke, I love you so much! Hold me, my dearest, hold me!"

"You're mine, *desperada*!" he breathed raggedly as he possessed her. "Never forget it! Never!" There was jealousy in his voice.

As she surrendered to his lovemaking, more ardent than ever this night, she knew in her heart that his fervent command was unnecessary. She was his—body, heart, and soul—only his! She did not have to have been loved by other men to know that he and only he was the man for her. There would be no man in her heart but Luke, with his smoldering dark eyes; Luke, with his fiery kisses; Luke . . . Luke who was everything!

Amidst the golden tide of her passion, through thoughts and emotions that tumbled chaotically through her like windswept leaves in the frenzy of a whirlwind, a small voice cried out from deep within her for him to say he loved *her*, needed *her*, as fiercely as she had come to need him in this short span of time since they had met.

But her silent plea remained unanswered and unsatisfied.

Long after Promise had fallen asleep upon his chest, Luke remained awake. He watched the shadows of the cottonwoods that lined the *plaza* make dark lace patterns against the whitewashed walls of the room. He heard the muted chords of a guitar and the tinkle of glasses and soft laughter from a nearby *cantina*. He felt the gentle rise and fall of her soft breasts against his chest, her warm breath fanning his cheek, the brush of her silky hair against his skin, and sleep evaded him. Something constricted his breathing as he recalled the expression on Promise's face when she had looked up at Joaquin in the square while they danced, and he felt again the anger—and fear—that he had experienced in that moment of seeing them together, laughing, enjoying each other's company. Jealousy, that's what it had been, jealousy that she could

215

look with such fondness on another man when she was his woman; that Joaquin could bring a smile of such enjoyment and delight to her lovely face, while he had only filled her eyes with pain. He had known in that moment that he had been lying to himself these past weeks. The enormity of what that implied was too great, to unsettling to contemplate while sober. He needed a drink, he decided, and badly.

He untangled her slender arms from about his neck, and gently lifted her sleepy head from his chest. Then he dressed and quickly left the *posada*, heading for one of the many *cantinas* that lined the dark, winding streets leading off the main square. He turned into the first one he came to, a dingy establishment that reeked of liquor and sweat. Smoke wreathed the tables, and the laughter of the saloon girls was loud and raucous. It suited his mood. Perhaps here he could put things back in their proper perspective. He took a table in a dark corner and called for a bottle of tequila and a single glass. The girl that brought it for him wore a red rose in her hair. Full breasts swelled from the neckline of her red blouse. Her black eyes offered him a sultry invitation, which her seductive hips repeated as she sidled up against him. "Will there be anything else, *señor*?" she asked throatily, bending down to afford him a glimpse of her cleavage.

"Nothing, *muchacha*," he said curtly.

She laughed. "Are you quite certain, *hombre*? It is not good to be alone when there is a *fiesta!*" Her dark eyes sparkled, and she licked her rouged lips, drawing his attention to her mouth. "It is a night for kisses and love, *señor!*" she cajoled him.

He fished in his pocket for a coin and flipped it to her. "Then find someone else to celebrate with, *muchacha*."

She pouted. "As you wish, *señor*. Perhaps you will change your mind when you have seen me dance, yes?"

He smiled faintly. "Perhaps." She nodded and moved away from his table, hips swaying seductively beneath her ruffled black skirt. Other patrons reached out to pinch her tempting bottom and raise her skirts as she passed, but she thrust them all away and looked back over her shoulder in his direction with a secretive smile.

The bottle of tequila was half-empty when the dancing she had spoken of began. The *cantina's* customers moved back, leaving a large, sanded area free for the girls to dance; and dance they did, high-heeled slippers drumming a staccato beat against the adobe floor, castanets clacking furiously as they whirled about the room. Their shadows partnered them on the white gypsum walls, dipping and spinning in silhouette. When it was the girl's turn, the crowd grew hushed. She stepped into the circle proudly, light flashing off her golden earrings and glittering in her dark eyes until they seemed afire. The music began slowly, and slowly she moved, reaching up almost lazily to click her castanets in time to the languid rhythm. Her eyes found and feasted on Luke where he sat and remained on him as she danced. The music quickened. Her ripe body stirred its sensually slow movements to match it, and he knew she danced for him and him alone, yet the thought gave him no pleasure. When her dark hair sprayed about her shoulders as she twirled, he saw a shimmering curtain of cornsilk floating in the torchlight. When she flashed her black eyes, it was slanted green eyes that beckoned him, green fringed with gold. When she temptingly drew down the top of her blouse and drove the other men to frenzy with glimpses

217

of her rounded shoulders and taut, tawny breasts, or shook her skirts in her fists to reveal maddening flashes of petticoats and strong, firm, tanned thighs, he saw the curve of downy, golden shoulders, the smooth pearly white of another's breasts, the satiny pallor of another's thighs, and turned his head away.

The bottle of tequila was empty now, and yet it might have been water for all the effect it had had on him. He was still aware, still sober. As the music ended and a pouting Luz offered her charms to a more appreciative man, he threw back his head and laughed bitterly, drawing startled looks from other drinks nearby. Patrick O'Rourke had won, after all, even after death! His winning card had been the lovely face, the sweet smile, the generous and giving heart of his darling daughter, Promise! How could he continue to pretend it was only vengeance he sought when he took her in his arms and kissed her, made fiercely passionate love to her? How could he continue to refuse the love she offered him, when everything within him hungered to reach out and accept it, and to repay the gift with the offer of his own love, his own heart?

Damn you, my darling Promise, he cursed silently. *Damn you and bless you for being the woman you are!* If only she had been someone else, another woman— one he could have used and hurt without guilt or love getting in the way of the revenge he had sworn to take—it would have been so damned simple! But she was not just any woman. She was Promise, his golden Promise, whose loveliness and goodness had made him forget his desire for vengeance.

He raised his glass. "To you, my golden Promise," he murmured, "and to your father, may his soul rot in hell!"

Perhaps he was a little drunk after all, he thought as he called for another bottle.

The *cantina* was almost deserted when Luke left it some two hours later, the drinkers and drifters having long since staggered off to whatever cot or alley they called home. Luke tucked a coin down the gaping front of Luz's blouse and blew her a roguish kiss as he left, shouldering his way through the swinging half doors and stepping out onto the boardwalk and into the night.

His stilt-heeled boots made little sound as he headed back through the narrow, shadowed streets of Santa Fe, toward Señora Diego's small *posada*. The squall of mating cats and the barking of dogs were the only sounds that broke the silence. Thumbs tucked into his belt, head down, he was deep in thought when a man stepped from a shadowed alley to stand before him, blocking his path.

"It's been a long time, half-breed!" the man drawled nasally.

Luke tipped back his Stetson, dark eyes narrowing as they assessed the man before him. A faint, mocking smile curled his lips. "It sure has, Colter," he agreed coldly. "But not long enough . . . !" He made to step past the older man, who reached out and gripped his shoulder.

"What's your hurry, *amigo*? Grown too proud t'pass the time of day with your old partner, boy?"

A muscle in Luke's jaw tightened. "Take your hand off me, Jake," he said softly. "My patience hasn't improved any over the last two years."

Jake Colter laughed, but his gray eyes were without humor, cold and expressionless as he dropped his hand to his side. "Say so, Luke, old friend? How about your memory? Has that improved some?"

Luke's dark eyes flickered to the shadowed alley at

Colter's back, where the bulks of several men showed dark against the gloom. Casually, one hand slid down from his belt and folded about the handle of his gun, fingers flexing. "I'd say my memory's as good as it ever was, Colter. State your business—or get the hell out of my way."

Jake Colter clicked his teeth and rubbed his stubbled jaw. His blunt features twisted into a sneer. "What's your hurry, boy? Someone waitin' for you, maybe?" He chuckled nastily. "A pretty little gal with long, yellow hair, say?" His grin broadened. "Oh, yeah, I seen her, Steele, over in the *plaza*. The two of you looked mighty cozy dancin' together. She your fancy-woman, half-breed?"

So swiftly Colter never saw it coming, Luke's fingers came up like lightning, knotted in Colter's bandanna, and twisted the kerchief tight about his throat. He slammed the older, heavier man up against the adobe wall, in the same instant drawing his gun and nudging the barrel into Colter's paunchy belly.

"Like I told you, old friend, my patience hasn't improved any since I saw you last," Luke gritted, black eyes burning. "Now, tell your *compadres* to back off— real slow and easy. If not, you're looking to find yourself with an extra belly-button, *partner*. *Comprende?*"

"You heard him, boys!" Colter said tensely, and there was a scuffling of feet as Colter's sidekicks spilled out of the dark alley. There were six of them in all, Luke saw, Mexican and Anglo, each one with the hard-bitten, menacing cast of an outlaw.

"Boss?" growled one.

"I said git!" Colter snarled. "You heard me, Starr, damn your fool hide!"

Muttering an oath, the one named Starr moved away, and the rest followed.

"Right," Luke breathed. "I reckon that was a real smart move on your part. Let's see if you're smart enough to take some advice from an 'old friend,' as well. Don't take it into your head to try making trouble for me, Colter, because that boy you locked up back in Denver's a grown man now, and he don't ask questions—he shoots first! You get my meaning?"

"Sure do," Colter acknowledged. "And I reckon we'll find out by and by if you're really a man, Steele—or still a thieving, half-breed pup!"

Luke's jaw tightened. "Try me," he challenged softly and released Colter's bandanna, spinning his gun back into the holster as he stepped away from the man and sauntered down the boardwalk.

He didn't go directly back to the *posada*; there was no telling if Colter or one of his sidekicks was following him. He circled around some, then cut through a crowded *cantina* and ducked out the back door, doubling back to watch the swinging doors. Sure enough, one of Colter's henchmen skulked in the shadows outside the door, lounging against the wall and smoking a long *cigarillo*. If he was waiting for him to come back out, he was in for a long wait, Luke thought grimly as he cut around behind the man. He drew his gun and tapped him across the back of the skull. With a grunt, the man folded to the dirt. After a quick glance about him, Luke vanished silently into the shadows.

Back at the hotel, he slipped into Promise's room, locked the door, and loaded both of his guns before stretching out alongside her.

She was still asleep, moonlight spilling through the

221

grilled window and patterning her lovely face like a veil.
Her lips were curved in a smile. He brushed his mouth
against her bared shoulder, then traced the outline of her
lips with his calloused fingertip.

"Sweet dreams, *desperada*," he murmured before
settling down to keep watch, his guns loaded and ready at
his sides.

Chapter Twelve

It was mid-morning of the next day before they left Santa Fe. There was a market in the *plaza publica*, and the town was thronged with people, horses, oxen, coops of poultry, and wagons. All jostled for space amongst the stalls, many of which were no grander than a blanket or matting spread upon the sandy ground.

Luke noticed the wistful, eager expression on Promise's face that morning as she looked down onto the square from the grilled *posada* window, and he knew she was itching to be below, amidst the crowd. Despite his aching head and unsettled stomach, he suggested they go below and explore. He was rewarded by a brilliant smile that made up for the effort the offer cost him after a sleepless night awaiting an attack that never came, and too much tequila!

He instructed Black-Strap and Joe to wait, while he took Promise's elbow and led her amongst the stalls. A careful perusal of the faces of the marketgoers revealed no one unusual, and his concern that Colter and his men might be lying in wait for him eased a little. They were night people, using the darkness and the shadows for their evil deeds. He would be surprised to find men of their kind in the sunlit brilliance of the *plaza*.

It was the first such market that Promise had ever seen, and she looked around her eagerly, like a little girl let loose to go to the fair.

There were magnificent horses for sale, with fine, aristocratic heads and glossy coats, whose blood was as pure and fiery as any *hidalgo*. There were silver buckles, necklaces, and bangles set with vivid turquoise stones; delicate *mantillas*, or shawls, of exquisitely worked lace; combs of pale ivory or cleverly carved wood; reed baskets, clay pots, leather work of the finest craftsmanship, with braided *las riatas* and saddles decorated with silver; hats and chaps of goatskin; boots and belts; statues of the Blessed Virgin or the beloved saints; food stalls that offered all manner of tasty fare, from spicy rice and *frijoles* to sweet and tempting *flan*. Oh, the array was endless, Promise thought, drawing her attention away from a *mestizo*, Spanish Indian, selling rattlesnake hatbands to where Luke was pointing. The stall before her was no more than a woven blanket spread upon the ground, strewn with silver baubles. An old Indian man squatted cross-legged beside his wares, wrapped in a striped blanket and smoking a fat cigar, an incongruity that amused her.

"Choose something," Luke was saying. "A present for your birthday," he added.

She smiled. "What I want can't be bought, Luke," she said softly. "Besides, my birthday isn't for another three weeks." She grinned. "Seventeen! I'll be an old woman then!"

He smiled down into her radiant face. "I've always liked my women older. They're like fine wines—they get better with age!"

Despite the flippancy of his words, the expression in his eyes—so different, so tender, this morning when compared to the dark anger in their depths the night before—did peculiar things to her heart. She blushed and looked quickly away, pretending to inspect the bracelet of twisted silver ropes the old Indian man thrust into her hand. It was pretty but too heavy and ornate for her taste.

"If you won't choose, then I'll have to choose for you," Luke threatened, slipping his arm about her shoulders.

She smiled shyly and studied the sparkling array before her for several moments before crouching down and selecting something. "This one," she said at length, "if it's not too expensive?"

It was a belt buckle, he saw as he took it from her, a dainty oval filigree of silver flowers and vines. The center of each flower was a tiny, turquoise, round stone. He nodded his approval. The piece suited her perfectly, far more than the ornate brooches and necklaces she could have chosen. "It's yours, *desperada*," he agreed, pulling a sheaf of bills from his shirt pocket and paying the old man.

He tucked the buckle into his pocket and took her elbow, leading her away. "You can have it later—on your birthday," he promised, dark eyes twinkling.

"Thank you, Luke. It's lovely," she told him, her face flushed and happy. "But . . . shouldn't you have tried to bargain with that old man?"

He shrugged. "Maybe. But I figured you were worth it, whatever his price." Embarrassed that he had spoken so honestly, he muttered, "Come on! It'll be dark before we reach the Casa del Ombras," and hurried her across the sandy *plaza* to the wagon, where Black-Strap and Joaquin were waiting.

*　　*　　*

The *hacienda* far outdid anything Promise had expected. She'd envisioned a small adobe house, much like the *jacales* of Santa Fe. In reality, it was a sprawling adobe building, whose weathered, mellow, adobe walls glowed a soft beige-pink in the afternoon sun. Red tiled roofs and gracefully arched doorways gave the *casa* the elegant look of old Madrid. Pots of bright geraniums added a splash of gay color to heavy wooden doors studded with black-headed nails and black wrought-iron grills at the windows. Live oaks laden with gray moss sheltered the *casa* where it nestled in the lap of a shallow valley. Beyond the gracious house were corrals filled with mustangs, barns, and outbuildings, and beyond these, the hazy-blue magnificence of the mountains on one side, and far in the distance, the silver ribbon of the Mora river. It was lovely, and she said so.

Luke nodded, pleased by the delighted expression on her face. "*Doña* Candida, my father's first wife, brought the Casa del Ombras to him as her dowry when they were married. She was the only surviving member of her family, which originally came to Mexico with the conquistadors. It is said she turned down the proposals of over twenty wealthy men to marry my father, Thomas Steele, an Anglo."

"Did he love her very much?" Promise asked.

"He did," Luke confirmed.

"Then I'd say *Doña* Candida was as wise as she was rich," Promise decided.

"Would you?" Luke said amusedly. "Climb down, and I'll take you inside to meet Margita."

Promise nodded and got down from the wagon, suddenly nervous as Luke set her carefully on the ground. Margita, she knew, was his housekeeper, yet he had spoken very little of her, and Promise had no idea if

226

she were young and beautiful, or old and ugly, or somewhere between the two. She had wondered from time to time if she were Luke's woman, and if that were so, what would become of her when Margita learned of her relationship with Luke these past weeks?

Her fears were unfounded she saw when they entered the cool, high-ceilinged rooms of the *casa*, and Margita bustled out to welcome them. She was a short, plump woman of middle years, with a broad, handsome face and sternly shining black eyes. Though she treated Luke with the respect due *el señor*, it was respect mingled with a maternal quality that Promise warmed to immediately. Luke introduced the two women, then left them alone while he went to confer with his foreman. Promise's initial shyness was quickly dispelled by Margita's warmth and friendliness. Although it was apparent by the way the housekeeper's eyebrows had arched that a young Anglo woman was the last person she had expected *Señor* Steele to bring to the *rancho*, she quickly shrugged off her doubts and showed Promise to a room overlooking the courtyard.

"I was not expecting a guest, *señorita*, but the room is clean. We need only air the linens and dust a little, yes? *Momentito* . . ." She returned shortly with a broom and dust cloths, and began bustling about. With Promise's help, the room was ready in a matter of minutes, and Margita nodded in satisfaction. "There! I will have my son, Paco, bring you water for washing, and you will be comfortable here. Have you any bags?"

"A trunk. I believe it's still outside on the wagon."

"No matter. Paco will see to that also. He is a very fine son!" she said with enormous pride. She smiled broadly. "*Bienvenido, Señorita Promesa!* Welcome to the Casa del Ombras! It is my hope that your visit will be a

227

happy one."

"*Gracias*, Margita, I'm sure it will be," Promise agreed, returning her smile. She was aware of the unspoken question in Margita's eyes as to what she was doing at the *rancho*, but she chose to ignore it for the time being. After all, she wasn't exactly sure herself what she was doing there! She could hardly tell Margita that *el señor* had at first forced her to accompany him to New Mexico, but that she would now willingly follow him to the ends of the earth, if need be! Somehow, she was certain that Margita would not understand such frivolous trains of thought, and even if she did, she would certainly consider them improper, if not downright immoral!

Supper that night was *al fresco*, set upon a long table of trestles erected under the starlight in the courtyard. Luke's cowboys and *vaqueros*, hair slicked down, clean shaven, and dressed in their best, came in from the bunkhouse to welcome the new arrival. Promise, who had never known the pleasure of a meal shared by a large, convivial family, thought it would be much like what she was enjoying this evening. She sat with handsome Cay Cantrell, the ranch foreman, dancing attendance to her every whim, on one side, and Luke, unusually relaxed and good humored, on her other. Barbecued beef and great platters of rice or potatoes were passed from person to person, as well as the inevitable beans and cornbread, and there were literally gallons of coffee to wash it all down. After they had eaten, the wooden benches were pushed back, and one of the cowboys, Shorty Price, produced an harmonica. Another found his battered guitar, and a third a squeaky fiddle that had seen better days. Flushed and happy, Promise was asked to partner each of the cowboys and *vaqueros* in turn, unable to refuse their invitations to dance when they reminded her with soulful eyes that they "didn't get t'see a purty young woman way out here too often, let alone dance with one!"

Margita snorted. "Am I not a woman, then?" she asked, feathers ruffled.

Shorty Price grinned and tweaked her plump cheek. "You sure are, Margita, honey—a purty *old* woman!" The words did not come out the way he had intended them to, and the company laughed as Margita threatened to crown the red-faced cowboy with the bean pot she was carrying.

The gathering was dispersed shortly after the moon came up, the cowboys joshing and talking as they made their way back to the bunkhouse, Margita humming as she straightened her kitchen before retiring for the night. Luke took Promise's elbow and together they walked out to the corral. The mustangs herded within it milled restlessly with their approach.

"The boys get up before sunrise," Luke explained, slipping his arm across her shoulders, "so they like to bed down pretty early."

"I think I'll join them," Promise said ruefully. "I'm beat."

He turned her to him and cupped her heart-shaped face in his hands. "What do you think of it—the *casa* and the Shadow S?"

"I love it!" she murmured sincerely. "It's like a great, happy family here, and I never had much of a family after Pa was killed. There was just Mama and me."

He nodded, reaching up to touch the arrow-shaped scar that showed white against his temple. "I—"

"Yes?" she asked, gazing up into his handsome face.

He shrugged. "Nothing. It wasn't important." He drew her against him and kissed her gently full upon the lips. "Good night, *desperada*!" he murmured huskily.

"Good night, Luke," she answered him. "I'm going to turn in now. Are you coming?"

"Go ahead. I think I'll have a smoke before I turn in."

She nodded and walked away from him, back to the *casa*. Luke watched her go as he drew a cheroot from his pocket and lit it. He inhaled deeply before turning back to the corral. He'd wanted to tell her that he loved her, but somehow the words had stuck in his throat.

"Fishing?" Luke repeated, his eyebrows rising like black commas above his amused, dark eyes. "What kind of a birthday celebration is that? I figured you'd want to have a small *fiesta* or something?"

Promise shook her head stubbornly. "No. I've hardly seen you since we came here a month ago. You spend so much time out on the range. You promised me anything I wanted, and that's it: a whole day alone with you, fishing for those cut-throat trout you're always bragging the mountain streams are filled with! I'd say you're aiming to go back on your word, *señor*!" she accused teasingly.

He grinned. "No, I wouldn't do that. I guess if that's what you want, then that's what you'll get," he agreed, still surprised by her request. "I'll see to the horses and meet you out by the corral. See if you can sweet-talk Margita into fixing us a picnic knapsack to take with us." He turned and left the room, grinning at the smile of pure delight on her face at his agreement.

Promise flew across the room and flung open the lid of her trunk, burrowing beneath blouses and skirts for her men's pants and an old white shirt. She'd worn nothing but blouses and skirts since she'd come here to the Casa del Ombras and she'd missed the freedom of wearing pants as she had on the long journey to the Shadow S.

230

She grimaced. She'd also missed riding all day and helping the men with their work. Margita seemed to think that simply because she was female, she should by nature love to clean and cook and sew—but she didn't! The six months her mama had been sick and she'd done all the laundry and cooking and cleaning had only served to bring that fact home with a vengeance. She'd vowed the day that Todd had tried to force himself on her that she'd do what she wanted henceforth, and she intended to do just that! If all went well, she'd be able to make Luke see things her way, too, she thought with a smile . . .

Hat perched jauntily atop her curtain of flowing hair, she walked through the high-ceilinged rooms of the *casa*, boots ringing on the glossy adobe floor in which she could see her own face. Luke's *casa* sure was pretty, she thought idly. Wide stone fireplaces in which resin-scented *piñon* boughs crackled were in almost every room. Knotty pine beams protruded from the ceiling and drew the eye upward to where sconces made of curling black iron jutted out from the walls or to the ceilings, from which hung heavy wooden wheels that held many candles. The floors were warmed with the bright colors and geometric patterns of Indian rugs—Navajo Indians, Luke had said—and beautiful clay pots filled with vivid geraniums that Margita had nurtured so carefully brought a splash of sunshine into dark corners of the house. One might tease Margita about her cooking, but never, never about her beloved geraniums, for she became a screaming virago if anyone maligned them. They sat in half-tubs against the beige adobe walls, nodding their brilliant orange, red, or pink heads in the sultry air. They sat in still more tubs in the open courtyard between the four galleried walls of the *casa*, where, Margita had told her, Luke's father's first wife, *la doña* Candida, had loved to sit in the cool, sweet afternoons and enjoy their beauty. The *doña* and her stillborn daughter were buried under the shady live oaks that curved about the red-tiled adobe house like protective arms, and Promise had taken to gathering wild flowers and placing them beneath the stone angels that marked the resting place. She wondered if anyone back in Cherry Creek had done the same for her mama's grave beneath the apple tree? Surely Sarah Crowley would have, and Arthur Morgan, too.

She found Margita in the vast kitchen, as always, humming as she plucked a chicken clean for the pot. As the plump woman caught sight of her in her men's attire, her olive face registered amazement. "Promise, where are you going like that?" she asked with a frown. "It—it is not fitting for a young lady to dress so!"

"*El señor* and I are going fishing, Margita, up in the mountains. A skirt would just get in the way," she said airily. "I was wondering if you could find something for us to take with us to eat?"

Margita snorted, her lips pursed in disapproval. "*Si*, you know very well that I can. Aiee, dios! *Siempre las chicas. . . .*"

She launched into a muttered diatribe against all young women nowadays, which Promise steadfastly ignored. When at last she handed Promise a bulging *maleta*, a knapsack, crammed with food, Promise kissed her plump brown cheek and raced outside to the corral, leaving Margita staring after her, trying to hide her pleased smile.

A cloudless blue sky arched above them as they rode up a narrow trail through the foothills of the Sangre de Cristos. Blue spruce and *piñons* flanked the path, and bluebirds and magpies chattered an alarm in their boughs

232

as the two riders approached. They let the horses set their own pace and talked easily of the Casa del Ombras, of Margita, and Luke's *vaqueros* and cowboys.

"I thought Margita would explode when I went into her kitchen dressed this way!" Promise said, ducking to avoid a low-hanging branch. "Oh, look—through there!" She reined in her mount to watch as a startled elk bounded away through the undergrowth.

"Margita is very much Spanish," Luke answered her comment. "If she had her way, she'd hire a *duenna* for you and have me run off the *rancho* with a shotgun!" He grinned.

Promise clicked to her horse and rode up alongside Luke. "Maybe that's not such a bad idea," she teased, "since you don't seem the marrying kind." She raised her eyebrows inquiringly, then hastily looked away as she saw his easy, relaxed expression grow suddenly wary and tense. "Neither am I," she added quickly, knowing in her heart that she lied. Maybe she had said that marriage wasn't for her a while ago, but that was before she had met Luke, had begun to feel the way she did about him.

They carried on in silence for a while, and Promise sought desperately for something to say that would bring back the easy companionship they had shared earlier.

"I remember having a birthday when I was about, oh, six years old, maybe," she began, "and I'd seen a pretty doll with a china face in a toyshop in town that I wanted so bad I couldn't sleep nights! I knew I didn't have a hope of getting it. Pa hadn't sold much of his elixir there, and we'd been run out of the last town we'd ridden through on account of one of the town elders getting the heaves after trying Pa's snake oil!" She grinned. "Anyway, you know how it is with little children. Even when it seems they have about as much hope of getting what they want as they have of touching the moon, they still wish real hard. For as long as I could remember, I'd always believed that if I wished for something hard enough and long enough I'd get it. So, I wished and wished for that little doll with the painted face and the pretty satin dress with ribbons and lace all over it, and you know what? When I woke up on the morning of my birthday, there she was, just as pretty as I'd imagined! I overheard Mama and Pa fighting later on, and I heard Pa say he'd sold his gold pocket watch to buy the doll for me, and Mama was real mad. She said that it wasn't right for him to be buying fancy presents when I didn't have a decent pair of boots to my name, or a petticoat or a pinafore that didn't have rips in it. Pa said that he knew that, but that every little colleen should have one special thing she'd wished for, that dreams and wishes were what being a child was all about. He said there'd be time enough when I was grown to worry about how I looked." She sighed. "I loved my pa so much! You would have liked him too, Luke, I know it! He—he was gunned down outside of Fairplay when I was ten years old. He didn't have a chance."

The muscle in Luke's jaw worked violently. "Is that so?" he said with difficulty. "Things aren't always what they seem when we're children. There's too much we don't understand." He gathered his reins in his fists and touched his toes sharply to the blue roan's flanks. "Let's get on. The day'll be half over before we get there!"

Puzzled, she leaned forward over her pony's neck and cantered after him.

The stream was set in a small clearing, bowered with hazy blue spruce and *piñons*, chokecherry bushes, *manzanitas* with their dusty leaves that looked as if they had been powdered with silver, and furry pussy willows.

In the long grass the wild bluebonnets showed their pretty heads, as did the Indian paintbrush, with its blue blossoms shading into pink or lavendar. The sun slanted through the treetops and made dazzling sunbursts on the water. The boulders that had tumbled down from the mountains years before baked in the heat, and deflected chill sprays of water against their steamy faces.

They dismounted and tethered the horses, then Luke found himself a comfortable spot in thick grass in the shade of a willow tree and lay back, his hat covering his face, giving every appearance of a man who intended to sleep. Promise drew the willow-switch fishing pole from her saddle and deftly baited it with scraps of chicken fat Margita had provided, then casted a disgusted eye at Luke. "You call yourself an Indian!" she exclaimed. "Huh! What sort of Indian is it that sleeps while a woman fishes?"

Under his hat, Luke smiled. "A lazy one, *desperada*!" he drawled lazily. "Besides, fishing is woman's work. If you'd rather go hunting, then I'll oblige you."

She snorted as she hauled off her boots and socks and rolled up the legs of her pants to her knees. After braiding her hair, she scrambled down the banks and perched herself atop a flat boulder, casting her line into the stream. Dragonflies dipped and skimmed over the water, as the droning of insects in the tall grass hummed in her ears. The flash of many fish darting in the cold mountain water fascinated her. She soon forgot Luke and devoted all her attention to the fish that gleamed tantalizingly below the surface and seemed to flirt with the bobbing bait she trailed temptingly past them. Minutes passed without a bite, and she leaned back and resigned herself to the wait for that tug on the line.

If she craned her head just a little, she could see the

Shadow S cattle far below, a dark, uneven blot on the yellow and rust of the range. In the far distance, a cloud shaped like a sailing ship scudded across the horizon upon a beautiful, calm blue sea. She'd thought that nothing could compare with the loveliness of her beloved Rocky Mountains, but New Mexico surely came close with a savage beauty all its own. Her daydreaming was rudely interrupted by a sharp tug on the line. She jerked her fishing pole back, then whipped it sideways, landing a gleaming trout effortlessly in the grass, where it flapped its tail in a ferocious but futile effort to escape the hook. Quickly she scrambled over the rocks to the fish, withdrawing a knife from her belt and a length of twine from her pants' pocket as she went. She quickly gaffed the fish, then threaded it on the twine which she fastened to a bush and then let trail in the water where the trout would keep fresh and cold. She glanced across at Luke, hoping he'd seen her, but he still appeared to be asleep.

With a shrug, she returned to her spot. By midday, there were an even dozen cut-throat trout dangling from the twine, and her belly was growling. She set aside her pole and went to where the leather *maleta* lay in the grass, taking out spicy *chorizo*, a thick wedge of cheese, fried *tortillas* and plump loveapples, tomatoes that still smelled of warm sunshine. There were also two generous slices of Margita's flaky peach pie and some pieces of crispy fried chicken. The housekeeper had done herself proud, Promise thought, spreading out the food on the white linen cloth that had been tucked around the *tortillas*.

Luke still appeared to be sleeping. She smiled and took up a piece of the chicken, wafting it under his nose. As she expected, he stirred and sat up, muttering, "Is it chow time already?"

"It is indeed, *señor*," she teased, loving the way he

looked when he had just awakened. His black hair was tousled and his eyes were heavy lidded and dreamy looking. His face seemed less hard, less tense than usual, softened by sleep. She held out the chicken leg to him, and he took a hefty bite from it before taking the whole drumstick in his hand, flashing her a smoldering look from his dark eyes that, peculiarly, made her blush to her hair roots with its intimacy.

"Thanks, *desperada*. We'll make a housekeeper of you yet!" He grinned and winked, chucking her beneath the chin.

"Not if I can help it, we won't!" she retorted indignantly. "I—I've been meaning to talk to you about that, Luke. See, Margita doesn't need another woman in the *casa*, not with you riding the range so often. I'm just dead weight, as far as she's concerned, though she'd never admit it." She paused.

"And?" Luke asked, dark brows cocked.

"Well, I got to thinking. I can ride pretty well now, and I love being on a horse all day," she explained eagerly, "so I was thinking maybe I could . . . well, help out with the herd?" Her expression was pleading, her eyes large and hopeful.

He frowned. "Be a *vaquero*? A woman?" He laughed. "No way, *desperada*! You have no idea how dangerous it can be, for all that the men make it look easy. There's roping—can you use a lariat?" She shook her head dismally. "There's cutting—do you know what that is?"

Again, she shook her head. "No, I don't. But I can learn! I can shoot as well as most of your men, I'll bet, and I'm strong, for a woman. I won't spend the rest of my life dusting and scrubbing and cooking!" Her green eyes shone with determination now. "I just won't."

He said nothing as he swigged water from the canteen

and handed it to her in turn, eying her speculatively. "If I were to say yes, there'd be no special treatment for you because you're a woman. You'd have to fend for yourself, just like the men. And they won't take too kindly to working with a woman. You'll have to win them over, too."

"I could, I just know I could. Will you let me try?"

"Maybe. Maybe not. I'll think on it a while."

"Give me your word that you will," she persisted.

"Consider it given, *desperada*," he agreed. "How was the fishing?"

"Everything you promised." She scrambled to her feet and padded quickly down to the stream, lifting her string of trout from the water to show him. "See?" she asked proudly.

He nodded his approval, eying the pretty picture she made with wisps of cornsilk hair escaping her braids and framing her sweet face like a halo. The shirt she wore was damp now and clung to her rounded breasts, and the men's pants clung little less snugly to the pert globes of her bottom. Just looking at her as she perched there, smiling triumphantly, filled him with a hunger to hold her, make love to her, that was heady in its intensity. "Come here," he drawled lazily, watching her through slitted dark eyes. "Come here and I'll show you a better way to spend a lazy summer's day than fishing!" His black eyes twinkled wickedly.

"Perhaps I'd rather fish!" she retorted pertly, planting her hands on her hips and giving him a challenging look.

"And perhaps I can make you think otherwise!" he threatened, uncoiling to stand.

"You're welcome to try," she offered, grinning cheekily as he sauntered toward her.

She waited until he was less than three feet away

before dashing to one side, but he anticipated her move and leaped at her, swinging her up into his strong arms, laughing as she pounded her fists playfully against his chest and kicked her legs in an effort to evade his arms. "There! I'd say my 'catch' beats yours any day, honey!" He ignored her furious demands to be put down and carried her away from the stream and into the lush grass, starred with wildflowers, beneath the trees. There he set her down, before dropping to his knees beside her.

She looked up into his lustrous black eyes as he gazed down at her. "Well, mister? Cat got your tongue?" she demanded teasingly when he simply looked at her, saying nothing for several long moments.

He shook his dark head slowly, a smile starting in his eyes and spreading to his chiseled lips. "No, baby," he breathed as he gathered her into his arms. "I was just enjoying the view!" He kissed her, twining his hands in her braids to hold her head still for his ardent lips. Her eyes were sparkling with merriment when, breathing heavily, he drew his head away, a smoldering expression in his eyes that she knew well.

"If that's what you call enjoying the view, you can look at me *any* time, mister!" she murmured breathlessly, brazenly, reaching out to toy with the buttons on his shirt and squirming her hand inside it to stroke his chest.

His lazy smile deepened. "Didn't I tell you there were better ways to spend a lazy afternoon than fishing?"

Her laughter tinkled on the deep green hush of the forest. "I seem to recall you did!" she agreed. She lay back in the tall grass, and their gazes met and held. Slowly, seductively, she trailed her fingers to the buttons of her shirt and, watching his face, watching the way his eyes grew darker and darker in his desire for her, she leisurely unfastened each one until she was barebreasted in the grass. He lay upon one elbow beside her and loosened her cornsilk hair from its braids, combing its silky length through his fingers. Reaching into the depths of the grass, he plucked a wildflower, tucking it between the gleaming strands, then another and another. Soon crimson and blue-violet blossoms garlanded the wanton tumble of silk that framed her lovely face. A small posy of wildflowers he tucked in the valley between her breasts. The nipples rose at the brush of his fingertips to stand eagerly erect.

"Oh, baby," he murmured as he lowered his head to taste each one, carefully, delicately trailing the tip of his moist tongue across the very tip of each until they honeycombed, thrust impudently against his lips. He sucked each jutting crest, circling, darting, drawing their sweetness ever deeper into his mouth until she moaned softly at the rising hot-spring of desire fountaining through her. Gracefully, she stood and removed the rest of her clothes, enflamed by the knowledge that he was watching her as she did so, and adding new and subtle undertones to their love play with the inviting, teasing expressions of her face, the movements of her body, as she seductively undressed for him. Straight ribbons of shining hair streamed down over her body when she was at last unclothed and standing shyly barefoot in the grass like a wooden nymph with the wildflowers cascading about her. The sunlight that spilled down through the treetops above dappled her pearly body with green and gold light, enhancing the green of her eyes. She curled her arms about the rough trunk of a tree, watching Luke as he undressed. When he was done, he strode through the thick grass to stand before her, straight and tall as a young pine, glossy black head set upon broad, muscled shoulders that tapered to lean, hard flanks. He untangled her arms from about the tree and caught her about the waist. She rose on tiptoe to press her lips to his, darting sweet kisses against his mouth, his jaw, and down his throat to his chest.

Gooseflesh rose all over his tanned torso as she copied his delicious torture of minutes before against his flat male nipples with her own eager mouth, and he growled deep in his throat, his fingers digging into her smooth, satiny skin as his desire surged, his nipples becoming hard little nubbins of flesh, his manhood rising firm and heated against her flat belly as he gathered her up into his arms and lowered her to the ground. Their kisses and embraces lost their lazy quality. They clung fiercely to each other now, mouths hungry, hands feverish as they explored, caressed, stroked each other. Limbs became entangled; her softly thrusting breasts were crushed beneath his hard male chest, her velvet female belly burned against his rougher male torso forested with springy black hair. When he parted her firm thighs and trailed his hand downward from the golden pelt at their joining to caress between them, he found her moist and ready for their union, and he lay back, lifting her astride his throbbing length.

The dappled light, the singing of the stream over the boulders, the sweet warble of the birds in the treetops, the drone of the insects melded together to become one glorious rhapsody, Nature's lovesong to the pair in the long, flower-starred grasses. Together they moved in the ancient rhythms known by men and women since time was born. Like the wild things of the forest about them, they answered the call of their blood to join, to create. Eyes closed, breaths mingling, they moved faster, ever faster, toward rapture, their bodies one, without beginning or end. Soon, he rolled her beneath him, took her fiercely, ardently, driving between her thighs with ever deeper strokes, strokes she matched measure for measure with her own body arching upward to meet his, until she cried out, a savage cry of sheer delight that spiraled up through the green and golden boughs of the trees to float on the wind.

Sweat dewed his tanned body like tiny beads of gold as he gripped her in a passionate embrace, pressed hungry kisses over her throat, her breasts, her closed eyelids, her lips . . . until, with a wild roar of release, he thrust one last, glorious time and fell shuddering to her side. Still now, both within and without, they caressed, kissed with tenderness, the heady fires of their passion for the moment extinguished. Curled together in the grass, her fair head pillowed on his chest, their hands clasped, their legs entangled, they slept.

When they awoke almost two hours later, the sunlight was gone. To the east loomed a great, menacing gray cloud, and the fluffy white clouds scattered and fled before it like sheep before the wolf.

"It looks like we're in for some rain," Luke observed, buttoning his shirt. "You'd best get dressed, honey." He leaned across her and pressed a light kiss to her nose before he stood and carried the leather *maleta* to where the horses grazed, fastening the knapsack to his saddlebag.

While Luke tightened their saddle girths for the long ride back to the *hacienda*, Promise hurriedly dressed, eying the sky dubiously.

As he had said, it looked like rain. The golden sunlight that had sparkled on the water earlier was dimmed now behind a vast blue-gray cloud that hung low above them. The air was heavy and humid, filled with the tension that

precedes a thunderstorm, as they rode back down to the
foothills. Before they had gone very far, huge raindrops
splattered down, soon increasing to heavy sheets of rain.
Water poured from their hatbrims and plastered their
clothes to their bodies. The angry rumble of thunder and
blue-white forks of lightning filled the lowering sky, and
the buckskin pony that Promise was riding tossed its
head and sidestepped skittishly on the muddy, narrow
trail. She was hard put to control her horse. Luke reached
down and grasped its bridle, leading the pony firmly after
his own.

"There's a hut near here—the western line camp. It's
not much, but at least we can stay dry until this lets up,"
he shouted over his shoulder.

"Sounds good to me!" Promise yelled in agreement,
gasping as a sudden gust of wind swirled a sheet of rain
into her face and took her breath away.

They reached the hut in minutes. It was made of
rough-hewn pine logs, roofed with sod. Luke urged
Promise to go on in while he tied the horses against one
wall for shelter. When he followed her inside shortly
after, ducking to enter the low doorway, she was kneeling
by the stone hearth, piling the *piñon* logs stored alongside
it into the fireplace.

"If you've a dry match, we can get a fire started," she
said.

He fished in the breast pocket of his blue shirt, still dry
beneath his leather vest, and found a box of sulphur
matches. The resiny scent of pine filled the small hut as
he touched a lighted match to the dry kindling. Soon the
fire caught and crackled in the hearth, illuminating their
faces and casting their shadows on the walls. Through the
single square window, paned with oiled paper, the storm
could be seen, lightning filling the small opening with

white light from time to time.

"Mmm, it's real cozy now," Promise murmured, unbraiding her dripping hair and combing it with her fingers. Her shirt clung wetly to her body and she plucked it away with a grimace of distaste. A loud crack of thunder sounded very close at hand and she flinched, eying the window apprehensively.

"Scared of storms?" he asked. It was his first real effort at conversation since they had left the stream.

She shrugged. "Yes and no. I like to be warm and dry someplace with a storm raging outside. I like to watch it—it's so wild and sort of beautiful, too. But yes, the lightning scares me! I was always afraid it would strike our cabin in the night, and we'd be burned alive!" She laughed self-consciously, as if to make light of her fears.

"Cheyenne legends say that the thunder is the sound of the beating wings of the Thunder Bird as he flies through the air. He flies with his eyes closed and when he opens them, the lightning flashes and fills the dark sky!"

"That's pretty," Promise said, smiling. He returned her smile and edged closer to her.

"And so are you, *desperada*." He pulled her backward to lean against his chest, and side by side in silence they watched the writhing flames do their strange dance in the hearth, changing color continually, now yellow, then blue or green. Occasionally raindrops managed to find their way down the short chimney, and the water sizzled and made the fire smoke.

"We'd better get these wet clothes off before too long," Luke said at length. He unbuttoned his damp shirt and held it up to the fire's warmth, smiling to himself as Promise watched enviously. It amazed him that a woman who could be so bold and passionate in their love-making—even brazen as she proudly bared her body for

244

his pleasure—could be so darned modest or bashful at other times. When his shirt was dry, he handed it to her. "Put it on, and take off your wet clothes."

Gratefully, she did so, laughing as he did at the picture she made in his oversized shirt that came almost to her knees, and nothing else. Her slender legs were pale gold in the meager light, her drying hair a gleaming sheaf. "You'd look good in a flour sack, baby," he breathed, pulling her down beside him once more. Smiling, she leaned back and rested her head on his shoulder.

It was wonderful to sit there, warm and dry before the fire, with Luke's arms about her, his strong body cradling her weight, and the fury of a late-summer storm howling about their haven. The flashes of lightning and the cannonball crashes of thunder ceased to frighten her with him beside her. She felt sleepy and relaxed, as close as she had ever been to being perfectly content. If only Luke had told her he loved her, if she could only be sure of his love, her happiness would be complete.

Later, when her clothes were dried and—much to Luke's displeasure—she had dressed herself again, he went to the leather *maleta* and the saddlebags he had set just inside the door when he had come in.

"Are you hungry?"

"No, thank you."

He returned to sit beside her, and she saw that he was hiding something in his hands.

"Remember the buckle you chose in the market at Santa Fe?" he asked. "I promised to give it to you on your birthday. Happy birthday, *desperada*!" He pressed the gift into her hands.

She saw that it was indeed the pretty silver buckle set with turquoises that she had chosen, but that now there was a belt attached. It was worked with the narrowest

245

strips of rawhide she had ever seen, intricately braided on either edge and woven down the center. "Who—"

"I did," he acknowledged. "Like it?"

Her mouth dropped open in disbelief that he could ever doubt it. "Like it? It's the prettiest thing I've ever seen!" she cried. Her green eyes shone with pleasure. "No one ever gave me anything like this before, Luke. Thank you." She leaned across and kissed his cheek, surprised to see that he appeared embarrassed by her praise, and perhaps a little tongue-tied. Excitedly, she made to try it on, but Luke grinned and spread his large hands over her two slender ones.

"Don't worry, honey, it'll fit," he promised with a smile. He placed his hands upon her waist and drew them away, still shaped to her figure. "It was made to measure just for you, ma'am!"

She curled her arm about his neck and drew his dark head down to hers, ruffling the thick, damp, dark curls at his nape as she kissed him. "You're just like my pa," she murmured, snuggling against his chest. "You spoil me, Luke, just like he used to do." Was it her imagination, or did her words cause him to stiffen?

He untangled himself from her arms and got to his feet, muttering that he wanted to check on their horses. She shrugged and watched him move away from the fireplace to the door. As he swung it open, the blue-white brilliance of the lightning filled the doorway, silhouetting his dark head and throwing his handsome, chiseled features into half-shadow. His expression was tight and angry, and his dark eyes glittered with a cruel, black fire that stirred some long forgotten memory in the depths of her mind. The memory slipped away before it was ever fully grasped, yet its brief emergence filled her with unease. For some reason she did not understand, she was suddenly short of breath.

"Oh!" She gasped in pain and looked down to find that she had been clutching the silver belt buckle in her palm so tightly, the pin had pierced her skin. She sucked away the trickle of blood, and a shiver ran down her spine like a thin stream of icy water. What on earth was wrong with her? It was as if someone had walked over her grave . . .

Luke returned minutes later, bringing a gust of wind and rain with him into the cabin as he fought the door shut.

"The horses are fine. I'd say the storm'll blow over before long." He drew a cheroot from his pocket and leaned over and lit it from the fire. Exhaling thin spirals of smoke from his nostrils, he glanced across at Promise. "Something bothering you, honey?"

"Me? Oh, no, nothing," she said quickly, smiling across the hearth at him. She hugged her knees and gazed into the crackling fire, cornsilk hair falling about her cheeks and hiding her thoughtful expression from him as she stared into the flames. The feeling she had had moments earlier was still strong, yet how could she explain that to Luke?

She felt his hand upon her shoulder and gasped, turning wide, frightened green eyes up to look into his face as he came to sit beside her.

"You're kind of jumpy, aren't you?" he murmured, stroking her back. "Is the storm still bothering you?"

"No, it's not that." She bit her lip. "Luke . . . do you believe that sometimes people—or places, too—can feel as if you've met them or been there before, when you know you haven't?"

He grinned. "I don't recollect ever having given much thought to such things, *desperada*. Is it the cabin?"

"No. It's . . . you." She laughed selfconsciously. "For

a second, when you were standing by the door, I had the strangest feeling I'd seen you looking just that way, a long, long time ago. It was the craziest feeling!"

He tossed his cheroot into the fire, lay back, and pulled her across his chest. "Maybe you have seen me before, baby—in your dreams!" he teased, sweeping aside the tickling strands of her hair that fell down about his face to gently kiss her lips. When he broke the kiss, she smiled down at him and her pensive expression was gone.

"I'd say that's probably so," she whispered huskily, and there was a sudden, desperate light in her eyes. She leaned up and unbuttoned her shirt, watching him seductively, reveling in the surprise—then pleasure—that flitted across his chiseled features. When she knelt bare-breasted before him, she took his hand in hers and drew it close to cover her breast. Her eyes still drawn to his, she murmured, "I want you, Luke! Love me, love me now!"

In answer he used a strand of her gleaming hair and pulled her down to lay at his side. He pressed hungry kisses to her face while she clasped him fiercely about the neck and whispered for him to hurry, please, hurry! Somehow, she wanted him as urgently as if this would be their last time together; as if some inner clock was ticking off the precious moments they had left . . .

Luke responded to her urgency, to the wild, abandoned loving she showed him there in the cabin while the thunder crackled outside and the rain lashed the sod roof and turned the ground to a morass beyond their haven. The brilliant white lightning revealed a Promise he had never seen before, a lovely, wild creature, a tempestuously passionate woman who made the blood race like rivers of fire through his veins. She kissed him, touched him, caressed him as if starved for his body, whispering her love for him again and again, and he responded to her with an ardor, a hunger, that left them weak and empty when it was satisfied. Breasts heaving, gasping with delight, she lay in his arms when it was over.

"Never leave me, Promise!" he commanded huskily, knotting her hair in his fingers.

"Never!" she echoed fervently.

In minutes, they were asleep, limbs entangled, Luke's fist still laced in her tumbled hair.

When Luke awoke, the storm had passed. There was a golden radiance in the sky that filled the window, and the sweet warbling of birds bathing in the muddy puddles outside the cabin rose melodiously on the air.

He woke her with kisses and they dressed in silence, without looking at each other, both shy after the stormy abandon of their lovemaking. When Promise looked up, she saw Luke smiling down at her. Whatever it was she had glimpsed fleetingly in his expression earlier was now quite gone.

"Ready to go?"

"Yes," she agreed, picking up her damp hat as he helped her to her feet.

They left the cabin hand in hand, laughing as they leaped the puddles and slithered in the mud.

"Enjoy your birthday, *desperada*?" Luke asked, grinning, a roguish expression in his dark eyes.

"You know better than to ask—" Her voice ended on a cry as a bullet whined between them and pinged off a rock at their backs.

"Get down!" Luke roared, grasping her hand and hauling her after him toward the cabin. No sooner had they fallen inside than another bullet ripped into the pine door itself. Luke cursed. "What in the hell . . . !" he growled, crawling across the cabin floor and drawing his gun as he went. He cautiously peered over the window.

"Who is it? Why are they shooting at us?" Promise asked, wriggling on her belly to his side.

Luke shrugged and ducked down to sit beside her. "I don't know, honey, but I reckon we'll find out soon enough!" he said grimly. "Keep your head down."

She nodded, heart racing like a speeding horse.

"Steele!" came a voice. The name echoed. "Come on out—an' bring your woman with yer!"

Colter, Luke realized and cussed under his breath. "The hell I will, Colter!" he yelled back.

"You know who it is?" Promise asked him.

Luke nodded. "I'm afraid I do, honey," he said regretfully. "It's Jake Colter and his boys." He grimaced. "Me and Jake are old friends," he added grimly.

"Steele! I done told you once, boy! Come out of there reaching, or we'll come in shootin'," came Colter's voice a second time. A bullet ripped into the frame of the window, sending splinters and the smell of gunpowder into the cabin.

"Damn if that rattlesnake doesn't have us pinned down," he growled. Keeping low, Luke crawled to the rear of the cabin. He considered the pine-log wall momentarily before drawing a knife from the leg of his knee-high moccasins. Crouching down, he began working at the boards, levering them loose. When he had pulled free enough to open a sizable hole, he beckoned across the cabin to Promise. "C'mon, *desperada*, out you go. The horses are back here. Ride back to the Shadow S and get help."

"No! What about you? We can both go!" she argued.

Luke shook his head. "Colter would figure it out if no one answers his fire." He grinned, black eyes dancing wickedly. "It'll stick in his craw if you get away and come

back with help. Go on! I'll be fine, baby. And Promise—
be careful!"

"I will," she promised, ducking under the ragged hole.

Once outside, she kept low and sprinted the last few
yards to where the horses were tethered. She untied the
buckskin's reins and sprang quickly astride him, knotted
the reins in her fists, and lashed them across his back.
The skittish pony rocketed forward like a bullet from a
gun, and Luke grinned again before quickly returning to
the window. He watched the foliage beyond the cabin,
waiting for some sign as to where Colter and his men were
hidden. The ground in front of the cabin rose in rocky
stages back up into the Sangre de Cristos. Colter had
picked himself a perfect spot for an ambush, he realized.
There was a flash of color from above one bush, and Luke
squeezed back on the trigger. The bullet whined toward
its target and there was a yelp of pain as it hit home.

"We're not coming out, Colter!" Luke yelled. "You'd
best make ready for a long wait!" He crawled across to the
door, opened it, and squeezed off another shot.

"Ain't no hurry, Steele!" Colter bellowed. "We got all
the time in the world!"

Promise galloped the buckskin pony down the slick
trail. Her heart felt as if it had risen clear up into her
throat with her fear for Luke's safety. "Come on, boy!"
she urged the pony, drumming her heels into its sides.
"Get up there!"

She neither heard nor saw the man between the trees
sitting the chestnut horse until it was too late. There was
a whirring sound suddenly, and something snaked about
her body and jerked her from the saddle. The breath was
knocked out of her as she slammed to the ground and lay

there, stunned, the lariat biting into her arms. The buckskin careened on. She struggled to sitting, clawing for the rope that pinned her upper arms securely to her sides, stopping abruptly as she saw a pair of worn boots with jingling spurs come to a halt before her. Slowly, her gaze traveled up the man's corduroy pants, past the heavy gunbelt that rode low across his hips, and finally to the leering face set on broad, muscular shoulders. The man was smiling, showing yellowed teeth. His jaw was dark with the beginnings of a beard, and his eyes were the palest blue she had ever seen, almost without color. They were cold, cruel eyes, she thought with a shiver of foreboding.

"I guess Colter was right for once in his miserable life," the man drawled, and spat into the dirt. He reached down and grasped the lariat, hauling Promise roughly to her feet. He grinned, and his pale, pale eyes filled with an evil light. "I guess that half-breed'll be eatin' out of our hands once he finds out we got his woman!" Spittle sprayed onto her face as he spoke, and her disgust and contempt were obvious on her face.

He cursed foully and shoved her hard in the back, forcing her toward his horse. Like a flour sack, he flung her across his saddle before swinging astride the animal himself.

"We'll see jest how much pride you got in you later, gal, see if we don't!" he said hoarsely as he spurred his horse. "Ain't no woman too fine for Billy Starr, an' don't you forgit it!"

Billy Starr rode with Promise in a wide circle around the log cabin where Luke was pinned down, up into the hill behind the line camp. There were several rough-looking men huddled behind the trees and rocks, their guns trained on the cabin below. One of them left his cover and scurried across to Starr's horse as he dismounted, hauling her to standing after him.

"It worked, jest like you said, Boss!" Starr told the man with a grin. "She came out the back like you figured!"

Colter grinned. "Like I said, Billy, them half-breeds are as slick as wolves!" He reached out and tweaked Promise's cheek, laughing when she jerked her head away as if burned. "Let's see how ole Luke feels now we got you, gal!" He sprinted back to the rock behind which he'd been hiding. "Steele!" he yelled. "We got the gal! Come on out, or she gets it!"

While Colter waited for a reply, Promise almost stopped breathing. Her palms were slick with sweat, as was the valley between her breasts. Colter jerked his head in Starr's direction and the outlaw shoved her forward to stand in clear view upon the rise, where Luke could not fail to see her.

"You hear me, boy?" Colter yelled again. Again, silence answered them. Then suddenly, two shots in rapid succession whined down from the rocks above them, and Promise's heart leaped with excitement. Two of Colter's men threw up their arms and fell to the ground. Colter cursed.

"Let her go, Colter!" came Luke's voice in back of them. "Or the next bullet's for you!"

"Goddamn!" Colter spat, whirling about. "Starr, take the gal and ride for home! I don't wanna see you for dust, *amigo*! Git! We'll follow you!"

Starr nodded, wrenched Promise around by the wrist and roughly pulled her after him, jerking her arm painfully when she tried to pull free. He tossed her up onto the back of a huge gray horse, tethered with others under the trees, then mounted his own chestnut.

253

Grabbing the reins of her mount, he dug his spurs into his horse and led the gray after him as he rode swiftly away. Promise held on to the high pommel for dear life as they left the foothills of the Sangre de Cristos behind them and Starr kicked his horse into a wild gallop. Her horse followed suit. Behind them, she could hear gunfire, the sharp reports echoing between the foothills. The sounds grew fainter as the distance they had traveled stretched, and soon she could hear them no more.

An hour of hard riding had passed before Starr slackened the pace; the horses were tiring. They came suddenly into a massive canyon. Walls of sheer perpendicular rust and ochre rock loomed menacingly above them on either side, yet it was not the canyon itself that caused Promise to gasp in shock; it was the enormous *pueblo* that seemed to be suspended from its walls! Hundreds of small, flat-roofed adobe dwellings sprouted from the cliff face like limpets clinging to a rocky wall. As she looked closer, she saw that narrow rock walkways led between them. The dying sun threw sharp black shadows everywhere, and the scene seemed painted in chiaroscuro, light and shade, the flat rooftops washed with the blood red of the sunset while the interiors appeared dark and gloomy and malevolent. The countless, small, slitted window-openings in each one of the adobe dwellings, some of which boasted three or more stories, seemed like black and sightless eyes. She had the eerie sensation that despite their blind aspect, they were watching—and waiting.

"This is it, gal," Billy Starr announced, reining in his horse with a vicious yank on the reins. He grinned, relishing the expression of dismay and apprehension on her face. "La Ciudad de Los Perdidos!"

"The City of the Lost!" Promise translated in a

whisper, not realizing she had voiced her thought aloud until the man chuckled nastily.

"I reckon you could call it that," he agreed. "But those that live here call it the City of the Damned!" He waved to the guard that stood silently upon the canyon wall, rifle in hand, and was waved onward. "C'mon, gal."

He led her horse after his, down into the pueblo. Promise saw that there were many living there, men for the most part, Anglos and Mexicans and a few *mestizos*, Spanish Indians. The men paused in what they were doing and whooped and jeered and cat-called when they saw her, and her face flamed at the things they called out as she rode past. Several women in evidence tending cooking fires were Mexican in appearance, clothed in the vivid colors of *cantina* girls, and there were a few Indian women, similarly clothed. They watched her through slitted eyes, saying nothing as she followed Billy Starr, their expressions blank. But like the windows, their eyes seemed filled with hostility, a hostility that was alive and reached out to her.

With a sudden chill, she knew what Billy Starr had meant when he had called this the City of the Damned. This rat's nest was the hideout of outlaws, gunslingers, murderers, and thieves: the lawless ones! She licked her dry lips, inwardly bracing herself for whatever came next as Billy Starr swung down from his horse. If Luke had escaped Colter and the rest of his men, would he come after her and try to free her from this awful place? Lord, she hoped so! Failing that, she must try to escape herself—and soon!

Chapter Thirteen

Luke scrambled down the hillside, small rocks showering underfoot as he raced after Jake Colter. When the tall, mean-looking *hombre* had ridden off with Promise, Colter had waited a while and then sent his last two men after them, one by one, staying behind himself to hold Luke off. It was just the two of them now, Luke thought, and Jake had a lot to answer for.

He raised his gun and fired as the older man suddenly broke from cover and zigzagged for his horse. The bullet ricocheted off a rock, and Colter vaulted astride his horse and lashed the reins across its rump. Cursing, Luke sprinted for his own roan, Sky, still tethered in back of the log cabin. He was halfway to the animal when he stopped. The two men he had shot earlier still lay where they had fallen, one draped across a boulder, the other sprawled in the dirt. The first man was obviously dead, but as he'd passed the second one, the man had rolled over and moaned. Luke looked from him, and then back to the cloud of dust in the distance, thrown up by the racing hooves of Colter's horse. The sun was already hanging low in the sky, the light beginning to dissolve to the mellow gold of late evening. Damn! The chances of catching up with Colter before dusk were slight, and he couldn't track him in darkness.

Features tight and angry, eyes as black and hard as jet, he turned to the wounded man and squatted on his haunches alongside him.

"No, *señor, por dios*, no!" the man begged, shivering away from Luke. His eyes were white and riveted on the smoking gun in Luke's fist.

Luke unknotted the bandanna about his throat and lifted the man's *serape*, revealing a splash of dark crimson that had soaked through the coarse white cotton of his loose shirt. "You're wounded, *amigo*," he observed, pushing up the shirt and pressing the bandanna over the wound to staunch the bleeding.

The man wetted his lips with his tongue. "Why—why are you doing this?" he stammered.

Luke chuckled, yet the sound was without mirth. "Why?" he echoed. "Well, *amigo*, Colter's got my woman . . . and I aim to get her back—*pronto. Comprende?*"

"And what have I to do with that, *señor?*" the Mexican, narrow features grayed from loss of blood, queried thinly.

"You're going to show me where those bastards have taken her," Luke said calmly.

The Mexican shook his head vehemently. "Me? Ah, no, *señor*, is impossible! *El señor* Colter, he would kill me if I did!"

Luke pulled back the hammer of the gun in his free hand. There was an ominous click. "And I'll kill you if you don't, friend!" he said, grinning. "It's your choice . . ." He pressed the gun barrel to the Mexican's temple.

*   *   *

La Ciudad de Los Perdidos was the stronghold of over fifty outlaws, men who freely or through adversity had chosen the lives of fugitives. They were gunslingers, rustlers, murderers, and thieves, men who lived by the gun and would someday die by it, whether it was held in the fist of a marshal or ranger, or one of their own kind. From time to time, they left Los Perdidos to ride south into old Mexico, returning days later with whiskey, guns, and gold they had robbed from the townships into which they had ridden. They left a trail of bloodshed and terror in their wake. In the canyon city, they were welcomed back like heroes returning from a war, for here, the law of the wild prevailed. The strongest and most ruthless preyed on those weaker than themselves.

It was to the former group that Jake Colter belonged. In Los Perdidos, he was King, and that suited Jake just fine. He figured life owed him something, independent of any effort on his part. All his life he had looked for the easy way out, the easy road to riches and authority. Here, he had found just that. He saw. He wanted. He took. Those that got in his way were gunned down with less compunction than if he had trod a scorpion under his boot heel. Hell, it was their own damned fault for getting in his way!

Billy Starr was equally deadly, for Billy enjoyed killing, pure and simple. The feel of the cold handle of a gun in his fist rivaled the soft body of a woman in his arms for the sensation of ecstasy he experienced at that moment. The power to choose the very second of his victims' deaths fired an unholy rapture in him that couldn't be equaled by anything else. He relished the abject terror in their eyes, their pleas for mercy, their screams as his bullets found their targets and they reeled to the dirt with blood spouting from the bullet holes in their bodies. At that moment, he reckoned he knew what it felt like to be God—if there was a God somewhere, which he doubted.

It was in the company of such men, and others, that Promise found herself when night fell. She sat huddled in the corner of an enormous room, the only room the adobe dwelling contained. They had reached this room by climbing a ladder onto the flat roof of the building, then a second ladder down into the cavernous room below. The opening in the roof appeared to be the only way in or out. A fire crackled in a shallow pit in the center, casting grotesque, looming shadows on the far white walls and lighting with a malevolent ruddy glow the hard-bitten faces of the men huddled about it, smoking and drinking. If she strained her ears, she could just make out Colter's and Billy's conversation.

"You tellin' me you mean t'send a man out to the Shadow S with a note askin' ransom fer the girl?" Billy spat. "You're a goddamned fool, Colter! That half-breed ain't gonna pay t'get her back—not when he can have any purty li'l whore he's got a hankerin' fer in Santa Fe, for a tenth of the price you're askin'!"

Unmoved, Colter shrugged. He tipped back his Stetson and grasped the neck of the liquor bottle before him, tilting it to his lips. He gulped greedily, then wiped his wet lips on the back of his hand. "Ahh!" he sighed. "That's good. About Steele—I reckon you're wrong, ole Billy-boy. You saw the two o'them dancin' and cuddlin' up in the *plaza* that night, same as I did. I'm tellin' you, I knew that half-blood bastard when he were a boy, and I can read him better'n anybody. What he feels fer that yeller-haired gal is different. He'll pay to get her back safe an' sound—and he'll pay plenty."

Starr grinned slyly. "But he won't get her back no

matter how much he pays, right, Colter?" His pale eyes met Colter's, and he saw an answering gleam of evil pleasure in their depths.

"Right, Billy," Colter agreed. "When he comes, I have a score to even with him, yessir. I'll have the money, and him!"

"What happens to the girl when we don't need her no more?" Billy asked, casting a speculative look in Promise's direction.

"I figure you'll know what to do with her, *amigo*. She's pretty enough, ain't she?"

Billy smiled. "Yeah, I know what to do with her, all right!" He wiped his lips on his fist and winked at the other men, who grinned back nastily.

Promise stifled the frightened cry that had sprung to her lips at Billy's words, her mind racing. Dear Lord, they'd double-cross Luke, and then after they'd finished with her, they'd kill her! If she wanted to get out of this rattlesnakes' nest alive, she was on her own. Maybe she could get away in time to warn Luke not to trust them— but how? There was no chance of escape from this vast room with its single entrance. For several moments she huddled there, trying desperately to come up with a plan. Yet all her ideas were as full of holes as a gold-panner's sieve. Finally, she decided to take a chance. After all, she had nothing to lose. By doing nothing, she was as good as dead anyway. . . .

She stood up, wincing as the blood rushed back into her numbed feet, and smoothed down her hair and blouse. Then she made her way hesitantly toward the circle of men about the fire.

"Mister Colter, sir?" she murmured.

"Yep?" Colter asked, grinning at her. Hell if she wasn't a good looking woman, yessirree! he thought, looking her up and down.

"I—I have to go outside for a spell," she stammered, lowering her eyes modestly.

The men sniggered and nudged each other.

"The hell you do!" snapped Colter. "You set that pretty little backside of yours down, and shut that mouth. I'll say when you get to go outside, gal, not you."

With a sinking heart, she made to turn away, making sure she stepped close to Billy Starr as she did so. Though she had half expected it, she gave a shrill cry as his hand snaked out and coiled about her ankle. With bated breath, she stood quite still as his hands slid up over her boot, rising steadily higher until he was stroking her thighs and flanks through the heavy cloth of her men's pants. "Ain't no need fer you t'talk t'the li'l lady like that, Colter," Billy drawled. "I don't reckon she can help a call of nature, can she, now? I'd be more than happy to escort you outside, ma'am," Billy offered, and the other men let out great belly laughs at his courteous tone.

"Why, thank you, Mister Starr," Promise forced herself to whisper. "I'm much obliged to you."

"You see, Colter—you have to treat ladies real pretty," Billy said, uncoiling to standing. His eyes roved over Promise as she stood there, the firelight gleaming on her tumbled cornsilk hair, her green eyes wide and reflecting the flames of the fire. Lust stirred like a snake in his belly as he eyed the thrust of her breasts against the cloth of the men's shirt she wore. Hell if they weren't just beggin' to be set loose! He licked his lips in anticipation and grinned wolfishly down into her flushed face. "C'mon, gal. This way."

Colter chuckled. "Go to it, Billy, you son of a bitch! Give me a yell when you're done."

"Sure will, Boss," Billy agreed. He eyed Promise

261

slyly. "I reckon there's plenty of what she's got to go around!"

He urged her up the rickety ladder of lashed cottonwood poles, pinching her buttocks as she climbed up onto the roof ahead of him.

The night air was cool and sweet compared to the smoky mustiness below, Promise found as she stood on the flat rooftop. Above, millions of tiny stars glittered fiercely, like glimpses of candlelight seen through the rents in a vast indigo velvet curtain. The silvery half-moon was shrouded by wisps of gray cloud. Promise looked furtively about her, yet she could discern only the angles of still more adobe dwellings in the gloom in the few seconds it took for Billy to clamber up to stand beside her. He growled at her to climb down below.

They had scarcely set foot on the rocky pathway that led between the *jacales* when Billy grasped her by her shirt and shoved her back against an adobe wall, hands fumbling for her soft curves before she had time to catch her breath.

"Here we are, baby. I reckon this is good enough. We can be all alone here—just the two of us!" He lowered his head to kiss her, and she almost gagged at the sour smell of whiskey on his lips.

She thrust him back. "Here? It's—it's not very comfortable here, is it? I'd—I'd hoped we could find somewhere a little more cozy than this, Billy . . . ?" she breathed, forcing her voice to sound husky and seductive in the shadows.

Billy's thin lips split in a wide grin. He shoved back the brim of his black Stetson, eyes glinting like silver as he stroked her pale face. "Sure," he murmured as his hand trailed down the long sweep of her cornsilk hair, "we can find a better place. But first, how about a little kiss for

Billy, hmm, baby?" He grasped her by the upper arms and pulled her against his chest, smothering her lips with his own hard mouth. His teeth scraped against her soft lips as he kissed her. Promise tensed momentarily, unable to steel herself against his loathsome embrace and his repulsive, cruel kisses, but then she forced her body to relax and submit. If she didn't, she couldn't hope to lull him into trusting her, couldn't hope to escape! Disgust swept through her as he thrust his tongue inside her mouth.

"Real nice, honey," he breathed as he broke away, his hands molding her soft curves, "real nice!"

He took her by the wrist and led her after him down the sloping rock pathway. His breathing was rapid and heavy as he pulled her into an adobe dwelling like the one they had left, except that this one had a crude doorway hacked from one wall. The soft nicker of horses and the pungent scent of their sweat, hay, and straw filled the shadows.

"How's this?" he asked.

"Better," she lied. "But . . . I sure would like a drink." She laughed nervously. "It—it would put us in the mood, wouldn't you say, Billy?"

Billy chuckled. "I don't need puttin' in no mood, honey," he rasped. "You got yerself a real man this time, not that yeller-bellied half-breed!" He licked his lips and dropped to his knees in the straw, pulling her down alongside him. "Take off them men's clothes, gal, and let's see what you got underneath for ole Billy-boy!"

His hands reached out for her, but she edged nervously away. "What's your hurry?" she asked, trying to keep the fear from her voice. "I'm not going anywhere. Come on, Billy, how about that drink?"

He ignored her request, saying instead, "You're right

there, gal—you ain't going any place at all!" His fingers knotted in the collar of her shirt and yanked hard. He wrenched again at the worn fabric and there was a shrill rending sound as it tore.

"No!" Promise cried as Billy's hand covered her bared breast.

"I jest knew you was play-actin'!" Billy hissed. "I ain't the fool you mean t'play Billy Starr for, gal!" He gave her a hard shove that sent her sprawling onto her back in the straw. Before she could recover from the force with which he had pushed her down, he had torn the shredded remnants of her shirt from her back and was reaching for the braided leather belt looped through her pants' waistband. He cursed as the ornate silver buckle hampered his fingers momentarily, then loosened the pin and tugged the belt free, tossing it aside in the straw. He grasped the sturdy band of her pants and pulled. Buttons popped as the fastenings tore. She flailed her hands at his face, knotted her fingers in his mousy brown hair and tore it out by the fistful. She kicked and squirmed as she tried desperately to free herself from the outlaw's iron grip. Billy threw his heavy weight across her and held her two wrists in one of his meaty hands. She craned her neck forward and clamped her teeth down hard into his cheek. He yelped and instinctively drew back, reaching up to his face to feel if it were bleeding. He cursed as he felt the warm trickle of blood on his fingers.

"Bitch!" he snarled. "Damn wildcat bitch! You're gonna pay for that, baby," he threatened. "You're gonna pay!"

The guard patrolling the south entrance to the canyon of Los Perdidos tossed the butt of his cheroot to the ground and stamped on it.

Above, the moon was hidden behind several streamers of cloud and cast a diffused silvery light upon the silent canyon walls below. The spilled moonlight rounded the tops of spiny cactus-candelabras and distorted everyday shapes of brush and chaparral into weird and grostesque shadows. The guard's head shot up as he caught the soft thud of hooves from below. He strained his ears as the sound came again, closer this time.

"Who's there?" growled the guard, straining to see in the darkness. He shouldered his weapon and jerked back the hammer. "Sing out or I'll shoot!" There was no answer, yet the horse plodded doggedly closer. The guard squeezed back on the trigger, and a shot whined through the silent night, echoing between the walls of the canyon.

"Please, no, *señor*! It is only me—Pepe!"

"Colter's man?" the guard queried. "You don't sound like Pepe to me."

"I—I am wounded, *señor*!" the man cried weakly. "*Señor* Colter left me for dead!" With a groan, he slithered from his horse's back and thudded heavily to the ground.

The guard muttered a curse. "Goddamned greasers!" he growled as he clambered down from his lookout point high on the canyon walls, heading toward the crumpled body.

Beside the man, he struck a lucifer on the heel of his boot and held it up to illuminate the wounded man's face. It was not the Mexican Pepe's face he found himself looking into, but the hard, angry face of Luke Steele. The match burned down and singed the guard's fingers. His yelp of alarm was coupled with a yelp of pain as Luke's hands came out of the shadows and knotted about his throat.

"You ain't—!" His outraged cry ended in a strangled gurgle as Luke's fingers tightened their grip. In desperation, the guard brought up his fists and chopped them down against the hands at his throat. The numbing force succeeded in breaking Luke's hold. The second the guard was free, he twisted about and lunged for the rifle he had carelessly set on the ground earlier. With catlike grace, Luke sprang to standing and leaped after the man, grasping him about the waist and bringing him crashing heavily to the ground with an explosive, "Ooof!"

The man struggled to escape, but Luke's weight as he straddled the man's shoulders made it impossible. He opened his mouth to yell an alarm, but in that instant Luke's clenched fist slammed down across the back of his neck in a hefty punch. He uttered a heavy sigh as he passed out.

Quickly, Luke drew several rawhide thongs from his pants' pocket and securely tied the guard, dragging his body by the heels to the cover of some thorny chaparral. Tethering his horse close to the canyon mouth alongside Sky, his blue roan, whom he had concealed there before riding toward the guard, he darted a furtive glance over his shoulder.

There were no signs of any outcry; no signs that the outlaws of Los Perdidos had been alerted to his presence despite that single shot from the guard. He could make out the wavering light of fires within some of the adobe dwellings, hear deep male laughter and the soft strumming of a guitar while a woman crooned a melancholy ballad. There was also the occasional nicker of a restless horse in the hush. Satisfied his entrance into the outlaw stronghold had gone undetected, he sprinted down the narrow, rocky pathways that led through the heart of the cliff *pueblo*. Getting into the canyon had been the easy part, he thought grimly. Freeing Promise and getting her away could prove rough.

He was hugging the shadows as he passed several adobe houses when he heard a strangled cry from within one of them. The desperate note froze him momentarily, but then he pressed back against the wall and edged along it. This house was different from the others in that it had been converted to a stable by the simple means of hacking an opening in one wall. The pungent odor of horses filled his nostrils as he stepped into the doorway. In the pale bars of moonlight that streamed through the slitted window, he glimpsed the profile of the one called Billy Starr, features twisted into an ugly leer. Even as he watched, he saw the man raise his fist to strike at something beneath him in the straw and heard Promise's cry yet again. So swiftly that the action was without conscious thought, he drew a knife from his belt and sent it singing through the shadows. Starr's back as he poised to strike the girl offered a perfect target. The blade thudded home, and Billy threw up his arms and rolled to the ground.

Luke padded silently across toward Promise as she scrambled to sitting.

"Oh, thank God!" she whispered fervently. "I thought it was all over for me!"

Luke cupped her deathly pale face in his large hands. "Did that bastard hurt you, *desperada*?" he demanded anxiously, his voice husky in his concern. He was relieved when he saw her shake her head.

"No. You got here just in time. He tore my clothes some though," she added ruefully, gathering the remnants of her shirt over her breasts.

Luke drew Pepe's bloodstained white tunic over his head and thrust it into her hands. "Here, put this on and let's get going. There's a chance someone will come looking for Starr if it seems he's been gone too long." He took her cold little hand in his own large one and drew her after him toward the doorway.

"Wait!" she whispered and returned for the belt he had given her, fastening it hurriedly about her waist. She saw the flash of his teeth in the shadows as he grinned, and she grinned back, adding, "Well, it *is* my birthday!"

He nodded and kissed her lightly on the nose. "I'd bet you never thought it'd end up like this!"

"No, sir!" she agreed vehemently.

Together they slipped through the darkened maze of buildings, ducking hurriedly into the shadows when a woman came out of one of them to empty a pitcher of water into the dirt. Holding their breath as they pressed up against a wall, they waited until she had gone inside again before continuing.

Scant seconds later, three shots rang out and the sound of angry male voices sliced through the silence.

"They've found Starr!" Luke hissed. "Here." He shoved one of his guns into her hand. "Head for the canyon mouth. You'll find horses there. Get the hell out of here, *desperada*, and don't stop 'til you reach the Shadow S."

"No, Luke!" Promise refused. "That's what I did last time, and look where it got me! We're going out of here together—or not at all!"

"Don't argue with me, Promise," Luke warned angrily. "I'll cover you! Now, go!"

After opening her mouth to make a retort, she thought better of it and started running in the direction he had indicated. Let him think she had obeyed him, if that was what he wanted. There was no way she was riding out of here without him!

Ten minutes, and she was at the canyon mouth, looking frantically about for the horses. "Sky!" she called softly, and gave a low whistle. Luke's horse responded with a whinny of greeting from some bushes behind her. She untied the reins, then scrambled astride him, gasping as shots rang out from deep within the canyon. Reaching down, she grasped the other horse's reins and wrenched them free before riding back into the canyon leading the second mount.

Through the darkness she could see yellow spurts of fierce light as Colter's men, ranged on rooftops and rocky outcroppings, tried to pin Luke down. He was still where she had left him, except he had clambered up onto the rooftop of one of the buildings to return their fire.

"Let's go!" she cried as she cantered the horses toward him. A shot whined over her head and carved a ragged trough on the adobe wall behind her. She ducked low over her horse's neck as she neared Luke. As the two horses drew level with the adobe house, he leaned from the rooftop to the back of the racing horse, took the reins in his own fists, and kicked his horse after Sky and Promise.

As one, they wheeled their horses about and arched forward over the high pommels of their saddles as a hail of bullets spewed hot lead all about them. Colter's men were scrambling down the rocky walls with the agility of mountain goats, heading for the stables and their horses, firing as they went.

Manes and tails streaming, the horses took the bits in their teeth and stretched out, thundering from the canyon with Luke and Promise yelling for them to go faster. All too soon, the sound of hooves behind them signaled that Colter's men were in hot pursuit. "Follow me, honey!" Luke yelled over his shoulder, and Promise

PENELOPE NERI

swung Sky's head around to do so.

Soon they came to what appeared to be a sheer wall of
solid rock with a dark fretwork of thorny bushes huddled
around its base. Luke slid from his horse's back and ran
to the bushes. To Promise's surprise, he lifted them
aside. "Climb down and lead Sky inside," he urged.

Obediently, she did so, finding herself inside what
appeared to be a huge cave. Luke led his horse inside after
hers, and there was a rustling sound as he replaced the
bushes at the cave mouth, effectively concealing their
hiding place.

They both tensed as the sounds of many sets of hooves
rumbled outside the entrance to the cave. Luke's hand
found hers in the darkness and he squeezed it reassuringly. Soon the sounds faded as Colter and his men
rode on in pursuit of them.

"There!" Luke pronounced cheerfully, taking her in
his arms and pulling her against his bare chest. "I'd say
we're pretty safe here, at least until daybreak." He kissed
her long and hard, hands roving her back and stroking
her tousled hair as he did so. "Oh, baby, I thought I'd lost
you!" he breathed into her ear when he had broken the
kiss. "I thought that damned Colter had—"

"Shh, I'm fine," she whispered, pressing her finger
against his lips to silence him. She stood on tiptoe and
kissed his stubbled chin. "You don't know just how glad I
was to see you! That—that Billy!" She shuddered. "I—I
couldn't stand the thought of him . . . well, you know!"
In the pitch-black darkness, she sensed him nodding, felt
the anger that tensed his body. "What is it that Colter has
against you, Luke?"

"Sometime I'll tell you the whole story, *desperada*, but
not now," Luke hedged. He laced his fingers through her
windswept mane of silky hair and buried his lips against

270

her throat. "Not now . . ."

A soft sigh of pleasure came from her lips as Luke sat down and drew her onto his lap, kissing her gently along the line of her jaw, teasing the downy curve of her cheek with his tongue tip before tentatively delving between her parted lips to explore the mysteries of her sweet mouth. She grew still in his embrace, and he knew that she waited for more.

"It's kind of hard, all these rocks," he murmured, and she knew by his tone that he was smiling even as he said the words.

"We'll find a way to get comfortable, Mister Steele!" she said impudently. She flung her arms around his neck and pressed her mouth heatedly to his.

Shaken by the fierce ardor she aroused in him, ardor born of fear that he had lost her as much as desire, Luke silently acknowledged that she was probably right . . .

Chapter Fourteen

The cowboys of the Shadow S perched on the top rail of the corral fence, hooting and whistling and making bets on just how long Luke, their boss, would stay astride the snorting, bucking broncho beneath him.

Dust rose in great clouds from beneath the pony's wicked hooves, drifting away in the light September breeze. Drops of sweat sprayed from Luke's brow as the broncho kicked up its heels, then twisted viciously sideways with a cunning flick of its rump, screaming in fury as the man astride him remained in place. More sweat ringed the blue denim shirt Luke wore as the pony bucked again and again, rocketing up in the air then back down to earth with a jolting thud. Black-Strap, who had been acting as hazer, rode away at a signal from Luke with a yell of, "He's all yours, Boss!" The men on the fence held their breath, awed by the savage poetry of the pony's furious battle for freedom and the man's determination to dominate. Luke and the pony seemed as one, the graceful arm raised to balance his torso all an extension of the wild beauty of the horse, his movements perfectly synchronized to the lunges and bucks of it so that, to the casual eye, there seemed little effort on his part.

The liver-and-white wild stallion was the pride of a

small herd of mustangs that Luke had corralled weeks before. The pony's small, well-formed head showed the proud blood of his Arabian forebears. He tossed it furiously from side to side, up and down as he fought, nostrils flared as he screamed his fury. The flowing mane and tail that streamed when he flailed his hooves were creamy white, sharply contrasting with the glossy markings of his body, deep brown painted on white. His shrill cries rang out like a challenge on the air, and Promise looked up from the pump where she was filling a bucket and shaded her eyes to watch.

The cords in Luke's neck and the muscles in his upper arms and thighs bulged beneath his clothing as he rode the seesawing broncho and the cowboys cheered when finally the pony shuddered to a standstill and stood in the center of the corral quivering slightly, muscles rippling under his smooth coat. He snorted once and pawed the dirt with a dainty hoof, seeming to admit only to a temporary defeat. The cowboys whooped as Luke touched the pony's sides with his moccasined feet, urging it to walk a full circle about the corral fence.

"You done broke him, Boss!" Black-Strap yelled with a broad grin.

The black wrangler ducked under the rail to take the hackamore from Luke as he swung down from the saddle. "Ah reckon you got yourself a fine li'l cayuse there!"

"Not me, Black-Strap," Luke denied with a weary grin. His black eyes gleamed, and his teeth flashed white against the dusty, deep tan of his face. "A broncho like this is a mite too pretty for a man to ride," he added, glancing across to where Promise stood transfixed, and noticing how very still she had gone suddenly. "Nope, I reckon this little fellow belongs to *desperada!*"

The cowboys grinned and exchanged amused glances

273

as Promise let go of the water bucket and flew into Luke's arms, kissing him soundly on his dirt-streaked cheeks.

"He's for me? Really, Luke?" she demanded breathlessly, green eyes shining. "Oh, thank you! Thank you! He's beautiful!" she cried as he slowly nodded. "Does— does this mean you'll let me try my hand at riding with you and the men?"

"I guess so," Luke agreed ruefully. "I reckon it's the only way I'll get you off my back! You and the pony should make a good team, honey—the two of you are both stubborn as mules!" Since her birthday, not a day had passed that Promise had not reminded him to consider her request, had not wistfully expressed her desire to do something other than help Margita in her housekeeper's duties about the *hacienda*. He had finally given in to her pleading. She had a natural talent for riding, he had seen during their long journey to the ranch, and a violent aversion to the more feminine pursuit of keeping house. Besides, her life had been filled with such drudgery. He sensed she had had little time to enjoy being a child. Her father's death and her mother's endless struggle to make ends meet had seen to that. It was guilt over his part in her father's death, combined with his wanting to make her happy, that had resulted in his decision to give her her way. It eased his conscience some, for still he had not been able to tell her of his feelings, or been able to get up enough guts to tell her that it had been he who had shot her pa. When she looked up at him that way, eyes shining like brilliant stars, a smile of pure delight curving her uptilted, lovely face, cold sweat beaded his palms. She once must have looked up into Patrick O'Rourke's face in that adoring way, he knew. She would never be able to forgive what he had done . . .

"When?" she continued eagerly. "When do I start, Lu—*Boss*?" she amended, her smile deepening to form pretty dimples in her cheeks.

"Tomorrow. By branding time, we should have made a real *caballero* of you," Luke said, smiling a smile he didn't feel. He wiped the sweat from his brow and neck with the kerchief from around his throat, then peeled off his tight black riding gloves. "Cantrell!"

Cay Cantrell, the tall, fair-haired ranch foreman, strolled across to the pair. He tipped his hat to Promise. "Mornin', ma'am!" he greeted her. His blue eyes lingered on her lovely, flushed face a fraction too long for politeness alone.

Promise smiled. She knew that Cay had been attracted to her since the first evening she had arrived at the Shadow S. When she was around, the tall, broad-shouldered cowboy, usually so collected, became as nervous and clumsy as a new-born colt. "Good morning, Cay," she returned.

"Promise will be signing on as one of the hands as of tomorrow," Luke said, hiding a grin at the astonishment on Cay's face. "You've got more patience than most, so I figured you'd be the best man to teach her the ropes. What do you say?"

Cay sputtered. "Me? Teach a—a *woman* cowpunchin'? No, sir! I reckon you'd be the best one for it, Luke!"

"I'd say you're right, at that," Luke agreed, laughter twinkling in his jet-black eyes. "But the fact is, I don't have the time to break in a new hand. Promise can ride the buckskin for now, being as she's used to him, and maybe the two of you can work with the paint there until he's ready?" Luke glanced at Cay inquiringly.

"I guess so," Cay agreed doubtfully, still shaking his head.

With a laugh, Luke walked away and headed for the bunkhouse to wash up, leaving Promise and the ranch foreman considering each other. Cay dropped his gaze first and looked away. He had turned beet-red.

"We-ll, I guess I'll be seein' you tomorrow mornin', then, ma'am. Say, around six?"

Promise shook her head, a determined glint in her eyes. "The other men get up at three-thirty, four o'clock, Cay, and you know it. I'll see you then. And it's Promise, not 'ma'am'! I know it bothers you that I'm a woman, but I aim to work real hard, just like everyone else. I don't want you to show me any special favors or be less hard on me because of it. If I'm to make this work, I have to do it fair and square. I'd count it a favor if you were to treat me the same way you'd treat any other green hand." She smiled. "Please, Cay?"

He tipped his hat to her. "You've got it, ma'am— Promise," he agreed before striding rapidly away in the direction Luke had taken, an argumentative light in his eyes.

Still smiling, Promise refilled the bucket, pumping the water with a will. She might as well get used to Cay's discomfort at the idea of a woman riding with them. He wouldn't be the only one. If she were not mistaken, the majority of the cowboys and *vaqueros* would be whole-heartedly opposed to the notion that a woman could even come close to doing their job. As far as they were concerned, womenfolk tended house, birthed babies, and washed clothes, all the while looking dainty enough for a sharp breeze to blow them away! She set her jaw determinedly as she toted the heavy bucket across the yard toward the kitchen door of the *casa*. They'd learn different soon enough, she thought firmly. She'd had enough of washing clothes and keeping house back in

Cherry Creek to last a lifetime! Now that she'd found something she really wanted to do, and Luke had given her the chance to try it, she'd give it everything she had, or go under in the attempt. In a few months they wouldn't look down on her as a soft, fluffy little thing, good for nothing but cooking and sewing, not if she had her way!

"*Hola, niña!*" Margita sung out as Promise stepped through the arched doorway, on either side of which hung strings of scarlet peppers, drying in the mellow sunlight. "You were so long, I thought perhaps you had gone to Santa Fe for the water!" Her chocolate-brown eyes twinkled in her olive face.

Promise grinned and emptied the water into the wooden washtub set upon the table. "No. I was talking with *el señor*. He's given me a beautiful horse, Margita!" She eyed the housekeeper expectantly, adding, "And tomorrow he said I'm to trade my petticoats for chaps!"

Margita frowned. "What is this?"

Promise laughed merrily and took up an embroidered *camisa* to wash. "He's finally agreed to let me try my hand at learning to be a *caballero*. Isn't that wonderful?" She wrinkled her nose. "No more laundering after today!" she added, nodding her head at the tub of sudsy water and the pile of clothing to be scrubbed, wrung out, rinsed, and rinsed again before being spread in the sunshine to dry.

Margita clucked her disapproval like an indignant mother hen.

"A *caballero*! A woman? Pah! *El señor* must be *loco* to even consider such a thing! Women are flowers, *niña*, to be treated with gentleness. A woman should do things that are fitting for a woman to do—not wear *pantalones* like a man and ride her horse astride! Aiee, *diós*! Next you

277

will tell me that you will chew the tobacco like *Señor* Charlie, or smoke the *cigarillos* like Manuel!''

An impish grin puckered Promise's face. ''Maybe I will, at that,'' she said defiantly, scrubbing the *camisa* in her hands with such ferocity the cloth threatened to tear. ''The way I see it, if women can give birth to babes, do a wash that would make a man's back feel ready to break, chop kindling, and fetch water, then I reckon we can't be such delicate little flowers after all! Be honest, Margita,'' she coaxed. ''Wouldn't you say we work as hard as they do?''

Margita shrugged, but the smile playing at the corners of the Mexican woman's mouth betrayed the fact that Promise had made her point. ''So,'' Margita said innocently, ''you will have no need of the so pretty, so *womanly* dress that I took the time to finish sewing for you this morning, before even the sun came up over the mountains?'' She arched her dark brows questioningly.

''You finished it? *Gracias*, Margita, *gracias*. You're an angel!'' Eyes sparkling, Promise hugged the plump housekeeper, deaf to the woman's laughing protests that her hands were covered with soap bubbles. Tonight, they had all been invited to a small fiesta on the neighboring ranch, Tierra Mora, run by Don Luis de Cordoba y Luz, to celebrate the birth of his first son after siring three pretty, dark-eyed little daughters. There was to be music and dancing, all manner of foods to eat and wines to drink, and contests in riding and shooting and roping for the *vaqueros* and cowboys. When Don Luis's foreman had arrived with the invitation, Promise had panicked, wondering what she could wear. Belatedly, she recalled the pretty green gingham Luke had bought for her at Bent's Fort weeks ago. With Margita's help, she had cut and sewn the cloth into the prettiest dress she had ever owned. All that had remained to be done on it before the *fiesta* this evening had been the hem, and now Margita had finished that too! She hummed happily as she washed the remainder of the clothes, thinking that today had turned out to be one of the nicest in her entire life.

The two women hurried to complete their chores that day, so that they would have time to ready themselves leisurely for the *fiesta*. They prepared dishes of chicken and rice flecked with red and green peppers, and pans of warm cornbread to take with them to Tierra Mora, to add to the many dishes that Doña Estrellita's serving women would no doubt have prepared. It was late afternoon before Margita would finally admit that they were done with their work and allow Promise to go to her room to bathe and dress.

The green-and-white checked dress lay spread across the bed in the high-ceilinged chamber, and Promise held it up before her and twirled about, noting delightedly how the flounced hem flared as she spun around. The neckline was cut in a deep curve at both back and front, and edged with a flounce of crisp white lace patterned with tiny holes that Margita had called *broderie anglaise*. Full, puffed sleeves edged in the same snowy trim would set off her golden, slender arms. The gathered skirts fell bell-shaped to the floor when supported by several layers of starched petticoats and boasted two bands of the same expensive edging. A wide satin sash of dark green would draw attention to the narrowness of her waist. It wasn't by any means the fanciest dress Promise had ever seen, nor was it the most expensive. But it was very pretty and, compared to the hand-me-downs and cast-offs she'd owned in her seventeen years, it was the most beautiful dress in the entire world! She carefully set it aside and undressed, stepping into the warm water that Paco,

Margita's son, had poured into the enamel hip bath set upon cloths on the polished adobe floor.

Leaning back and sighing blissfully, she cupped handfuls of warm water and let them trickle down over her body. The hasty knot into which she had pinned her long hair let loose tendrils that spilled like shining, straight ribbons of gold about the slender arch of her throat and rounded shoulders, curling slightly as the humidity of the water dampened them. She had best make the most of such luxury, she thought dreamily. After today, she doubted there would be much time for the pleasure of lounging in a tub! River water would be more what cowboys were accustomed to!

Humming, she gathered up a cake of the yucca soap she and Margita had made the week before, and she lathered her face until it squeaked with cleanliness, then extended one slender arm and swiftly soaped that, too. Next came her breasts, firm and taut from the warm water's caress, and she blushed as she recalled the way Luke's hands felt upon them, warm and gentle and infinitely arousing.

The soap fell unnoticed into the water as she lay back, eyes closed. Recalling their lovemaking the night before filled her with warmth and tingling pleasure. In her mind's eye, she could see Luke as he had been last night, his lean, tanned body etched in silhouette against the white-washed walls of his bedchamber. Moonlight and the flickering radiance of a single candle had gleamed in the blue-black shadows of his hair, was reflected in his night-black eyes, and cast a sheen of gold on the light veil of sweat that dewed his body. She had watched as he came slowly to the bedside, reveling in the male beauty of his body, his catlike grace, reaching up to trace the dark furring of his chest down to the hard, flat plain of his

belly and almost fainting from sheer anticipation as he
drew her into his arms and kissed her. A tingle of
excitement darted through her even now, and her
breathing became shallow and quick as she relived that
night in memory. "Luke, oh, Luke!" she heard herself
whisper to the shadowed room, "Love me, my dearest,
oh, love me!"

But it was only in her imagination that she heard him
respond with the whispered words she yearned to hear. It
was only in her dreams that he breathed, "Yes, yes, my
only one, I love you!" For in reality he had said nothing
last night, had only murmured his desire for her as he
slowly drew the silken sheets from her body and bared
her to his sensual dark eyes. They had made love fiercely,
wonderfully, as always, but afterward she had felt
strangely hollow and bereft as she nestled against his
chest. Made love. Making love. Didn't the pleasure they
shared mean that he must love her? Didn't the way he
sighed her name as he caught her hungrily into his arms
imply that he felt the same as she? No, a small voice
jeered mockingly inside her head. No. Naïve as she was,
she knew nonetheless that love and lust were not the
same. Men—and women, too—were capable of giving
and receiving pleasure from each other's bodies without
the added element of love between them. She sighed
heavily. Perhaps she was a fool to yearn for more.
Perhaps there never would be more between them than
there was at this moment. That thought filled her with a
deep, pervading sadness. The knowledge that Luke might
never come to love her as she loved him tainted the
golden aura that surrounded their lovemaking, tarnished
the pleasure. *He's using you*, the little voice whispered.
*And when he tires of you, he'll find another to take your
place.* Did that explain his gentleness these past weeks

since they had come to the Casa del Ombras? Was this his way of letting her down gently? Had he already tired of her? She'd noticed that at times he seemed preoccupied, would start to say something to her and then stop himself, seeming to think better of it.

She swallowed the knot of pain in her throat and forced her thoughts to the moment at hand and the *fiesta*, willing herself not to ponder Luke or her feelings and fears again. To do so invited only pain and doubt, and she wanted to enjoy an illusion of happiness tonight, even if a part of that happiness was edged with sorrow. She wanted to forget the bitter-sweet passion they shared in the small, dark hours of the night, and she would—with flirting and dancing, music and song, drinking sweet, rare wines and sampling delectable treats with never a thought given to the hopelessness of her love for Luke.

Her bathing completed, she wrapped herself in a rough linen towel, poured fresh water from the jug into a porcelain basin, washed her hair vigorously with the yucca soap, and briskly toweled it dry. Feeling clean and refreshed, she donned her camisole and petticoats, long white pantalets, and black stockings that gartered at the knees, then finally slipped the green gingham dress over her head, smoothing down the crisp folds almost reverently. She gasped as she looked at herself in the cheval glass mirror, tilting it in order to catch her reflection from every possible angle. Why, she scarcely recognized herself, she realized with a thrill of pleasure! Instead of a gawky girl, a poised young woman stared back at her. The dress fitted perfectly, skimming her slender shoulders and cupping her young breasts before billowing to the floor where the deep, lace-edged flounces swept the polished adobe in grand style. The color brought out the true depth of green in her eyes and seemed to accent the cornsilk hue of her hair and the pale gold of her complexion. Oh, how Luke's eyes would widen when he saw her, for until now he had seen her only in her men's clothing, or the shabby funeral dress! Surely he would find her pretty, if not exactly beautful.

She ran quickly out into the wide hallway, picking up her full skirts as she went, calling for Margita. After several moments, the woman came, hands filled with hairpins and trailing shiny, wide green ribbons.

"I am coming, I am coming, *niña!*" she grumbled. "*Por dios*, have you no patience at all? Did I not promise that I would help with your hair?"

Promise's merry peal of excited laughter filled the gloomy hallway of the *hacienda*. "*Si*, Margita," she acknowledged, twirling about so that the skirts of her dress billowed and revealed a teasing glimpse of petticoats. "Well, how do I look?"

Margita's irritable expression softened. "*Muy bonita, niña!* Very, very pretty indeed! I think I shall have to become your *duenna* for this evening, for I am certain that all the *vaqueros* will wish to dance the *fandango* and the *cuadrilla* with so charming a *señorita!*" She grinned slyly. "*El señor* will burn with jealousy!"

The impish smile upon Promise's face wavered momentarily and became wistful. "Do you really think so?" she asked in a small, doubtful voice.

"Hope so? I know so, *pequeña loca!*" Margita said firmly, shooing her back into her bedchamber and pressing her down into a chair as she took up a silver-handled bristle brush.

Promise squirmed with excitement while poor Margita endeavored to brush every last tangle from her hair until it shone like a curtain of beaten gold leaf. She sighed with impatience while the housekeeper braided two narrow sections in the front and swept them back to be tied in the green ribbons behind, a style that revealed the pretty angle of her profile to its best advantage. A heated curling iron was fetched from the kitchen fire and applied to the ends of her hair so that they fell down her back in artful, loose curls. The laborious process made Promise squirm still more.

"Aiee, *niña*, you must sit still!" Margita grumbled. "Else how shall I finish? *La doña* Candida, *Señor* Thomas Steele's first wife, was never this way. She would sit as still and patient as a statue of the Blessed Madonna Herself until Margita was done, as befits the great lady of the *hacienda*."

Promise grimaced. "And what of *Señor* Thomas's second wife, Singing Wind? Did she also sit still while you dressed her hair?" she asked curiously.

Margita's strained expression softened. "Ah, *si*, of course! I would braid her lovely hair and coil it about her head like a crown," Margita recalled.

"Was she beautiful?"

"Very beautiful, *si*," the housekeeper acknowledged. "And also possessed of a sweet nature that all who met her came to love. At first, I was unhappy to learn that *Señor* Thomas had taken an Indian woman for his bride. I felt that perhaps she would not prove a good wife for him, or a *patrona* of the *hacienda*. *Gracias à diós*, I was wrong! *Señor* Thomas, he loved her very much. When the message came from her people that she had died of the cholera, it was as if *el señor* had been struck by a bullet. He broke down and wept like a baby before all. He loved *Doña* Candida, for she was a good wife to him and a true lady of this *hacienda* which she brought to him upon their marriage. But it was my belief that *el señor—diós* grant his soul peace—loved his little Indian bride the most, for she gave him a son, the son that *Doña* Candida was unable to give him in all the years of their marriage."

"*Señor* Thomas must have been heartbroken when *Señor* Luke was imprisoned," Promise remarked casually, hoping to learn more of Luke's past from the house-keeper, for she had never been able to coax Luke into telling her much about his life.

"Ah, *si*, he was like a madman," Margita agreed dolefully. "He tried everything a man could do to see his son set free, but—"

"Margita!" cut in a sharp voice from the open doorway.

"*Si, señor?*" Margita answered, flushing guiltily to have been caught gossiping by *el señor* himself.

"We'll be leaving in a few minutes. If you intend to come with us, you'd best get ready."

"*Si, señor,*" Margita agreed contritely, pulling Promise's hair in her haste to flee the room. She gathered up the curling iron and the pan of hot coals and fled.

Promise's eyes widened as Luke stepped inside the room, for he was a Luke she had never seen before. He wore a tailored black short coat and matching trousers that fit his hard, lean body impeccably and accented the broadness of his shoulders. Beneath it, a snowy white shirt and black string tie could be glimpsed from under a pearl-gray satin vest. The effect was that of an elegant man of the world, a side of Luke she had never seen or even guessed at! She gaped wide eyed at him, forgetting her plan to behave in a poised and elegant manner herself in her surprise. A blush pinkened her cheeks as she felt his dark gaze upon her. She rose self-consciously from the chair, feeling awkward and schoolgirlish as she swept across the room toward him.

"I'm ready to leave," she murmured huskily, heart

thudding. Surely he would offer some remark about her appearance, she thought. But the unfathomable expression in his eyes never changed, and her hopes died.

"Good. Then let's be on our way," he said curtly. "Bring a shawl with you. It'll be cool later, coming home."

Hurt filled her as he turned on his heels and left the room without further comment. She angrily snatched up a white lace *mantilla* that Margita had loaned her and stormed after him.

The *hacienda* of Don Luis and Doña Estrellita was much like that of Luke's. The red-tiled adobe *casa* was set about a large courtyard with covered walkways giving access onto it. Today a huge spit was being turned over the glowing coals of a fire in a shallow pit in the center of the courtyard, and the succulent aroma of barbecued beef floated tantalizingly on the air. Trestle tables lined the walkways, groaning with the weight of platters laden with *tortillas* and spicy-hot *salsa, albondigas, arroz con pollo*, and other exotic and appetizing dishes that Promise had never seen before. Wooden boards held loaves of bread, ripe cheeses, and various fruits: oranges, limes, peaches and plump, sweet grapes. Tubs of fragrant gardenias spilled their heady perfume into the warm air.

The *vaqueros* of both ranches were resplendent in black, flat-topped *sombreros* trimmed with silver braid and *conchos*. They had relinquished their colorful *serapes*, white cotton pants, and goatskin chaps in favor of short, dark jackets and narrow, dark pants worn with elegant high-heeled boots ornamented with silver.

The Anglo cowboys of the Shadow S, not to be outdone, sported their fanciest silk shirts of vivid colors, set off with pearl buttons and narrow string ties. They wore vests that were painted with various designs or had edges laced through with colorful braid. Their Stetson hats had also been made festive for the occasion with bands of rattlesnake skin, cougar fur, or linked silver *conchos* about the crown.

When the two groups from their respective ranches met, considerable good-natured bantering and bragging occurred, for the Shadow S and Tierra Mora had long been friendly rivals. Soon challenges to ride the Mora's bronchos or shooting contests had been arranged, and there were whoops and laughter as the two groups strove to outdo each other. Mescal, the liquor made from fermented agave, flowed freely as did tequila and whiskey and wine. Taciturn cowboys turned verbose and rowdy. Quiet, dark-eyed *vaqueros* grew bold and drew out their guitars and fiddles to sing and play, and their wives, daughters, and sweethearts danced and swirled to the stirring music.

Promise set aside her irritation with Luke as he led her to meet Don Luis and his wife. Doña Estrellita proved to be an exquisitely beautiful woman with the flawless complexion of a creamy camellia and luminous dark eyes. Don Luis, her husband, was by contrast a short, wiry fellow with the fierce, darkly handsome looks of a Spanish *hidalgo*. Luke made the introductions and both greeted her warmly, then the *doña* excused them and led Promise away to show her the *casa* and the infant son in whose honor the *fiesta* was being given, little Christolphe.

The child was sleeping peacefully in a cradle of carved dark wood within the lovely *hacienda*, a tiny silver crucifix pinned to his blankets after the Spanish custom, to ward off evil. He was tended by his nurse, a very wrinkled *mestizo* woman who could have been anywhere from sixty to a hundred years old. The baby's hair was a curly mop of jet-black. His cheeks were chubby and flushed with the heat of the day as he slept, sucking lustily upon a tiny thumb. Lashes dark as ebony curled against his flushed cheeks, and his little mouth puckered like a rosebud as he stirred and sighed dreamily. Promise was entranced by the beautiful child, and *doña* Estrellita was proud and pleased by her lavish compliments. She smiled. "Come, *Señorita* Promise, we will let Christolphe sleep for now. When he awakens, you shall hold him, *si*?"

Promise nodded in pleasure and followed Estrellita from the room. They found the *doña*'s three little daughters sitting primly in the leafy shade of a spreading oak tree, dressed in lacy white frocks and pinafores, with white stockings and black leather slippers. Each wore differently colored ribbons in her long dark hair. They stood at the urging of their *duenna* as their mama approached, and they giggled and lisped their greetings to Promise as they curtsied with the introductions.

"You have a delightful family, *doña* Estrellita," Promise remarked as they strolled back toward the courtyard.

Estrellita smiled. "*Gracias.* I am very proud of my children, and Luis, he dotes upon them all! Now, if you will permit me, I must see that all goes well in the kitchen. *Señor* Luke, he is over there, see?" When Promise nodded, the *doña* smiled. "We will continue our visit shortly, I promise you. Please make yourself at home for the short time until I return." She then squeezed Promise's hand in a warm, friendly manner and left her to her own devices.

Promise took a seat upon a wooden bench set beneath

yet another shady oak, spreading her full skirts across it. She leaned back, watching Luke through half-closed eyes. Despite the *doña's* urging, she had no wish to join him, nor to intrude upon his conversation with Don Luis and the foreman of Tierra Mora. If he chose to behave as if she did not exist, then so be it, she thought waspishly. She was not about to force him to pay attention to her. She frowned. What could have happened to cause him to be so cold, so distant to her? This morning when he had announced that the paint pony was to be hers, and that he had decided to allow her to try her hand at learning ranching, he had seemed indulgent and good tempered. A sigh escaped her. Despite her love for him, his mercurial changes of mood since they had come to the Shadow S both puzzled and annoyed her.

A shadow fell across her, and she opened her eyes to see Cay Cantrell standing there beside her. He took off his white Stetson as she glanced up, and shot her a bashful smile.

"I hope I didn't wake you?" he murmured, fidgeting with the hat held in his hands.

"No," she denied, "I wasn't sleeping. Just . . . thinking."

He cleared his throat nervously, the action incongruous considering his tall, big-boned frame and strong, handsome face, for he appeared capable of handling any situation, Promise thought. She swept aside her skirts. "Won't you sit down?" she offered.

"Thank you, ma'am," he accepted, taking a seat beside her. "You sure look pretty, if you don't mind me saying so, ma'am—I mean, Promise."

"Why, thank you, Cay. It's real nice of you to say so," Promise said, blushing with pleasure at his compliment. At least Cay had noticed her appearance, unlike *some* men, she thought.

Nodding, he replaced his hat. "I was wondering if you'd eaten yet, Promise? I'd be happy to fetch you a plate . . ."

"I haven't. Why don't we go together?" She paused. "Unless you've already finished?"

Vigorous shaking of Cay's head and his broad, triumphant grin confirmed that he had not. He took her elbow and escorted her through the knots of people in the courtyard to the heavily laden trestle tables, where *la doña*'s serving girls stood ready to assist the many guests with the vast selection of dishes.

As Promise pointed to the various foods she wished to try, she was acutely aware of Cay's warm blue eyes upon her, watching her every move with an attentiveness that was flattering indeed. Why couldn't Luke treat her this way, she wondered silently? Why couldn't it be him dancing attendance on her? Was he ashamed to be seen with her, was that it? Oh, she liked Cay well enough, and there was no denying that the tall, fair-haired cowboy was handsome, but . . . well, he wasn't Luke. She forced a smile of thanks for Cay as he took her elbow and led her back to the bench where he had found her, a bottle of a golden liquor tucked under his arm.

They ate in amicable silence while the stirring rhythm of a *fandango*, played on many guitars, throbbed on the late-afternoon heat, the rich, vibrant chords and the cries of the musicians coupled with the stamping of heels and the whirring chatter of castanets and cries of "*Bravo!*" As Promise ate, she recalled the night she had gone to the *plaza publica* in Santa Fe alone and danced with Joaquin there. How furious Luke had been! Though he had laughed when she had suggested it, she was still convinced that some of his anger had been the result of jealousy . . .

"Want to try some of this, Promise?" Cay asked, grinning.

He held a shot glass between the fingers of his right hand, and on the ridge of skin between his thumb and index finger was a white, grainy powder that looked like salt. In the other hand he gripped a wedge of fresh, green lime.

"What is it?" she asked, wrinkling her nose.

"*Tequila*. I'll show you the right way to drink it." He smiled. "The true Mexican way, not the way of us *gringos*!"

She laughed as he rolled his eyes, watching curiously as he quickly sucked the juice from the lime wedge, licked the salt, and tossed down the deep-golden *tequila*. "There!" he exclaimed, grinning. "Your turn!"

"It looks kind of difficult," she said doubtfully. "I don't know if I should—"

"Here. One won't hurt you," he insisted, pressing a fresh glass into her hand, a piece of lime into the other. "Hold still," he cautioned as he sprinkled the salt onto her hand, no easy feat as she fought to control her laughter. "There!"

"First the lime, then the salt, and then the *tequila*, right?"

He nodded, and she did exactly as he had done minutes before. She spluttered as the fiery liquid, somehow smooth as well as burning, ran down her throat and lodged like a fireball in the pit of her belly. "*Jésus!*" she gasped.

Cay threw back his head and roared with laughter. "Spoken like a true daughter of Mexico, honey!" he said at length.

She flinched at the easy, natural way the endearment

291

had come to his lips, knowing she should have insisted he call her Promise instead. But somehow, there was a pleasant, mild buzzing in her ears and a tingly numbness to her lips, and she couldn't quite bring herself to scold him, not when he seemed so happy. "Let me try that again," she murmured, holding out her glass.

Cay frowned. "No, Promise, I reckon one is plenty for you. You look kind of—flustered!"

She scowled at him and tossed her hair over her shoulder.

"Flustered! You and Luke both think I'm a child, don't you?" she accused. "Well, I'm not! If I can punch cows starting tomorrow, I can drink like a cowboy, too," she declared recklessly. "Come *on*, Cay, another one won't hurt me!" She giggled. "I'm a big girl!"

She pouted prettily and all Cay's resolve to remain firm dissolved. He shrugged and poured more tequila into her glass, eyes widening as she downed it even faster than the first. She licked her lips delicately, tasting lime and salt upon them.

"Mmm," she said appreciatively, "that one was even better!" Her eyes were growing greener and brighter by the minute. Her cheeks were flushed, her voice was a little throaty, and her words just a fraction slurred. Hell, she was drunk, Cay realized! There'd be the devil to pay if Luke saw her this way, he knew, and for Promise's sake, he figured it was time to call a halt. Inwardly he cursed himself for urging her to try the strong liquor in the first place. He held the bottle up to the fading light.

"See, honey, it's almost empty. Another shot, and that little old worm in there is gonna be in your glass. Time to call it quits!"

"Worm?" She peered at the bottle and giggled. "Why, so there is!" She eyed him solemnly. "Do you know what's worse than a worm in a bottle of tequila?" she asked him, and when he shook his head she giggled again and said, "A half a worm!" Cay smiled despite his anxiety. "*I know an old lady who swallowed a worm . . . ,*" she sang exuberantly. "Come on, Cay, don't be a spoil-sport—sing with me!" she urged.

"Nope, I can't carry a tune," he insisted, looking apprehensively over his shoulder for Luke.

"Then let's dance!" she insisted, jumping to her feet and taking him by the hand. "I just love to dance and dance and dance!"

He wavered only fleetingly. "We-ell, I'm not much good at dancin', either, but we'll give it a try!" he agreed.

He took her arm and led her back to the courtyard, thankful to see that Luke was nowhere in sight. Several people were leaving the area set aside for dancing, laughing and breathing heavily and calling for glasses of wine to refresh themselves. Cay bent to whisper in one of the musicians' ears, and the *vaquero* guitarist grinned broadly and nodded. Smiling, Cay drew Promise into his arms as the lilting strains of a waltz with a peculiarly Mexican rhythm filled the courtyard. Cowboys from the Shadow S each found themselves a pretty *señorita* and joined Cay and Promise as the music played on.

Promise leaned heavily against Cay, smiling up into his handsome face as they drifted about the courtyard on a sea of music. She was dimly aware of the feel of his hand resting against her waist, of the sure, comforting strength of his other hand enfolding her own. But, she realized sadly through the tequila's fuzzy effects, Cay's nearness had none of the jolting electricity to it that she felt when close to Luke. It was the liquor that made her feel dizzy and weak at the knees—not Cay.

Cay held her still closer as the musicians changed

293

easily to a second waltz, scarcely able to believe he was dancing with the beautiful young woman whose face had filled his dreams and most of his waking hours these past few weeks. He rested his chin lightly in her hair, wondering if she'd slap his face if he dared to kiss her. "You sure are lovely, honey," he murmured huskily. Promise could feel the slight tremor that ran through his body as he said the words, and she guessed that his feelings for her were very close to the surface now. "I know I've said it before, but you look like something out of a man's dreams!"

A deep sense of guilt swept through her, eroding the rosy veneer of the tequila. How could she allow Cay to hold her so close, to give him cause to hope she felt as he did? She mustn't lead him on; it just wouldn't be fair. She was bitterly ashamed now of the brazen way she'd begged him to dance with her, and she knew that at the back of those urgings had been her desire to make Luke jealous. "Cay, I feel a little dizzy," she lied. "I—I think I've had enough dancing for now!" She broke free of his arms and wove her way a little unsteadily between the couples still dancing, not stopping until she had left the courtyard far behind and had reached the rear of the barn. She leaned against the wall, closing her eyes and taking a deep breath, startled on opening them to see that Cay had followed her from the courtyard.

She turned away from him, but he took her by the shoulder and gently swung her around to face him. "What's wrong, honey? What did I—"

She placed her finger across his lips to silence him. "You didn't do anything, Cay," she cut in. "It's just that I—I know how you feel about me, and it's no use, because you see, I don't feel the same. I like you very much, Cay, I think you know that, but it's Luke that I love. I can't help it."

His blue eyes darkened with pain. "Do you think I can't see that? Hell, watching you with him—it's like someone's digging a spur into me each time I see you together! But Luke's only using you, believe me, honey," he continued earnestly, grasping her by the arms and shaking her slightly. "I—I know things that you don't, about Luke. We've been friends for a while, and I've always respected him, 'til now. I'm tellin' you straight, Promise, he'll use you and when he's done"—he shrugged—"he'll put you out of his life!"

"No," Promise denied fiercely, fists clenched in the folds of her gingham skirts, "I don't believe that! I'll make him love me, I will! You'll see! What is it you know that I don't? Tell me!"

"I can't," Cay said grimly. "I gave my word." He paused, obviously torn. "But I will tell you this much—"

"Tell her what?" cut in Luke's voice, and Promise flinched.

Cay swung about to face Luke. "We have to talk," he said heavily. "I've stood by and kept quiet too long, I reckon."

Luke nodded, his expression dark and unreadable. "I'd say it was time," he agreed. He turned to Promise. "Estrellita is looking for you, *desperada*." Dark eyes flickered over her flushed face and overly bright eyes. "She said something about the baby having awakened, and that she'd promised you could play with him?"

Promise nodded coolly. Turning to Cay she murmured, "I appreciate you keeping me company, Cay. It was fun," she added before picking up her skirts and heading back toward the *casa*. As she left, she caught Cay's angry voice: "Goddamn, Luke, if she's who I think she is, I reckon I know what sort of game you're playin'!"

Luke hooked his thumbs in his belt. "She's who you think all right," he agreed. "O'Rourke's daughter! And this is none of your business, Cantrell!" he warned, his lips thinned to a long, straight line as he glowered at Cay. When he'd gone to wash up after breaking the paint pony earlier that day, he'd overheard two of his hands laying bets on whether Promise would stay with him or transfer her affections to Cantrell, the foreman. Finding the two of them alone here behind the barn had done little to improve his temper . . .

"I mean to make it my business, Steele," Cay growled, his good-natured face hard with anger. "I like Promise, Luke—I guess you could say I care for her. I don't aim to stand by and look on while you tear her apart for something she had no part in!"

A muscle in Luke's jaw twitched. "Maybe things aren't what they seem, Cantrell," he snapped, his voice like the crack of a whip. "Why don't you tend to your own business and stay out of mine? This doesn't concern you, damn it!" His black eyes glittered with fury.

"If it concerns Promise, it concerns me," Cay insisted stubbornly. "You're only using her, Luke, when any fool can see she's in love with you. I reckon she deserves better than that!" His blue eyes narrowed. "I've decided to take her away from you, friend, and I give you fair warnin', I'll do it any way I have to. You ain't playing by the rules with her, so I don't reckon I need to stick to 'em either!"

"Has Promise said she feels the same about you?" Luke asked, gritting his teeth.

"No," Cay replied honestly. "But I aim to ask her to marry me anyway. See, I'd be proud to give her my name!"

"After she's been sharing my bed all these weeks?"

Luke taunted cruelly.

Cay flushed. "I know that. I'm not blind. But I blame you for it, not her. She's a fine woman, Luke. Her past doesn't matter a damn to me. It's her future I'm concerned with." He smiled suddenly. "Say, it seems like you're stoopin' pretty low bringing that up, Luke, old friend? Afraid that I might come off the better man in Promise's eyes after all? Hell, it's every man for himself. If you want her, then you'd better stay on your toes!"

Luke sprang forward, drew back his fist, and cracked Cay solidly under the jaw. Cay reeled backward, thrown off balance by the force of the blow.

"Stay away from Promise, Cantrell, or you'll answer to me!" Luke growled jealously.

"The hell I will!" Cay threatened, lunging forward, fists raised. He slammed a punch into Luke's cheekbone, sending him rocking back on his heels.

Luke recovered and feinted a right, hooking Cay with a sharp left that brought a surprised grunt from the cowboy. The cracks as fists met flesh and bone and the gasps and curses of the two as they fought filled the air, the only sounds here behind the barn save for the rasping of their heavy breathing and the cooing of the doves. Blood trickled down Luke's chin and dripped onto his snowy white shirt front, a legacy from Cay's vicious punch to his jaw that had smashed his lip into his teeth. Cay's cheek was sporting a livid welt and his right eye was swollen shut, yet both his and Luke's faces were dark more from anger than brusies. At length Luke ducked Cay's powerful fists and slammed his knuckles up under the cowboy's chin, clipping him solidly beneath it. He succeeded in laying Cay out in the dust. Stars filled Cay's vision in the few seconds it took him to come around. He attempted to stand, then slumped back as Luke hung over him menacingly, wiping the blood from his chin.

"I'd say I've proved who's the better man, wouldn't you, Cantrell?" he panted.

Cay squinted dazedly up at him and managed a lopsided grin despite his swollen cheek and one closed eye. "You haven't proved a damn thing, Steele," he said amicably. "See, it's Promise who has to decide this—not you or me!" His grin widened. "I'd say you messin' up my pretty face is liable to better my chances with her—you know how tender hearted these little gals are!"

Despite his anger and his jealousy, Luke grinned back at him. He reached out and hauled Cay to his feet. "Maybe it would work with another woman, but not with Promise, friend," he said softly. "It's me she wants."

"We'll see," Cay said confidently, standing and dusting off his fallen hat. "Like I said, it's every man for himself. I won't tell that little girl what I know. I gave my word and I mean to keep it." He put on his hat and began to stride away, adding over his shoulder, "But if you mean to tell her the truth, you'd best tell her real soon. If you're still playing her for a fool when the brandin's all done with, word or not I'm tellin' her the truth!" He left for the liquor table, where he intended to get good and drunk.

"You're right there, friend," Luke muttered under his breath. "I have to tell her!" He'd already waited too long.

Promise spent the next hour playing with little Christolphe on a vividly striped blanket of Indian weave that Estrellita spread on the dark, polished wooden floors of the bed chamber.

The baby cooed and gurgled, trying to capture her shining cornsilk hair in his chubby little fingers and thrusting strands of it eagerly into his mouth when he succeeded. Promise picked him up and held him close, nuzzling his sweet face and dark, shining curls and inhaling the lovely baby fragrance of his skin. Oh, how she would love to be Luke's wife, to give him a child, to hold their son close this way! she thought wistfully. She bit her lip. Perhaps Cay had been right. Perhaps she was fooling herself in hoping Luke would change. The way things stood between them now, she shared only his bed, not his name and not his heart, either. Damn! Where was her pride? Had he taken that, too, along with her innocence and her heart, and left her with only the painful obsession of her love for him?

Tears welled in her green eyes, threatening to spill over onto the baby's dark head. A lump in her throat suddenly pained her. Sharing Luke's bed without carrying his name, she was now everything that Hollander and Todd Plimmer had ever accused her of being! She gently handed little Christolphe back to his mother. "I really should be going now, *Doña* Estrellita. It's later than I thought. See, they're lighting the torches outside. I think *Señor* Steele must be looking for me."

Estrellita nodded. "Ah, *si*, you are right." She smiled and kissed Promise's cheek. "I am most happy to have met you. You must come often to Tierra Mora now that we are friends. I have a feeling we will be close *compadres*, you and I!" Her luminous dark eyes twinkled. "Perhaps when next we meet, it will be on the occasion of your wedding, *no*?"

Promise forced a smile. "Perhaps," she agreed in a small, doubtful voice, wanting desperately to leave. In minutes she had made her farewells and hurried away, leaving Estrellita waving after her from the arched doorway, Christolphe in her arms.

She was unusually silent as she and Margita rode the buckboard home to the Shadow S. It was a long drive, over two hours, yet she offered no more than a few words of conversation for the duration of the drive. Luke rode ahead of the buckboard with the *vaqueros* and cowboys, who were singing and bantering good-naturedly with each other as a result of the liquor they'd downed and the good time they'd had. But before he had ridden off she had seen the bruises that darkened his face and knew that he and Cay must have come to blows, and that they had probably done so on account of her. Cay, she had learned from Margita's idle chatter, had drunk a good deal more than he was used to, and had been bedded down in the bunkhouse at Tierra Mora, to return in the morning. Poor Cay, Promise thought. He had fallen for her, and yet her love for Luke precluded her loving him in return, while Luke cared nothing for her love, seeking only the ease and pleasure she could offer him with her body! It was a cruel thing, this love, she thought miserably, for it made a captive of the heart, however willing a captive it might be.

She was glad when the lights of the Casa del Ombras glimmered through the darkness, and she knew that they were almost home. The thought of her room, where she could think and hurt and feel in private, was a welcome one. She lost little time in bidding Luke, Margita, and the others a hurried good night once the buckboard had halted, escaping swiftly inside.

Later, she lay sleepless in the vast Spanish bed, staring up at the shifting shadows the trees cast upon the white-washed walls of her room. How much longer could it last, she wondered? How many more days, weeks, before Luke tired of her? She drifted into an uneasy sleep, wondering dreamily in the few seconds before she succumbed what it was that Cay could have meant by the words she had overheard that afternoon, when she had left him and Luke together . . .

She awoke to the feel of Luke's lips gliding over her bared shoulder, the touch of his hands upon her body beneath her nightgown.

"No, Luke, don't!" she protested sleepily, thrusting his hands away.

In answer, he laughed softly in the shadows and entrapped her breast in the cup of his hand, thrusting up her night chemise to cover the dark-rose crest with his lips.

Involuntarily, she gasped as his mouth worked its damning magic on her vulnerable flesh, bringing her fully awake to the awareness of desire. He leaned up on his elbows and looked down at her. His eyes were aglitter in the shadows, shimmering dark pools that reflected the moonlight spilling through the grilled windows and patterning his bare chest with bars of shadow.

"Do you still say no, *desperada*?" he asked huskily, slender fingertips drawing lazy circles on her breast.

In answer, she sighed and reached out to stroke the hard curves of his shoulders as he rested beside her, feeling the muscles rippling under the smooth, warm flesh like taut cords, already lost in the sensation of his caresses. He dipped his dark head and pressed his lips to hers, his tongue parting her mouth and delving into its velvety depths in a kiss that sent fiery tingles eddying from her loins and rippling through her belly. His lips tasted of the sweet, heady wines he had drunk; his scent was an intoxicating mixture of soap and the faint but pleasant aromatic scent of tobacco, a male musk that was uniquely his. She shivered as those lips trailed down across her cheek and past the curve of her jaw, seeking and finding the delicate hollow in which throbbed her pulse. As he kissed her, his hands traveled lingeringly over the curves of her body, as if he would learn each texture, each mystery it presented, and commit them to memory by touch alone. Her heart beat a little faster, the pulse fluttering and rapid as a small, frightened bird against his lips. Yet beneath his lightly furred chest, her crushed breasts tautened and pressed voluptuously against him. His manhood rose, hard and demanding against the softness of her belly in answer to their ardent embrace.

He drew the chemise from her, the breath catching in his throat at the picture she made in the moonlight, bare upon the pallor of the sheets. The moonlight was caught like a golden fish in the net of her hair, and it glinted with a magic luster. Her eyes were dark emeralds, slanted and mysterious in the shadows, filled with the poignant longing of her heart and body. His own eyes grew hazy with desire as he gazed upon the pale gold of her body, and involuntarily her name broke from his lips like a long, drawn-out sigh.

"Promise . . . ," he breathed, and she reached out and cupped his handsome, bruised face in her cool palms, drawing his lips down to hers. Pain, as real and agonizing as any physical pain could ever be, filled him as she sweetly kissed him, arching her lovely body against the hardness of his own. An image of her—his woman—with Cay Cantrell flashed before his eyes and filled him with jealous pain. No, Cay would not take her from him, never! he silently swore, kissing her hungrily and leaving her weak and breathless in his arms. Later, when she was still and sated from his loving, he would tell her all . . .

Never had he made love to her as he did that night, Promise thought, waves of rapture wafting throughout her as he trailed burning lips across her body, kissing every inch of her flesh until she feared she would swoon with the pleasure of his caresses. He would not take her, would not cease his maddening love play even when she moaned with sheer delight and implored him to take her, please take her! Instead he brought her inch by quivering inch to the pinnacle of ecstasy, then skillfully brought her gently back down until she writhed like one demented under his touch, tossing her head to and fro upon the pillow so that her hair billowed about her like a silken sea, and her breathing came rapid and husky from between her moistly parted lips. He plundered the very fount of her womanhood with his touch and his kisses, his lips nestling momentarily against the golden fleece that shielded the treasure between her thighs, before tasting the nectar hidden there. Only then, when she grew still and whimpering in the sweet prison of his desire, did he gather her into his arms and claim her with his body. He drove deeply into her liquid, throbbing heat with a groan that wrenched itself from his lips and was lost against the soft cloud of her hair.

For a few moments, she remained quite still as he moved with ever-increasing ardor between her thighs, yet soon the flames of desire rekindled, and she embraced his lean lips with her long, lovely legs and began to move with him, meeting the driving, delicious force of his powerful body and adapting her movements to the sensual rhythm of his. She twined her fingers in his thick, dark hair, whispering her love for him over and over as he bore her skyward on a whirlwind of rapture.

She knew even before she felt the convulsive arch of his body that he had found his release, and with a fierce joy she felt her own body pulse to match the throbbing ecstasy of his. For one glorious moment, it seemed they were one being, without beginning, without end. As he fell heavily across her, his black head cradled in the valley between her breasts, she heard the words she had never thought to hear, murmured as if torn from his lips: "I love you, little one, my golden one! I love you!"

Goosebumps rose the length of her arms, and her heart began to pound crazily. Tears of joy glimmered in her eyes, and she was so filled with emotion she felt close to bursting from the happiness inside her.

"I—I've waited so long to hear you say those words, my dearest Luke!" she whispered, stroking his cheek. "Say them once more, so that I know I wasn't dreaming!"

Too late, he realized what he had said, yet the emotion within him at that moment had thrust aside all wariness and caution. He leaned up and looked down at her radiant face, at the love and trust mirrored in her beautiful green eyes, and for the first time in his life, he was afraid. If he told her now that he loved her, and she learned later that it was he who had killed her father . . . If she remembered that spring night and recognized the face of the man she loved as that of her father's murderer . . . He could not bring himself to repeat the words he'd said, not this way! And so he lied, took the easy way out, and hated himself for it, for the little death she died when he told her.

"I said that I loved your body, *desperada*," he murmured and died a little death of his own, despising himself for his cowardice. "I love every curve and hollow, my golden one; your lips, your eyes—everything." And he kissed her.

When he drew his lips away, Promise rolled apart from him and curled upon her side as far from him as the width of the wide bed would allow. *I hate you, Luke Steele!* she cried silently. *I love you, but I hate you too, damn you!*

It was useless, she thought woodenly. He would never feel for her the deep and enduring love she felt for him. Somehow, she must free herself from the hold that love held over her. If not, it would destroy her. Or he would.

Chapter Fifteen

"Go get 'em, *caballera*!" yelled Cay, and Promise grinned and spurred her pony after the bellowing yellow cow who was steering her calf to a tangle of chaparral farther down the valley, away from the cowboys, the fire, and the frightening odor of singed hide and the smoking branding iron.

The cow pony beneath her responded to the slightest gesture of thigh, knee, or hand; indeed, there were times when Promise was convinced he didn't need her guidance at all! He came up alongside the cow and crowded her on her left shoulder, forcing the stubborn creature to turn while maintaining a safe distance from her wicked, long horns. The calf dogged its mother's hooves, bawling loudly, and Promise turned the pair back toward Cay.

There was a swift, whirring sound as the loop of Cay's hemp lariat snaked through the air and circled the calf's hind legs. The calf rolled over and lay there, struggling to rise, while Cay hitched the end of the lariat twice about his saddle horn and ordered his pony back, tautening the line. Then he sprang down from his saddle and swiftly hogtied the calf's forelegs together. The calf bellowed loudly in fear at such treatment, and his mama trotted forward, snorting, toward Cay.

Swiftly, Promise angled her pony toward him, yelling and waving her Stetson in the air. The confused cow looked across at the cowboy, who had stepped silently away from her calf, then back at Promise, who now seemed by far the most threatening of the pair with her yelling and waving. She swung around to face the oncoming pony, pawing the dirt and lowering her spread of long cracked horns to charge. The cow pony nimbly sidestepped the cow's enraged attack, and Promise rode away, the cow following her in a crazed rush back to the main body of the herd.

Promise wheeled the pony about and trotted him back toward Cay, who had mounted up again after relinquishing the roped calf to the branders. "Good work, Tequila. Good work, boy," she murmured to the liver-and-white paint pony, patting his neck. Once again he'd lived up to his name, she thought with a smile. He was every bit as fiery as *tequila* and capable of doing the darnedest things—also like the liquor!

"Nice ridin', *caballera!*" Cay praised, grinning. He swept off his hat in salute. "Reckon I must be a pretty good teacher, wouldn't you say, if you can handle yourself like that in less than two months?" He winked.

She nodded shyly. "The best!" she agreed, flushing with pleasure at his praise.

Cay kneed his horse to stand alongside her own. "There's other things I'd sure like to teach you, Promise, honey, if you'd let me." His deep blue eyes roved her golden-tanned face, the love in them as blatant as the tender timbre of his voice. "Do I get that chance?" he asked, his voice catching huskily.

"No, Cay. I'm sorry," Promise told him gently. "You know how it is."

He smiled bitterly. "Yep. I reckon I do. Hell, honey, if Luke weren't the closest thing I've ever had to a friend, I'd do something about it, too. I just hope that damned half-breed realizes what he's got in you, Promise, honey. I sure hope he does!" There was no malice in his tone, despite his words. He shrugged regretfully at Promise, clicked to his horse, and rode off to round up more calves for branding, leaving Promise alone, sitting her pony atop the crest of a gentle hill.

She unfastened her bandanna and mopped her damp face and throat, tossing her sheaf of fair hair over her shoulders. It had been a long day, though it was not yet noon. They'd been riding and cutting and branding and roping since dawn and weren't half-finished yet. Still, she wouldn't have traded what she was doing or anything about the new life Luke had given her for all the gold in the world. She loved him, she loved the Shadow S, and she loved her work.

In the past few weeks since she had joined the cowboys of the Shadow S, every day had been a struggle, a challenge to prove herself in a man's domain. She'd had to grit her teeth when the going got rough, to keep doggedly at it when she was aching and bruised from a fall off her pony or was simply exhausted from long hours spent in the saddle. There had been days when she was bone-weary from sunup to sundown and nights when she'd wanted nothing so badly as to sink into the soothing warmth of a hot bath and forget that the words "horse" or "cow" had any part in her life. Nevertheless, she continued to ride herd all night 'til dawn the next day.

Yes, prove herself she had, and the doubt and mockery in the eyes of Luke's men that a slip of a girl should even attempt their job had gradually given way to reluctant admiration for her spunk, grudging acceptance, and more recently she had detected the first overtures of friendship. She could ride nearly as well as the best of them now, and she and her pony, Tequila, performed as one, drawing the respect of the other hands. Cay, at Luke's bidding, had taught her the rest: how to cut a fractious cow from the remainder of the herd, how to turn a herd that looked ready to stampede, how to ride down a calf and rope it for branding, how to brand a cow correctly so that the overlapping double S of the Shadow S brand showed sharp and clear. All of this she had learned and so many other new things that she needed to know! And at night, under the stars or in his bed at the *hacienda*, Luke had taught her other things—sweet, wild things, she recalled, heat stealing through her.

Despite her fatigue each night, she was never too tired for his love-making, for the heady warmth of his kisses that seemed to sear her to her very soul. Nor did she ever weary of losing herself in the shimmering dark depths of his night-black eyes. When she came into his arms and curled her softness against him, she felt alive as she never felt when they were apart. It was as if she were but a shadow without him, needing his presence to give substance to that shadow. However many times she swore that she would leave him, leave the Shadow S and New Mexico, he had only to look at her in that special, intimate way, and her resolve to do so melted. Lying secure in his embrace, watching the moon scudding across the star-filled sky above, listening to his words of passion as soft as the night wind against her cheek, she had only fallen deeper and deeper under his dangerous spell . . .

The Shadow S lay northeast of Santa Fe, the beauty of the snow-capped Sangre de Cristos on one flank, the silver ribbon of the Mora River on the other. Longhorns covered the grasslands for as far as the eye could see: fractious cows, ornery bulls, and bawling calves, their colors red and brown, rust and yellow. All bore the Shadow S brand burned into their hides. Around them rode the Mexican *vaqueros* and the Texan cowboys who called Luke Steele "Boss," men as hard and tough and weathered by their rough, outdoors existence as the cows they rode herd on—maybe tougher. Their mounts were the sturdy *bronchos*, wild mustangs whose endurance and ability to survive against all odds had been inherited from their ancestors, the fiery Arabian and Andalusian horses who had escaped the Spanish conquistadors of Mexico centuries before. These ancestors had been bred for the endless deserts where water was scarce and the sun relentless, and through their proud blood they had bequeathed similarly hardy traits to the *bronchos*. Man might rope the wild *bronchos*, bend them temporarily to do his bidding, but they were rarely, if ever, truly domesticated. A *broncho* was as likely to buck his rider off his back one day as he was to nuzzle his pockets for treats the next, or save his life from a charging bull with a catlike whip of his hams. A man might never dote on his *broncho*, treat it as a pet like the city folks back east treated their horses, but he learned to respect it. Together, cowboy and *broncho* made a team unmatched for cowpunching.

Arthur Morgan had told Promise, on that morning when she had—literally—first run into Luke Steele, that he estimated Luke ran close to a thousand head of cows on his land, yet Promise had quickly realized that Luke had branded three or four times as many longhorns. She had taken her turn at riding the range boundaries and been awed by their numbers, and by the wild, beautiful length and breadth of the land he called his own, land that seemed as much a part of him as he was of the land.

She had also seen that here a man was measured by his worth, his guts, his knowledge, and his character, rather than by the color of his skin or the race of his parents. Outside of the Shadow S, Luke had been called a half-breed, feared but looked down on with contempt. Here, he was simply "boss" to his Texan cowboys, or *el señor* or *el jefe* to the *vaqueros*. He asked no more of them in the way of hard work than he was willing to give himself, showed no favorites, and put down trouble that came up from time to time with a stern but fair hand. As a consequence, he had earned the respect and loyalty of the men who worked for him, though they were few who had gained his friendship for he was by nature a solitary man.

Could a man with such a nature ever love a woman, Promise wondered? Would he ever say that he loved her as she loved him, or would he fear such an admission would entrap him, harness his spirit, which was as free as the wind, until it chafed to be released? But she didn't want to tie him down, to curb that side of his nature; it was part of what she loved most about him! She only wanted for him to love her. . . . Her sunny smile faded, and her green eyes filled with sudden, desperate longing.

Cay's shout for Promise to cut a "loco" steer from the main herd cut through her daydreaming. She signaled that she would, gathered Tequila's reins in her fist, and spurred the cow pony toward the skittish, one-eyed creature. Its crazy antics—pawing and snorting and sidestepping—had been disturbing the herd all morning, and there was a definite threat that such an animal could start a stampede.

When she had separated it from the rest, Tequila

weaving and twisting beneath her with an instinct that was uncanny, she herded the steer toward Cay, who drew his rifle from its saddle holster and shot it between the eyes. He ordered two of the cowboys, Sam and Manuel, to see the carcass skinned and delivered to Joaquin at the chuck wagon for butchering.

Promise grimaced. She'd learned over the past weeks to smother any pangs of pity she might have had for the dead animal. To allow it to live and disrupt the herd could ultimately cause the death or injuring of one or more of the cowboys, herself, included. Instead, she looked forward to the fire-broiled steaks that would come their way that night, smoky and delicious after a long day's riding, and her mouth watered. Yes, sir, it was a hard life but a good one, and to survive one had to learn to become hard, too. She felt she'd grown up a great deal since she'd joined the Shadow S.

Joaquin's strident banging with a metal spoon upon the backside of a frying pan and his loud cries of "Chow, *caballeros*!" was passed down the line to Promise, who eagerly headed Tequila for the chuck wagon about a mile back. The herd was calmly grazing for the time being on the fresh pasture to which they had been driven early that morning, and, if all went well, they would continue to do so for the next hour.

The flap board of the chuck wagon had been let down when Promise rode up, and the cowboys, shirts stained with rings of sweat, faces streaked with dirt, were flocking to it with good-natured cussing and bantering.

"Hell, Miss Joaquin, ain't you got nothin' but this ole hoss meat again today?"

"Shoots, Pete, that there ain't no hoss meat! I reckon that's Manuel's old chaps—sure tastes tough enough and smells like goat an' all!"

"Goat, hell! Goat'd taste mighty good compared t'this mess!" The cowboys sniffed at his tin plate of cold grub. "What y'got in here, Miss Joaquin—fried rattlesnake?"

Joaquin grinned. "You guess right, *señor!*" he quipped, and the cowboys laughed and moved away to squat in the dirt and eat.

Promise took her plate and got in line, greeting the cowboys with nods and smiles as they greeted her. She saw Luke sitting apart from the others, leaning up against the trunk of an oak smoking a slim cheroot. He felt her eyes upon him and turned to look her way. As their eyes met, a thrill ran through her that she was powerless to control, and she quickly averted her eyes. They had agreed that while working, she would be just another of his *caballeros*, but Lord, it was hard to look at him and not let her feelings show in her face! Eyes still downcast, she took her plate of *chile con carne* and fried *tortillas* and sat a few yards away from him, surprised when he beckoned her to sit beside him.

"You look tired, *desperada*," he murmured, eyes raking her. "Rough morning?"

She shrugged, smiling. "No worse than usual, *señor!*" "Cay and I had to put down a *loco* steer, but apart from that it was just the usual—bawling calves and angry mamas."

He nodded, tossed the butt of his cheroot aside, and reached out a booted foot to ground it under his heel. "Seems like you and Cay work well together," he commented, dark eyes fastening on her face.

She flushed. "He's taught me a lot, Luke," she said, a defensive edge to her tone. His words had had an accusatory ring to them, and she wondered if he were not a little jealous of Cay's feelings for her. The foreman had made no attempt to hide them. The notion that Luke

313

might be jealous made her heart do flip-flops in her breast. Surely he wouldn't be jealous unless he cared, just a little?

He grunted, his smoldering dark eyes sliding uneasily away from her as he stood up and bent to retrieve his gray Stetson from the grass. "Just be sure he doesn't teach you anything 'cepting what he's paid to teach you, honey," he said darkly and strode away to the *remuda* for a fresh horse.

Promise bristled at his words, tempted to cuss him out for his insinuations. Instead, she shrugged and contented herself with making a face at his retreating back. They had to work out here together, after all. That work could become very uncomfortable if there was bad blood between the two of them. Better let sleeping dogs lie and hope Luke could shake off his jealousy with hard work in the afternoon. After all, she'd never done anything to encourage Cay, no matter what Luke might believe. Why should she be put in the position of having to defend herself to him? A bitter smile curled the corners of her mouth. For a man who had never once said he loved her and had insisted she never tell him that she loved him, he certainly was possessive . . .

By late afternoon, all the calves born during the past spring and the unmarked mavericks had been hauled to the fire and branded. The remaining few would be marked the next spring, before the cattle drive into Denver. The mood of the men was relaxed and festive. The steer Cay had shot earlier that day had been butchered, its meat cut into fine, big steaks, or strips for drying to make jerked beef; the organs had been simmered for son-of-a-gun stew, and the savory smell of it wafted out over the grasslands, mingling with the less pleasant but ever-present odor of cow manure and horse sweat. One by one, the cowboys rode slowly back to the chuck wagon for the evening's chow, grimy, weary, and eager for a smoke and a good meal before turning in for the night. It had been a long day.

Promise spurred Tequila lightly after the other horses, her belly growling. Luke's thinly veiled warning earlier that day had spoiled her appetite for lunch, and she felt hungry enough to eat a bear. She was lagging behind the others when she heard the plaintive bawling of a calf somewhere off to her right. She sighed wearily. Oh, well, it looked as if supper would be a little later than she'd expected, she thought resignedly as she wheeled Tequila toward the sound.

She found herself in a *cajón*, a box canyon, perhaps half a mile in length and as wide as it was long. Great boulders littered an *arroyo*, a dried stream bed, and thickets of pines and cottonwoods grew along what had once been the creek's banks. The mellow late-afternoon light gilded the tops of the aspens upon the foothills of the mountains above, burnishing their golden boughs with still more gold and touching the pines' somber green with brilliant light. Promise shaded her eyes and stood up in the stirrups, looking for the stray she had heard. The bawling had ceased for the time being, and she could not get a fix on the sound she had heard. She walked Tequila deeper into the canyon. The drone of insects and the twittering of birds settling down to roost for the night were the only sounds. She frowned. Had she imagined the calf after all or somehow mistaken the direction of its bawling?

She swung around at the sound of hooves behind her, alarm in her eyes momentarily before she saw that it was only Cay. He was riding from the canyon with the calf slung across his horse and waved a greeting as he saw her.

315

Promise waved in return and kneed Tequila onward across the dried stream bed toward him. Suddenly, Tequila let out a shrill whinny of terror and reared up, hooves scraping air, before he lunged forward and bolted. Promise, caught unaware, rolled heavily from his back, hitting a boulder with her shoulder as she landed in the creek bed. Pain filled her vision with white-hot stars. Winded, she lay where she was for a few seconds before trying to sit up.

"Don't move, honey," Cay cautioned, his voice low and strangely tense. "Stay right where you are!"

Promise opened her eyes and froze. Not a foot from where she had landed, a rattlesnake lay coiled, its head raised to strike, the dull click-clicking of its rattles ominous and deadly in the canyon's sudden hush. The drone of the insects stilled. The birds ceased their twittering. Even the breeze held its breath.

Cay's shot, when it came, was so sudden that Promise screamed once involuntarily and twitched, despite his warning. A cloud of dust rose where the rattler had been, and Promise saw the snake fly backward like the lash of a whip and lie coiled and still in the dirt. Cay left his pony ground-tied, the calf still slung across it bawling again now, and he swung down from his saddle. His bright blue eyes were darkened with concern as he crouched over her. He shoved back his Stetson.

"Are you hurt, honey?" he asked.

"Uh uh. I'm fine," Promise insisted. "Just a little winded, I think—ahhh!" As she used her arm to push herself off the ground to sitting, pain burned in her shoulder, so sharp she had to clench her teeth hard to keep from crying out again.

"The hell you're fine!" Cay gritted, helping her to sit. He peeled off his leather gauntlets and reached for her shoulder, his hands gentle as he touched her. "You must have hit those rocks on the way down. Can you move your arm, honey?"

"I think so." Promise tried, wincing as she did so. "There. I don't think anything's broken."

"I reckon not," Cay agreed. "Still, I'd bet you won't be using that arm for a spell, broken or not." He unknotted the red bandanna from about his neck. "Let's take a look at it."

Embarrassed, Promise unbuttoned the pearl fastenings to her blue shirt, using her good arm to pull the collar down and bare one shoulder. Already an ugly, huge bruise was spreading angry red and purple across the creamy pallor of her skin. Cay reached out and gingerly touched the swelling, the expression in his eyes tender and hungry all at once. He raised his blue gaze to look into her eyes. "Damn it, Promise, honey, I can't go on this way—" he said huskily.

"Cay, don't!" Promise said sharply. "Don't make it harder for me than it already is! Please?" Her green eyes were imploring.

He nodded and swallowed, turning back to his horse and fetching his canteen. He doused his bandanna with water, wrung it out, and folded it into a cool pad which he pressed against the bruising on Promise's shoulder. She muttered her thanks and buttoned her shirt, looking up to find his face scant inches from her own, aware in that instant that he intended to kiss her. Her good arm came up and the palm lodged firmly against his chest, pushing him from her. "No, Cay, I can't!" she cried, shaking her head and scrambling away from him.

"Why not?" Cay persisted. "I love you, Promise! Does Luke? Has he ever said he loves you—or only that he wants you? Come away with me, girl! We could get ourselves a little place, something small at first, but together we could make it grow. He's only using you, honey. When he's finished, he'll drop you like a hot iron. I'm offerin' you a life, with a man who loves you. A home. My baby growin' inside you. Can't you see, honey? I want to marry you, not—"

"No, Cay, no!" Promise cut him off. "Can't *you* see, it isn't that easy? I don't love you—but I *do* love Luke, no matter what he feels or doesn't feel for me. I can't stop it. I can't help it! That's just the way it is. I'd never had a friend, Cay, not 'til I met you. Can't we keep it that way? Can't we just be friends?"

Muscles worked furiously in Cay's face as he fought for control over himself and his emotions. His expression was bleak as he slowly stood up. He took off his hat and ran his fingers wearily through his fair hair. "I guess it's that or nothin', right?" he said flatly.

She nodded, standing with difficulty, casting about the creek bed for her fallen hat so that she wouldn't have to face the hurt in his eyes.

"I'll get your horse," Cay offered brusquely, and Promise knew that he couldn't meet her eyes either.

Tequila had recovered from his scare and was cropping the dry grass farther down the canyon, reins trailing. Cay rode out after him and led him back. When he reached Promise, she saw that Cay was looking fixedly at something beyond her. She turned and followed the direction of his gaze, seeing Luke sitting his horse behind them. His hat rested on its rawhide cord across his shoulders, and in the mellow light his hair glinted with blue lights and his tanned skin bore the reddish hue of copper. His features seemed carved from rock, hawklike and cruelly chiseled to a savage, rugged handsomeness that took her breath away. She knew that his eyes would

318

be black and glittering. How long had he been there, she wondered suddenly? How much had he seen of her accident and Cay's attempt to kiss her? She wetted her lips nervously.

Cay got down from his horse and helped Promise to clamber astride Tequila. When he was certain she was safely in the saddle, the reins firm in her good hand, he motioned her to follow him with his eyes and rode down the canyon toward Luke. The two men's eyes met. Promise saw the expression in Luke's eyes and shuddered. Cay calmly got down from his horse and took off his gloves.

"Well, Luke, I guess this is the end for you and me," he said heavily. "I don't reckon I can stay on here at the Shadow S, feelin' the way I do about Promise, you bein' my friend, an' all. I'd like for you to get down from that horse, so I can show you how I feel about what you're doing to her before I leave."

Luke slowly dismounted, left his horse ground-tied, and strode slowly across the dirt to Cay.

"No! I won't have the two of you fighting on my account!" Promise cried, kneeing Tequila forward. She stopped dead, the look in Luke's eyes as he glanced up at her draining her courage.

Cay's fist came out and cut Luke under the jaw with a ringing crack. Luke reeled backward, staggered, but kept his balance. He made no attempt to return the punch, only stood there, a strange expression in his black eyes, a trickle of blood running down his neck from the fresh cut on his jaw.

"If you're done, you'd best be on your way before dark," Luke said softly.

Cay flexed his fingers, nodded curtly, and swung astride his horse. He looked down at Promise as he gathered the reins into his hands. "So long, honey," he murmured. "You ever change your mind, you come looking for me, understand?"

"So long, Cay," Promise said huskily, without answering his question. "*Vaya con dios, amigo mio!*" she added, misery in her tone.

With her farewell, Cay quirted his pony and lit out of the box canyon, dust billowing in his wake. Promise watched him go, an aching in her heart. He had been a good friend and it troubled her to think that, because of his feelings for her, he and Luke could no longer be friends; that he had to leave the Shadow S and the work he had loved.

"He's good at what he does," Luke said, as if reading her mind. "He'll find another spread someplace else—Texas maybe, or Wyoming, where he came from."

His casual, uncaring tone infuriated her. "Is that all you care?" she snapped, angry tears springing into her eyes. "Doesn't it mean anything to you that Cay was your friend, that he won't be coming back?"

Luke's jaw hardened. "He should have thought of that before he let himself get sweet on you. He knew you were my woman."

"Your woman!" she flung at him. "Huh! Being your woman means warming your bed at night, that's all. You've never said you loved me, Luke, never. Every time I've tried to tell you that I love you, you hush me up. At least Cay offered me more than his bed—he wanted me to share his life with him, his name!"

"Go on after Cay, then, if it's him you want," Luke said cruelly. "There's nothing holding you here. If you want him, ride on out after him, honey!" He saw the anger drain from her face to be replaced by hurt.

"You know that it's you I want, Luke," she whispered

brokenly, "but it seems you don't want me. I won't let you use me any more. I won't let you make love to me again, because it's not love for you, is it? It's only those needs you have that I satisfy! I'm leaving here, Luke. I'm leaving you and the Shadow S. I've been a fool. I should have gone a long time ago." Her expression was bitter.

"Then you're going after Cay?" Luke said jealously.

She shook her head. "No. I'm just . . . leaving." She gathered her reins in her fists and made as if to kick her pony into a gallop.

He reached out and grasped her reins, pulling Tequila's head around. "No, I can't let you go like this, *desperada*! You're my woman!"

"No, Luke, I'm my own woman—not yours, not Cay's, not anybody's but my own! Let go of my horse, damn you!" When he would not let go, anger rose through her like a crimson tide. Her breasts heaved against her cotton shirt, her hands shook on the pommel of her saddle. Cursing him under her breath, she reached swiftly for the quirt tucked into the loop at her belt. With a snap of her wrist, she cut him sharply across the shoulder, air zipping over the braided rawhide lash with a high-pitched whirring sound that ended in a sharp crack when leather met shirt and skin.

Her hand had not even begun its ascent to strike him a second time when his fingers snaked out and curled ruthlessly about her slender wrist and squeezed. Fingers numbed by his vicelike grip, she yelped and let go of the quirt. He dragged her from the saddle and roughly held her in his arms, breathing heavily. "I thought you said you loved me, baby," he growled. "Then how come you're running out on me?" His black eyes smoldered with rage.

"I do love you! But there's no future for me here with

you! What I want from you you're not prepared to give—"

"Maybe you've already had what it was you wanted," he taunted, cruel in his jealousy. "Maybe you're aiming to go on after Cay and see if he's got something better to offer you? Is that your idea of love, *desperada*?"

"Bastard!" she ground out through clenched teeth. She lashed out with her booted foot, intending to kick him. She squirmed sideways and tried to wrench her wrists free of his punishing hold on her, but his arms were like cords about her and she could not break free. She screamed with rage against his mouth as it covered her own, beating her small fists against his hard chest even as he kissed her. But neither his arms nor his kisses could be evaded. He kissed her until her senses reeled, until she tingled from her hair roots to the tips of her fingers and toes, until her feet left the ground with the intensity of his embrace. His tongue parted her lips and claimed the velvet terrain of her sweet mouth with arrogant mastery, withdrawing only to dart hotly within again and again, nibbling and teasing until her furious cries became whispers and her raging blows became caresses as her hand burrowed between his shirt buttons to stroke his chest. "Bastard! Bastard!" she moaned, head flung back as his mouth left her lips and trailed fire down the column of her throat.

He laughed deep in his throat and caught her up into his arms. Pausing only to drag his bedroll from the back of his blue roan, he carried her to where several boulders offered some privacy and laid her down.

She bit her lip as she watched him towering above her, fiery dark eyes holding hers captive as he slowly unbuttoned his shirt and dragged it from his arms. Barechested now, he dropped to his knees beside her and kissed her again, lacing his long fingers in the mass of cornsilk hair that spilled about them. She moved her mouth hungrily against his, her hands roving feverishly over his broad shoulders, relishing the feel of his muscles rippling like sinewy cords beneath his taut flesh. He broke the kiss and pressed her down upon the blanket, reaching for the buttons of her shirt and slipping them one by torturous one from the buttonholes. When they were all unfastened, he slowly lifted the shirt fronts away from her breasts, like a child unwrapping some wonderful gift and taking pleasure in the suspense of the unwrapping. "Please . . ." she breathed huskily, fierce stabs of desire prickling in the pit of her belly. "Please . . . ?"

He shook his head slowly, drinking in the loveliness of her before him. Even as he swept her body with his burning dark eyes, the rosy crests of her breasts surged and stood erect and impudent, offering themselves as sacrifice to his lips. He leaned over her and brushed his lips against those vulnerable peaks, first one and then the other. The brush of his mouth was as fleeting as the velvet beat of a butterfly's wings against her body, and she shivered with delicious anticipation. Her lovely body writhed as he repeated the maddening caress again and again until she ached, burned for more, for the feel of his warm hands molding her flesh, for his touch upon her. His black hair tickled her as he buried his face between her breasts, pressing light, hot kisses to the valley between them, then trailing down across her rib cage, still further down to where her belt impeded his lips. Holding her still now, for she arched helplessly against him, he darted his tongue beneath her belt, ran the tip under the edges until she came close to fainting with the intensity of her desire.

"Undress, honey," came his low voice, and she nodded shakily.

She rose and unbuckled her belt, began shoving down the heavy men's pants she wore with feverish fingers. A curtain of fair hair hid her flushed face from him, and for that she was glad. Oh, Lord, he made her feel wild and crazy inside! He made her lose touch with herself when he kissed her just that way! She shivered as he came to kneel at her feet and pushed her hands away, drawing her pants down the slim columns of her legs, then the knee-length white pantalets, giving her a little nudge to step from them and stand bare before him. He cupped her taut buttocks in his hands and pulled her against him, kissing her belly as he had seconds before, darting the moist flame of his tongue into and around the miniature well of her navel until she shook uncontrollably. His mouth moved inexorably lower, skimming across her quivering thighs momentarily before returning to the flaming golden pelt at their joining. "No-oo!" she moaned as he tasted the very essence of her being, sending shock waves of dazzling pleasure throughout her. Her hands knotted spasmodically in his thick, black hair as his mouth worked its dangerous magic upon the throbbing core of her body. Her legs began to buckle beneath her. He bore her down to the blanket and parted her thighs, coupling the rhythm of his mouth with the delicate, rhythmic pressure of his hands, moving deeply into the honeyed warmth until she could stand it no longer. Her body tensed, and small, birdlike cries broke uncontrollably from her lips as she pulsated with pleasure and release and finally relaxed, utterly spent, upon the blanket beneath them. Her green eyes were heavy lidded and dilated to huge, dark pools as he unfastened his clothing and loomed above her. His entry made her gasp, and she reached up to clasp him about the neck, drawing his mouth down to hers, tasting her own musk upon his lips as he kissed her hungrily.

He leaned up and looked down at her as he moved strongly between her thighs, his dark head etched sharply against the gaudy splendor of the setting sun beyond, its ruddy light bathing his profile in liquid copper. "You're a witch, *desperada*, a damned, lovely witch! You make me feel things I don't want to feel, baby!" He gathered her up into his arms and kissed her ardently, crushing the softness of her breasts beneath the expanse of his chest. His release was violent, explosive, full of all the anger and desire within him. His fingers dug into the soft flesh of her upper arms as he roared out his pleasure, head flung back as he drove one last time into her. He rolled to her side, darting a fleeting kiss against her shoulder as he lay back, waiting for the tumultuous racing of his heart to slacken to its normal, even beat.

With a sleepy sigh, Promise rested her head upon his chest, her arm curled across it, listening to the cicadas' rusty trilling in the grass, the cry of a nighthawk, the twittering of little birds settling down to roost for the night. The sounds, coupled with the even, comforting beat of his heart beneath her ear, were like a lullaby. Their quarrel earlier now seemed like a bad dream only dimly remembered in the morning. Her head lolled heavily against his chest, and her eyelids drooped as sleepiness crept through her.

Luke stared up at the fiery sky above, eyes wide open, features sternly set in thought. "Promise," he said softly, "don't sleep, not yet. We have to talk."

"Mmm, later," she mumbled drowsily, snuggling closer to him. He gently disengaged her arms and sat up.

o, now," he insisted. "I've put this off long
ough."

"You talk, I'll listen," she offered with an impish
smile, still lying beside him.

He leaned across and grasped her firmly by the chin.
"Right now," he repeated as her eyes fluttered open to
look at him. His tone brooked no refusal. Sighing, she sat
up, reaching for her discarded clothing and pulling it
about her lower body.

"Well," she said with a smile, "what is it you have to
say?" She watched as he dressed, wondering how she
could have so recently vowed she would leave this man.
Her threat had been a hollow one at best, she knew. She
loved him; she loved every line and angle of his
magnificent body; she loved the deep timbre of his voice,
the sweet ardor of his kisses—everything! To leave him
would mean to leave a part of herself. What could have
brought this serious mood upon him so soon after they
had made love, she wondered?

At length he turned to her, his face grave, his eyes so
dark and brilliant, filled with apprehension. "I—I have
something to tell you, Promise."

She felt a flutter in her heart. Hope soared within her.
"Ye-es," she breathed, "go on, Luke. I'm listening."

"It's about why I brought you here with me, to the
Shadow S," he began. "After you've heard what I have to
say, you might feel differently about me, but I have to say
it."

She frowned but nodded nevertheless. "I see."

He took up a fallen twig and scratched circles in the
hard dirt, seeming uncertain of where to begin.

"Well," he said at length, "I wasn't being straight with
you when I threatened to turn you over to Sheriff
Harding for robbing the bank. I never intended to turn

you in, honey. I just used that as an excuse to get you to come with me to New Mexico. See, I intended to bring you here whatever it took. There—there was a reason."

She smiled. "I think I know what it was," she ventured hesitantly.

He shook his head. "No, honey, my wanting you was only part of it then," he said regretfully, his tone strangely gentle.

He stood and paced back and forth several times before turning to face her once more. "See, it all began a long time ago," he started. "I was young and itching to prove myself, and my father was wise enough to give me free rein to do so.

"My grandfather, Yellow Rock, had told me many times since I was a young boy of the gold to be found in the Rockies. He knew places where, he said, it glittered in the sunlight, just waiting to be panned. As a child, he had found nuggets himself, and it was for this reason he had been named Yellow Rock.

"As a half-breed, I'd been trying to prove myself all my life, first at the mission school my folks sent me to in Kansas and then on the ranch. When the gold rush started in the Colorado territory in '58, I remembered what Grandfather had told me and decided to make my own fortune without any help from my father.

"There was an older man working here on the ranch then, name of Jake Colter. He could rope and break mustangs better than anyone I'd ever met—better even than the Cheyenne. I looked up to him. When I was ready to leave the Shadow S, I told him what I planned to do, and he said he'd come with me, that we'd be partners.

"We went to Fairplay, to the mining camp there, and using my grandfather's directions, we struck color within days after we arrived. It seemed Jake and me would be rich men by the time we were ready to leave! But then, one spring night it all went sour.

"I went down to the dance hall, leaving Jake drinking in the saloon with a man who'd come in earlier. When I came back later, I heard they'd left for our tent with a fresh bottle and a new deck of cards. I went back to our tent and found Jake out cold on his cot. He'd been slugged across the head as he slept, and the pouch he kept about his neck that held our gold nuggets was gone! On the floor was a broken bottle of something dark and sticky, and I knew right there and then who had robbed Colter of our gold! I made certain Colter was only stunned, then lit out on horseback after his drinking partner. I figured enough time had gone by that that rattlesnake could be halfway to Denver City. But he wasn't. I found him only a few miles outside of town, camped with his family pretty close to Fairplay."

Promise's heart lurched at these last words, missing a beat. It began to thud audibly in her ears, growing louder and louder. She clenched her fists over the clothes thrown carelessly about her hips, heedless of the heavy, cold weight of her guns still in the gun belt resting across her thighs.

"I rode into his little camp," Luke continued. "The man greeted me, invited me to warm myself at the fire, and offered me coffee." He saw her face grow paler with every word he spoke.

"*Get on down from your horse, stranger, and pour yourself a cup o'coffee. 'Twill take the chill from your bones, an' that's a fact!*" Patrick O'Rourke's voice suddenly sounded loud in Promise's ears. She felt herself a child again, standing in the bushes and watching the dark stranger ride into their camp, shivering with the chill of the night air and the urgent need to relieve herself.

As if Luke's words had torn away a curtain that had hidden the stranger's face from her all those years, she saw it again as it had been that night, dark and angry, black eyes glittering in the firelight and shadows. The memory that had eluded her the day of the storm was suddenly sharp and clear, as if etched in crystal. "You!" she hissed hoarsely, and it was a duplicate of her father's shocked gasp, echoing down through the years and finding voice again on her trembling lips. *"It was you!"*

Grimly, Luke nodded. "Yes! I challenged your father. I told him to hand over the gold he'd stolen, and that would be an end to the matter. He panicked, drew his gun, and fired. It was a case of kill or be killed. I fired back. You know the rest."

"You killed him!" she cried in a strangled voice, face working uncontrollably. "You killed my pa!"

Eyes somber, he said softly, "I did. I told your mama why I'd come, and we searched the wagon for the gold after we'd laid your father to rest, but we never did find it—"

"Of course you didn't find it, damn you!" she cut in. "My father was no thief, God rest his soul. You shot an innocent man that night. I know it!"

"Wrong, honey," Luke denied, pain in his expression. "It was him. He'd sneaked back to our tent that night after he and Jake parted ways and slugged Colter with a bottle of his snake oil while he slept. Then he took the gold and ran."

"Someone else made it look like him then!" she sobbed, her voice shrill and crackling with emotion. "My father was a rascal, yes, but he wasn't a thief—he wasn't!"

Luke's eyes flickered over her, but he said nothing in answer to her anguished outburst. "Let me finish,

329

honey," he asked, and she gave him a tight, cold nod. "I rode back to Fairplay empty handed, to find Jake Colter waiting for me. He was nursing his cracked head and cussing me out for a thief! He'd never seen who hit him, but it turned out that several people had seen me riding hell-for-leather away from the mining camp. He'd put two and two together and come up with six!

"He and his lynch party were liquored up and ugly, in no mood to listen to reason or logic," he continued, his face darkening as he remembered that night. "There were over twenty of them to my one, and those were odds only a fool would have gambled with. I handed over my gun belt and said I'd go with them quietly. I figured I'd wait on the Miner's Court to hear my say and turn me loose. They were all greedy men, jealous men who'd envied the rich pickings Jake and I had come by. They said a hearing was too good for a goddamn half-breed and egged Jake on to let them string me up. They tied me up, set me on my horse, and looped the noose about my throat. I figured it was all over.

"But at the last minute, Jake said no. He said he reckoned he'd hold out for a hearing after all. He wanted the gold he figured I'd stolen, see, and he knew that with me dead, he'd never find it. There was a hearing, and I was found guilty. They sentenced me to be locked up until I told Jake Colter where I'd hidden the gold." His fists were knotted so tightly at his sides the knuckles were bleached white and bloodless.

"They threw me into a cell they used to hold rowdy drunks overnight. It smelled like death. It was so small, I couldn't lie down. There was only one small window, way up above my head. They put irons on my ankles and bolted them to the wall. That was my world for the next four years. When Colter remembered, he tossed food

330

into me. I slept on a dirt floor; I ate on that dirt floor; and I figured sooner or later I'd die on that dirt floor. From time to time, Jake and his pals would come and rough me up some, hollering at me to tell them where I'd hidden the gold. Four years I spent in that stinking hell-hole— four years of my life! I was barely twenty when they locked me up, but I felt a hundred when the creek flooded and they were forced to let me die or turn me loose. The Cheyenne found me, took me back to the ranch. I reckon seeing me the way I was when they brought me back helped put my father in his grave."

Legs braced apart, arms akimbo, he towered there, frightening as the anger surged through him anew. "There was only one thing that kept me alive all those years, honey, just one thing: revenge! I wanted to get even with O'Rourke for what he'd done, for what I'd had to go through on account of it. But he was already dead. He'd gone beyond paying, damn his soul! To my mind, he'd gotten off too easy! Then I remembered a little girl with blonde pigtails, the little daughter who'd wept over his body and whom he must have loved in return. I knew then how I could have my revenge on him. I could make those he'd loved pay in his place, so that in the end they'd come to curse his name and his memory forever!

"I had to put aside what I planned to do after my father died in order to get the ranch back on its feet. Every year since then, I've been going back to the Rockies to look for the gold Patrick O'Rourke stole that night. The last time was back in July. I didn't find the gold, but I found something that to my mind was even better—O'Rourke's little daughter! I didn't know who you were, not at first. It wasn't until after you'd robbed Hollander's bank that I found out from Henry just who my *desperada* was. I knew then that I could use what I knew to force you to come to

331

New Mexico with me. I reckoned I'd take my time and make you pay for what your father did, slow and easy—"

"By making me love you!" she whimpered, her lips drained of blood as the import of all he had told her sank in. "By making me give myself to you, my father's *murderer*. It all makes sense now, all of it! Oh, what a fool I've been! Dear God, I've been loving the man that murdered my pa all these months!" The blood pounded in her ears, growing deafening with its throbbing beat. "That was your revenge, wasn't it?" she gritted through clenched teeth. "You used me, my heart, my—my body, to get your twisted revenge on a dead man, a man who's been dead for six years! You dirty sidewinder! You damned—half-breed—savage—low-down—bastard!" Her tone had grown suddenly low, yet she spat the words with vehemence. "You should have died in Fairplay!" she hissed. "They should have strung you up good and left you to rot!" Her eyes were the only color in her face, a fierce, deadly, glittering green against the ashen pallor of her skin as her hand swept down to the gun belt that lay across her thighs.

Luke found himself looking down the barrel of Promise's six-shooter, held in a fist that shook with rage. Her face was the color of chalk, and there was a wildness to her green eyes that he knew was the result of the shock his words had caused. A dull ache started in his temples, and the arrow-shaped scar her father's bullet had left him with throbbed visibly. He set his jaw, his night-black eyes riveted to hers.

"Let me finish, Promise," he urged softly, taking a step toward her. "Put the gun down, honey."

"Give me one good reason why I should, mister!" she cried shrilly. Tears suddenly splashed down her pale cheeks. "All those weeks—all those nights that I loved you! All those times I hoped, *prayed* that one day you'd say you loved me too! Every touch, every kiss—they were all lies! Lies! *Damn youuu!*"

He saw the expression in her eyes change, saw the blinding, mindless rage and hurt within them, and knew even as he leaped toward her that she meant to fire. His lunge knocked her backward yet in that same instant her finger jerked convulsively against the trigger. There was a deafening explosion between them. The acrid odor of cordite burned their nostrils. Luke felt a searing, hot pain in his side, the gush of warm blood against his fingers, and knew he'd been hit.

"Promise . . . I—!"

Promise stood up, backing away from Luke as he slumped to the dust. She stared blindly down at the spot where he lay sprawled for some time. He moaned only once, then lay very still. His body was twisted like a fallen rag doll. His eyes were closed, and his blue-black hair was powdered with dirt. His hat lay a few feet away, where it had rolled when he fell. Blood bloomed dark from under his vest to pool on the ground beneath him.

She looked at the gun, still clutched in her fist, as if she had never seen it before, and a low, keening cry escaped her lips. The six-shooter fell heavily to the ground as her fingers relaxed and her knees gave way. She sank down, staring at Luke's body, shaking her head numbly from side to side. She began to shiver then, teeth chattering uncontrollably as she knelt there, still naked. But it was shock, not the chill of approaching night, that caused her to do so. "Papa! I did it for you!" she whispered. "Help me, Papa!"

Eyes vacant, mind blank, she crawled shakily to her feet, dressed herself as if in a trance, and retrieved the fallen gun and slid it into the holster at her belt. She looked down at Luke one last time.

"You didn't ought to have killed my pa," she said in a child's frightened voice. "You didn't ought to, mister!"

Then she spun about and ran to where the horses were grazing, grasped Tequila's hackamore, and swung herself astride him. She dug her toes into the cow pony's flanks and gathered the reins into her fists before urging him swiftly from the canyon into the night.

In the foothills of the Sangre de Cristos, a wolf threw back its shaggy head and sniffed the night air eagerly, catching the warm, sweet scent of blood on the wind. He howled his pleasure, yipping to his pack to follow him. Like gray shadows, they padded swiftly down the *arroyos* in the direction of that warm, sweet smell that promised food.

Chapter Sixteen

Promise crouched in the mouth of a deep cave, hugging her knees and crooning. It was a mournful, tuneless, monotonous singing that went on and on, and her slender body rocked back and forth in time to it. Her face was streaked with dried tears, clean rivers of pale flesh amidst the dust that caked her face. Her glorious cornsilk hair was a tangled, wild mane. How long she had sat there, rocking, singing, she neither knew nor cared. Her mind wavered in and out of the past and the events of the evening before, childhood memories strangely confused with Luke and Jake Colter or Cay Cantrell and Matt Hollander. When she went too far back in time, to the long-ago spring night in '58 when Luke had shot her father, she could now see the dark face with the glittering dark eyes that had eluded her for so many years, and she rocked harder and harder and faster and faster to block out that face from her mind. She felt no pain, no grief, nothing; for what she had learned had left her numb. In the place of her heart there was now a yawning emptiness that was sometimes briefly replaced by a heavy weight, as if a great boulder had wedged itself in her breast.

She was still there, rocking and singing tunelessly, when Joaquin found her that morning, in the cave carved into the rock formation known as the Caldera del Diablo, the Devil's Cauldron. Her pony still wore his hackamore and saddle as he stood, head low and dispirited, ears flicked back, at the cave mouth. Lather had dried on his haunches, as well as blood from the furious whipping his rider had given him in her flight from the box canyon. There it was they had found *Señor* Steele lying in a pool of his own blood, while the golden eyes of the wolves gleamed in the moonlight all about him.

He sighed heavily and dismounted his coyote-colored pony, looping his reins about the chaparral that framed the cave. *Madre de Dios!* Why had *Promesa* shot *el señor?* he wondered. What could have passed between them to cause such a terrible thing? He approached the cave warily, the tuneless crooning grating on his nerves. Manuel Santos and Shorty Price had ridden back out to the herd when *el señor* and Promise had not returned to the *hacienda* for supper as expected, despite Black-Strap's sly comment that it was a pretty night, and the two were more than likely busy courting! They had returned with *Señor* Steele slung limply across Shorty's saddle, a makeshift bandage binding his wound. Margita had not been optimistic about his chances for recovery.

"He has lost much blood!" she had pronounced dolefully after they had cut his clothing from him and she could see the awful wound with the powder burns about the edges. Her plump, olive-complexioned face had paled, and she had crossed herself. "I do not know if *el señor* can survive this, but with the help of God, I will do what I can. Come, Joaquin, help me! First, we must get the bullet out!"

Get it out they had, but it had not been easy, for the bullet had lodged firmly between two ribs, saving the *señor's* life but making its removal difficult beyond belief.

For over an hour Margita had probed the ragged wound, urging Joaquin to pour mescal down Luke Steele's throat to dull the pain when her doctoring brought him, moaning, back to consciousness. At last, she had pried the bullet free, had bandaged him and gathered up the pile of blood-stained clothes, offering a fervent prayer that he would live. Soon after, Joaquin had slipped from the bunkhouse carrying two canteens of water and some rations tucked into a leather *maleta*, determined to go after the *señorita*. He could not believe it had been she who had shot *el señor*, for all that he had mumbled her name constantly in his pain. No, it could not be so! Anyone who had eyes with which to see could not have helped but observe that the *señorita* loved him, for her feelings showed in her face, her voice, whenever she came near to him. He would find her, help her if she needed help, for had she not saved his life before, when the Comanche arrow had lodged in his neck?

He edged closer to the gloomy mouth of the cave, nostrils flaring as he caught the rank odor of mountain lion at the cave entrance. Rocks and the bones of small creatures littered the cave mouth, further evidence that this place had indeed served at some time as the lair of *el cugar*. He stopped as he saw Promise crouching in the shadows. Concern furrowed his kind face as he looked down at her, and tears misted his gentle brown eyes. *Pobrecita!* What could have done this to her? What? She appeared a demented woman, dirt streaked, vacant eyed, lips cracked and moving feverishly as she crooned that endless, eerie tune. He entered the cave and crossed to her, leaning down and shaking her gently by the shoulder.

"*Señorita! Señorita Promesa!*" It was as if the hand on her shoulder had never been, as if she had not heard the words he had spoken. He crouched down before her and grasped her by the chin, tilting her face to his. "It is I, Joaquin, *niña*," he whispered softly, as if to a child. Green eyes stared past him to some point beyond that only she could see. He cursed under his breath, drew back his hand, and slapped her hard across the cheek, then slapped her again across the other.

Her head rocked with the force of the blows, and the imprints of his palms rose instantly on her pale, dirty face as bright, crimson welts. She gasped, and a deep shudder ran through her. Tears of pain welled in her eyes and flowed down her cheeks to mingle with the dirt. He clutched her to him as the dam inside her burst, stroking her tangled hair while she sobbed against the rough fiber of his *serape*.

"*Calma, niña, calma*," he soothed. "It is all right. I am your *amigo, no*?" Relief flooded through him as he saw that her eyes were now filled with pain and awareness, no longer empty of all emotion and life as they had been minutes before.

He lowered her carefully to the ground and covered her with his *serape* before fetching the canteens from his pony and soaking his bandanna in water to bathe her burning, grimy face. She continued to weep even as he did so, and he made no attempt to stop her tears. It was better, he knew, that her hurt be cried out, else it could remain locked inside her to fester like a poisoned wound that is not drained. When she was comfortable, he left her to gather brush with which to build a fire and hung a coffee pot over it on a rack of three forked branches. When the water boiled, he tossed a handful of coffee grounds into it and when it was ready, he carried a well-sweetened mug of the scalding black brew to the girl.

"Sit up, *niña*, and drink this. It will do you good, *si*?"

His voice was unusually stern.

She sat up obediently, seeing Joaquin for the first time. She looked about her, nose wrinkling in distaste as the rank smell of some wild animal reached her nostrils. How had she come here, to this place, she wondered dully? Had Joaquin brought her here for some reason? She passed a trembling hand across her brow, wincing as her shoulder protested the movement with fierce stabs of pain.

"You are wounded?" Joaquin asked.

"My shoulder," she whispered. "I—I fell, I think. It's just bruised."

He nodded. "When you have finished your coffee and rested a little, we will ride to Santa Fe. *Mi madre*—my mother—she will see to you," he said confidently.

A bitter smile hovered at the corners of her cracked lips. "Your mother? You would take me to your home, knowing what I did? I shot *el señor*, Joaquin, or did you think it was someone else?"

"*Si*," he said softly, "I knew it was you."

"Don't you even want to know why I did it?"

"Not unless you wish to tell me. If you feel that I should know, you will do so when you are ready," he said simply. He stood up from where he had been crouched by the fire. "I must see to your *caballo*. He does not look so good."

There was no reproof in his tone, but Promise felt guilty nonetheless and astounded that she could have quirted poor Tequila so mercilessly in her mindless rage. Yet everything that happened after the gun had gone off in her hand seemed blurred and out of focus, as if seen through a pane of crimson glass. She didn't even recall finding this cave, though she supposed some instinct must have guided her here, to sanctuary.

She sipped the hot, strong coffee, feeling its warmth spread through her stiffened limbs and revive her a little. Joaquin's expression had been guarded at her mention of Luke. Had she killed him, she wondered? Was he dead? Her hands shook on the tin mug and the coffee slopped over the rim and burned her fingers. There was a part of her that hoped so . . . Not only had he killed her father, but he had killed something fine and vulnerable inside her that could never be resurrected. No, never! He had trampled her innocence underfoot with no more compunction than if he'd simply stood upon a fragile prairie wildflower. He had betrayed the trust she had put in him by offering him her heart on a platter. Even should she have been able to find it in her to forgive him for shooting her father, she could never forgive him for that! What sort of man was he to have conceived such a terrible revenge, then had the cold-blooded gall to carry it out to the last letter? A savage, she acknowledged bitterly, a sly, scheming, heartless, bloodthirsty savage! It was the act of someone not quite human, someone beneath those of white blood who could never, she was certain, have done such a thing. Hate burned like an acid river through her. She wanted to hurt him as badly as he had hurt her! She wanted him to know what it was like to feel such pain! Now she, too, wanted revenge!

Joaquin returned then, carrying a white cloth in which were wrapped several fried *tortillas* filled with beans, meat, and cheese that he had packed in his *maleta* on leaving the Shadow S. He insisted that she eat something to regain her strength, and Promise reluctantly agreed to do so. To her surprise, she discovered that she was ravenous once she tasted the spicy rations.

The sun was a spinning yellow disk directly above the Caldera del Diablo when they finished the noonday meal, and their bodies cast no shadows upon the ground as they left the cave. They made their way to the horses, which Joaquin had tethered in a clump of thorny chaparral. Promise approached Tequila slowly, expecting the paint pony to shy away from her in fear. To her immense relief, he nickered softly as she came toward him and nuzzled at her hand as he always did. She clasped him about the neck and pressed her cheek against the rough, creamy-colored mane, murmuring that she was sorry for the ill-treatment she had given him the night before.

"When it is a little cooler, we go," Joaquin announced.

She nodded, content to let him take charge for the moment. Her body still ached with weariness, and heat burned behind her eyes as if she had taken a fever. Had she slept at all last night? She couldn't remember—couldn't remember very much at all of what had happened after she had ridden from the canyon. "Joaquin . . . ?"

"*Señorita?*"

"Is—is Luke dead?" She had to know, *had* to!

"I do not know, *señorita,*" Joaquin replied honestly, and was shocked by the expression of disappointment that flitted across her pale face. He had thought that whatever had come between them to cause such violence the night before might perhaps have dissipated with the coming of morning. With a sinking heart, he realized that it had not. "He lost a great deal of blood, both before and after we found him . . ."

She nodded, inwardly cursing herself. If she had not wavered last night, if she had not weakened when she gazed into his face, swayed by her deep love for him, she could have fired before he leaped at her, made certain he was dead. Somehow, she'd make him regret what he had done to her, she vowed. Somehow . . .

Joaquin shuddered as he read the look of hatred in her burning green eyes, repulsed by the naked hunger he recognized within them. His revulsion was quickly followed by a feeling of overwhelming sadness. For some reason, the beautiful Anglo girl he had come to admire over the past few months for her spirit and her courage coupled with gentleness and honesty was gone. Would she ever return, he wondered? Or would this bitter, hate-filled woman remain forever in her place? He sighed heavily. She was like the mountain lion in whose cave she had sought unerringly to hide in her confusion and her rage, deadly and filled with the desire to hurt. *La puma*, a female mountain lion, wounded and, deep inside, very much afraid—the most dangerous of creatures! Except that *Señorita Promesa* bore her scars on the inside, where they could not be healed.

He got heavily to his feet and kicked dirt over the fire, emptied out the coffee pot, and eyed the position of the sun. It was already beginning its descent toward the west, its fierce, glaring heat abating somewhat. He picked up his *sombrero* from the ground and pulled it down on his head, then gathered up his *serape* and his bandanna from the reeking cave.

"We go, *señorita*," he said gravely, and saw her nod in agreement.

Chapter Seventeen

Promise ducked through the low doorway of *Señora* Paloma's *jacal*, her hair brushing against the hanging scarlet strings of chili peppers left there to dry. She wore a *camisa* of unbleached cotton, the gathered low neckline embroidered with flowers in vividly colored silks, and a full skirt of heavier dark red cloth. Were it not for the shining curtain of cornsilk-blond hair that flowed down her back, she could have been mistaken for a Mexican *señorita*. In one hand she carried a clay bowl of Indian design, in which lay several pieces of the delicious, paper-thin, cornmeal bread called *piki* by the Hopi Indians who made it and from whom she had just bought it in the *plaza publica* of Santa Fe. In her other hand she carried a small, woven basket filled with pine nuts, whose scent mingled with that of the *piñon* logs burning in the fireplace of the small adobe dwelling, perfuming the air with a woodsy fragrance.

Señora Paloma looked up from her embroidery as Promise came in smiling. She set aside the magnificently decorated *colcha*, or bedspread, which she had been sewing for the Governor of Santa Fe's wife, and hurried to take Promise's purchases from her.

"*Buenos tardes, Promesa,*" she greeted her warmly.

"How was it at the market?"

"Very crowded, *señora*," Promise responded ruefully. "I wasn't able to get some of the things you asked for. Three Conestogas had arrived this morning, and everyone had gone to the *plaza* to see the newcomers." She shrugged. "They had also bought up everything by the time I reached there!"

Señora Paloma laughed, and Promise thought how much she resembled Joaquin when he smiled. "It does not matter, *niña*, she consoled the girl. "We have enough rice and enough flour to last us until next week. Then you may try again, *no*?"

Promise nodded, yet she did not return the smile the woman flashed her. By next week, she vowed, she would no longer be here, in the *jacal* of *Señora* Paloma. In the three weeks since Joaquin had brought her here, she had determined to avenge herself on Luke Steele, and no words from Joaquin, however heatedly whispered when his mother was not in earshot, could dissuade her from her purpose. She had forced from Joaquin only two days ago the knowledge that Luke had recovered from his bullet wound. Indeed, not only had he recovered; he was again riding and seeing to his business about the Shadow S!

With each day that passed, an idea had grown stronger and stronger inside her, watered by the bitter tears of his betrayal of her love, warmed by the fierce heat of her hatred for him, and taking firm hold in the fertile soil of her need for revenge. She had determined that she would ruin him, wrest from him the lands he held dear, and the cows that were his claim to wealth. She would reduce him to no more than a common half-breed, destined to wander everywhere, belonging nowhere, as other half-bloods were forced to do. With his lands and his beasts would go his pride and his self-respect as a man, and she would then, and only then, account them even!

She had not told *Señora* Paloma the truth when she had blamed the crowds on her inability to obtain all of the supplies the woman had requested she should purchase. She had slipped away from the market in the *plaza* and gone to the gunsmith's, where she had traded one of her guns for ammunition. With the change from her trade, she had purchased two sturdy canteens and another heavy blanket. At first light tomorrow, she would leave the *jacal* and head back to the cave in the Caldera del Diablo where Joaquin had found her the morning after she had shot Luke. From there, she would be perfectly positioned to wage a full-scale war on Steele's herds without threat to Joaquin and his mother by their unwilling involvement in her plans. Insofar as she knew, Luke had no knowledge of her whereabouts and believed Joaquin made his usual weekly treks into Santa Fe to visit his widowed mother. She preferred he should continue to think so. *Señora* Paloma and Joaquin had been kindness itself to her these past weeks, and she could not leave them to bear the brunt of Luke's anger if he learned they had taken her in. Yes, tomorrow she would go, when it was still dark . . .

Luke's eyes were as black as the bottom of a deep, dark well as he glared at his cook. "I won't ask you again, Joe," he said softly. "Is the *señorita* in Santa Fe, with your mother?"

Joaquin looked down at his feet, misery in his heart. He said nothing, though he expected at any moment to feel *el señor*'s fist against his jaw. Nevertheless, he would not betray *Promesa*, never!

Luke laughed harshly. "Your silence is as damning as anything you could say, Joe! I know she's there—but don't worry. I don't aim to hurt her." He smiled.

Joaquin raised his head slowly. Despite the *señor*'s words, he felt far from comforted, for the tone of Luke Steele's voice had been ruthless, completely without mercy. "If you do not wish to hurt her, *señor*, why is it that you are trying to find her?" His boldness surprised even himself, and he flinched as Luke Steele strode across the wooden floor of the *sala* of the Casa del Ombras and poured himself a drink.

"Why?" Luke sipped his whiskey, swirled it in the glass, and admired its rich color as he held the glass up to the light. "That, *amigo*, is between myself and the *señorita*. Go now, back to the chuck wagon. When you leave in the morning, I will be coming with you to Santa Fe."

Joaquin swallowed, nodded, and hurried from the room, not half so cowed as his appearance suggested. A friend was always a friend. He could not permit *el señor* to arrive at his mother's *jacal* and surprise *Promesa* in the morning, for she would believe that he, Joaquin, had betrayed her. No, he must leave this afternoon and give her warning!

He looked about for the coyote-colored pony that he had ridden in from the herd on receiving Luke's summons to the *hacienda*. It was gone! Just then Black-Strap rode out from behind the bunkhouse, leading the bronco as he rode his own buckskin mount.

"Ah sure am sorry, pardner," Black-Strap said ruefully, "but the boss done give me orders t'see you goes back t'the herd. He figured mebbe you'd have it in mind to ride to Santa Fe, if Ah wasn't here to see to it that y'didn't."

Joaquin gave him a look like thunder and mounted his pony.

"No hard feelin's?"

In answer, Joaquin muttered a curse under his breath.

Black-Strap chuckled. "Yep, Joe, Ah know how yuh feel! Ah had a soft spot for Miz Promise maself, yessir, poor li'l gal. Whatever she done to Mistah Luke, I've a notion he musta asked fer it, somehows. Git up there, hoss!"

The two rode from the *hacienda* to the herd, which was watering and grazing on the banks of the Mora River, two miles from the rocky basin known as the Caldera del Diablo.

Promise tossed restlessly on the blanket-strewn pallet of straw by the fire in *Señora* Paloma's *jacal*. Tomorrow Joaquin would come again, and she wondered if she would be able to hide her intention to leave from his gentle, brown eyes that somehow saw—and understood—everything. If he guessed her intention, she knew he would insist that she stay, for he had often given her stern council on the dangers that lay in wait for a young woman alone, both in bustling Santa Fe and in the wilds.

From across the room, *Señora* Paloma snored, deeply asleep. Promise pushed back the blankets and stood up. She dressed quickly in the shadows, donning once again the clothing she had worn in the box canyon when she had shot Luke, now washed and darned. Tiptoing about the gloomy *jacal* with only the flickering firelight against the whitewashed adobe walls to give her light, she rolled up both her blankets, tucked some of the *piki* bread in her shirt, and, carrying her boots in her hand,

347

slipped outside.

Tequila nickered softly at her approach and strained against the hobble to greet her. She sat down, pulled on her boots, and fetched her saddle from the small, rickety lean-to that served as tack house and chicken coop. Then she pulled out the ammunition and two canteens she had purchased earlier that day from under the straw where she had hidden them. She quickly saddled Tequila, lashed the bedroll to his back, mounted up, and walked him through the narrow, winding streets of Santa Fe.

Despite it being the wee hours of the morning, the streets were not deserted. Painted saloon girls lolled in some shadowed archways, looking up hopefully as she rode past. A drunken bullwhacker snored in a gutter, sleeping off the effects of too much mescal. From the opened doorways of the rowdy gambling halls, amber light spilled out along with warm air, heavy and oppressive with the odors of sweat, liquor and cheap perfume. The whirring sound of a roulette wheel, the tinny plink of a piano, and raucous laughter carried in the hush. In the area of the silent *plaza publica*, the weary oxen teams from the Conestoga wagons that had arrived that morning rolled in the warm sand and luxuriated in their release from the shafts.

She held her breath until she was clear of the town, realizing suddenly—and gratefully—that there was a full moon floating in the dark heavens above, washing the trail with silvery, clear light. She bit her lip. Before leaving, not once had she even considered how she would see to find her way in darkness! If she intended to survive, she would have to be careful to note such things as wind and weather and the moon, she decided firmly.

She rode on for what she estimated to be almost two hours, letting Tequila walk in order to conserve his strength, though Tequila had been ridden little in the past few weeks and she sensed that he was eager for a gallop. Ahead, she could discern the sharp, black angles of many buildings, silhouetted against the lighter sky beyond. It was the abandoned *pueblo* to the north of the town, deserted now and strangely forlorn in the shadows. She decided to pass the rest of the night here, rather than go on. In the morning, she'd be better able to gauge her direction.

With Tequila securely tethered to a low bush, she found an adobe house that still had a ladder leaning alongside it. The only entrance to such a *pueblo*'s many-storied, apartmentlike dwellings was through an opening in the roof, she recalled Luke telling her when they had passed through here en route to the Shadow S for the first time. In this fashion, the Indians who had lived here had been easily able to defend their homes against their enemies.

She shivered as she recalled her captivity in such a building in La Ciudad de Los Perdidos. She took a blanket from her bedroll and clambered up onto the roof, finding the opening easily and a second ladder leading down into the gloom of the room below. Placing her feet cautiously, she fumbled and slipped her way down. Inside was pitch black, save for gray fingers of moonlight that streamed through the aperture to puddle at her feet and reflect ghostly glimmers of light on the gypsum walls. The room smelled musty, as if many small wild creatures had taken shelter there over the years, even as she was now doing. Turning about and groping with her hands, she brushed aside fallen fragments of adobe and dirt that littered the hard floor, spreading her blanket on the cleared space. Her hand brushed against something large and knobbly in the darkness, probably some household utensil

349

forgotten by the former inhabitants, she decided, setting it carefully aside and rolling herself into the blanket.

She lay looking up at the sky through the opening above her, at the silvery brilliance of the moon and the bright frostiness of myriad stars, before falling into a fitful sleep. In the few seconds before she drifted over the chasm between wakefulness and slumber, she caught the sigh and moan of the night wind searching through the many empty rooms of the *pueblo*, like the whispering voices of the Hopi Indians—now long dead—who had once lived there.

The sun was shining full in her face through the opening when she awoke the next morning. She yawned loudly and sat up, groaning. The floor had been hard beyond belief, and strange dreams and fancies had plagued her sleep. Instead of feeling rested, she felt more tired than she had when she had come here the night before!

She dragged herself to standing, her eyes falling on the object she had brushed in the darkness last night and mistaken for a household tool discarded there. Yet it was no tool; it was a mask of some sort, she realized, picking it up and turning it over. The painted and carved face that grinned back into her own was that of some ferocious wild animal, perhaps a lion or a cat, she guessed. Slanted eye holes allowed the wearer to see, and there was another hole where the mouth opened in a silent roar, through which the wearer could breathe and speak. She held it up to her face and dared a low growl, smiling in self-conscious embarrassment as she lowered the mask, despite being alone. She'd never seen anything like it before! Tucking it under her arm, she rolled up her blanket and clambered back up the ladder to the rooftop. She'd take the mask with her, she decided. Perhaps it would bring her luck in her revenge against Luke Steele.

She rode from the *pueblo* through an early morning shower that would, she hoped, wash away her tracks should Joaquin try to follow her.

Chapter Eighteen

The strident clamor of Joaquin's skillet pounding, calling the cowboys to the chuck wagon to eat, carried across the open grasslands to where Promise quietly sat her paint pony, blond hair riffling in the breeze like a golden banner. She had made no attempt whatsoever to disguise her appearance. Let Luke or his men see her flowing hair and know by it that it was she who would, little by little, bring ruin down upon his head!

She squinted across the river and grinned with satisfaction. As she had anticipated, most of the cowboys from the line had answered the call to chow and only two remained to see that the herd was held in check. Patting Tequila's neck, she urged him down the sloping riverbanks and into the water which was only a few inches deep after the long, hot summer months. Gaining the opposite bank, she spurred him into a swift gallop, broke from the cover of cottonwoods and junipers that lined the river in a wild rush and a vivid blur of color, and careened straight for the dark herd of longhorns that grazed placidly on the grass. As she neared them— Tequila's patterned forelegs working like pistons beneath her—she swept the battered brown Stetson from her head and brandished it.

"Yah! Git up there! Yah! Yah!" she screamed, waving the hat as she galloped nearer and nearer to the herd.

Shorty Price, the man who had replaced Cay Cantrell as foreman, stood in his stirrups, eyes narrowing as the slight figure on the paint pony neared the distant perimeters of the lead cows. "What in the hell . . . !" he growled, and lashed his quirt across his horse's hindquarters, spurring and whipping it furiously in Promise's direction.

Several fractious cows set up a nervous bellowing and searched anxiously for their calves as the rider neared them, rolling wary eyes in her direction. Old bulls with cracked horns pawed the dust and added their enraged bellows to those of their cows, while the more spirited, younger bulls broke away from the main body of the herd to charge after the paint pony that nipped and tucked and bobbed and weaved like the expert he was to evade their wickedly curved horns. Promise drew her six-shooter and fired two shots over the herd, and all hell broke loose.

The cows, which had been peacefully grazing scant minutes before, reacted to the sharp reports and began running, picking up speed as fear replaced reason, and they became governed only by the instinct that urged them to flee! Dust rose in great, blinding clouds as thousands of hooves churned the sere grass underfoot and the cows thundered up the gulch toward the river-banks that, if calm, they easily could have negotiated. Long, curved horns carved bloody troughs from tough hides as each beast jostled those nearest for room, and screams and bellows and snorts of rank fear were joined with those of pain. Calves went down under the surging mass and were churned to a bloody pulp as the stampeding tide swept over them.

Shorty Price and Manuel tasted and smelled the fear

353

on the air as they galloped their horses desperately to the river in an attempt to turn the crazed beasts before it was too late. Yet they had gone no more than half the distance when the first cows poured over the shallow drop, legs broken, necks twisted, a chaotic tangle of hooves and horns resulting as the second, third, fourth, and still more waves of animals crashed down atop them. The flood of dying and wounded beasts grew, and the cowboys' faces went white as they realized that there was no way on earth to save them all.

The outside of the herd surged toward the middle where the gully narrowed, and it seemed as if the cowboys would be caught in the crush. Promise held her breath until the thick dust cloud had settled and she saw them safe where their horses had carried them, slipping and scrambling up the steep bluffs on either side. For all that she burned to ruin Luke, she had no wish to harm his men, for they had offered her their knowledge and their friendship.

She watched as the two men careened back down from their cover and began cracking their blacksnakes over the herd to divide it into two parts, the only means left to them to save as many of the animals as possible. With a low laugh of triumph, she wheeled Tequila's head about and turned back for the Caldera del Diablo, where she had camped the morning before. "This is just the beginning, Luke!" she promised under her breath as she rode away.

Later that night, she sat hugging her knees before a small fire, staring into the flickering amber flames that lit the rugged walls of her cave and feeling overwhelmed with loneliness. Here, alone, with the night pressing close all about her and her belly squeezing with hunger, the knowledge that she had put her plan into action and had begun to bring Luke down was scant comfort.

She shivered, for the night had grown achingly cold, and pulled the blanket more tightly about her as wolves howled at the moon from the timbered foothills of the mountains. For all that her gun lay loaded and close at hand, she was afraid. The faint rustling of night creatures foraging for food in the brush and thorny chaparral about the cave filled her with anxiety. The dark had never scared her before, but now it did, seeming to be filled with threatening half-images, too vague to put names to but frightening nevertheless. She thought of what Margita had told her, of the village of Mora's reputation for having several witches numbered amongst its people. The Caldera lay on Tierra Mora land . . .

Tequila's cough, loud on the silence, sent her head jerking about in the direction of the sound, eyes wide open and seeking desperately to plumb the blackness. She glanced over into the corner of the cave where her canteens and the painted mask she had found in the abandoned *pueblo* lay. Tossing aside the blanket, she scrambled across the rock rubble toward them and returned to the fire with the mask. Somehow, its nearness comforted her despite the fact that the carvings were grotesque. Strange that it should, she thought, lying down rolled in her blanket once more, the mask propped up where she could see it. Firelight gave life to the snarling *puma*, and as the flames writhed in the draft and cast shifting light over the carvings, they seemed to move. Eyelids grown heavy at last, she fell asleep, only to dream she found herself in a deep, dark pit below the earth.

She sensed the presence of many bodies pressed close

355

all about her. The odor of perspiration and excitement, mingled with fear, was sharp and rank in her nostrils. Through the pitch-black, oppressive darkness came the slow, hypnotic beat of drums and the whirring click of shaken rattles and gourds. Torches of *piñon* wood hissed and flared, casting flickering light on bodies that glistened with paint and sweat as they danced, throwing giant, leaping shadows on the walls of the sacred *kiva* . . . The dream receded, the gyrating figures dissolving into images of Luke. In sleep, she clung to him anew, felt the searing warmth of his kisses on her flesh, cried aloud her love for him. But her arms closed on air. Only the rough blanket beneath her received the warm pressure of her lips; not him. No, never him, ever again . . .

As the night wind prowled the cave, the craggy walls threw back the vibrating tremor of its current, and it seemed to make a low, purring sound, like that of *la puma*. The sound reached Promise even through her uneasy slumber and the sticky web of dreams in which she had become entangled. Her restless tossing and turning ceased. Her whimpers of loneliness and fear were silenced. A small smile played about the corners of her mouth as she slept, deep and undisturbed now.

Luke's eyes were hooded as he gazed into the fire of fragrant *piñon* boughs that crackled in the hearth. Where is she, he asked silently. Where?

He had gone with Joaquin to *Señora* Paloma's *jacal* in Santa Fe and had seen the apprehension in Joe's eyes increase steadily as they had neared it. Apprehension had been replaced by a mixture of relief and concern when, on being pressed, *Señora* Paloma had reluctantly admitted that the *señorita* had indeed been there but had left earlier that day while it was yet dark. She had no idea where she could have gone. Luke, watching Joe's face, had been willing to bet that Joaquin had no more knowledge of where Promise was now than he did.

They had followed her tracks to the abandoned Hopi *pueblo* north of Santa Fe, but then her tracks had given out, washed away by an early-morning shower. Had she determined to go back to the Colorado territory alone, the little fool? His wound pained him, and he ground his fist against it to dull the ache, recalling the expression in her green eyes in the second after the gun had fired—an expression of hatred so fierce its heat was palpable. No, he doubted she would have left New Mexico without first attempting to get even with him, not when she had learned from Joaquin that she had not killed him as she'd hoped. He was half persuaded that it was Promise who had started the stampede that had resulted in the slaughter of close to fifty head of cows that afternoon. Neither Shorty Price nor Manuel had been able to get a good look at the rider in the chaos and dust, but Shorty had thought he recognized the pony and believed he had glimpsed the rider's long, blond hair streaming in the wind behind her as she rode. Luke smiled mirthlessly. In many ways, they were well matched, she and he . . .

He stood and reached for a fresh log from the fuel box, laying it atop the glowing fire. Flickering light played on the brightly patterned, vegetable-dyed, woven rugs and on the smooth adobe floor that had the texture and appearance of oiled leather. Protruding beams of pine, the *vigas*, gave interest to the high ceiling. Beside the stone fireplace stood his mother's rocking chair, and across from it the heavily carved chair which had been his father's, and where he now sat.

How many nights had he sat here, as a small boy at his

father's feet, and watched how the firelight played on his mother's blue-black hair or lit the dusky beauty of her face as she worked at her sewing? How many nights had he watched, awed, while his father whittled a figure from a scrap of pine—a ferocious bear perhaps, or a coyote with its head raised to the moon—or while he braided thin strips of rawhide together to fashion a lariat? If he closed his eyes, he could imagine they were here still, his father's face, so stern in concentration, softening as he smiled down at him; his mother's gentle smile as she held up a shirt she had been working on, to check its fit against his small chest. They had been good times, filled with security and the warmth of belonging, of being part of a family. There had been many times since he had brought Promise to the Shadow S when he had felt that warmth again, had looked across the fireplace to where she sat and had seen the way the firelight struck gold in her hair and touched her downy cheeks with its warmth. Then he had not known the bitter, warping emotion of vengeance, but the tender yearning of love.

His fingers clamped about the arms of the chair so tightly the knuckles showed white against his tan. Why hadn't he told her how he felt? Was he such a coward that he'd had to keep putting it off until it was too late? Yes, damn it, *yes*! For he had known deep in his heart that to tell her all, to reveal his identity to her, was to risk losing her. And lose her he had! He, who was afraid of no man, who feared nothing on this earth, had been afraid to tell the truth to the woman he loved. That fear had cost him dearly. . . .

He stepped across the cavernous room, wincing as the healing wound in his side stretched and began a dull aching that was now familiar. He rested his arms on the window sill and gazed bleakly from the arched window.

Moonlight washed the white manes and patterning of the mustangs in the corral beyond. A lamp spilled golden light from the bunkhouse, set at right angles to the *casa*, and the soft lament of Shorty's harmonica carried through the darkness. The Sangre de Cristos were a looming, dark sentinel over the silent valleys and *mesas* below, light reflecting here and there as if upon glass where the moon's gentle radiance touched the snow-capped peaks. The snarl of a mountain lion suddenly splintered the hush, and the mustangs milled about, stamping nervously.

The sound filled him with foreboding. An uneasy image of Promise's face, pale and frightened in the shadows, filled his mind. Where are you, my golden one? he asked himself. In the far distance, a pair of dogs set up a furious barking. Are you alone out there? Are you hurt? Was she even now dead? The latter suggestion sent chills spiraling down the length of his spine. It was a thought he could not bear to consider, yet she was a fragile woman in a strange and savage land, and that land had destroyed far hardier beings than she . . .

The enormity of what he had done encompassed him then. In his lust for revenge upon her father, he had destroyed the only woman he had ever loved. He had broken her proud spirit and trampled upon her tender, loving heart—exactly as he had set out to do! He cursed himself bitterly, then turned and strode rapidly across the room, pausing only to buckle on his gun belt and jam on his Stetson. He'd be damned if he'd wait 'til sunup to go out and look for her again. Sunrise was hours away yet. He'd find her, he vowed, find her and convince her that he loved her, that it was no lie—not any more!

Chapter Nineteen

Hunger outweighed even Promise's desire for revenge by the fourth day after she had left *Señora* Paloma's *jacal* in Santa Fe.

Back in the Colorado territory by the Cherry Creek, game and fish had been plentiful most of the time, and she had been a good hunter and provider for her mother and herself. Squirrels, rabbits, and even an occasional small antelope had fallen to her rifle and found their way into the stewpot. But here, in this strange country where there was so little vegetation, she had no such luck.

Soon after daybreak, she had ventured out from the cave in the Caldera, painfully hungry and weak because of that gnawing need. Gathering up her blankets, her canteens, and the mask, which comprised the sum of her possessions, she had clambered feebly astride Tequila's back and ridden him down to the muddy trickle of the Mora River, where she and the pony had quenched their thirsts under the willows. In the distance, the hazy dawn sunlight had glinted between the spreading oaks and reflected off the windows of the *hacienda* of Tierra Mora. For a second or two, she had been torn between riding there and going on. Perhaps she could ask *Doña* Estrellita for food. It had seemed at the *fiesta* that a friendship between them had already begun. She was certain that the *doña* would not refuse her—but she would ask questions. Too many questions, Promise decided ruefully. If Luke had men out searching for her, the *doña* could tell them that Promise was in the vicinity, and she would be quickly found. No, it was better to go her own way without help, at least for now. Trembling from lack of food, and feeling the vast quantity of muddy water she had drunk in a vain attempt to fill her belly press heavily against its narrowed walls, she mounted Tequila again and urged him onward to the green-and-rust foothills of the snow-capped Sangre de Cristo range. Surely she would find game there, amongst the trees.

The chatter of a pair of noisy magpies seemed to mock her some hours later as they watched horse and rider from the cover of a vivid, gold-leafed aspen.

A young female deer had exited a heavy thicket of bushes into the clearing where Promise crouched, waiting, and moved daintily to within feet of her hiding place. She had lifted her velvet nose warily to catch the breeze and any alien scents upon it before lowering her head to graze. Promise had quivered all over with excitement, and saliva had gushed into her mouth as she envisioned the deer rapidly transformed to venison by her skinning knife and a hot fire. She had carefully drawn her gun from her belt and raised it to shoulder level, steadying her right hand with her left when the gun trembled with her excitement and weakness. Sighting down the short barrel, she had taken aim at the motionless deer, certain her shot could not fail to bring the doe down. Holding her breath, she squeezed gently but firmly on the trigger, careful not to jerk the gun in any way. A hollow click had followed instead of the deafening report she had expected, not overly loud but enough to startle the nervous doe, which had bounded back into cover.

Promise had muffled a sob and hurled the empty gun across the clearing in her frustration. How could she have been so darned stupid; how *could* she! Some moments later, her anger vented, she had hurried to retrieve the gun and load it, deciding that if one deer had shown itself, there could well be others about and that if granted a second chance, she would be ready. But, despite two hours of patient waiting, squatting uncomfortably on her heels, no other deer came to the clearing.

Promise was forced to content her growling belly with a few handfuls of bright red chokeberries that had gone unnoticed by the birds, and a few handfuls of *piñon* nuts, which, in her hunger, were the very devil to shell, although delicious. She even tried tasting the large, shiny beads of dried resin that had dripped and hardened upon the trunks of the *piñons* but found their gummy texture and resin flavor made her feel sicker than ever.

Dispirited and still hungry as a bear, she again left the spruce and aspen-covered foothills and returned to the vast, sagebrush-littered prairie below, hoping against hope to find an unwary jack rabbit enjoying the afternoon sunlight or a prairie dog rash enough or bold enough to poke its head from its hole. Yet what she did find was far larger—an Indian herdsboy tending a vast flock of sheep and goats! The sheep grazed the grama grass, while the lad, who was barechested and wore several chains of pretty blue stones and silver about his neck, leaned against a large boulder and opened a buckskin pouch. From it he withdrew several small things that looked like little cakes wrapped in leaves and began munching happily.

Food! Promise realized, and saliva again filled her

mouth. She had, on spying the flocks from a distance, toyed with the idea of running off one of the sheep and butchering it for food. But the prospect of those little cakes was so much more immediate, she could not bear to wait. The boy, who could have been only nine or ten years old, stood then, and Promise saw that he carried a wicked-looking, long-bladed knife in his belt. He strutted across the ground, picked up a rock, and hurled it with startling accuracy at a sheep whom he had decided had strayed too far. Promise wetted her lips. For all that he was quite small, he appeared independent and very protective of himself and his flocks. She was certain he wouldn't simply hand over his noonday meal to her without a fight, and she was reluctant to hold a gun on a child . . .

It was then that she recalled the mask, still strapped to her saddle. Guiding Tequila into the cover of a clump of thornbush, she reached for it and drew it over her head before cantering from cover directly toward the herds-boy. Her strange appearance had an even more dramatic effect on the Hopi boy than she could ever have hoped for. He looked up and saw her, and his dusky face paled as she careened toward him, whooping. His food spilled from his hands and he let out an unearthly shriek.

"*Kachina! Kachina toho! Nata'aska!*" he babbled. "Aieee!" With that, he fled through the rabbit brush, stumbling over rocks and clumps of sagebrush that barred the swift flight of his moccasined feet. The flock baahed and milled uneasily about as its herder fled screaming at the top of his lungs, and the goats bleated and dashed nimbly away to what they felt was a safe distance, watching curiously with their bearded faces turned toward Promise as she slipped from the back of her pony and fell upon the leaf-wrapped corn cakes like a starving wolf.

There were only three of the cakes left, and she quickly devoured them, reaching eagerly for more into the buckskin pouch the Indian boy had dropped in his haste. She found only segments of what looked like the flesh of some sort of cactus, again wrapped in leaves. With a shrug, she stuffed that into her mouth, too, reasoning that since it had been carefully tucked inside the food pouch, it must also be some kind of food favored by the Hopi. It tasted far from pleasant, but she chewed it gamely.

Tequila whinnied then, and she looked up to see dust rising on the prairie in the distance. Her heart lurched. Surely the boy could not have brought his elders back here so swiftly. Yet it seemed he had, for the ponies drew steadily nearer, and as they did, Promise glimpsed Indian riders upon their backs between the clouds of dust thrown up by their mounts' hooves.

Keeping low, she scurried back to Tequila and slipped quickly astride him, turning him back toward the cover afforded by the foothills. She rode deep between the trees for over an hour, until she figured she had thrown off any would-be pursuers with her circuitous ride and dropped wearily from Tequila's back. Her full belly filled her with a sense of well-being that even the threat of being followed had not taken away. She felt extraordinarily drowsy now, as if her eyelids were weighted, her limbs loaded down with enormous burdens. Yawning hugely, she curled up in a niche between several boulders and fell asleep.

She slept more deeply in that hour between afternoon and dusk than she had in the past three nights. On awakening, she scrambled to her feet and stood there, swaying gently. Her body felt peculiarly light now, as if it lacked all substance, and the trees and boulders nearby seemed to bend and waver in her vision. She rubbed her eyes, and yet the detached, unreal feeling persisted. A nearby aspen seemed to grow up and up and up, like the beanstalk that Jack had planted in the fairytale, she thought, giggling. Giggles turned to peals of merry laughter, and she flung her arms wide and twirled around and around until she sprawled, dizzily, to the ground. Tequila flicked back his ears and shied away from her as if she were a stranger. Yet another giggle exploded from her lips, and she laughed until tears streamed down her face. What on earth was wrong with the paint pony, she wondered? While she slept, his ears had grown longer and longer, his nose had become more rounded, until he looked like a—a donkey! "Poor donkey! Come, little long-ears donkey, come to Promise!" She staggered to her feet and reached out toward him, managing on the second attempt to grasp the trailing hackamore. "Bad donkey," she scolded sternly, wagging a finger at him. "Bad, bad, *bad* donkey! I ought t'take a switch t'your tail for tryin' to run away from me!"

She mounted him clumsily, then lifted the mask and set it solemnly atop her head. "Me heap big medicine man!" she announced gravely to the forest, a peal of laughter following her words. Birds fluttered from the trees and took flight, and Tequila sidestepped nervously. "Git up there, li'l donkey!" she urged and kneed him forward down the hillside.

She sang as she rode, snatches of songs her mama had taught her and cowpunching songs she had learned from the cowboys of the Shadow S, her voice deep and muffled beneath the mask's fusty confines. Interspersed with her singing were bursts of wild laughter that seemed to bubble up from somewhere deep inside her like an

365

irrepressible spring.

Tequila halted of his own accord at the top of a gentle rise, and through the giddy feeling of euphoria that filled her, Promise was dimly aware of the vast herd of cows spread across the floor of the narrow valley below. She smiled broadly beneath the mask. Lord, how that li'l Injun had run when he'd seen her! She'd just bet the mask would scare the pants off of Luke's men, too! 'Sides, it made her feel good wearing it, kind of sleek and powerful and fierce, like the animal it stood for. She made a deep, purring growl far back in her throat and touched her heels to Tequila's flanks. Laughter bubbled again from her lips as she imagined the cowboys' faces paling, their horrified gasps loud on the hush as she rode toward them through the half-light of dusk. She slipped from Tequila's back and flung herself behind one of several huge boulders, from where she could watch the line camp. And wait.

Manuel Santos and Juan Moreno had ridden hard all day, carrying out to the letter *el señor*'s instructions to be extravigilant since the recent attempt to stampede the herd. They were glad to reach the tiny cabin that nestled in the foothills of the Sangre de Cristos, marking the line of the western range of the Steele lands.

The light was rapidly fading to the amethyst and gray of dusk as they finished their *frijoles* and *tortillas* and settled down by their campfire. They talked idly of the upcoming *fiesta* at the end of the month, the feast day of the gentle, wise San Gerónimo, on the last day of September. Manuel's dark eyes were merry as he recalled past *fiestas* in the *plaza publica* of Santa Fe; how the women had danced, beautiful as flowers in their brilliant dresses and fringed shawls, bright paper roses setting off their dark hair and flashing dark eyes! Juan, younger than he, nodded eagerly. Manuel continued in his low, musical voice, describing the lovely *Señorita* Dolores who awaited him in Santa Fe, the memory of whose beauty and voluptuous figure made the blood flow hot and swift through his veins even on a night as chill as this! Her eyes, he said tenderly, promised him that their marriage bed would be more *caliente*, hotter, than the fiery red chili peppers Margita hung to dry outside the kitchen *portal* of the Casa del Ombras!

Juan let out a great roar of laughter and slapped his goatskin chaps. He cautioned the love-sick Manuel to be certain the lovely Dolores' mother never heard him talk in such a fashion. "*Amigo*," he said solemnly, "if *la vieja* heard you speak so of her innocent, untouched flower of a daughter, it is very possible she would take up the *machete* and turn *mi amigo* Manuel, the bull, into Manolito, the steer!"

Manuel grinned and lit a slim *cigarillo* with a sulphur match struck upon the heel of his silver-trimmed boots. "*Si*, Juan," he agreed, "but first *la bruja vieja*, the old witch, has to catch me!" He winked slyly. "It would seem that the chaparral bird merely stands still when compared to the swift feet of *Señor* Manuel Santos!" The image of the beautiful *Señorita* Dolores' ancient mother, whose joints were permanently knotted with arthritis, careening through the streets of Santa Fe in pursuit of a spry Manuel with a *machete* brandished aloft in her scrawny hands made both men laugh.

They sat, wrapped warmly in their *serapes* in companionable silence, watching as the moon rose and cast her silvery light in patches through the gnarled trees. Juan added more of the brush they had gathered earlier to the fire when it burned down. From behind the tiny log cabin at their backs, their ponies whinnied and snorted, moving restlessly about. Juan got to his feet to be motioned down again by Manuel, who was already standing. "I will see to them, *amigo*," he offered. "It is probably only the wind carrying the scent of wolves down from the mountain. Pour me another cup of coffee, *por favor*."

Juan nodded and poured two mugs of the thick, black brew, while Manuel, whistling softly, stepped around the cabin toward their horses.

They were rolling their eyes whitely in the moonlight and fighting the *remuda* rope stretched between two trees to form a portable hitching post that held them in place. He murmured to the ponies softly until they had calmed a little before untying them and leading the pair back toward the campfire. The fear that had filled the horses had communicated itself to the herd now, Manuel sensed, the cows' shift in mood palpable to the *vaquero*'s sixth sense that he had sharpened over the years. His expression was uneasy as he heard several cows snort and saw others begin to mill nervously about.

"We must mount up again, Juan," he murmured. "There is something wrong! I can feel it in my—"

"Look!" Juan cut in. "Over there!"

Manuel looked and caught a glimspe of what it was Juan had seen disappearing between some boulders beyond their camp. Moonlight had shone down on something lithe and large and golden bounding gracefully between the rocks to vanish amongst them. "*La puma!*" he breathed, reaching for the repeating rifle he had left by his place at the fire.

Juan nodded and pulled on his gloves, reaching for his own rifle before leaping astride the pony Manuel held

368

ready. They rode off in opposite directions, fearful that the mountain lion's presence would cause a stampede, singing softly in an attempt to calm the already restless herd while keeping their eyes upon the rocky wall where the animal had disappeared.

All was quite for some time, and their unease abated a little. But then, suddenly, they heard the spitting snarl of the mountain lion, loud in the shadows and the hush. Manuel reined in his pony and looked up. The lion was crouched atop a bluff of yellow rock ahead of him, her jaws parted in yet another loud snarl. Eyes that were not amber as other cougars, but a fierce, shining green, gleamed down at him through the gloom. *"Madre de dios!"* Manuel hissed under his breath. Across the narrow valley, on the other flank of the herd, Juan's words echoed his.

It fell on Manuel to shoot the massive creature since he was the closest of the pair and his position would afford him a clear, killing shot. He raised his rifle to his shoulder and took careful aim, yet in that very second he saw the great mountain lioness bunch up her rippling muscles and hunker down, preparing to spring upon a bawling calf below the bluff.

He aimed at the beast's breast and pulled back on the trigger, but in that moment *la puma* snarled again, and Manuel's pony shied. Bullet and beast exploded at the same time, the lioness soaring gracefully through the air in a gigantic leap that seemed ungoverned by the laws of gravity that bound other beasts. Her effortless grace was marred as Manuel's bullet, thrown off course by the movement of his pony, took her in the front leg. The beautiful creature crashed clumsily to the ground, rolling heavily onto her side. For a second she lay quite still, and Manuel smiled in satisfaction. But then, with a snarl of pain and fury, she struggled to standing, turned tail, and loped swiftly away. As she fled, Manuel could see the dark splash of blood that stained the tawny gold of her magnificent, rich coat. He muttered a curse under his breath and raised his rifle for a second shot, but in the short time it took for him to do so, *la puma* had vanished between the rocks from where she had appeared, and was no more.

He turned his pinto back to the herd toward Juan, calmer now that the mountain lion had gone. "*Amigo*, you must ride to the next camp," he ordered quickly. "I only wounded *la puma*! She will be back, and we will need help to handle the herd when she comes. Go *amigo*, go quickly, and with God!"

Without pausing to question or disagree, Juan gathered his reins in his fist and spurred his pony away. After he had gone, Manuel looked apprehensively about him, half-expecting to find a pair of shining, slanted green eyes staring unblinkingly down at him through the shadows. He shivered and drew another *cigarillo* from his pocket. Those eyes had seemed more the eyes of a she-devil than the eyes of a creature of God! He hoped fervently that *la puma* did not return before Juan and the other men arrived.

Chapter Twenty

Promise stumbled through potholes and gullies, clutching her belly and moaning as she fought the waves of nausea that crashed over her again and again. The euphoria of hours before had fled. In its place now lodged an overwhelming sensation of doom. Tequila had gone, where she did not know, and she was lost. Her canteens were lost, her blankets and the mask were lost with him. The night was cold, and her teeth chattered uncontrollably. There was a dull ache in her shoulder that wouldn't go away. Oh, Lord, she'd die out here, she just knew it! She sank to her knees upon the cold, sandy ground and sobbed. Mama was gone. Pa was long dead. All her friends—Sarah, her daughters, Arthur Morgan, his sister Ginnie—were miles away. And Luke—Luke didn't love her, but, God forgive her, she still loved him, no matter what he had done to her, or her pa! This kind of love wasn't a blessing; it was an evil, a hungry obsession that consumed like fire and left only destruction in its wake!

Her tears flowed into the dirt until they were spent and she was empty, could cry no more. She pressed her flaming cheek to the cool, moist earth and lay there, exhausted, not caring if she ever moved again.

Luke glanced up from his seat by the fire as Juan, a young *vaquero* from the west line camp, galloped up to the chuck wagon. He rose quickly to his feet and strode to meet him, grasping the bridle of the snorting pony as it slid to a halt alongside him.

"What is it, Juan? Another stampede?" he demanded grimly.

Juan shook his head. "No, not yet, *señor*. Manuel sent me to bring help. A mountain lion came down from the foothills into our camp! Manuel shot at her, but she got away. She is wounded, *señor*, and he is certain she will come back. The herd is already restless. If *la puma* returns, I do not know if the two of us alone could hold them in check!"

"Black-Strap, saddle up some fresh horses. Shorty, you and Charlie mount up!" Luke ordered.

In minutes, Luke and the others were riding swiftly westward to the line camp Juan had left. Hell, Luke thought angrily, if it wasn't one damned thing it was another! He had spent night and day searching for Promise, scouring the prairies without sign of her. Now, a mountain lion was bothering the herd! It was as if he had been attracting bad luck like a magnet since that night in the box canyon, he thought fatalistically. His mother's people would have called a *shaman* to him to dance away the evil forces that surrounded him with their strong medicine. He smiled grimly. Maybe that wasn't such a bad idea, at that.

Manuel rode out to meet them when the party reached the line camp. Luke was relieved to hear the lion had not come back. He listened to Manuel's description of how he had winged the creature and knelt to examine the drops of blood where it had fallen. "We'll track her come sunup," he said at length, "and finish her off." The other men nodded agreement. A wounded predator such as *la puma*, unable to run down her prey, would return to the herd for an easy kill when she was hungry, they knew. It would be better to shoot her before that happened, so each man kept his rifle within easy reach as they rode herd that night, just in case the animal returned earlier than they expected.

Luke and Manuel set out the next morning on the trail of the wounded lioness. The blood had dried during the night, but Luke, with his skill at tracking, was able to follow the dark, rusty spots for a little over a mile, when the sign tapered to the imprint of a paw here and there, or a flattened clump of dry grass.

"*Dios*, she moved in circles, no, *Señor* Steele?" Manuel grumbled, tilting back his *sombrero* and scratching his head.

Luke nodded. "Could be the pain's making her act that way."

"*Si*," Manuel admitted. "Or—she is just very clever, *señor*, and hoped to throw us off her trail!"

His boss snorted. "She's a lion, not a woman, Manuel, amigo!"

Manuel gave a shrug, yet his expression was guarded. "Yes, *señor*, but there was something very different about this one! What, I cannot explain . . ."

Grinning, Luke mounted his roan. "Superstition from you, Manuel? I wouldn't have expected it!"

Manuel appeared affronted. "You would not speak of superstition if you had been there, *señor*. *La puma*'s eyes, they were like green glass and seemed to see straight into my soul!"

A chill swept through Luke, passing as swiftly as it had come over him. Apprehension suddenly filled him. "Green eyes?" he echoed hoarsely. He turned in the saddle to face Manuel, his expression dark and stern. "Are you certain it was a puma you saw last night, man? Would you stake your life on it, if it came to the question?"

Startled, Manuel nodded. "*Sí*! Of course, *señor*! First, Juan and I, we glimpsed her bounding between the trees. We heard her snarl, and the animals, they were afraid, *señor*. Later, I looked up and she rose above me, ready to spring. When she jumped, I shot her!"

"And you were worried about the herd, and it was dark," Luke added grimly. He lashed his reins across his horse's back. "Come on! I hope I'm wrong, but I've a feeling it was no puma you shot at last night."

Behind him, Manuel spurred his own horse, his expression set in a fierce, dark scowl. Let *el señor* believe what he would, he thought. He had seen what he had seen . . .

An hour's riding brought them to a shallow arroyo, and below Luke saw the liver-and-white paint pony he had given Promise weeks ago, reins trailing, its saddle still hung with canteens and blankets. He and Manuel rode down to the pony, and Luke dismounted. He ran his hands knowledgeably over the animal but could find no injury which might have caused Promise to leave it and go off on foot. He straightened and looked about him. There was little cover here where she could be hiding or sleeping, nothing but sandy, hard earth stretching as far as the blue horizon and a few sagebrushes and cottonwoods to break the monotony.

"*Qué es esto?*" Manuel asked thoughtfully, stooping to

pick up something from the ground. He held it out to Luke, who took it from him and turned it over.

The mask of a *kachina* spirit grimaced back at him, its features carved into the fierce snarl of a mountain lion. The chill swept over him again, and the dark hair on his neck rose. Now, more than ever, he was certain that his suspicions were correct! "It's a *kachina* mask," he told Manuel. "The Hopi believe that the *kachina* spirit comes to earth several times a year, to give blessing to the crops. While here, he lives in the bodies of the men who wear the masks that represent the *kachina toho*, the mountain lion *kachina*." He gave Manuel a long, level stare, obsidian eyes piercing.

A dark, angry flush rose up in Manuel's face. "I know what it is that you are thinking, *señor*, but it is not so! It was not the *señorita* that I shot, but *una puma*, I swear it on the Blessed Virgin's name!"

Luke nodded. Whatever the truth might be, it was obvious to him that Manuel truly believed it had been an animal he had shot the night before. "I sure hope you're right," he said softly before they rode on, leading the paint pony behind them.

Promise dragged herself to standing from where she had sprawled most of that long, cold night. She felt as if she stood upon the crumbling edge of a narrow chasm, that if she took a single step she would plummet into the yawning black abyss below. She held out her arms on either side of her for balance and took a tentative step forward. *Don't look down*, a small voice cautioned. *If you do, you'll fall!* She licked her lips, afraid to move. *Go on, take a step! Look down and see what's below. There's nothing to be afraid of, nothing at all!* a second, sly voice wheedled in her ear.

Perversely, the urge to look down grew overwhelming. She lowered her head and looked, and there was the yawning black abyss she had feared, alive with wriggling snakes of enormous lengths, pink and purple and silver! Each one had its mouth wide open, and she could see the droplets of golden venom that clung to fangs like huge pollen grains. Their mouths opened wider and wider, until each one was a vast cavern of scarlet, the walls slick with glistening saliva . . .

She screamed in terror and felt herself falling, twirling as she dropped like a rag doll tossed over a steep cliff toward those waiting mouths below. She braced herself for the bone-crushing agony of the impact, yet no such agony was forthcoming. Instead, she flailed wildly with her arms, felt a rushing current of air lift and carry her upward, upward. A wild, exultant peal of laughter tore from her lips. She could fly! The flesh of her arms was now gloriously feathered, and she flapped her new wings in wonderment, feeling new currents of air eddy under them and soar her to incredible heights, up and far out of reach of the snakes who waited hungrily below.

Higher and higher she rose, like Icarus, toward the orange sun that spun in a deep purple sky above, and about which silver stars careened in dizzying orbits. A moon of shimmering lime green lay on its back to the far west, and she turned and soared toward it, reveling in the delicious sensation of weightlessness that having wings imparted. As she neared the lime-green moon, she saw that a man sat upon it, swinging his legs. In his hands he held two bright ropes wrought of the moonbeams, and their light was dazzling as he swung gently to and fro.

She giggled. He must be God, she thought incredulously, for who but He would take such liberties as to make a swing from the moon and the moonbeams? Yet as she neared the moon swing, she saw above a dark, threatening cloud. From the midst of it stretched a hand, and in that hand was held a glittering giant knife!

For a second, she faltered and dropped down, forgetting to fly in her horror. Whoever it was that held the knife so threateningly couldn't do that, she thought in dismay—he couldn't cut the swing ropes and send God crashing into the snakepit below. He just *couldn't*!

She arced upward, arrowing directly for the knife with all the speed she could summon. Air rushed past her in a sibilant hiss as she soared straight for the knife that threatened to plummet the bearded old man into oblivion. From somewhere came the whistling of a mighty, rushing wind, and the dark cloud was torn aside, the remnants whirling away like shreds of a dark veil. Eyes wide with horror, she found herself gaping into a darkly handsome face lit by dark-satin eyes that burned like twin dark coals, smoldering, singeing her with their heat. Their magnetism drew her inexorably deeper into their fiery depths. Dear God, *Luke's* face, *Luke's* eyes! She couldn't draw back, couldn't escape the hold he had upon her—couldn't fight it—couldn't!

The knife rose with a shimmer and a glitter of steel as she fluttered helplessly there as it came down and plunged deep into her breast. Scarlet ribbons of blood fountained from the awful wound, rising and bubbling as they unfurled and raveled away. "How could you do this to me!" she screamed. "I loved you, damn you! I loved you—but you betrayed me!"

She flapped her wings but found that they were no more. They had become simply arms again, unable to keep her aloft. She trembled fleetingly in space for one long moment before beginning to fall . . . fall . . . fall.

"Noooo!" she screamed, and Jake Colter, squatting beside her, jerked back, startled by her vehement cry.

"Calm down, gal, it's only yer old friend, Jake. Remember me, gal?"

Her dark gold brows drew together in puzzlement. She passed a limp hand across her brow. "No, no, not Jake . . . Luke! Yes, Luke!" She sank back and in seconds appeared as deeply asleep as when he had found her seconds before.

What in the hell was she doing way out here, alone, and with no horse that he could see? Jake wondered. He grinned. Maybe there was still a way for him to get even with Luke after all! The grin vanished as he recalled the way the girl had stared at him, terror in her wide green eyes. They had been focused on something beyond him— something Jake was real glad he hadn't been able to see. He felt her brow, but it was cool. What was it she'd taken? He smelled her breath. It wasn't liquor. He rocked back on his haunches and considered her thoughtfully. Loco weed, maybe, or peyote—one of the two. Whichever, he reckoned he had a while yet before she came around from it and got troublesome . . .

"Come on, li'l gal," he panted, hooking his arms under her shoulders, "you an' me are going t'take ourselves a ride!" He dragged her toward his horse, left ground-tied cropping the sparse yellow grass. She hung as dead weight in his arms when he lifted her and only gave a low moan at his clumsy handling when he hoisted her across his saddle. One foot in the stirrup, Colter made to swing astride his mount behind her. As he did so, a shot rang out, pinging into the dirt inches from his horse's hooves and raising a miniature dust funnel.

"Freeze!" barked a voice, and Colter's head snapped around as if jerked by a string. He grinned as he saw Luke and a *vaquero* sitting the slight rise at his back.

"Go ahead an' blast me, Luke, *amigo*!" he challenged. "This li'l gal is gonna get my first bullet if you do! Is that what you want, partner?"

Luke's dark eyes narrowed. Manuel glanced anxiously across at him. "What do you think, Manuel?" Luke asked without turning to look at the *vaquero*.

Manuel squinted against the light to where Colter sat with the *señorita* held before him in the saddle like a shield. "Too risky, *señor*!" he offered at length. "You might easily hit the girl. She seems unable to help herself, *no*?"

Luke nodded grimly, eyes riveted on the pair then briefly dropping down to the gun now held in Colter's fist, leveled at Promise's head. As he watched, she whimpered and thrashed in Colter's arms. The diversion of Colter's attention gave Luke the scant second's opening he was looking for. As Jake struggled to keep her from slipping from his horse, Luke kicked his blue roan in the sides and Sky exploded from the crest of the rise like a steely blue thunderbolt hurled from the sky, Luke riding low in the saddle and drawing the black-snake whip from its loop as they raced toward the pair.

Colter glanced up, the alarm and fear obvious in his face as he saw how very close Luke's horse was now. He swung his gun hand around, realizing belatedly that if he shot the girl, they would both jump him and he'd have nothing left to bargain with. "Back off, Steele!" he yelled. "Back off or she—"

Even as he spoke, there was a sharp cracking sound and something long and black snaked through the air and coiled itself about his wrist. The bone snapped clean in two, and with a yelp of agony Colter was torn from his saddle and crashed heavily to the dust. Promise, freed of

Colter's tight grip, slithered to the ground, and Manuel kneed his horse toward her as Jake began running for his life, Luke kneeing the roan after him.

Colter scurried crablike toward a rocky outcropping, fumbling for his other gun with his good hand. His face was contorted with pain as he drew it free and dived behind a boulder, and he was wheezing for breath as he rested the gun barrel on the rock and leveled it at Steele. Again came the crack of the whip, as loud as any shot on the silence, and Colter's Stetson flew off, caught by the eager tongue of the flying lash.

"Hold yer fire!" Colter yelled. "I give up! I'm coming out, damn you!"

Luke hauled on the reins and Sky reared up. "Then come out reaching!" Luke snapped, watching with hooded eyes as Jake Colter edged his way out from behind the rocks. As Luke had half-expected, the man still held the gun in his fist, and as he reappeared he raised his arm once more to shoot. It was the last time he was ever to squeeze a trigger. As his muscles flexed, the lash cracked and Colter's face turned blue as it zipped through the air and knotted about his throat. The snap of his neck was echoed by the blast of his bullet as his muscles twitched and their convulsions fired the gun in his hand. The bullet scored harmlessly into the dirt as Colter rolled over and lay still.

With a grim expression, Luke turned Sky's head and cantered the horse back toward where Promise lay, Manuel crouched at her side.

"He is dead?" Manuel asked, dark brows raised.

"He sure is," Luke confirmed, swinging down from the saddle. "His neck's broken."

Manuel nodded. "Then, the past is laid to rest, is it not, *señor*?" he murmured.

A bitter smile hovered about Luke's lips. His eyes came to rest on Promise where she lay, still deeply asleep to all appearances. For the past to be laid to rest, he still had to make his peace with her—and that promised to prove the hardest thing he had ever done! Would she listen if he told her that he loved her? His shoulders slumped. He coiled the blacksnake, still dangling from his hands, and stuck it back in his saddle loop. "No, *amigo*, it's not all over yet," he said heavily. "Not by a long ways! Let's rig a *travois* to carry her home. She can't ride double in the condition she's in."

"I will cut poles, *señor*," Manuel offered. Luke nodded and crouched beside Promise while the *vaquero* went to do so.

As he had expected, there was a flesh wound in her shoulder, no worse than a nick. Her brow felt cool, yet she slept as if in the depths of some fever-sickness. Had Colter slipped her something, some poison, maybe, he wondered? Minutes later, he and Manuel lifted her onto the framework of cottonwood poles covered with his bedroll, which would be drawn by his horse. Whatever was wrong with Promise, Margita would know how to deal with it, he was certain.

"Come on, *amigo*, let's get her home."

Margita folded back the crisp linen sheet and tucked it in. "There, *señor*, she is sleeping now, *pobrecita*. The dreams, they are gone."

"They will not return?" Luke asked, looking down at Promise.

Margita shook her head, earrings swinging. "No, *señor*, not if it was indeed the flesh of the peyote that made her this way. After a few hours of . . . madness, it is gone."

Luke nodded. "*Gracias*, Margita. I'll sit with her now. You go on to bed."

"*Si, señor. Buenas noches.* If you need me, you have only to call." Margita turned down the lamp and left the room.

Luke looked down at Promise and sighed heavily. As Margita had said, she appeared to be sleeping peacefully now. The swell of her breasts rose and fell against the bedcovers, and her body was relaxed. The tension had drained from her lovely face, leaving it unlined, vulnerable, and almost childlike as she slept. He knotted his hands into fists, remembering her expression in the box canyon in the seconds before she had fired the gun. How she must hate him! And yet, he could not blame her for that. He had brought it upon himself, had he not, when he deliberately set out to make her want him, need him, love him? A bitter laugh came softly from his lips. And in so doing, he had lost his own heart.

He stood and paced back and forth across the bedchamber, aware that her fragrance filled it, reminded poignantly of the scent of her warm body nestled snugly against his own in the cool of the morning, or of that same body languid from his love-making in the heat of the night. *Promise, my love, how can I mend this thing? How can I undo the wrong I have done you?*

If only she had permitted him to finish what he had intended to say in the box canyon that night—if she'd only waited until he had reached the part where he had planned to tell her that his desire for revenge had been lost in his love for her! He scowled in the shadows and poured himself a drink from the bottle Margita had brought earlier. What good were recriminations and might-have-beens? It was the here-and-now that counted. He would tell her anyway, he determined, hold her still and *force* her to listen if he must. Or else he would run the risk of losing her forever, knowing he had done nothing to prevent her from leaving him. He could live with the knowledge that he had failed, but not with the rancor of knowing he had never tried!

She awakened the next morning to find him still there beside her, dark shadows upon his unshaven cheeks, fatigue deepening the tiny creases alongside his eyes. A slow smile spread across his face, hiding his uncertainty.

"Welcome back, *desperada*," he murmured.

The sleepy expression on her face ebbed. Her eyes became hard where minutes before they had been large and liquid with sleep. She turned her rosy face away from him.

"Welcome back to what, *señor*!" she flung at him. "Why did you bring me here? You must have known it would be the last place on earth that I would wish to be— here, with you!"

Slowly, he nodded.

"Then why was it, I ask again, *Señor* Steele, that you brought me here? More revenge? Do you plan to use me again? If so, I give you fair warning, Steele—I shot you once, and I would do so again!" She sat up and swung her legs over the side of the bed, sitting there glowering at him, green eyes like shards of emerald glass.

He reached for her. "Promise, I want—"

"Don't touch me!" she snapped, flinching away from him. She jumped to her feet and stalked across the chamber. "Don't ever touch me again!"

The muscle in his jaw twitched. He nodded. "Okay. If that's what you want, I won't touch you. But . . . you have to promise me something in return. Will you?"

She shrugged. "I suppose so." She looked over her shoulder at him warily. "It depends on what it is you want me to promise."

"Nothing hard. Just that you'll listen to what I have to say."

"There's nothing you could say that I'd want to hear. Didn't you say enough that last—that last time we were together?" She wore her hurt on her face like an open wound.

He ached to take her in his arms but knew if he took one step in her direction she would turn on him like a wild cat. "No, *desperada*, not nearly enough. I didn't get the chance to finish what I had to say that time." He smiled faintly and touched his side. "Something . . . came up, remember? Will you let me say my piece now?"

She nodded irritably. "Go ahead."

"Well," he began, hesitating as he sought for the words, the right words. "It was like I told you. I wanted to make Patrick O'Rourke pay for those four years of my life. And, I decided to do that through you, his daughter." He turned from her, unable now to look her in the eyes. His grandfather's, Yellow Rock's, vision came back to him then. ". . . *I saw the dove flutter free, and the hawk was lying still upon the ground where before the dove had lain*," the old shaman had said. The muscles in his jaw flexed and tautened. Now he understood. He understood only too well! "It didn't work out the way I had it planned, *desperada*," he continued heavily. "I saw the look in your eyes, knew that you loved me, and yet I couldn't bring myself to say what you wanted to hear, that I loved you, too, because *it was true.* I couldn't admit that, not even to myself! I even tried to talk you out of loving me, told you what you felt wasn't love but physical need. You see, I knew that I'd failed, honey. I'd set out to destroy you by making you love me . . . and ended up loving you back! That's what I wanted to tell you that night: that I couldn't go through with what I'd planned. I love you, *desperada*!" At the latter words, he turned to her and gazed unflinchingly into her eyes, willing her to believe him against all odds.

Silence hung heavily between them for several long moments after he had finished speaking. He saw tears well up and fill her eyes. Her mouth worked soundlessly. Finally, she shook her head.

"No, Luke. I don't believe you," she said flatly. "It won't work any more. That Promise, that innocent little fool who loved you—who would have believed you—she's dead, don't you see? And you killed her, just like you killed her pa! This Promise will never make the mistakes she made. No, sir!" Her slender shoulders shook with the fervor of her outburst, and her breasts rose and fell raggedly against the cloth of the nightgown in which Margita had dressed her. She turned away and leaned against the window, staring blindly out at the courtyard beyond. Birds were making a dustbath below her window sill, fluttering and chirping noisily. Margita's scarlet geraniums made a vivid splash of color against the sandy earth, defying the arid land from the fertile safety of their tubs of dark, rich, mountain soil. Yet Promise saw none of this, blinded by tears that refused to fall.

Luke cursed under his breath. His arms were around her before he realized that he had crossed the room. He pulled her back against his chest and buried his face within her hair. "No, Promise, no. It's not a lie, not any more. I love you, baby, I love you!" He turned her to face him, his mouth surging over hers and silencing her protests with his kisses. He encircled her shaking body with his arms, stroking her gently until she ceased to shake and grew still. Joy filled him as she yielded to his kisses, her mouth beginning to move sweetly against his, the hands that had initially sought to thrust him away from her now reaching up to twine in the dark commas of hair at his neck. But suddenly she gave a short, sharp, anguished cry and twisted from his embrace.

Alarm ran through her as she stood there, looking fearfully up at him. Oh, how quickly her body had responded to his touch! How easily she had forgotten the pain this man had given her, betraying her vow never to make the same mistake again for the price of a kiss, a caress, a whispered promise of love that was only a lie! "No, no, no!" she cried. "I feel nothing, *nothing* for you, Luke, not any more!" Let him not guess that she lied, she prayed fervently. Oh, how she lied!

His broad shoulders slumped. His jaw worked as he fought to master his emotions. He reached out to her then let his hand fall slackly to his side. "I guess I was a fool to have expected more," he said heavily. "You'll be wanting to leave here?"

"Yes," she agreed, lowering her eyes.

"Where will you go?" he asked, feeling a deep, aching pain begin in his heart.

She sighed. "I don't know. Back east, maybe. I have kin back there that I've never met. Maybe I'll see if I can find them."

He nodded and bent to pick up his hat from the night stand, running the brim through his fingers in the only agitated gesture she had ever seen him make. "Then I'll see to the arrangements," he said, his voice hoarse. "It may take a day or so. Will you—would you stay here until then?"

"If you'll let me, yes," she murmured in a small voice.

Without further words, he turned sharply on his heel and left the room. She stood there unmoving for several minutes; then came the drumming of hooves and she knew that Luke had ridden away from the Casa del Ombras. She walked back to the high Spanish bed and sat down upon it. Her lips still tingled from Luke's kisses. Her body remembered the touch of his slim brown fingers upon it. Her heart ached with a pain unparalleled by any she had ever known. She flung herself across the bed and buried her face in the pillow, seeking the cleansing release of tears. Yet even in her anguish, she remained dry eyed, for tears would not come, not now, when they were so desperately needed.

Chapter Twenty-One

Major Edward Wynkoop stroked his mustache thoughtfully as he held aside the lace curtain and looked down into the dirt main street of Denver City. How different the street appeared today, compared to what it had been back in June, when some ghoul had ordered the mutilated bodies of the Hungate family, massacred at Box Elder Creek, to be displayed in the back of a wagon. The result had been near panic among the citizens of Denver and the arousal of great hostility toward the Indians in general, friendly or otherwise.

Ned felt a great deal of warmth for Denver, for he—as a member of the Leavenworth-Lecompton gold-rush party—had helped to found the town back in '58. He and another man had followed the Platte Trail in bitterly cold weather and across unmarked plains to secure a charter for the new settlement. He was proud of the part he had played in Denver's history. After mining for a while, he had run for and been elected to the office of sheriff, and later, when the Colorado First Regiment had been formed, he had been appointed Captain of Company A. He had later distinguished himself at Apache Canyon where he and A Company had been instrumental in aiding then-Major Chivington in outflanking the Texans and capturing their Confederate baggage train. For this, he had been promoted to major, with Chivington moving into the position of colonel. All in all, he was pleased with the progress he had made in his twenty-six years. Ned Wynkoop was convinced that if handled with the delicacy and diplomacy required, the coming negotiations with the principal Indian chiefs would further advance his career, for a successful meeting would mean the prevention of a full-scale Indian war that could take the lives of countless innocent white settlers. Yes, he had come a long way from the security and almost boring conformity of his well-to-do Pennsylvania origins and proved himself in his own right, he thought with satisfaction. He turned back to Governor Evans and raised his eyebrows inquiringly.

"Well, sir? Will you give me your answer? Will you meet with the chiefs, or no?"

Evans's face creased in displeasure. "Wynkoop, you ask the impossible! Damn it, man, these sly red devils have declared war against the United States! What becomes of them now is in the hands of the military authorities. If we were to make treaties with the Cheyenne and Arapahoe now, without first seeing them severely chastised for the atrocities they have committed against the whites this spring and summer, it would appear that we consider ourselves bested by them!"

Wynkoop smiled. "Whipped—by a handful of savages?" He chuckled. "I think not, sir! I have brought the chiefs over four hundred miles to meet with you, and in answer to proclamations *you* yourself made, sir, guaranteeing that all Indians friendly to our cause of peace will not be harmed should they agree to assemble at rendezvous points you have selected, be willing to accept the protection of the military, and obey any and all instructions they shall receive from it. Black Kettle, White Antelope, and the others have agreed to do so. They will be here in Denver in two days. You must hear them out, Governor!" Wynkoop braced his palms upon the table at which Governor John Evans was seated, his expression earnest.

"Your timing is most unfortunate, Ned," Evans insisted. "I have promised to leave tomorrow for the Ute Agency, and as superintendent of Indian affairs for Colorado, I feel I must keep my promise. Perhaps, when I return . . . ?"

"Sir, I must insist that you stay here and tend to this matter, first!" Wynkoop cried, his handsome face reddening with anger. "I have spoken with the chiefs at great length, and I am convinced that they are not only ready but very willing to parley for a lasting peace. They have even demonstrated their willingness to accept the conditions of your proclamation by giving up several white children and a white woman, Laura Roper, that their people had taken captive. This may be our only chance to avoid an Indian war of devastating proportions!"

Evans appeared unconvinced. "Doubtless they have heard that I have caused Washington to raise and equip the Colorado Third Regiment here, and they now fear reprisals for their raids and murders this year. This, Wynkoop, is why these red devils sue for peace—they are afraid!" He took a long swig of whiskey from the glass before him and scowled, wishing Wynkoop would disappear and take his talks of an Indian peace with him. Damn it all, the Colorado Third had been raised at his insistence, based on his urgent representations to Washington that the unit was desperately needed to fight hostile Indian factions committing murder and rapine in

390

the Colorado and surrounding countryside! If he did as
Wynkoop was urging and sued for peace now, it would
appear he had exaggerated matters here and lead
Washington to believe he had put them to needless
trouble and expense. His credibility in the future could
be severely weakened!

Wynkoop straightened up, fists clenched at his sides.
"Very well, Governor. I have done my best to persuade
you to hear the chiefs out. I can do no more. If they take
affront at your refusal to parley with them and decide to
go on the warpath as a result of it, the lives they take will
be upon your head, sir. I would like it to go on written
record that I urged you to see them, and that you
refused."

Evans sprang to his feet, his face thunderous. He
opened his mouth to blast the young major with a
scathing reprimand, then thought better of it. His
shoulders sagged. "Oh, very well, then, damn you,
Wynkoop! I suppose I shall have to see them," he
muttered.

Edward Wynkoop hid a smile and nodded. "Thank
you, Governor Evans. I knew you could be relied upon to
do the sensible thing, sir." Evans only snorted his reply.

A wagon bearing the principal chiefs of the Cheyenne
and Arapahoe tribes rolled into Denver City's main street
two days later, on the morning of September 28, 1864.
Emotions in the town were divided, with some eager to
welcome the chiefs and see the peace treaties quickly
made, and others angry that the hated Indians should go
unpunished for the several raids and massacres that had
broken out at varying times during the year: the Hungate
Massacre at Box Elder Creek, where the two Hungates

and their small children had been brutally murdered and their bodies horribly scalped and mutilated; the raid of the Little Blue Settlement in August, when fifteen were killed and several white women and children taken captive—the very captives that Major Wynkoop had in part succeeded in freeing as a result of his talks with chiefs Black Kettle and White Antelope of the Cheyenne; and numerous other bloody incidents.

Several carriages arrived to meet the chiefs, who were stiff from the long ride in the cramped wagon and appeared ill-at-ease to find themselves in the very heart of a white-eyes' wooden village, surrounded by the very people who had invaded their lands and forced them into the gameless land reservations, who had driven away the buffalo upon which their lives depended with their many settlements and their wholesale killing of the herd for their skins. Black Kettle stared stoically ahead, his deeply lined, copper face impassive as they were taken to Camp Weld to meet with the bluecoat chiefs sent there by the Great White Father in Washington. When all were assembled, John Smith, the interpreter who would translate their words into the tongue of the white man, came to stand at Black Kettle's side. The Indian chief looked curiously about the gathering. There were many of the bluecoat warchiefs here today, as well as the man named Wyn-koop who had brought them here. One, who had the girth of a buffalo bull, towered above all the rest, and Black Kettle fancied that this one held his people in special hatred, for there was a certain light in his eyes that boded ill. This one's name, he had heard, was Chiving-ton. Another man scratched with a feather dipped in black paint upon white leaves fastened together in a great pile, while other white men, not in blue uniforms, looked on.

392

"You have come here today to speak of peace," Governor John Evans began sternly, "or so you would have us believe. We are prepared to listen to what you have to say. Mr. Whitely," he added, turning to the seated Ute agent who was acting as the recorder for the meeting, "it behooves you to take down everything as it is said here, without omissions and with no embellishments of your own. The outcome of these talks may well decide whether or not there will be a full-scale Indian war in this territory." The Agent, Simeon Whitely, nodded solemnly and waited, pen poised, for the council to begin.

Black Kettle rose to standing. He cast his blanket aside and folded his arms over his chest. John Smith moved closer as he began to speak in order to catch every word. He translated:

"We, the chiefs of the Cheyenne and Arapahoe, have come here in trust, following the men that Major Wynkoop assigned to lead us like men going through a great fire with their eyes closed. We are here to ask for peace with the white man. We wish to clasp our hands together in brotherhood and friendship, and put an end to the black cloud that has overshadowed our lives since war between our two people began. Those who have come here with me today are of the same mind and the same heart. It is our wish to return home to our villages today with the glad news that henceforth we may live in peace, that we may sleep without fear. We wish to be looked upon as friends of the white man, not his enemies. My words are true and without deceit. My people will rejoice when I go back to them and tell them that I have clasped hands with you and all the white chiefs here in Den-vah. We have come here freely and without fear of being harmed at your hands."

"Well, I do not believe you, Black Kettle," Evans

countered grimly. "We have heard that you and the chiefs of the Arapahoe have made alliances with the Sioux, and that you intend to unite and wage a great war against the white man, to rid these lands of all of us! Is this how you repay the Great White Father in Washington for the many thousands of dollars he has spent to feed your people and to teach them how to farm so that they will not starve now that the buffalo herds are few? No, Black Kettle, I do not believe your offers of peace. We are not fools!"

Black Kettle's eyes gleamed with anger in his seamed, dark copper face. His lips tightened. "I do not know where you have heard this, but it is a lie!" he said vehemently, after John Smith had translated the governor's words.

The other chiefs spoke all at once then, adding their denials to that of Black Kettle. They insisted that they had made no alliances with the Sioux, nor had they agreed to go to war with any tribe against the whites.

Governor Evans conceded that perhaps they spoke the truth as they perceived it, but that their hostile actions since the spring of that year did not bear out their words. The chiefs acknowledged that this might appear so, but they explained that the older chiefs all wished for peace. It was the young warriors who were hungry for war.

"I have no desire to talk peace with you at this time," Evans told them bluntly. "Soon the plains will be dark with soldiers of the Union. Any peace agreed upon now would be founded on fear of our force alone. What assurance can you give me, Black Kettle, that your braves will not just keep the peace through the winter, when game is scarce and the white man's rations are easy to come by, only to forget the promises you have made in the spring, when game is again plentiful? You may believe that, united, you and the other tribes can rid these lands of the whites, but when the civil war with the rebels in the South is over, the Great White Father will have more than enough soldiers to rid the Plains of all the Indians who oppose him! Remember the proclamation that I made in June, Black Kettle, and show not only by your words but also by your *actions* that you are truly on the side of the government—and our friends!"

"To be on the side of the government—what does this imply?" asked one of the other chiefs.

"You must give assistance to the bluecoat chiefs, act as scouts for them, and do all that they tell you to do. In this way you will prove that you are friends of the white man, by helping him find those Indians who are still fomenting war," Evans explained.

The chiefs conferred together. Finally, Black Kettle spoke for all of them. "I and my brother chiefs will return to our villages and tell the young men what you have said. I cannot speak for them, but I believe it will not be difficult to persuade them to help the soldiers. Our people are weary of fighting. They are hungry. I will speak to them."

"See that you do, Chief," Evans said sternly, "for if they do not come to some agreement with our government, they will be considered our enemies and will be killed." He spoke at length then, urging the chiefs to talk to their people and agree to surrender themselves and submit to military protection until a peace agreement could be drawn up. He asked them to help the government in fighting those tribes who would not enter into a similar agreement with the whites. Old White Antelope, who like Black Kettle had long counseled peace with the whites, then asked, "How can we be certain that our people will be protected from other bluecoat soldiers, should we agree to surrender?"

Governor Evans instructed them all to make arrangements with the military commanders in their respective areas, to insure their safety. He added that they would be under military direction, not his.

The talks continued, Evans trying to determine how many the warring factions of the Apaches, Kiowas, and Comanches numbered, but White Antelope replied that he could not be certain, although there were a great many. Evans then went on to discuss the several atrocities committed by the Indians throughout that year, in an effort to fix blame for these on specific Indians who were suspect.

Though the Cheyenne and Arapahoe chiefs admitted that their people were responsible for some of these, and that they could no longer control some of the fierce, warring societies of young braves within their numbers, they cited the Sioux, Kiowas, and Comanches as being responsible for many others. Bull Bear, who had been silent until this point, added that it was the desire of the Sioux to rid the country of whites. He also pledged his people to fight for the whites and added that he thought peace and friendship between the two would be a good thing.

Colonel Chivington then rose to have his say. The shadow of his massive body, clothed in the dark blue uniform of a colonel of the Union Army, fell across the faces of the gathering. When he spoke, his voice was deep and resonant, as if he yet preached from the pulpit where he had been a Methodist minister before asking for a fighting command. "If you chiefs are ready to lay down your weapons and sincerely wish to keep peace, you can go to Major Wynkoop here, at Fort Lyon, since he is closest to your villages, and surrender to military protection. Be warned that I am not a great war chief, but nevertheless all of the bluecoat soldiers in this area are mine to command. It is my rule to fight all enemies until they are beaten, and willing to surrender and submit to military authority!" His eyes glowed fiercely as he looked at the circle of chiefs.

On this threatening note, the meeting was concluded and the council was adjourned. Embraces and hand-shakes were exchanged between the Indian chiefs, Governor Evans, and Major Wynkoop, and the chiefs agreed to pose for their pictures to be taken.

Edward Wynkoop, returning to his command at Fort Lyon, was well satisfied with the outcome of the proceedings. He held another council with the chiefs there at the fort, urging them to move their villages closer to the fort so that it could be clearly seen that they were under military protection until such time as a peace treaty could be drawn up and officially recognized. The chiefs agreed and further more promised to obtain the release of three more white captives held some distance away.

Ned was understandably pleased with the results of his negotiations and relieved at the promise of peace with the Cheyenne and Arapahoe at least. He believed the old chiefs meant to adhere to the conditions made at Camp Weld, and he intended to fully uphold his side of the agreements.

Six weeks later, Major Edward Wynkoop was relieved of this command and ordered to report to District Headquarters at Fort Riley, Kansas. It transpired that there had been complaints that Indians were running Fort Lyon, and not Major Wynkoop. He was replaced by Major Scott B. Anthony, who carried strict orders to have nothing to do with the Indians whatsoever, to make them no promises, and above all to keep them away from the post. Anthony urged the Cheyenne of old chief Black Kettle to remain where they were camped, along the banks of the Sand Creek, and promised that he would see that they received rations. Black Kettle agreed, although he had planned to move his camp to the Purgatoire.

Ned Wynkoop was greatly perturbed by these events. But having extracted Anthony's promise that he would uphold and follow through with the agreements made by him to the Cheyenne, he left Fort Lyon as his orders had instructed. With him on the stagecoach he carried letters, testifying that all the officers at Fort Lyon supported his policy made with the Indians, and that they felt he had followed all proper courses open to him in his dealings with them. Another letter, signed by many of the civilians who lived in the Arkansas River valley, expressed praise and appreciation for Wynkoop's efforts to avoid bloodshed.

Six weeks later, Major Scott B. Anthony, the new commanding officer of Fort Lyon who had promised both Wynkoop and the Cheyenne that he would uphold all conditions of the treaty of Camp Weld, sent a letter to General Curtis at Leavenworth. In it, he stated that he was adhering to those treaties for the time being to keep the savages subdued, for he had insufficient men to fight them on their own ground. He added that he intended to let matters remain dormant until enough troops could be sent out to take the field against all tribes . . .

Todd Plimmer scowled as he stepped out onto the street from the seedy boarding house in which he had taken lodgings. He had come to Denver from Cherry Creek to get away from his father's persistent harping that he find himself some decent employment and give up his drinking and wild ways. And what had he found in Denver? He snorted. Everything he'd expected, at first. There were saloons and dance halls aplenty here, and the dance hall girls had come running each time he'd crooked his little finger—'til the money his father had staked him with had run out. Then they'd laughed at him. And now, that fool Chivington had established martial law, and everything was closed down, including the dance halls and the saloons. Only the medical dispensary was open, and even the damned grocery store closed up shop after three hours a day! He would have liked to leave Denver and move on to someplace else, but even that was forbidden. Not so much as a wagon was permitted to leave the territory—and for what? So that Chivington—that pompous ass—could complete the enlistment for the newly raised Colorado Third Regiment, that's what, he thought disgustedly. Contractors had been filing into Denver all week in the hopes of securing contracts to equip the new regiment. He'd seen Henry Crowley just yesterday with two of his boys, no doubt after a blacksmithing contract. He spat and cursed under his breath, watching sour faced as a handful of new recruits came swaggering down the main street sporting new uniforms and shouldering the outmoded muzzle-loading muskets that were all the military had been able to acquire to outfit them. Damn fools! he thought, turning away and ducking down an alley. He had one lousy dollar left. Maybe he could buy himself a drink from the back door of one of the saloons. The idea cheered him. He needed a whiskey.

Where the two sidewinders who jumped him at the end of that alley came from, he was never to discover. He woke up an hour later sprawled in the dirt amidst heaps of refuse, with an aching head, a cracked rib or two, and a gash in his chin. His guns, his hat, his dollar, and even his boots were gone. As he dragged himself to his feet, cursing foully, he thought back over the past few months and realized suddenly that everything had been sweet as pie until the day Promise O'Rourke and her half-breed savage had showed him up in front of half of Cherry Creek. Yessirree, everything had been just fine until that day! She'd jinxed him in some way, she had, and he'd never gotten a chance to get even for what she and that Steele son of a bitch had done! He grinned nastily, the effect even more horrific with his swollen, bloody face. She'd better pray she never ran up against him again, by God, or she'd be sorry! And so would he . . .

He halted at the end of the alley, sagging groggily against the clapboard wall. Tarnation, what in the hell was he to do now—without money, without even a pair of goddamned boots to his name? His gaze fell on the recruiting office across the street, and he hesitated only briefly before limping toward it. Inwardly, he shrugged. If you couldn't beat 'em, it was better to join 'em, he supposed. Hell, he didn't have much of a choice!

Chapter Twenty-Two

Promise stood looking at herself in the cheval glass mirror that Margita had brought to her room earlier. She wondered how it could possibly be that her reflection could look so unfragmented when she felt splintered into millions of tiny, sharp shards that could never be put together and made whole again.

Her reflection revealed a slender, composed young woman, clad in a divided skirt of butterscotch-yellow buckskin. A matching short vest, fringed at the lower edges, contrasted well with a plaid blouse of brown and yellow. The braided rawhide belt with the fancy silver buckle set with turquoise stones emphasized her small waist. She wore a dark brown Stetson and knee-high boots of tooled Spanish leather. The colors of the outfit complimented her pale golden skin and the fall of cornsilk hair that swung in a shining mass down past her shoulders, yet she could find little pleasure in her appearance. *That girl in the mirror isn't me*, she thought. *She's someone I don't even know!* The essence of being that had been Promise O'Rourke was lost; it had been left wandering out there somewhere, beyond the *casa*. All that remained of that vulnerable creature now was the shell she had lived in, the love she felt for Luke Steele, the man who had destroyed her, and, oh, yes, her hatred of him! Strange, that the love should linger even now. Perhaps that was her punishment for giving herself to him while knowing in her heart that he was only using her.

She turned and crossed the room, kneeling before a Spanish dresser of dark wood and pulling out the drawers. From them she took the worn skirts and blouses, bodices, pantalets, and stockings she had brought with her to the Casa del Ombras. She piled her belongings haphazardly into the open trunk beneath the window sill, then went to the heavy armoire in one corner and took out the beaded moccasions Flattens-Grass had given her in Black Kettle's camp weeks before. There. That was it. She was ready to go. She made to close the trunk, then paused, spying the walking stick with the horse's head that had belonged to her pa propped in one corner. She frowned. She must be even more fragmented than she had thought to have forgotten that, the only thing, the only personal thing, that she had left of him. She put the walking stick in the trunk atop her clothes and shut and fastened the trunk with an air of finality.

"*Promesa*?"

Looking up, she saw Joaquin standing at her window.

"Joaquin," she said softly as she walked to the window. Dear Joaquin. "Did you come to say *adios*?"

He shook his head. "No, *niña*. I came to ask you not to do this thing! Your place is here, at the Shadow S, with *el señor*." His gentle brown eyes were grave, earnest.

"You're wrong, Joaquin. My place is nowhere—certainly not here with Luke!" Her tone was bitter.

"It is here," he repeated stubbornly. "Whatever may have passed between you and him, he truly loves you, *Promesa*. And you love him! Do not deny it, little

402

one. Can there be so much pain in a woman's eyes if there is no love in her heart? One of you must reach out, mend that which is broken. A man tries to be hard; always he must be strong, even when something inside him cries out to be tender, to put that which is inside him into words. It is not easy, for in doing so a man fears that something of the man in him will be lost. But a woman is all feeling! She does not hide behind strength; she does not need to pretend that she is always strong, always in control. She can cry. She can hurt inside. She can say the words to restore a man's faith in himself, or soothe a baby's tears. Say them now, *Promesa*! Tell him that you love him; that you forgive him!"

"No. What you ask of me is impossible, Joe. I can't do it!" she cried, clenching her fists. "The hurt is too deep. He took everything from me, don't you see? I gave him my heart and my trust. I forgot my self-respect and my pride in doing so. Nothing mattered but having him in my life, loving him, even if he didn't love me! And he destroyed me. He *used* me!"

"At first, *si*, it was so. But I know him, *niña*. I know *el señor* very well. As the days passed, I saw the confusion in his eyes, the jealousy when *Señor* Cantrell looked at you. He wanted to halt what he was doing, to put a stop to it. But by the time he had found the courage to do so, it was too late. He could have said nothing. He easily could have let you believe he had simply come to love you as you loved him, for you did not remember him as the man who shot your *padre*, did you, *niña*? He did not take this easy way. He knew that for you to forgive him, for all to be right between the two of you, he had to tell you the truth. Does that count for nothing?"

"*Truth!*" she spat out. "He doesn't know the meaning of the word! I could forgive him for what he did to my

403

father," she gritted, "but never, never for what he has done to me! I hate him, do you hear me? I hate him!" Her breasts heaved against the plaid shirt, and her eyes glittered with fierce emerald fire. "I know you mean well, Joaquin. You've been a true friend to me when I needed one the most. But you are wasting your time, *amigo mio.*"

The gentle brown eyes looked upon her with such sadness she felt as if she had struck him.

"You are right," he said softly. "I am wasting my time. The *Promesa* that I knew has gone, as I feared. I do not think she will ever come back. . . . Try to find her again, *niña.* She is a woman worthy of the search. *Adiós. Vaya con dios, señorita!*"

With that, he turned on his heel and strode from the window, leaving Promise staring after him. Her hurt at his curt farewell was replaced by anger. What right had he to speak to her so, to try to tell her what to do? *The right of a friend who cares*, the nagging voice of her conscience insisted, but she smothered that little voice with arguments born of pride.

In a matter of minutes, she would be leaving the Casa del Ombras and the ranch that she had grown to love. In a matter of hours, she would be joining the wagon train that would carry her back the way she had come just two months before, and on to Fort Lyon. There she would take a stage east toward an uncertain future. Her trunk stood closed and ready. Farewells had already been said the night before to the *vaqueros* and cowboys, and to Margita, bless her, all of whom had become a part of her life in such a short space of time. There was nothing else left to do except to pick up the little drawstring purse, in which Luke had tucked her pay as one of his hands, and leave here. She had refused his offer of any money other than that which she knew was her due. She would make it on her own from here on. Somehow. A dry lump lodged in the back of her throat as she looked out of the window for the last time. Never would she have dreamed it could be so hard to leave here! But it was . . .

"Ready, *desperada*?"

She turned to see Luke standing in the open doorway.

"Yes," she acknowledged, rapidly pulling herself together. "There's just my trunk to be loaded onto the buckboard."

He nodded. "I'll see to it." He looked her up and down, yet the hunger with which his dark eyes had always raked her was now replaced by an intensity of a different nature. It seemed as if he was trying to commit each detail of her appearance to memory. "You look beautiful," he said huskily. "My mother would have been pleased to see someone wearing those clothes at last. She made them for a trip to San Francisco she and my father planned to take, but she died before she ever wore them. You do them justice, *desperada*."

"Thank you, but I feel wrong wearing them. Perhaps I should—"

"No," he cut in, "we went over this yesterday. Singing Wind would have preferred that they be put to good use. She hated waste of any kind. And I know she would have approved of my giving them to you. My father put all of her things away after she died, saying he couldn't bear to look at them. I guess the pain of remembering when he looked at them was just too much for him." A bleak look came into his eyes, as if now he knew how Thomas Steele had felt. He turned abruptly away and went to the trunk beneath the window. "Let's be going, then," he said, his voice strangely hoarse. He lifted the trunk onto his shoulder and strode from the room.

Promise looked for one last time about the room, then

hurried after him.

Two hours later she was seated on a rolling wagon beside a bonneted young woman by the name of Carol Bushley, staring straight ahead but seeing nothing as the cumbersome Conestoga, drawn by four sturdy yellow oxen, rumbled out of Santa Fe.

Carol kept up a lively stream of chatter, not seeming to notice Promise's silence in her own animation.

". . . and so Larry and me were real happy to have you along, isn't that so, Larry, honey?"

Larry Bushley, a tall, stocky man with an attractive, weather-beaten face that seemed perpetually creased in a smile, winked and nodded at his wife from the back of the enormous brown horse he rode alongside the wagon. "Sure is, Carol. Excuse me, ladies. I think I'll ride on ahead and have a few words with the wagon master."

He rode away, and Carol turned to look curiously at the pretty little thing beside her, surprised to see that she appeared ready to cry. She reached out and squeezed Promise's hand. "There, there. It'll be all right, honey, you'll see," she reassured her, not knowing what it was that was upsetting her so.

Promise nodded, then looked back over her shoulder, hoping against hope to see Luke still there. But no, he was gone, rider and horse swallowed up by the noisy crowds of the *plaza's mercado*, market, this morning.

The wagon train rolled down out of the foothills of the mountains, and the massive Conestogas that had seemed so large and cumbersome were suddenly dwarfed by the endless expanses of the plains. Promise listened half-heartedly to Carol's chatter, of how the Bushleys had intended to go on to California but had decided to return to the Colorado Territory and settle there instead, since the wagon trails west had been closed because of Indian trouble. She had added a few comments about the beauty of Colorado and its mountains for the sake of politeness, and Carol had beamed and seemed even more taken by excitement.

"Of course, the colonel in Santa Fe wasn't too pleased that we all decided to go on back," Carol said with a dismissing shrug, "but our feeling was that there's safety in numbers, right? Why, there's twenty-one wagons in all, and over thirty men, not to mention women and children! It's not like we were heading over the plains alone. What could possibly happen to so many of us?" She grinned, her snub nose wrinkling amidst a sunny spattering of freckles that went with the pretty red-gold of her hair. "We've enough bullets and rifles to fight off a whole parcel of Injuns!"

Promise nodded, yet Carol's airy confidence did not still the doubts that fluttered in her own breast. "Wait, *desperada*, please," Luke had implored her a few days earlier. "Stay here 'til the spring; then I'll see you safely to Fort Lyon myself and onto the stage. Colonel Wharton told me the Comanche are attacking anything that moves out there on the plains!" But she had refused to wait, knowing that if she stayed until the spring, she might fall under his dangerous spell yet again and succumb to his lies. She was still too painfully vulnerable to his kiss and caress, her hatred of him too fragile a shell about her heart, to run that risk. "No," she had told him stubbornly, "I'm leaving, Luke, one way or the other. If you won't make the arrangements for me, I'll see to them myself. I won't—*can't* stay here!" He'd suggested finding her some lodgings in Santa Fe, but yet again she had shook her head, and finally he had realized that she could

407

not be persuaded. Reluctantly, he had inquired about a wagon train of disillusioned pioneers heading back toward the Colorado Territory, and he had found her a place with it and with the Bushleys, a young couple he had felt would prove good traveling companions. And so, here she was. Even the possibility of an Indian attack on the train had not terrified her as much as the thought of staying at the Shadow S with Luke.

The days blurred and ran together as the wagon train moved steadily northwest, and the very monotony helped Promise to shake off the numbness that had enveloped her like a cocoon on leaving Santa Fe. She took turns at driving the oxen team with the Bushleys, and when their wagon fouled on a steep incline and had to be pushed, she added her shoulder to theirs to see it safely up and over. The wagons ahead and behind became neighbors to their own on the trail, and their supper each night was a shared meal, the three families congregating about the fire within the drawn-up circle of wagons to eat, to talk, to sing, and share hopes and dreams for the future. Promise quickly became a popular member of their circle, for the women admired her willingness to help with anything that needed doing, and the children ran to her for stories or games or to be rocked to sleep in her arms as she hummed them a lullaby. The men found her lovely and were pleasantly surprised to find her character had none of the pertness and pridefulness that pretty misses were reputed to be full of.

Yet despite her acceptance and her popularity, she was of them, but not one of them. The women had their husbands, their children, their families, while she had no one. They had futures to look forward to which would be shared by those they loved, while she saw only a question mark on her life's horizon.

She took her shawl from the back of the wagon and went to the fire to tell Carol that she planned to walk for a spell before turning in. It was a crisp, cool night, and the sky was filled with stars. From other campfires in the circle came the sleepy voices of children and the low talk of their parents. Carol and Larry sat side by side, her head resting on his shoulder, a glow in her wide blue eyes that Promise recognized as the radiance of love and desire. There would be no protest if she left the two of them alone, she knew.

"I think I'll take a walk," she told Carol. "It sure is a pretty night."

Carol looked up at Promise, then uncertainly at Larry. "Give me a minute to fetch my shawl, hon," she said. "You shouldn't go off on your own."

Promise pressed her back down. "No, I'll be fine," she insisted. "Stay right where you are."

She walked quickly away from them, down the circle of wagons. People called out in greeting as she passed by, offering her companionship or coffee or both. Smiling, Promise refused them all with thanks, saying that she needed to stretch her legs after riding all day on the wagon.

She went between two wagons and left the protective circle the train had made, wanting to be alone with her thoughts. She gazed up at the stars, remembering nights when she and Luke had marveled at their glittering beauty together in the afterglow of making love. The night wind brushed against her cheek, cool and sweet and evocative of his breath against her face. She shuddered. *Luke!* She clasped herself about the arms. *Luke, oh, Luke!*

"Promise?"

The voice sent her spinning around, coinciding so perfectly with her silent cry that for one, joyful second, she thought it was he. Her eyes plumbed the shadows, seeing the glint of blond hair from beneath a Stetson, the profile of a familiar face in silhouette.

"Cay?" she asked hesitantly, coming toward him.

"It is you!" Cay exclaimed, taking two rapid strides to meet her. He bent and swept her into his arms, twirling her once before setting her down upon the ground again. He held her in a fierce bear hug and gave her a smacking kiss full upon the lips. "Hell, girl," he growled huskily, "you don't know how many nights I've lain awake wanting to do just that!"

She laughed happily. "After that kiss, I can guess, I do believe!" she teased. "What are you doing here, with the train?"

"I hung around in Santa Fe for a while," Cay told her, "sort of hoping you'd take me up on my offer and come after me. When you didn't, I figured to drown my sorrows in liquor," he confessed, "and spent a night or two in the calaboose for my trouble! After that, I knew I had to put distance between myself and Miz Promise or go *loco*. I hired on as an extra gun with the train. How about you?" He looked over his shoulder, sudden apprehension in his eyes. "Where's Luke?"

Her shoulders sagged. "He's not here. I—I came on the train alone." She sighed heavily. "You were right, Cay, all along."

He nodded. "Maybe," he agreed noncommittally. "Maybe not." He chewed thoughtfully on his lower lip. "Were you—were you planning on looking for me?"

She looked up into his eager face, the hope shining in his blue eyes like the stars above them. "I don't know exactly what it is I'm looking for just yet, Cay," she told him honestly.

He grunted in understanding. "I guess I can understand that. I rushed you once, Promise. I won't make that mistake again." He grinned suddenly, his teeth showing white in the gloom. "But if you find you're ready to take me up on my offer while I'm busy 'not rushing' you, you be sure to let me know, you hear, honey?"

Her laughter tinkled on the night. She went up on tiptoe and kissed the rough angle of his cheek. "I will, you crazy cowboy, you!" she promised.

He took her elbow and they walked for a while, Cay telling her of his plans to start a ranch up in the Colorado Territory.

"I figured horses were more to my liking than cows," he said seriously. "See, that's how I came by my name, corralling and breaking horses back in Wyoming. When I was just a little shaver, my pa pinned the name Cayuse on me, seeing as how I couldn't stay away from his horses. The name stuck and got twisted around and shortened some, until it was Cay—as in Kay—Cantrell!"

Promise laughed, finding his good nature infectious. "What was the name that you were given when you were born?" she asked curiously.

Cay chuckled. "If you want to find that out, you'll have to marry me, honey!" he teased.

"You drive a mighty hard bargain, Mister Cantrell!" she teased him back.

"Whose wagon are you riding with?" he asked as they strolled along.

"The Bushleys," she supplied. "Do you know them?"

"I know Larry, the husband. Fine man, too—and damned good with a rifle."

"They're both real nice, and so kind to me," Promise agreed. She stopped and turned to him. "Their wagon's the next one down. I guess I'll say good night to you now, Cay. I'm real glad you're here. I don't feel as lonely as I did before," she confessed, darting him a shy, sweet smile.

"I'm happy to hear it, Promise," he said huskily. He reached out to put his arms around her, then thought better of it and instead bent down and gave her a chaste kiss upon the brow. "Good night, *caballera!*" he called after her as, cheeks pink in the shadows, she hurried back to the Bushleys' wagon.

"Good night, Cay!" she called over her shoulder.

Cay grinned. "Whhoo-whee!" he crowed softly. Face still split in a broad smile, he almost ran back to his horse to take his turn at riding sentinel on the train. He'd never put much faith in praying before, but by golly, it looked like it had come through for him this time! *Oh, sweet Promise!* he thought as he swung astride his horse and cantered off into the night.

Chapter Twenty-Three

Cay's presence on the wagon train vastly improved Promise's spirits. True, she still felt deeply saddened whenever she thought of Luke and knew it would be a long, long time before the pain of loving him and being betrayed by him wore off, if it ever did. Yet Cay's good-natured teasing and flirting made her forget, or at least dulled the ache in her heart whenever they were together. With a maturity she had not had before, she realized that she and Luke had never shared the easy camaraderie that she and Cay shared. The physical attraction between them had simply been too intense and volatile. She enjoyed the light-hearted banter with Cay when he came to their campfire each night, and she began to look forward to the evenings as the high points of her days. Their neighbors on the train, the Evans and the McDonalds, and the Bushleys exchanged knowing, pleased smiles when they saw the way the handsome cowboy looked at Promise, and the smile that lit up her lovely face as he took his seat at her side.

"I'd just bet there'll be a weddin' before long!" Carol whispered in her husband's ear. "I just know it!"

Larry grinned and tweaked his wife's cheek affectionately. "Don't you women ever let up on your matchmaking?" he teased. "How in the heck are they going to get married out here?"

"Reverend Simon can do it," Carol said firmly.

"Bob Simon's pa? He's a preacher?" Larry asked, this news a revelation to him.

"He sure is—as you'd know *if* you'd come to the services he holds every Sunday morning!" Carol said accusingly, though her blue eyes danced with merriment.

"Honey, you've told me so many darned times that I'm perfect, I didn't figure there was any need for me to go to church!" Larry quipped innocently and ducked as Carol tossed her calico bonnet at his head.

Cay and Promise exchanged smiles at the young couple's whispered bantering. The Bushleys had been married for only six months and still carried on like newlyweds, much to the delight of the wagon train members who derived great pleasure in good-naturedly teasing the two of them.

Carol jumped to her feet. "Promise, could you give me a hand? We're needing brush for the fire," she explained loudly. "Let's leave these two men alone for a while— give them a chance to miss us while we're gone."

Promise got to her feet. "Brush? But there's a whole heap of it—"

"Shush, now, don't you think I know that?" Carol chided, leading the way around the wagon. She stopped and whirled about to face Promise. "Truth is, I have a secret I want to share with you, sort of ask your opinion on!"

"What is it?" Promise asked, smiling.

"Well, I haven't said a word to my Larry yet, but Promise, I think I'm going to have a baby!" Her eyes shone.

"No!" Promise exclaimed happily. "When?"

"Not right now, silly," Carol laughed as Promise's eyes went immediately to her flat belly. "Around March of the new year, I reckon, if I've figured it right. My monthly hasn't come around for two months now. What do you think, Promise? Do you think I'm carryin'?"

Promise nodded. "I don't know what else it could be, Carol. Have you had any sickness of a morning? I recollect my mama saying it started that way."

"I've felt a bit queasy in the mornings, I do believe," Carol said thoughtfully. "Could that be it?"

Promise hugged her. "I'm sure it is! Oh, I'm so happy for you, Carol!" Carol grinned back.

"I aim to tell Larry tonight. He'll be like a speckled pup with two tails, he'll be that proud!" Carol said, looking decidedly proud herself. "Come on, let's go back to the fire."

Giggling, the two young women returned to the fire and Cay's and Larry's suspicious glances. Soon after, Carol and Larry said their good-nights to everyone and headed for the back of their wagon. Carol threw Promise a wink over her shoulder as they left, and Promise winked back.

She rested her chin in her palm and gazed dreamily into the campfire, smiling up at Cay as he rested his arm about her shoulders.

"I'll give you a penny for your thoughts," he offered. "And if you're thinkin' about me, I'll raise it to a nickel!"

"I can't lie, Mister Cantrell," she said solemnly. "I was thinking about . . . Carol and Larry!" He tugged her hair in mock anger and she giggled. "Truly I was," she insisted.

"What about them?"

"I can't say. It's supposed to be a secret." She pressed her lips firmly together. "Wild horses couldn't drag it out of me!"

"Maybe not, but I'd just bet I could," Cay threatened, "with a tickle or two!" He lunged toward her.

"Don't you dare, Cay!" she warned him, hurriedly backing away. "Stop it, now. Everyone'll be looking at us!"

"Let them!" Cay challenged. "Don't you know the entire wagon train is placing bets on how long it'll take us to ask Reverend Simon to tie the knot?"

He regretted his words the instant he had said them. It was as if a curtain dropped over her features at the mention of a possible marriage between them, removing her from him. He cursed inwardly, then clicked his teeth, muttering, "Darn it, why'd I have to go and bring that up?" He reached out and tilted her face up to his. "I'm sorry, honey. I promised you, didn't I, and now I'm rushing you all over again. I won't mention it any more."

She shot him a grateful smile. "Thanks, Cay. I know how hard it is for you, honest I do. But I feel like I've been turned inside out by Luke, and all the hurt is on the surface, raw and smarting still."

"Did he ever tell you that . . . well, what it was you wanted to hear from him?"

"That he loved me?" She smiled bitterly. "Oh, yes! When it was too late to make any difference. I didn't believe him, anyhow. Cay, how could I, after he'd told me why it was he'd really brought me with him to New Mexico? You know how I felt about Luke. I was so certain that one day he'd feel the same. When he told me it had all been part of his plan to avenge himself on my pa, I went crazy for a while, I guess." She told him in halting tones how she had come to shoot Luke, and of the days that followed. "I intended to ruin him, Cay!" she said with a little shiver of horror at her own lust for revenge.

"I stampeded the herd. I would have burned him out, too, if I hadn't gotten sick. When I woke up back at the Casa del Ombras, I realized that I was no better than he—that I'd better leave before my hatred took over and I lost myself in it."

Cay nodded. He glanced up at her, almost holding his breath as he asked, "Then you don't love Luke any more?"

Her expression cut him to the quick, filled as it was with a desperate yearning, a pain he had never noticed before, so well had she kept it hidden. "I didn't say that, Cay," she said quickly, her voice little higher than a whisper. She jumped suddenly to her feet and shook out her skirts, tossing back her loose hair with a quick, light gesture that succeeded in ridding her face of all traces of what he had glimpsed there seconds before. "I've a mind to walk a spell before turning in." She patted her belly. "That was some supper Carol fixed, wouldn't you say?" She smiled. "I figure a walk would help settle it some. Are you coming with me?"

He nodded and unstretched his great length as he set his Stetson atop his blond head, hoping she would not notice his silence. Truth was, right now words were just choking up in his throat, words he knew he'd never be able to say to her; not now; maybe never . . .

A full moon illumined the circle of wagons, and their canvas tops gleamed like great white ghosts in its silvery light as Promise and Cay walked. The merry strains of a fiddle sawed lustily by someone carried on the night air, as did the distant, eerie howl of coyotes. Promise pulled her shawl more tightly about her shoulders against the chill, matching two of her smaller paces to each one of Cay's long, easy strides. He'd gone quiet since they left the fire, and she knew his reason for doing so. Yet she was

417

hard put to think of anything she could say that would help and not at the same time give him cause to hope her heart would do a sudden about-face, and that she would return his love.

There was an awkwardness between them when they murmured their good-nights at the Bushleys' wagon later, and after he had left, Promise realized that Cay had not given her his customary farewell kiss upon the brow. She shrugged and clambered up the wagon's steps. Poor Cay. She knew how he felt. Oh, yes, she knew! She undressed in the shadows, aware of Carol and Larry across the wagon bed from her, arms entangled in a close embrace as they slept, their deep breathing filling the pitch-black darkness inside the wagon. How she envied them their certainty in the love they felt for each other, so blatantly obvious to everyone. Sometimes, she'd noticed, words were unnecessary between them, they were so perfectly tuned to each other's thoughts and feelings. Would she ever know that kind of deep and enduring love, she wondered, or would she, as her mother had, spend the rest of her life yearning for a man she could not have?

The day dawned fair and clear and unusually warm for the month of September. Before the pink flush of dawn had fully faded from the sky, the families of the wagon train were up and preparing their teams of oxen or mules and their wagons for yet another day's traveling. Women hurried to cook breakfast and shake out bedding before Joel Schooner, the wagon master, gave the signal to "Roll 'em!" The smell of frying bacon and corn bread wafted on the dewy morning air, and Promise stepped eagerly down from the wagon to give Carol a hand.

The young woman was humming as she worked, and she flashed Promise a smile as she came toward the fire.

"Well, Miss O'Rourke!" She grinned. "I'd about decided you were fixin' to deny us the pleasure of your company today!"

Promise stuck out her tongue. "How anyone has the right to be so darned perky first thing in the morning has me beat!" she scolded teasingly, then smiled herself, and added, "though I'd say you had more right than most, under the circumstances, Miz Bushley! Did you tell him?"

Carol nodded vigorously. "I did indeed! He went out of that wagon this morning with a strut that would have done credit to a prize rooster! 'Bye, Papa!' I told him, and I swear, Promise, if he'd smiled any wider, his face would have cracked clean in two! He was so tickled with the news, he kept me up half the night tryin' out names for his 'boy'!"

Promise laughed. "Where's the proud papa now?"

"He went to help the Fullers with their wagon. Seems they've been having trouble with it since yesterday," Carol supplied. "Coffee?"

Smiling her thanks, Promise accepted a mug of scalding black coffee from Carol. "Lord, that's good!" she murmured appreciatively. "Did—did Cay come by this morning?"

Carol hid a grin, stirring the skillet of sizzling bacon without looking up. "Yes, he did. He left word to tell you he'll come by the wagon later, when he gets back."

"Back from where?" Promise asked.

"He and some of the others are scouting the trail up ahead. He reckoned he'd be back before we bed down for the night." She gave Promise a sly side-glance from her bright blue eyes. "He sure is handsome, Promise, and he

419

seems real taken with you. Folks are saying—"

"I reckon I know what *folks* are saying!" Promise cut in. "But folks are wrong!" Her smile took the sting from her words and Carol rocked back on her haunches and looked at Promise with her spoon brandished in midair.

"He loves you, honey. It's as plain as the nose on his face. You could do a lot worse than a good man like Cay Cantrell. He dreams big, and I'd say he's got the guts to make those dreams come true, with the right woman at his side." She jabbed her spoon into the air to add emphasis to her words. "I'm a plain talker, Promise. I reckon you know that by now. He'd be better for you than Luke Steele! Your Luke's a mighty handsome man, and any woman that would say he isn't must be blind. But . . . he's a half-breed. What sort of future would the two of you have together, even if he does have a ranch and all? Why, as his wife, you'd be shunned by your own people, honey! You know what they say about women who take up with Indians! You'd best put any notions about Luke aside, for your own good."

"I already have," Promise said softly. "But, tell me this, Carol, would you give up your Larry just because folks badmouthed you?"

Carol appeared startled. "Larry? Why, no, of course not! I love him. I wouldn't give a hoot what folks said!" She frowned, realizing what Promise had been getting at.

"Nor would I have, Carol, not if things had turned out different. Now, we'd best get this fire raked over and our things put away. Mister Schooner looks ready to hit the trail."

Sure enough, Joel Schooner's bellow to "Roll 'em! Stretch out!" came within minutes of their packing the cooking utensils in back of the wagon. Promise ate a hurried breakfast while they rode, a piece of corn bread and a rasher or two of bacon. The rolling of the wagon left her feeling a little queasy after she had eaten it, and she wondered fleetingly if she were coming down with something.

The wagon train made good time that morning, moving like a centipede in a steady northwesterly direction. The shouts of the teamsters and the cracking of their bullwhips over the backs of their teams, the rattle and rumble of the wagons' wheels, and the steady drum of the horses', mules', and oxens' hooves were familiar sounds that had long since ceased to intrude upon either the two women's conversation or Promise's thoughts on the rare moments when she allowed herself to fall silent and pensive. From time to time, the wagon master would ride along the cavalcade of wagons and urge the stragglers to catch up. Promise took her turn at the reins, feeling sweat begin a slow trickling down her spine and in the valley between her breasts long before noon. She wiped salty perspiration from her brow with the back of her hand and grimaced at Carol, who was doing the same. "It surely is a hot one today," she remarked, and Carol nodded fervent agreement.

"I'm so glad I'm not further along with this baby," she murmured, fanning her sunburned, freckled face with her bonnet. "That poor Annie Fuller must be having a rough time of it, what with her being so far gone and all. Larry said her man told him the babe's due any day now. I'll bet she'll be real happy when it comes. Can't be easy tending her other young ones carrying that extra weight and having to sit all day on this darned wagon into the bargain. I swear, I've got callouses in places that aren't hardly decent to mention!"

"I know what you mean!" Promise laughed, remembering an adobe *posada* in Santa Fe where she had once

421

thought exactly the same thing.

They ate the noonday meal atop the wagon—leftover corn bread and beans from supper the night before. Larry rode up and tied his horse to the rear of their wagon, clambering up front to take the reins from Promise. He'd brought with him a small blue crock filled with fresh milk.

"This here's for you, little mama," he told Carol, planting a lusty kiss on her peeling nose. "When I told Annie Fuller our good news, she insisted I bring you some fresh milk from their cow and wouldn't take no for an answer."

"Why, that's real nice of her!" Carol exclaimed, sipping the creamy milk with relish. "When we stop this evening, remind me to drop by their wagon and thank her. Promise?" she offered, holding out the jug to her.

"No, thank you," she refused. "My stomach's a mite fickle today."

The heat waned a little as the day wore on, and by early afternoon the dazzling blue sky of morning was fluffed over with white clouds behind which the sun played hide-and-seek. Gray clouds streamed across the western sky, promising rain to come before nightfall. Still the wagon train crawled on, through miles of rock-littered, rolling land where only the hardy mesquite or Spanish dagger, sagebrush or tumbleweed broke the rolling amber of the plains. Carol was dozing in the wagon bed, and Promise lolled sleepily on the driver's perch beside Larry as he drove, when Joel Schooner's voice cut through her drowsiness like a knife.

"Close up! Close up!" he roared, and immediately the wagons began pulling around in a defensive circle.

Promise, jerked wide awake by both the cry and the edge of panic to it, sat bolt upright as Larry laid his whip across the oxens' backs. She heard him curse as he had never before cursed in her presence as he hauled on the reins to turn the team. Frightened cries carried now from the other wagons and from one of them a child set up a wailing lament.

"What is it? What's wrong?" she asked Larry anxiously, dread uncoiling in her belly like a rattler ready to strike.

"Look up there, on the rise!" Larry gritted. "You'll see what's wrong! Goddamn! Goddamn!"

Promise looked, and her heart skipped a beat, and her stomach churned over with terror. *Dear Lord, no! Not again, please!* she prayed silently, her fingers clenching over the folds of her skirts.

On the gentle rise ahead sat several dozen Indians. Even from this distance, Promise could see their long, black hair fluttering in the breeze, the eagle feathers atop their lances dancing in its current as, like statues, they looked down at the wagon train below from their ponies' backs.

"Get in back and wake Carol," Larry ordered thickly. "Then stay down and don't come back out!" He grabbed his rifle and hurriedly jumped down from the wagon.

Promise crawled in back and scurried over to Carol, shaking her shoulder to wake her, then spinning away toward her trunk which was stored by the rear opening. She flung up the lid, rummaging beneath her clothes and flinging them aside as she reached for her guns in the trunk's depths.

"What is it? What's wrong?" Carol cried, sitting up.

"Indians!" Promise told her, her breathing rasping and rapid in her panic. Fingers trembling, she found a box of cartridges and hurriedly loaded her six-shooters, cursing the panic that caused those fingers to be clumsier

423

than usual. "Do you know how to use a gun?"

"Dear God! Yes, yes, I do! Larry taught me how before we left— Oh, Promise, where is Larry?"

"He went to talk with Schooner," Promise told her. "He's fine. He told us both to stay here."

Carol swallowed. "Then give me a gun," she asked, her voice little more than a harsh whisper. "I don't plan to just sit here!"

"Me neither!" Promise said grimly.

They heard the furious tattoo of many hooves from beyond the wagon then, and the whooping of the Comanche as they swept down the hillside to attack the train. Promise and Carol crawled to the front of the wagon and peered out, and the sight that met their eyes drove the breath from their lungs in fear.

Over two dozen braves wheeled about the wagon train, which was spread in a horseshoe shape since the teamsters had not had sufficient time to form a defensive circle. Their faces were painted in garish, frightening reds, yellows, and black, and they were armed to the teeth as they rode.

"My God, look at them!" Carol gasped. "We'll never be able to—"

"Stop it!" Promise ordered sharply. "We outnumber them! We'll get enough of them to send the others running!" she said with far more conviction than she felt. "Get a hold on yourself, honey! We must keep a clear head and be ready to shoot when—if—the time comes."

Biting her lower lip fiercely, Carol nodded and stiffened her spine.

Now the whoops of the Comanche were interspersed with the sharp cracks of gunfire and the screams of horses. From their hiding place, Promise saw Joel

Schooner rise up from behind a wagon and take aim at the stream of braves as they careened about the train in a wide circle. She stifled a scream as an arrow took him full between the eyes and he reeled back and lay still, slumped across the shafts. The Comanche who had killed him leaped from his pony's back and straddled the lifeless body, and both women saw the flash of his knife in the sunlight as he took the wagon master's scalp and brandished it dripping above his head with a whoop of victory. Others of his war party leaped from their horses' backs now and sprinted lithely for the wagons. Some reeled to the ground, bullets halting them dead in their tracks; yet others leaped inside the canvas-covered sanctuaries that had now become little more than bloody coffins for the terrified women and children huddled inside them. Their screams ruptured the air as the Indians snatched them up like rag dolls and flung them to the ground outside to lie broken and bleeding and await the death that would be theirs. Promise let out a wail of anguish as she saw them murdered before her eyes: children she had played games with, told stories to about the campfire at night; their mothers, with whom she'd sat sewing and exchanging recipes and small talk. Some of the younger children were snatched up by still-mounted braves and flung across their ponies, too dazed by the horror of it all to protest or even cry as they were carried off.

Angus McDonald, a great, bearded Scot with the girth befitting his blacksmith's trade, bellowed with rage as the savages turned now to his wagon, where his wife Betty and his three little ones were hiding. Wielding his empty rifle like a club, he laid open the skull of one marauder and cracked another in the belly. As a third leaped aboard his wagon, he heard Betty's high, ululating scream and threw his full weight upon the brave. Furiously, they grappled in the dust, first one then the other on top, but at last Angus's great bulk lay still, his head lolling back from the enormous slash across his throat that had almost severed his head from his body. Carol retched, moaning softly as in seconds Angus's fiery red hair fluttered bloodily from the brave's lance. Then came a shot from the wagon, followed by a second and a third. Each one made Promise and Carol jump in fright. The Indian who had taken Angus's scalp leaped up to look inside the wagon turning away with disappointment clearly written on his face, and Promise knew that Betty and her children had escaped the Comanches forever.

Their own wagon rocked as Larry sprang up into it, his eyes wild. He immediately took up position and began firing shot after shot through the open rear of the wagon. His arrival galvanized the two stunned women into action, and they both began firing through the front-side of the wagon, taking turns to reload while each covered the other.

"Those red bastards!" Larry cursed, a sob of rage choking out from between his clenched teeth. "They're firing the wagons!" He began shooting again with renewed ferocity, whooping in triumph each time a Comanche fell under his bullet. "Save a shot or two," he ordered hoarsely, and Promise and Carol both knew why he had ordered them to do so without asking. They knew only too well . . .

The acrid odor of smoke grew as the minutes passed and more and more wagons were put to the torch. Whoops and yells of blood lust and victory continued, mingled still with screams and curses and shots. Promise's eyes smarted, and her throat was sore, making swallowing painful.

426

"Larry! We've only a few bullets left!" Carol cried. "What in God's name do we do?"

Larry turned to offer his terrified wife some words of comfort. His eyes widened in horror as he saw a Comanche brave appear in the opening behind the two women, tomahawk raised above his head. Hurriedly he jerked the rifle to his shoulder and fired, but it was empty.

"Damn you, *noooo!*" he screamed as he flung himself across the wagon, shielding Carol and Promise with his body.

Crushed beneath Larry, Promise gave vent to the long, high-pitched scream she had held in for so long, dimly hearing her own cry echoed by Carol's hysterical shrieks. Then something warm and wet and crimson came gushing down from the man above them, and Larry's head lolled back, eyes turned skyward. The Comanche hefted the body aside and grinned down at the two shrieking women below. As his hand knotted in Promise's hair, she saw his painted face split in a smile of animalistic pleasure. Then all went black and silent as she slipped mercifully into oblivion . . .

Chapter Twenty-Four

She came around minutes later to the sound of sobbing. Opening her eyes, she saw Carol sprawled on the ground just inches from her, shoulders heaving as she wept. Blood spattered her cotton dress; whether her own or her husband's, Promise could not tell.

Gingerly turning her head, afraid any movement might draw the savages' attention to her, she saw that there were other men, women, and children huddled nearby or lying on the ground as she was. Some were crying, but for the greater part they simply stared ahead stonily, frozen in the grip of shock. Smoke wreathed about them. Beyond, Promise could see the still-smoldering skeletons of their wagons, twenty-one in all that had bravely set forth from Santa Fe, now reduced to metal hoops and ashes. Comanche braves were ransacking their contents, which were heaped upon the ground. Whoops of delight could be heard at their discovery of a few bottles of whiskey, sugar, coffee. One warrior cavorted about with a great black umbrella that Promise recognized as having belonged to Reverend Simon, while another held up a whalebone corset and puzzled over its possible use.

Fresh screams rent the air as another of the Comanches dragged a young girl from the captives bunched together in the dirt and threw her down, cutting the clothes from her writhing body while others of the war party came to watch and laugh. Soon their grunts and gasps of pleasure replaced the girl's screams as they took turns upon her young body, and Promise turned away, ashamed that she had done nothing to help the girl, but afraid, oh, so afraid, that she might be their next victim. Tears coursed down her cheeks in silence, for she dared not make a sound that would draw attention to herself.

"Promise?" came a raspy whisper.

"Oh, Carol!" Promise whispered back, turning her face to her friend's. "Are—are you hurt?"

"I don't think so. Promise, they killed Larry, didn't they? He's dead, isn't he?"

"I—I don't know," Promise lied, the high-pitched quality to Carol's voice warning her to speak with caution. "Maybe he was only wounded. I passed out!"

"So did I!" came Carol's tearful whisper back. "They're goin' to kill us, aren't they, Promise, when they're done? I don't care—not if my Larry's dead! I just hope they get it over with fast!"

"Don't speak that way!" Promise hissed back. "You've got Larry's baby growing inside you, depending on you for its life. You give up, and that little baby can't live either!"

There was no answer from Carol, and Promise sighed and pressed her face back down to the dirt once again, turning it so that she could watch the Comanches, still looting.

One of the braves had found a calico bonnet and had perched it atop his head, laughing merrily as he cavorted about, much to his companions' delight. Her eyes widened as they wrenched the lid from another trunk and drew out a walking stick topped with a knobbly horse-head carving. *Pa's walking stick!* The brave who had found it jiggled it in his hand, muttering something to another brave that Promise took to be his liking of the carving. Fury raged through her, for the moment blotting out all thoughts of fear. Damn their black-hearted, murdering souls; she had nothing left of her father save this one thing! She'd be damned if they would take it for themselves! She had scrambled to her feet before any of them noticed her and flung herself forward toward the Indian who held the stick in his hand.

"Give that to me. It's mine, damn you!" she shrieked, grabbing at the walking stick.

The Comanche's painted face registered surprise, then amusement. He said something and lifted it above his head. Promise reached up, trying to knock it from his grasp, and received a stunning cuff across the ear for her trouble. Livid and mindless now, she drew back her foot and kicked him hard in the shins. The Indian laughed in her face and dealt her another sharp cuff, this one across her cheek. He jerked the walking stick toward himself and grunted something.

"No!" Promise ground out through clenched teeth. "It's not yours!"

She threw herself at him full weight, small fists bunched and raised aloft to flail at his painted face. Her surprise attack caught him off guard. He lost his balance and toppled backward with a grunt, Promise sprawling heavily atop him. Onlooking Comanches laughed deeply and jeered at the warrior good-naturedly as Promise writhed from his grip and snatched wildly for the walking stick, which had fallen from his fist as he fell. She held the stick to her breast, breathing heavily. The brave sprang lithely to his feet and stalked her, arms held out on either side of him, scalp lock swinging with its single eagle feather, a breechclout all that stood between her and his nakedness. A wickedly bladed knife, tucked casually into a rawhide sheath at his waist, was his only weapon.

He sprang at her with a wild whoop and instinctively she raised the walking stick to defend herself, striking it at his red-painted face with all the strength she could muster. There was a sharp snapping sound as it landed alongside the brave's skull, then the carved horse-head knob cracked and fell, dull brassy-colored lumps of metal showering after it from the hollow interior.

For a fleeting second she froze, transfixed by the sight of the hoard of golden nuggets and the import of finding them, but then she recovered and gaped wild eyed at the dazed Comanche as he reached for her. He fastened wiry brown arms about her waist and flung her, still struggling, over his shoulder.

Her body flopped limply up and down as he sprinted to a waiting pony and urged her with yet another slap and a sickening punch to her belly to straddle it. Sobbing and fighting waves of nausea, she did so. The brave sprang up onto the pony before her, gave a short yell, and touched moccasined toes to its sides. Promise lurched and almost toppled from the pony's back. With a sob, she clutched for the Indian's waist and held on for dear life as they galloped away.

They rode on throughout what daylight remained, stopping neither for food, water, rest, or to relieve themselves. Against all odds, Promise fell asleep from time to time, waking to find herself still clinging grimly to her captor's waist. Her fingers were cramped from clutching him so tightly, and her legs felt wrenched off from straddling the pony's broad rump. Her inner thighs were chafed raw beneath the thin cloth of her pantalets,

431

which was all that covered her legs with her dress hiked up for riding.

When at last they halted, she opened her eyes wearily to see moonlight glinting through the branches of several cottonwoods. She heard the guttural conversation of several other Comanche, and a child's distant whimpering that went on and on. Her body screamed with pain and stiffness, yet at least she was alive, she thought dimly. Could the same be said for Carol and the others? she wondered, gnawing her bottom lip.

Just when she feared she would slide from the pony's back, the Comanche turned and shoved her roughly from it. She landed hard on the stony ground with a thud that snapped her teeth together on her tongue. She tasted blood upon it as she swallowed dryly. The Comanche swung down from his pony and towered over her. Grinning through his war paint, he slowly drew aside his breechclout and she sucked in a terrified breath. *Dear Lord, he means to rape me!* she thought and shrank back, away from him. He laughed aloud as her face paled, and he urinated, the thin, yellow stream landing only inches from where she sprawled. His laughter infuriated her. Her lip curled back and her nostrils flared in contempt, and she scuttled across the ground to lean against the gnarled trunk of one of the trees, away from him.

With deliberate, easy grace he followed her and squatted down at her side. He gripped her chin in his fist and jerked her head this way and that, grunting in approval. When he was done with his inspection, he tore the ribbon from her hair and wrenched the cornsilk mass free about her shoulders. It seemed to please him, for he smiled not unpleasantly and tapped his chest, which was slick with some sort of grease and still more garish paint.

"Some name this one Fights-Wolf. What name white woman?"

Though surprised by his use of her own tongue, however crude, she allowed nothing of her surprise to show in her face. She stared ahead, without answering.

His brown fingers curled about her throat and he squeezed, forcing her down onto the ground. Her eyes streamed. Blood rushed to her head and pounded there agonizingly, until she felt as if the top of her skull would explode. She tried to breathe but could not as his hands gripped tighter and tighter. Just when darkness closed in, and she knew she would fall unconscious if he did not release her, he let go and repeated his question. Breathing deep, enormous gulps of air, she whispered, "Promise."

Fights-Wolf grunted in satisfaction. He drew two narrow strips of rawhide from his waist and roughly rolled her over, face down in the dirt. Wrenching her arms behind her, he bound her wrists together, then her ankles, and dragged her upright and hefted her roughly to where other captives lay, similarly bound, before letting her fall heavily to the dirt. Her escape made impossible, he left her to join the rest of the war party at the fire.

Promise lay very still. She had no choice, since her bonds permitted little movement, and what they did permit proved agonizing. From the campfire came the whoops of victory of the Comanches, bursts of harsh laughter, the smell of roasting meat, and, later, the screams of the tortured, high and ululating on the night air. She knew then why the men had been brought along by the other braves. For entertainment.

"Promise? Are you here?"

Carol! "Yes, oh, yes!" Promise whispered.

433

"When you ran at that Indian, oh, Lord, Promise, I thought they'd taken you away to kill you!" Carol murmured, a sob in her voice. "I never reckoned to see you again!"

"Are there others?"

"Yes. Annie Fuller's here. Oh, Promise, she's tied up, too, and she thinks the baby's coming! And—and there's Becky Skinner and her little brother, as well, right here next to me. They can't even cry any more. They saw their pa tortured and killed, and their mama was—was—" she couldn't go on, and a muffled burst of weeping followed her words.

"Don't cry, please!" Promise implored her. "We're going to get away. I don't know how just yet, but—but *somehow*! Don't give up, honey; you mustn't give up."

Annie Fuller started screaming then. Both Carol and Promise lay silent, listening to her shrieks yet helpless to aid her in any way. Soon, two of the braves came from the fire and carried her, still screaming, away with them. That was the last they were ever to see of kindly Annie. Exhausted and afraid, they dropped into a fitful sleep on the cold, damp earth.

Promise was awakened the next morning by Fights-Wolf's sharp kick in her ribs. She groaned and rolled over, her limbs bound so tightly that her wrists and ankles had swelled enormously, and the rawhide thongs had cut into her flesh until it bled. He squatted down beside her and jerked her to sitting, ignoring the low moan of agony she gave at his cruel handling. With one quick slash with his knife, he severed the thong at her wrists, then did the same to that at her ankles. Tingling pricks of fresh pain filled her hands and feet as blood surged back into them. She looked up into his arrogant, savage face, now free of paint. His features were well formed, with high cheekbones above which his eyes were black and shining as onyx, his skin a deep, shiny copper, and his hair loose to his shoulders and blue-black in color. He was barechested, clothed only in a short breechclout and fringed moccasins. About his neck hung a thong, threaded with beads and claws. Two curving white scars marred the smooth flesh of his torso.

"We go now, Prom—ise," he ordered, jerking his head in the direction of the coal-black pony they had ridden the day before.

She shook her head. "No." If they meant to kill her, rape her, then she would resist them until the end. She would not meekly do as bidden, like a lamb led to the slaughter.

To her surprise, Fights-Wolf threw back his head and laughed. His eyes were cruel and glinting with dark fires as he returned his gaze to her face. "White woman die, very soon now. Prom-ise woman, she pay!" he said thickly. "She kill brother to Fights-Wolf, three moons past. She die many ways."

Her face grew waxy under its layer of dirt, sweat, and tears. So, she was indeed to be killed, and slowly. Her heart missed a beat and continued to flutter with fear as he went to the pony and led it toward her. A squeezing knot cramped her bowels, and she screwed her eyes tightly shut until the paralyzing terror from his words had ebbed a little. *Give me strength, Lord!* she prayed silently. *Dear God in Heaven, given me strength!*

Fights-Wolf swung lithely astride his pony, then stuck out his arm, jerking his jaw in her direction to order her to mount up behind him as she had the day before. For a second, she was tempted to refuse, to run and force him to kill her quickly, but then another brave rode up alongside her captor, with Carol clinging to his waist behind him. Her pale face was blue in places where the other brave had struck her, and it was also streaked with tears. Her pretty red-gold hair was matted and tangled with twigs and leaves, her lips swollen and cracked. She looked down at Promise from her captor's pony's back, her expression pleading. Woodenly, Promise stumbled the few feet to Fights-Wolf's pony, groaning at the pain in her ankles, and clasped his outstretched hand. With little effort, he swung her up behind him. In minutes, they were riding onward once again.

It was dusk before Promise realized that they were nearing their destination. All that day they had ridden, stopping only once at about noonday when the Comanche pair watered their horses at a spring and ate of the pemmican they carried in their buckskin pouches. Added to the weakness from riding without rest and the several slaps and punches dealt them, the two women were further weakened by lack of water and food. Unwillingly, Promise felt saliva gush into her mouth as Fights-Wolf squatted down to devour his dried meat and berries mixture, and he turned and caught the yearning on her face. With calculated scorn, he cast the remainder of his food upon the ground, then stepped upon it and walked away. That—that animal! Promise thought furiously. He expected her to fall upon his leavings like a dog and devour them! She'd starve first! she thought defiantly and stayed standing where she was, flexing cramped arms and legs. Sure enough, Fights-Wolf glanced back over his shoulder at her and appeared disappointed to see that she had not moved. She'd had little time to relish this minor victory, however, for they'd soon mounted up again, and the ride had continued to where they now were.

The smell of wood smoke carried on the evening air, and with it the coppery smell of fresh blood and offal. As they neared what appeared to be an Indian encampment, Fights-Wolf and his companion stopped yet again to paint their faces. Then, before either Promise or Carol could react, the Comanches grabbed them, held them securely, and cut the clothes from their bodies. They looped long rawhide thongs about the two terrified women's throats and half-dragged, half-pulled the captives behind their ponies as they rode in the zigzagging path of victory into the Comanche village.

About a hundred tipis were ranged about them. A vast herd of many-colored ponies grazed far to one side. Dogs set up a fierce barking as they were pulled to the center of the village. One by one, people came out to gape at the arrivals, and as news of the war party's return was passed, women poured from every tipi to jostle forward and stare at the white women.

Never would Promise forget the feel of countless, mocking black eyes upon her, the cruel clawing of the women's fingers as they reached out to touch, to pinch, to hurt, the sharp pokes of the sticks they carried. As they harried the captives, hurling insults as well as blows, some began the yee-yeeing songs of victory; then all joined in, mocking the naked pair who huddled amidst them trying to protect themselves with their arms.

Carol shrieked and began batting their hands and their sticks away, imploring them to leave her alone. Her cries seemed to please the Comanche women, and their spiteful attack gained in fervor, Promise noticed, shielding her eyes with her hands as a stick jabbed wickedly close to them.

"Don't move," Promise urged her friend. "Don't move and don't cry. That's what they want us to do. If— if we stand still, I don't reckon they'll keep up with it." She hissed grimly, "It's not so much fun for them, see?"

437

Carol nodded. "I'll try." She stood quite still as Promise did, sucking in a breath instead of crying out as the women pinched her bare buttocks, her arms, her thighs, or jabbed their sticks cruelly at her tender breasts. It was a nightmare, but after a few moments with no reaction from the white captives, they turned away in disgust and left them alone.

Fights-Wolf had observed Promise's urgent command to the red-haired one, and his onyx eyes gleamed with admiration. For all that she was only a woman, and a hated white-eyes, she was a prize worthy of a warrior such as he. He admired the courage she showed now, as he had admired her attempt to take from him the strange medicine stick with the head of a war pony upon it. She would die well, he thought as he stepped through the beaming women of his village to her side. As he looked into her eyes and saw the fiery gleam of determination in their depths, he wondered if perhaps the grass color of those eyes gave her some powerful medicine that other female white-eyes captured and brought to their village had not possessed. He would lie with her before she died, he determined, and in so doing share in that powerful medicine. His manroot stirred at the thought as he took her roughly by the elbow and drew her after him between the rows of tipis.

Before almost every lodge stood racks on which strips of buffalo meat had been hung to dry, Promise saw as she passed. The smell of roasting ribs and humps filled the air, and her belly growled with hunger. She had not eaten anything since the corn bread and bacon atop the wagon yesterday, and then she had done so sparingly. Oh, what she would give for a piece of Carol's warm corn bread and a rasher of bacon and coffee . . . She sobbed inwardly. What she would give for a humble dipper of water and a

438

blanket to cover herself . . .

The fires within the tipis made them glow golden before the amethyst dusk like conical candles. The lodge poles were etched dark against the sky forming a strange, bare forest. Fights-Wolf halted before one of these and ducked under the tipi flap, dragging her after him. A slender, pretty Comanche woman came quickly to greet the brave, and Promise guessed correctly that she was his wife. A toothless old crone wrapped in a blanket huddled by the fire. While Fights-Wolf and his wife exchanged words, the crone looked up at Promise and gave a cackling laugh, muttering something through her gums and slack lips that sounded overtly malevolent. Promise quickly looked away, shielding her breasts and her womanhood from the old one's eyes with her hands.

Fights-Wolf turned to Promise. "Do as this one tells you," he ordered, nodding at his wife. With that, he left the tipi. As he strode proudly to join his fellow warriors, he smiled with satisfaction. His wife, Little Otter, would now look upon him with new respect. She would no longer regret that she had become his wife.

Little Otter's contempt for Promise was obvious in her pretty but sulky face. The old woman muttered something, and her expression changed. She looked Promise up and down slowly, heedless of the heat that filled the white girl's face, flung a few words at her, and flounced across the tipi. She snatched a buckskin garment from the rack that hung at the rear of the tipi and flung it at Promise with a harsh command.

Fingers shaking from lack of food, exhaustion, and fear, Promise picked it up and pulled it over her head. It fitted loosely like a sack without a belt to tie about the middle and was stained and torn, yet Promise was too grateful to have a covering of some kind to care. "Thank you," she whispered, pointing to the dress and nodding.

Little Otter appeared surprised, for she had understood the gesture and Promise's motions. She shrugged and turned away, busying herself with the preparations for the evening meal and ignoring Promise completely.

Promise retreated to one side of the tipi and sank down. She dearly would have loved to sleep but dared not in case it would anger the two women. Her body throbbed from the pinches and scratches of the squaws, her back pained her, and her throat was so dry she doubted she'd be able to swallow anything even if they did feed her. She wondered if they'd come for her tonight, and if she'd last long before she escaped them in death. She forced herself not to think of that and instead thought about the lumps of brassy-yellow gold that had tumbled from the walking stick knob when she'd cracked the Comanche brave across the head. Miserably, she realized that Luke must have been right. As he had said, her father had stolen the gold from him and his partner. *Oh, Papa, why?* All these years she had remembered him with such pride, such love. Both were tarnished now by the knowledge that he had been a thief . . .

That night, the village celebrated their hunters' successful kill. Many buffalo had been brought down and slain, and the women had sung with joy and praise as they ran to butcher the great, shaggy beasts, to drink of the fresh blood, and devour the liver as they worked. The meat had been carried home, the many *travois* piled high. Tonight they would celebrate with feasting and dancing, before the hard work of the next day. Strips of meat must be dried. Berries must be crushed and mixed with it to make *pemmican* so that there would be food in the snowy Moons-When-the-Babies-Cry-for-Food. Hides must be stretched and scraped and cut and sewn to make new lodge covers or fine warm garments or robes. Sinews must be prepared carefully for the making of sturdy cords or bowstrings; bellies and bladders must be washed so that they might be used to carry water or for cooking pouches. The horns and the full mane of the buffalo would go to make bonnets for the shaman, to add the mystical magic of the sacred buffalo to his already powerful medicine. No, nothing would be wasted as the white man squandered the creatures the Earth Mother gave them for food. The People would have full bellies this winter and the children would not cry with hunger; nor would the women be forced to seek the wooden lodges of the white man to beg for food like scavengers.

The drums beat their wild, frenzied tattoo of joy and sent the glad sound far across the plains. The hunters danced, and their women gave the yee-yee calls of victory. Tomorrow it would be the turn of the war party to boast of their triumph, to tell of the many *coups* they had counted against the hated white-eyes. But tonight— tonight was the night of the hunter.

Chapter Twenty-Five

Cay stood in the purple plains dusk, his mouth working soundlessly as he surveyed the destruction about him on every side. The ruined wagons still smoked. The personal belongings of the settlers that the Indians had not carried off with them were strewn in the sandy earth. He spied a little rag doll and a woman's hope chest, and tears of rage and frustration filled his eyes. He turned away then and forced himself to look at the broken and bleeding bodies he had been trying hard not to see. Angus McDonald lay, scalped, to one side. The buzzards had already been at him. There was Jan Van Klein and his woman, Minnie, pinned to the ground by Comanche lances. They hadn't died easily, from the looks of it.

When he had inspected all the bodies, he turned away and vomited into the dirt. Even a cowboy's tough existence had not prepared him for this! Only one question remained unanswered. Had the Bushleys and Promise perished in the burning wagons? Or had they and the others that were missing been taken captive by the savages? His shoulders sagged wearily. He didn't know whether it was better to hope Promise was dead and beyond pain, or to pray that she'd been taken captive, and that there was still a chance she could be found.

"Well, there ain't much we can do here, Cay," Ed Brown said as he walked up to him. Ed appeared green and red eyed. "I'd say they were hit just after noonday, wouldn't you?"

Cay nodded. "There're several women and a few of the men missing, Ed," he said wearily. "I'd say they took captives with 'em."

Ed Brown nodded. "Reckon so. We'd best ride on to the fort and get help to go after them."

"That would take days!" Cay growled. "No, I reckon I'll see if I can track them a ways, Ed. You ride on to Fort Lyon."

"Hell, Cay, come with me. Chances are if they took prisoners, they're dead by now! Leastways, if they're lucky they are," Ed argued.

Cay shook his head. After a few minutes, Ed Brown cursed, mounted his horse, and rode away. Cay stood there a while, watching him leave, then turned back to the ruin. Soon he found a place where it appeared many people had been dragged. The hard ground was scuffed up. Off to one side lay the raped body of a young girl. His gorge rose up in his throat once again, but he steeled himself to look and saw that it was not his Promise. He couldn't tell by her hair: she'd been scalped. The tracks of several ponies led away from that place, but each set of tracks led in a different direction. He knotted his fists and stood stock still, seething with impotent rage. No one man could track so many ponies! How the hell was he to choose the right set of tracks—the one which would lead him to Promise?

Muttering under his breath, he spun about to go after his horse. He pulled up, gasping with shock and reaching for the gun at his hip, for there was someone standing behind him. For a moment he took in the tan fringed buckskin shirt, the pants of soft tan kid, and the high-legged moccasins, and he thought it was an Indian before him. But as his gaze traveled up the length of the man to his face, he realized with a shock that it was none other than Luke! At first, neither of them spoke, the old jealousy rising between them like a wall.

"She's not here, Cay," Luke said at length. "The Comanche took her. You planning on going after them?"

"Yep," Cay nodded. "You?"

Luke nodded. "I was about to leave when you rode up. Promise told you about us?"

"She told me some," Cay admitted. "She told me that she never wanted to see you again. How come you're way out here?"

Luke's black eyes met Cay's blue ones without a flicker. "I reckon you know why, Cay," he said levelly. "I think you feel the same way. I give you warning. I'm going after Promise. If I find her alive, there's nothing I won't do to get her back!" Dark eyes smoldered now.

Cay grimaced. "Then I reckon we feel the same way, all right," he agreed. "Seems to me we'd have a better chance of doing just that if we worked together."

Slowly, Luke nodded. He crouched down and inspected the hoofprints in the dirt. "It doesn't matter much which tracks we choose to follow," he said at length. "The Comanche split up after a raid to make it harder to follow them. Any one of these sets of tracks will eventually lead to their camp—if they haven't moved on. Either way, we can follow them. Let's mount up!"

Cay nodded and headed for his horse. One foot in the stirrup, he hesitated and looked back over his shoulder at Luke. "Whatever she said, it's still you she loves, Luke," he said gruffly. "But don't feel too good about it! If— when we find her, I aim to change her mind!"

Luke nodded but offered no comment, unable to voice his fears that they wouldn't find Promise alive.

It was the Comanche custom to degrade their enemies by raping all women taken captive before returning to their village, to bind them cruelly, and to torture and kill the men. Those captives that survived days of rough riding on the trail to their camp were often further tortured, sometimes by the women, whose capacity for cruelty was often even greater than that of the braves. If they survived all of this, their strength and great courage—both values the Indians admired—resulted in their being kept as slaves or rarely, the women might become the wives of Indian braves.

Children fared better, as long as they were captured young enough to learn the Indian ways. Often they were given to couples to replace their own children who had died, for few families were blessed with more than two children. Such white children often grew to adulthood more Indian in thought and behavior than those born of the People. They fiercely refused recapture by their white kin, and when taken against their wishes often pined away and died. But Promise was no child. . . . Furthermore, he had recognized several of the arrows at the sight of the wagon train massacre. They had belonged to the Comanche war chief who had attacked Captain Hughes's men months ago. If the Comanche recognized her as the woman who had killed one of his war party, the one who had shot their young warrior with the nine toes, she was more likely than not already dead.

"We've about half an hour before the light's gone," he spoke at last. "We'd best put it to good use. Yah!" He kneed his blue roan away and Cay rode after him.

The moon rose soon after they left, spilling its light on the upturned, lifeless white faces of the dead that littered

445

the sandy earth below. The rising moon, known as the Comanche moon by the Spanish who had noted the Comanche favored its brilliant light for their raids, gleamed on the brassy lumps of gold beside the shattered walking stick. They lay where Luke had found them before Cay rode up. After six years of searching for the truth, he had found it. But at what price?

Promise awoke from a fitful night to the sounds of the Comanche village coming to life. Babies wailed to be nursed. Children tumbled out of lodges to play with the camp dogs. Women stirred to go down to the stream to wash themselves and hurry back to their tipis to prepare the morning meal. She lay very still, heart thudding, hoping no one had noticed that she had awakened. Last night, she had slept in the tipi with the grunts and sighs of Fights-Wolf's and his woman's fierce coupling filling her ears, combined with the snores of the wrinkled old crone whom she had guessed was Fights-Wolf's mother-in-law, though he never spoke to her except through Little Otter. The old witch had given her scraps of leftover buffalo meat from the evening meal the night before and some water, but neither had done much to ease the gnawing hunger in her belly—if it *was* hunger. Promise guessed much of her queasiness was caused by fear. There had been moments when all of this had seemed like a nightmare from which she was certain to awaken. Even Fights-Wolf's threats that she would die a slow and agonizing death had a strangely unreal quality to them. Drums had throbbed far into the night. Joyous singing had swelled throughout the village and filled the darkness, coupling with blood-curdling whoops. At any moment, she had expected to be dragged from the tipi and taken to where the people congregated, there to be tortured and killed. Yet even then she had felt detached from the reality of such a thing happening, as if it might happen to someone else but could never happen to her. Was that how the mind dealt with such terror, she wondered, by denial?

The old crone stirred under her sleeping robe, coughed, and finally rose and left the tipi. Soon after, Little Otter followed her. Only Fights-Wolf and Promise remained. She sensed that he was awake, and she lay there, heart thudding, breath bated, pretending to be asleep still.

His fingers closed about her wrist suddenly, and a small cry came from her, for he moved so silently she had not heard him cross the tipi. He flung her onto her back and loomed over her. There was the fierce glitter of lust in his eyes, and he was quite naked, his magnificent body silhouetted sharply against the wan light that filtered through the walls of the lodge. She drew in a shaky breath as she saw that he was very much aroused, his manhood rearing turgidly from his lean hips. He saw the fear in her eyes as she unwillingly looked upon his maleness, and he smiled. Her belly turned over sickeningly at the gloating manner in which he stood over her. Sweat made her palms slick. His smile struck terror in her heart and made it flutter feebly as if it were impaled on a sharp spike.

He dropped suddenly to his knees beside her, and she saw that there was a knife in his fist. He lay the sharp blade across her throat and cautioned her to be still. Her terror abated only a little when he did not slit her throat as she had feared but slit the buckskin shift down the center and flung it aside. Naked, she lay helplessly before him, her eyes enormous, slanted green pools as he gripped her thighs and pried them apart before kneeling arrogantly between them. He traced the knife point down from the fluttering pulse in her throat, between her breasts, and across the flat plain of her belly, laughing softly as she followed its path with her eyes. When he reached the silky golden triangle between her thighs, he hesitated, watching the terror in her grow and spread out to fill her, making her breathe as if she had run very far and was short of wind.

"You are brave," he said grudgingly, for she had not shrunk away from his blade, nor tried in any way to escape him. "But soon you will scream, as do all your people's women!" The contempt in his tone was blatant.

His tone stirred something inside her. "Perhaps," she admitted, fighting to control her erratic breathing, "but before I die, I will curse the name of Fights-Wolf and all who are dear to him!"

Taken aback by the vehemence in her tone, he wetted his lips, for once uncertain of himself. Was it possible that this woman could place such a curse upon him and his family? he wondered. He glanced into her face and found her eyes staring steadfastly back into his own black ones, with no shred of fear in their grass-green depths. He found that steady gaze peculiarly unnerving, and, without thought, he touched the sacred medicine bundle that hung on a thong about his neck, to counter the feel of those eyes upon him. Warily, he forced his gaze aside. She had no powers! He was like an old woman to fear this white captive who was soon to die! He turned his uneasy thoughts away and forced his attention to her body.

The pale gold flesh of her face and arms shaded into the white of the winter snows upon her breasts and belly, and it seemed to glow with the luster of moonlight. Only the faint blue shadows from the blows he had given her marred its perfection. His manroot throbbed with the pulsating urgency of his lust as he covered her full breasts with his hands and fondled them, marveling at their firmness and pleasing size. Such a woman could have suckled many little ones, have given a man great happiness with her body upon their robes. If she had not made the fatal error of killing his brother, the brave warrior Nine-Toes, and thus condemned his soul to eternal torment, he might have kept her for his use until he wearied of her fair body and its novelty. Little Otter was without fire. He had learned soon after they had become joined that she only submitted to his wishes and did not share and seek to increase his pleasure in their coupling. He leaned back, preparing to plunge his aching manroot into her body, eager to find a release from the pressure of his lust. He found himself drawn to look at her face once again, and even as he gripped her thighs and forced them apart in readiness, a shudder of fear coursed down his spine like a trickle of cold water from a mountain stream. He could not look away!

Promise willed herself to keep looking at him, for she had noticed his fascination with her eyes. Could it be he had believed her desperate threat to curse him? Did that explain his hesitation, the troubled and uncertain expression in his onyx eyes? She had no way of knowing—could only pray that she had by chance struck the superstitious core of him, and in so doing bought herself a little time . . .

A snarl forced its way through Fights-Wolf's twisted lips as his manroot slackened, hung limp, and shriveled against his thigh. Amazement filled him. Not once since he had lain with his first woman had such a thing happened to him! Always he had been as virile as the stallions with their mares upon the plains. Until now. Until *this* woman. He lunged for the knife that lay beside

449

them and raised it aloft, prepared to plunge it into her breast.

Promise's heart almost stopped beating. Death was imminent, mirrored in his blazing eyes. *Let it be quick, dear Lord!* she prayed, glassy eyed as she stared fixedly at him. She could not know that it was this transfixed look as she awaited certain death that saved her.

Fights-Wolf flung the bone-handled knife aside and struck her a ringing punch to her jaw. Stunned, she gasped and jerked sideways, stars filling her vision, darkness crowding in as they faded. For a second or two, all went black. When she recovered, he had gone. She let out a great, keening cry and buried her face in her hands, scalding tears spilling down her cheeks.

Little Otter and the old woman returned then, and the younger woman's eyes darted jealously from Promise, who still curled naked upon the ground, to the torn buckskin shift across the tipi and Fights-Wolf's empty buffalo robes. She shrieked and leaped at Promise, raining blows on the girl's body, slapping and pulling her hair. Promise raised her arms to ward off the blows and fight back, but before she could do much harm, the old woman spoke sharply and pulled the two women apart. She said something calming to Little Otter and jerked her grizzled old head contemptuously at Promise as if reassuring the Comanche woman that such a pitiful creature was no threat or rival for her husband's affections. Little Otter seemed somewhat placated. The old woman gestured to Promise to put on her torn shift and, when she had done so, gave her a vicious shove in the back, then gestured for her to leave the tipi.

The old woman shooed and shoved her toward the stream, snatching up a black iron kettle from outside the tipi flap as they went. Promise looked about her curiously. Everything here seemed very similar to Luke's Cheyenne camp save for the tipis being arranged a little differently. In a group of children playing with the camp dogs, she caught sight of Becky Skinner, naked as the Indian children. She broke free of the old woman's grip upon her arm and ran to the little girl.

"Becky, honey, where's your brother? Where're Missus Bushley and the others?" she asked as she crouched down before her.

Becky shrugged. "Billy's dead, ma'am," she said, lower lip quivering. "He was awful sick when—when the Injuns took us." Her eyes brimmed with tears. "This mornin' I tried to wake him, but he wouldn't get up! I don't know 'bout Miz Bushley. I saw Mister Rawley and Mister Evans, though. They're tied up in that tipi back there—"

Becky's voice died away as the old woman tugged Promise off. Promise shrugged her bony fingers from her arm. "Don't touch me!" she hissed. "Take your hands off me!"

A cackle of laughter came from the old crone, and others nearby smiled, too. They sure were strange, Promise thought. She'd expected blows when she'd shouted at the old woman but instead received only what appeared to be amusement and approval at her actions! They reached the stream then, and Promise saw that there were many women already there, bathing in the chill water or washing their children. In cradle boards propped up against rocks or tree trunks, dark-eyed papooses gazed curiously out at the world beyond their down-lined confines.

The old woman thrust the kettle into Promise's hand and gave her a shove in the small of the back, pointing upstream. As Promise set off in the direction in which

451

she'd been pushed the old witch followed at a slower pace, making certain to keep her in view.

At a spot where the water sang over numerous rocks, she jerked her head toward the stream and gave what appeared to be an order to fill the kettle. Promise stepped into the water, gasping at its chill at first, but quickly enjoying the soothing sensation on her aching body. She took her time, attempting to wash off some of the dust and dirt that streaked her before the old woman suspected her delaying tactics. As she cleansed herself, she glanced about her curiously, noting her surroundings with an eye to a possible escape, if the chance presented itself.

The stream burbled down from amidst a riot of vegetation. Cottonwoods lined its banks, as did junipers, sassafras, and a few pecans. Tangles of chokecherry bushes clustered about their trunks, and several Comanche women were gathering the red berries in their skirts or rooting along the stream banks or diving into its depths for the juicy greens that grew in the running water. Still others dug with sharp sticks amongst the trees for tasty bulb vegetables such as wild onions or collected nuts and herbs, chattering as they worked as women anywhere might do.

Despite what she had heard about the way Indian women were treated by their menfolk, the women here seemed neither badly abused drudges nor dull-witted creatures little better than slaves. They were attractively and cleanly dressed in buckskin shifts decorated after their own fancy in patterns of quills or trade beads. Their complexions were varied from deep gold to dark copper, their hair uniformly a shining blue-black, worn either loose about their shoulders or braided, the ends bound with fur or silver bands or rawhide thongs. Many had painted their faces and the partings in their hair. Their children appeared well cared for and happy as they splashed in the water, and though she never once saw their mothers scold or correct them in any way, she observed that they were little more undisciplined than white children of similar ages, a deal more spirited, and totally unconcerned by their lack of clothing.

The old woman screeched at her to come out then, and she did so, hastily filling the black kettle almost to the brim as she waded from the water.

They went back to the village the way they had come, and Promise's eyes widened, for there were many people up and about now. Frames of straight saplings had been erected outside many of the tipis, and women were lashing buffalo skins upon them, using lengths of rawhide or sinew to stretch them taut. Others had staked the green hides upon the ground, hairy side down, and were laboriously scraping the fat, muscle, and shreds of tissue from them with a toothed fleshing tool. At some hides more than one woman labored, talking as they worked, and for a second Promise was reminded of the sewing bees she and her mother had enjoyed in Cherry Creek. True, the Indians had many different ways from those of the white men, but surely they had many similarities, too.

When they reached Fights-Wolf's tipi, they found Little Otter busily fleshing a hide as the other women had been doing. The old woman snatched the kettle from her, slopping water to the ground as she did so, and pointed to yet another hide already pegged out on the ground. She ducked inside the tipi, returning with another flesher, indicating with a sharp barrage of words that Promise should do as Little Otter was doing.

She knelt down and began scraping the hide. The

flesher was made of elk bone tipped with metal to give a
sharp scraping edge. It was not pleasant work, she soon
found, or easy. The hide smelled bad, and, despite the
flesher, her fingers often slipped and were soon rubbed
raw from the friction. It was hard on the knees and back,
too.

While she worked, she stole a glance about her from
time to time, hoping she might see some of the other
captives. Where was Carol, she wondered? She hadn't
seen her since the day before, when they had arrived in
the village and had been poked and pinched by the
women. She bit her lip. She hoped they had not harmed
her.

There was some kind of commotion in the tipi at the
end of the row then, and many Comanches began going to
and fro through the opening. Soon a strange old man
arrived, dressed in the skin of a bear, its head stuffed to
form a mask. From the skin dangled the claws, feet, or
tails of many different animals, and in his bony hands he
carried a medicine bag of some sort of smooth, dark fur.
The women, children, and even the men grew silent as he
passed by, and from their respectful hush, Promise
guessed he must be a man of some importance in the
village. The silence was so absolute that the only sounds
in the sudden hush were the clicks of the animal claws
that dangled from his bear-skin robe and the tinkle of
metal cones that adorned its hem. When he reached the
lodge at the end of the row, he began chanting in a
quavering, eerie voice, and shaking his rattles rhythmically. From within the tipi came the loud throbbing of
a drum, like the steady, strong beat of a pulsing heart.
The medicine man—as Promise guessed him to be—
then chanted louder, emitting short yelps and growls that
sounded much like the bear from which the robe he wore

had come, until finally he ducked through the tipi opening.

The people continued about their business then, but they seemed more subdued to Promise's eyes, and she noticed that they glanced at the tipi in which the *shaman* had gone with apprehension in their expressions. Not long after, a woman's loud wail rent the silence, echoed by other shrieks and wails—cries of grieving that were unmistakable in any language. The medicine man exited the tipi and disappeared between the lodges. It appeared his magic had failed. Whoever he had come to heal had died despite his incantations and scaring away of the evil spirits.

Promise looked up, startled, to see Fights-Wolf standing over her. His eyes would not meet hers as he ordered her to go with him, and she knew that in some small measure, the great, ruthless warrior was afraid of her. She stood gracefully and followed him, a little nervous as he ducked into a tipi and harshly ordered her to follow.

To her surprise, a Comanche woman crouched beside a willow-framed sleeping couch on which lay Becky Skinner. The little girl had appeared pale and drawn earlier that day when Promise had spoken to her, but she had thought that this was due to the terror of being taken captive and seeing her parents brutally murdered. Becky's face was so ashen it appeared bloodless. Her eyes were two great, dark holes in that pallor. She was quite still, except for screwing up her face from time to time and pressing her little hands to her stomach.

"What is it, Becky, honey? Does it hurt here?" Promise asked, kneeling at her side and lightly touching the little girl's belly.

Becky bit her lip and nodded faintly. "I want my

mama! Mama! Mama!" She retched violently then, and the Indian woman who had been anxiously watching and crouching nearby thrust Promise away and placed a basin under the child's chin. Promise looked up at Fights-Wolf questioningly.

He shrugged. "It happens quickly. The girl falls. The other children bring her here, to her mother, Grey Blanket." He said the word "mother" with heavy emphasis, as if expecting Promise to contradict him. "Grey Blanket, my sister, has lost one daughter. This one was to take her place. Now the evil spirit of sickness fills the child. She is afraid she will also die. Grey Blanket feels white woman with powers has more medicine to heal white child than our *shaman*. You *will* make her well again!" His black eyes glittered as he made the threat. His arrogant, chiseled features challenged her to refuse him.

"And if I do?" Promise asked. "Will Fights-Wolf reward me?"

He nodded. "I will."

"And what will this reward be?"

"We will speak more of that when the child is again well," he said evasively.

Promise stood up. "No. We will speak of it now or not at all. If I can heal this child, will you release your white captives? Will you give us food and water and horses so that we will not die on the plains?" With bated breath, she awaited his answer.

He shook his head. "I cannot. The other prisoners are not mine to bargain with. I cannot speak for my brothers to whom they belong. Nor will I let you go, Pro-mise Woman. You killed my brother. I have sworn to take your life for his." He smiled slyly. "Is that not the teaching of your Black Robes? An eye for an eye—a life for a life? It is also my teaching! I can promise you only an easy death. Heal the girl, and you will be spared the tortures of the other white-eyes this night.''

His slight hesitation and his sly expression filled Promise with unease. Lord, it wasn't much of a bargain, and she did not trust him to keep it, yet what choice did she have? ''And if the girl dies?''

Fights-Wolf's jaw tightened. ''Then all will be as I swore before! You will beg for death many times before it is granted you!'' He saw her pale beneath the gold of her skin; saw her magic green eyes darken with dread.

''Very well,'' she murmured at length. ''I will do what I can.''

He grunted.

''I will need herbs and plenty of water, a kettle like the white man's kettle that Little Otter has, and cloth.''

''You will have them. What herbs do you need?''

''The one the white man calls the sassafras. It grows by the stream. The leaves are orange now and shaped so,'' she held up her hand and outlined a mitten shape. ''It is the bark of this tree that is needed.''

Fights-Wolf spoke with his sister. Grey Blanket nodded eagerly. ''My sister will fetch the things you need.''

''Thank you. Also, I would like the help of the woman that was brought here with me. The red-haired one also— also possesses great healing powers.'' She stared boldly at him, daring him to deny her request.

Fights-Wolf's eyes gleamed. He laughed softly. ''You dare much when you order a Comanche warrior to do your bidding, white woman! It is only for my sister's sake that I do not put you in your place!'' He gave Grey Blanket a fond look, spun about on his moccasined feet, and left the tipi.

To Promise's relief, Carol and the items she had

demanded arrived soon after. She quickly explained to Carol what she had done, preparing a tea from the sassafras bark while she spoke.

"It's small comfort, the bargain I made, but it was the best I could do," she finished.

Carol nodded. "It's more than I dared to hope for," she said huskily. She looked at Becky, so still and pale on the hide-covered couch, and sighed. "I hope you can do something for her, poor little thing. She looks real bad."

Promise nodded. "She told me this morning before she got sick that her little brother, Billy, passed away this morning."

"What? Of this same sickness?"

"I reckon so," Promise confirmed.

"But what if Becky dies, too?"

Promise sighed. "I don't know. We'll have to do our best and say a bunch of prayers that she pulls through!"

Becky Skinner whimpered and retched again, and both women smothered their fears and turned to nursing her. The child alternately vomited and passed vast quantities of watery stools, and it was as if she grew thinner and thinner before their eyes. By noonday, her eyes seemed to have sunk into the flesh surrounding them, and there were hollows where before there had been plump, rosy cheeks. Promise bathed the child again, refusing to let Carol touch her in her condition for fear she might lose the child. "If it's what I'm beginning to think it is, there's a good chance we won't have to worry about Fights-Wolf and his slow death, whatever happens to little Becky," she said grimly, tucking a warm buffalo robe about the child.

"What do you think it is?" Carol asked, blue eyes apprehensive as she awaited Promise's answer.

"Cholera," Promise whispered. "Someone died this

morning. I saw the medicine man go into the tipi. When he came out later on, the women were wailing and carrying on. Little Billy Skinner's dead, too. I'd be willing to bet there'll be others sick real soon if I'm right."

"But . . . if you are, there's no way Becky will get better!" Carol exclaimed.

"Maybe not. But there's a chance she will. Isn't that better than no chance—or would you rather accept being tortured?"

"Of course not! I don't want to die at all!" She shuddered. "I—I thought after last night—after that savage had finished with me—that death would be better. But—but not now." She clasped her hands over her belly and squeezed her eyes shut. "Whatever they do to me, I don't want to die!"

"Come on then, let's try to get some tea into Becky," Promise urged grimly.

Chapter Twenty-Six

Shortly after dusk, Grey Blanket brought food for the two white women, a stew of buffalo meat and wild vegetables. The two ate hungrily. All day they had bathed the little girl, cleaned up after her when she soiled herself, and diligently spooned water into her to replace that which she had lost. Coupled with their fatigue was the weariness that uncertainty and fear engendered, and when Fights-Wolf came to the tipi for them, bringing with him the scowling brave who had taken Carol captive, both Promise and Carol hoped that they would now be allowed to sleep. Their hopes were short-lived.

They were led to a large, open area about which all the people of the village sat cross-legged. The light of flaming torches lit the darkness, casting fearsome shadows on the painted faces. In the midst of the cleared area stood a tall pole, from which dangled many scalps, some old and others more recent, Promise realized, gulping as she recognized the curly thatch of fiery hair that had once belonged to Angus McDonald.

To one side of the gathering sat old men who appeared to be the village elders, their hatchet faces deeply clefted with lines, resembling ancient leather. On either side of them sat the young braves, the warriors who had attacked the wagon train. Their plunder lay heaped on the ground before them: guns and rifles, tools and provisions, small, fancy items that had caught their eyes such as looking glasses, strings of beads, and sturdy iron pots and kettles. Beyond the circle stood yet another pole, and to this was lashed the only two white men taken captive who had survived the ride back to the Comanche village, Martin Rawley and Thomas Evans, the two men little Becky had told Promise of earlier. Beyond them milled the horses taken by other braves during the raid.

Fights-Wolf led Carol and Promise to where the warriors sat before their plunder, and roughly shoved them down beside it. He sat cross-legged beside his fellows and totally ignored the two terrified women. Drums began to throb then, and one of the braves leaped into the cleared area and began dancing, acting out the daring raid the war party had made on the wagon train with wild whoops and a victorious chant that sent chills rippling up and down Promise's spine. Other warriors followed him, and they all grew wilder and more flamboyant as the fervor filling the onlookers incited them to even greater limits. When, bathed in sweat, they fell back to their seats beside the others, Fights-Wolf took their place. Promise watched his graceful dancing with the same fascination a rabbit feels when mesmerized by the sinuous gyrations and cold, compelling eyes of a snake about to devour it.

Fights-Wolf moved with the agile grace of an antelope as he danced, telling by his actions of the *coups* he had counted against the hated whites and of the prizes he had taken in both captives and guns. The torchlight glistened upon his oiled and painted copper body as he danced, emphasizing the play of muscles and cords rippling down his arms and across his torso. His short braids sprayed

461

about him, the single white-tipped eagle feather that dangled from his scalp lock bobbing as he moved, heels thudding against the earth in time with the heartbeat of the drums. His necklace of teeth and claws showed in sharp relief against his dark body as he moved in a wide circle, as the sun moves across the heavens in the direction of the hands of the white man's clock. In the shifting light, his face was terrible indeed, his chiseled features frighteningly painted in red and black—the Comanche colors of death. The crowd grew hushed to the last little child. The night air trembled in the wake of his chant and his blood-stirring dance. The women rose slowly to their feet when he was done, like sleepwalkers waking from a dream, to dance slowly in unison, gliding and shuffling after the manner of the women's dance, to sing their praises for mighty Fights-Wolf and the warriors. Soon the shrill yee-yeeing of their victory song reverberated to even the farthest corners of the village. The war ponies herded there whinnied and screamed their excitement and tossed their heads.

The white men lashed to the pole beyond the circle felt all hope flee their bodies as the song rose in intensity, inciting men and women alike to a fever pitch. Blood lust was a stinking musk upon the air. They smelled it, and they trembled.

The women's faces grew expectant; their eyes glittered with excitement as the captives were dragged out to the center of the clearing. Soon, the hated white-eyes would die! The deaths of the two captives would be a symbol of what would befall *all* white-eyes who drove the sacred buffalo from the Earth Mother so that her children, the People, starved—those who scarred and wounded the belly of the Mother and robbed her of her verdant forests to build their wooden villages and plant their fields.

Aiieé, yes, they would all die, to the last one of them! The People would see that it was done!

The first man, Martin Rawley, was spread-eagled upon the ground, his wrists and ankles lashed with tight rawhide thongs to stakes driven far apart, so that both arms and legs were stretched to the breaking point. His clothes were cut from him. Naked and helpless, he still uttered not a sound, despite the frenzied whoops from the savages all about him. The drums began to beat, faster, faster! Promise's stomach lurched sickeningly as she saw two braves come forward, knives raised in their fists. Horrified, she saw them reach for Rawley's groin, and she turned away so that she would not have to see what came next. He screamed then. The sound seemed to go on and on, rising higher and higher without end until she feared she would forever after hear it ringing in her ears. She wouldn't, couldn't, look. Carol, beside her, had likewise turned away and was sobbing.

Fights-Wolf leaned across and knotted his fist in Promise's tangled hair. He forced her head up and hissed at her to open her eyes and watch. Sick to her stomach, she had no choice but to do so. She saw the flesh peeled from Rawley's body and hot coals were brought and piled upon his bleeding belly and groin. The stench of burning human flesh was all about them, and she gagged violently but dared not turn away. Instead, she prayed for him to die, prayed with every ounce of faith and concentration she could summon for that gentle, serious man who had never, in-so-far as she knew, harmed any man—white or red or black. He had wanted only to teach school to the children of the settlers in the West. Never, not even when her mother lay sick, had she prayed for anything as she did for the death of that poor, broken man! Her head swam, her throat constricted, and she tasted bile in her mouth. Blood roared in her ears, and darkness edged in about her vision like the spread wings of a great black bird. Her scalp was afire from the cruel knot of Fights-Wolf's fingers. She hovered dangerously close to losing consciousness when Fights-Wolf released her. He smiled cruelly, eyes like shiny lumps of black coal in the torchlight.

"Where is your power now, Prom-ise Woman?" he jeered. "It is well. I have given my word to you, killer of my brother, or you would die as slowly as he!" He jerked his head in the direction of the bloody piece of meat that had once been Martin Rawley. The braves were dragging him away, and others were bringing Thomas Evans to take his place.

Thomas Evans. The Evans' wagon had been neighbors to that of the Bushleys on the trail. The two families and the McDonalds had shared suppers together, borrowed and traded countless little things, offered willing hands when the wagons fouled or the harness broke. Tom was a mild man, deeply religious, who had left the mines of his native Wales to sail to the land of America and find a new life for his wife and his children, away from the shafts and their lung-destroying dust. As they lashed him to the stakes, Promise heard dimly, through wild shrieks and whoops, Tom's calm voice. *"Yeah, though I walk through the valley of the shadow of death, I will fear no evil—"* The prayer ended abruptly in a gurgle as red-hot coals were applied to the soles of his feet and the tips of his fingers. Then he cried out in a voice that rang loud and clear, "God, have mercy!" His head lolled to one side, and the people all about groaned with disappointment. Water was brought and dashed over him to revive him, but it did not. Thomas's gentle heart had given out. By dying, he had cheated the savages of the sacred medicine such a ritualistic torture and death would have given them.

They mutilated and scalped his body, yet Promise watched with a stony face and did not turn aside. What they did now could not hurt Tom any longer. It didn't matter. His soul was with his loved ones and with God.

Soon after, they were returned to the tipi where Becky Skinner lay, tended by her new Indian mother, Grey Blanket. Despite what they had just witnessed, Promise was moved by the genuine love the Comanche woman felt for the little girl: her eyes were the eyes of any woman who fears the death of her child. Silently, Promise marveled that the two emotions—deep and abiding love and relentless cruelty and hatred—could live side by side in the same village. But then, did not both lurk in the hearts of all men, red or white?

Becky appeared to be asleep. By gesticulations, Promise and Carol learned from Grey Blanket that the child had not vomited since they had left earlier with Fights-Wolf. They managed to get a little more water into her, then Promise urged Carol to try to sleep for a little while, agreeing to wake her when she was herself exhausted. As Carol slept, Promise and Grey Blanket kept a vigil over the little girl.

It was three days more before Promise dared hope that Becky would live. On that third day, she sat up and asked for food. Though painfully thin and wan, it seemed that with care she would recover. Grey Blanket scooped the child up into her arms, murmuring endearments and rocking her like a baby. She hugged her so fiercely the girl gasped for breath. When she released her, she hurried to fetch food for the girl and shyly handed the two women choice pieces of roasted meat as tokens of her

465

gratitude. Promise and Carol accepted them with mixed feelings.

It was apparent that as far as Grey Blanket was concerned, their task as healers was over. They were no longer needed. Now, Promise knew, Fights-Wolf would come, and they would die as he had promised. She looked at Carol and knew by the dread in her eyes that that thought had occurred to her, too. "We'll try to buy more time," Promise said, squeezing her hand to comfort her. "We know that many people are sick. Perhaps we can talk him into letting us heal the others," she suggested, trying to keep the edge of desperation from her voice. Carol nodded and forced a smile.

"I'd say that's a good idea. The longer we can—can stay alive, the better chance we have that your Cay will bring soldiers looking for us."

Not long after, Fights-Wolf ducked under the tipi flap. It took all of the two young women's restraint not to cling to each other in terror as he towered over them. They both sat cross-legged upon the buffalo robes, hands clasped in their laps, demure as if they sat in church and awaited the minister's sermon. Yet inside, all was chaos and dread.

"You have done well, Prom-ise Woman," Fights-Wolf observed. He lifted Becky into his arms and saw how she regarded him curiously, her eyes bright now and no longer dulled with the wasting sickness. He said something to his sister, and Grey Blanket nodded and smiled as she took the little girl from him. Becky snuggled against her ample breasts as if she were truly her mother.

"My sister is well pleased with what you have done. She asks that you be allowed to return to your people . . ." He paused, relishing the flare of hope that ignited in both women's eyes. "But I have told her that

this cannot be. It was you, Prom-ise Woman, who struck
down Nine-Toes, our small brother, and condemned his
spirit to walk the Ghost Path when the Apache dogs were
given his body. His death must be avenged. It is our way.
I have promised my sister that I will give you one more
passage of the sun to live on Mother Earth to show you
her thanks. When the Sun next rises from his lodge and
begins his ride across the sky, you will die." With that, he
left the lodge. Promise and Carol, both the color of chalk,
gaped after him.

They were treated like honored guests by Grey Blanket
for the remainder of that day, but her kindness gave them
little comfort. The hours seemed to fly past as if they had
been given wings of quicksilver.

All too soon the moon rose, spilling her light over the
Comanche village. Huddled under warm buffalo robes,
the two women shivered with fear. Promise leaned across
and shook Carol by the shoulder. "We have to get away
from here tonight!" she hissed. "Are you game to try it?"

"Yes!" Carol whispered. "It's now or never!"

Promise peered through the shadows. In the firelight,
she saw Grey Blanket upon her robes with Becky curled
against her body. They appeared to be asleep. Grey
Blanket's husband snored loudly on his robes across the
tipi. Promise carefully lifted the heavy pelt from her
body and crouched there, waiting until Carol had slipped
from her covering. They crawled toward the tipi's
opening and were almost to it when Promise felt a firm
hand upon her shoulder. Heart almost in her mouth with
fear, she could make out the silhouette of Grey Blanket
leaning over them. The homely woman placed a finger
across her lips, warning them with the motion to stay
silent. She thrust something into their hands which they
found to be moccasins and a parfleche filled with

provisions, then she beckoned urgently. Pulling Promise by the arm, she crawled under the opening.

Promise and Carol needed little urging to follow her. Hearts thudding, they padded quickly in her wake, keeping to the shadows and avoiding the treacherous patches of silver-gray moonlight. By one tipi, Grey Blanket stopped and dropped to one knee, the two women instantly falling back to crouching positions behind her. They watched as a guard made his patrol past them only a few feet away, before he moved on to circle the village.

As soon as he had passed and it was safe to move again, Grey Blanket darted across the clearing toward the bushes. Carol and Promise sped after her. The rushing of the stream sounded somewhere nearby, and the breeze rustled the trees. Grey Blanket turned to Promise. She touched her breast, then reached out and touched Promise's own, gesturing her heart-felt thanks without need for words. Then the Comanche woman gave them each a little shove and murmured something in urgent, insistent tones, shooing them away. Her actions needed no translation. Promise thanked her and grasped Carol's wrists, tugging her through the bushes toward the stream.

"Come on! We have to get as far from here as we possibly can before Fights-Wolf learns we've escaped!" she whispered urgently. "We can follow the stream—he can't track us through water. Oh, Carol, we have a chance! We have a chance!"

Hand in hand, they forged over rocks and roots and into the chill water, creating diamond-bright sprays in the moonlight.

Chapter Twenty-Seven

Throughout that night, they struggled along the stream bed, heedless of the cuts and bruises their feet suffered from the sharp rocks in their panic to put as much distance as possible between themselves and Fights-Wolf. While it was yet dark, the stream gave out, seeming to go underground, though they could not be certain in the darkness. They sat and rested briefly, drinking as much water as they could before tying on the moccasins Grey Blanket had given them and battling their way through bushes and tree stumps across dry ground.

Promise had come close to laughing in hysteria when she had finally stopped to look at the moccasins, for they were the ones given to her by Flattens-Grass in the Cheyenne camp months ago, obviously Grey Blanket's portion of the booty taken from her trunk in the wagon train. Flattens-Grass had said when giving the gift that she hoped the moccasins would carry Promise many miles, swiftly and in comfort. Lord, she hoped so! The soft buckskin was like velvet to her battered feet as they ploughed on.

Promise figured they must have put over twenty miles between themselves and the Comanche camp by daylight,

469

but it was not enough. A swift pony could cover such a distance in less than half the time it had taken them, and she was certain Fights-Wolf would come in pursuit when he learned that they had escaped. Carol collapsed exhausted to the ground, insisting she could not go on. Grimly, Promise took her elbow and hauled her to her feet.

"We can rest later," she said firmly. "For now, we have to keep going, honey. I know you're tired. When it gets hotter we'll rest," she cajoled her. "I promise. Just a little farther . . ."

Biting her lip, Carol nodded. Holding on to each other, they covered a few more miles. Though it seemed to Promise that they traveled painfully slowly, she knew to force a faster pace from Carol might result in her losing the child or her falling down from exhaustion, never to rise again.

The terrain changed as they hobbled on in the direction from which the sun had risen, the east. The heavily wooded undergrowth of the lower mountain slopes upon which the Comanche had made their camp gave way to the bare stretches of the plains, where there were few shrubs or trees for shade. The only shadows available were those cast by great heaps of boulders that seemed to have simply erupted from the earth. The late September sky was a brilliant azure, so intense it pained the eyes with its brightness. The heat shimmered over the ground in a wavering, watery haze, distorting distances and clumps of sagebrush alike. Promise heard a thud behind her and looked over her shoulder to see Carol sink to her knees on the ground.

"It's no use, Promise," she moaned. "You can yell at me all you want, but I can't go on! Leave me here . . ."

Promise looked about her, shading her eyes against the

sunlight. There was a huge boulder up ahead where they could rest in the shade. She half-carried, half-dragged Carol to it and made her comfortable, taking off her dusty moccasins and massaging her bruised and blistered feet.

"Oh, Lord, that feels good!" Carol sighed. "Here, let me see to yours." Afterward, they opened the parfleche and found pemmican and little journey-cakes of corn. They ate sparingly, trying to conserve their scant provisions. There was no water to wash the food down with, however, and the dry beef-and-berries mixture seemed to stick in their parched throats.

Despite everything, they slept a little, too weary to fight the exhaustion that swept over them. Promise judged it was past midday when they awoke. She stood and flexed muscles that screamed with fatigue, denying her body's urges to sink back down and sleep again. She shook Carol awake.

"Time to hit the trail again, Carol. It's cooler now, so it'll be easier than it was this morning."

Stubbornly, Carol shook her head. "Later, Promise, please? I'm still so tired!"

Promise's patience snapped. "Have it your own way, then! If you want to stay here so that Fights-Wolf can find you and carve you into little pieces to feed to his dogs, then you go right ahead! But don't expect me to stay here with you!"

She swung about and marched determinedly away, hoping her ploy would work. It did. When she looked back, Carol was struggling to her feet and stumbling after her. She waited until the girl drew alongside, then slipped a comforting arm about her waist as they continued on. "I knew you could do it, honey," she murmured. "We're going to make it, I just know we are!" She gasped as she stubbed her toe against a rock. "We weren't that far from

471

Fort Lyon when the Comanche's attacked. I figure a day or two, and we'll be there. Maybe some soldiers will find us before then—wouldn't that be wonderful?" Her words lifted Carol's spirits some.

"Oh, yes!" she agreed fervently and smiled, looking a little more like her formerly optimistic and cheerful self.

Promise forced herself to smile back, though inside she was far from smiling. The Comanche had ridden for almost two days with their captives, to the west—two days riding from the easterly direction in which the train had been headed! If they were to reach Fort Lyon, it would take days longer than she had optimistically promised Carol. Inwardly, she shrugged. Oh, what of it? What if she had lied? It was worth it, if it kept Carol going . . .

As they plodded along, weaving from side to side with exhaustion, Promise thought about Luke, forcing her mind to dwell upon the days and nights they had shared rather than upon the endless amber plains that rolled away to the hazy blue horizon as far as the eye could see. She remembered the way he looked, the way he felt, the timbre of his voice. He had been right about her father. Oh, yes! Four years he had spent at the mercy of Jake Colter, four terrible years. She had spent less than a week as a captive in the Comanche camp, and look at what fear and abuse had done to her! Was it any wonder, in light of his prolonged captivity, that in his bitterness she had become the victim of his vengeance? She understood him so much better now! If, by some stroke of fortune or with God's will they survived this, she'd find some way to let him know that she forgave him everything. She couldn't alter what had happened to him as a result of her father's theft of the gold, but she could tell him that she was

472

sorry, deeply sorry, that it had. If only they could get out of this alive! If only . . .

Cay glanced at Luke, and his shoulders sagged. *Goddamn!* he cursed silently. *To have come so far for nothing* . . .

"When do you think they left?" he asked grimly.

Luke was crouching down, testing the ashes of an old fire.

"This morning; no earlier. These are still warm." He stood up. "They were afraid of the sickness spirit. I'd say the chances are they're miles from here by now."

The two men stood silently, looking about the deserted Comanche campsite. Tipis, horses, and people had gone, signs of their hasty departure everywhere. Tracks of travois poles crisscrossed the ground. In the treetops hung the bodies of several men, women, and children, wrapped tightly in green buffalo hides. The Comanches must indeed have been afraid, Luke thought. They had not even taken the time to build burial scaffolds for their dead but had prepared them for the star-path in the swift manner usually reserved for winter, wrapping the bodies and securing them high between the forked branches of trees.

For six days Luke and Cay had tracked and circled about, searching for the camp. The war party had covered its tracks well, and if not for Luke's skill in following what had seemed to Cay insignificant "sign," they would never have managed to follow them this far. To find the camp deserted now was a crushing blow to their spirits. Cay sighed heavily, took off his Stetson, and wiped his brow on the back of his hand.

"Do you think she's with them?"

"I'd say so." His jaw worked violently. "We haven't found her body. That's something to draw comfort from."

"That doesn't mean she's still alive. We—we could have missed it," Cay pointed out.

The look Luke shot him was murderous. "I won't believe she's dead, not until I see it with my own eyes!" he said grimly. "If you feel like giving up, then you go on to the fort!" He spun on his heels and went to his horse, mounting up and riding away in the direction the churned hoof marks and ruts of the travois poles told him the Comanche had taken.

After a few minutes, Cay jammed his hat firmly on his head and spurred his horse after him.

He would have given anything to find Promise, sweet Promise, alive and unharmed! But he had a growing certainty now that they were chasing a mirage. Given what Luke had told him of his conviction the Comanche who had taken Promise captive sought her life for the life of the brave she had killed in that other attack, he had lost all hope that they would find her unharmed.

It was late into the afternoon of that day before Promise became aware that they were being followed. At first she thought it was a trick her mind was playing, a result of exhaustion, little water, and the heat. But then the distant object came closer, and she saw that it was indeed a rider, mounted on a coal-black pony. He was quite far from them as yet, and his horse was no doubt tired, but she knew that if he chose, he could overtake them at any time and ride them down. Still they plodded on, moccasins torn now, feet numb and little more than unfeeling lumps of flesh, backs racked with pain. The rider kept his distance, never coming closer or moving away, doggedly following them. Anger swept through Promise, filling her with a little energy she had long since thought lost. She gripped Carol's elbow and hauled her faster, heading for the rocks up ahead. She knew who that rider was, knew that it was Fights-Wolf and that he was playing with them, like a cat playing with a pair of little mice before the kill!

Carol sensed her alarm and looked back over her shoulder to see its cause. She, too, recognized the rider.

"Oh, my God, no!" she whimpered, blue eyes widening in terror. She clutched wildly for Promise, fingers like talons as she gripped her arms. Hysterical laughter rolled off her cracked lips. "It was all for nothing, all those miles and miles! He's just waiting until we drop, then he'll kill us! He won't let us go! He'll never let us—"

Promise slapped her, hard. "Stop it! He hasn't caught us yet! There's only one of him and two of us. We—maybe we can kill him, take his horse—yes, his horse! Come on!"

They reached the rocks, and Promise scrambled about, picking up small boulders until there was a pile of them at her feet. Carol seemed to have decided that their only chance was to do as Promise said. She scurried about adding rocks to the pile.

"There. If that isn't enough, nothing will be," Promise announced. She shaded her eyes and looked back the way they had come. The rider had halted, his dark horse etched sharply against the yellow plains. He must be wondering what they were up to, she realized grimly. Well, he'd find out soon enough, if all went well!

"Well, what now?" Carol asked, leaning wearily against a large rock.

"Now," Promise said, heart racing and pounding in her ears like a drum, "comes the hard part. We wait . . ."

It seemed like an hour passed before Fights-Wolf rode on. Maybe it was less and fear made it feel longer, but it seemed an eternity that they watched that distant horse and waited for it to begin moving toward them. When it did, they almost cried out, unnerved by their flight, fear, and exhaustion. Peculiarly, Carol seemed better, not exactly resigned to their fate, but calmer and more determined looking. "Whatever happens, Promise, I want to thank you for everything—for sticking by me so that I could escape, too; for getting mad at me when I needed yelling at. You've been a good friend, Promise, a real good friend. Whatever happens," she said again, "I love you for that."

"Oh, Carol," Promise cried, and the two women hugged briefly before settling down behind the huge boulder to wait.

Unhurriedly, the coal-black pony came closer, the Comanche rider relaxed upon its back. Promise and Carol ducked down behind their hiding place, jittery now that the moment they had awaited was close at hand.

"When I give the word, start throwing those rocks at him for all you're worth!" she hissed, and Carol nodded, lips grimly pursed. The dull thud of the pony's hooves grew closer. "Now!" Promise screamed as its head appeared, picking up a rock and hurling it at the pony as it came into view. Carol stood and flung rock after rock at the animal, which whinnied shrilly, reared up, and galloped off. Too late, they realized that it was riderless.

Instinctively Promise whirled about to see Fights-Wolf, grinning evilly, poised to spring down from the rock above them. In the same instant that she drew back her arm to fling a rock at him, he sprang down, knocking

476

her backward to the ground with the weight of his body.

"Run!" she screamed to Carol. "For God's sake, run!"

But Carol wavered, a rock clenched in her fist that she was afraid to use as Promise grappled with the wiry Fights-Wolf upon the ground. She tore at his black braids, raked her nails down his greased chest and cheeks, struck desperately for his eyes as she fought for her very life, but all her efforts were in vain. He was simply too strong for her. A sob broke from her parted lips as she saw Carol, still waiting for her chance to club the Indian with the rock, and she knew with a feeling of defeat that Carol's moment would never come. Fights-Wolf would see to that! "No! Run!" she screamed one last, frantic time, before she saw Fights-Wolf raise his bunched fist to strike her. There was a sharp blow, an instant of pain, then all went black. She spiraled down into that dark void with the sound of Carol's terrified screams following her.

When she came to, she was aware of an excruciating pain in her arms and legs. Her eyes fluttered open weakly. Above her was the sky. Below, the hard, stony earth. She was not dead, after all, as she'd hoped. Oh, God, no. She was still alive! She turned her head and saw that Carol lay only a few feet away, her wrists and ankles lashed to stakes by tight thongs of rawhide as were her own. Looking up, she saw Fights-Wolf looming over them, a long-bladed knife clasped in his fist. A wave of terror swept over her. She was certain she could hear the screams of Rawley and Evans as the Comanches tortured them horribly that night, even smell the copper-stink of their blood in her nostrils. Soon, it would be her and Carol's screams that rent the air; their blood that spilled on the sandy earth.

Fights-Wolf's obsidian eyes glittered mockingly as he

saw the fear in her face. Silently, he cut the buckskin shifts from the two women and wrenched the tattered moccasins from their bruised and cut feet.

"You have shown great courage, Prom-ise Woman," he said softly, "more courage than I have ever seen before in a white woman. And, you have great powers! But I, Fights-Wolf, have proved the stronger! Where is your power now, Green-Eyed-One? It is nowhere—even as my little brother's soul is nowhere! If you survive the wolves, my brothers, that come with the shadows of night, you will not last beyond the midpoint of the mighty Sun's next ride across the sky! When you breathe your last, my brother's spirit will be freed to take the star-path. Die slowly, Prom-ise Woman, and die well! I will leave your bodies unharmed, in thanks for your healing powers!" And with that jeering promise, he sprinted away from where they lay and vaulted lithely astride his coal-black pony. He galloped away, emitting a shrill, triumphant whoop as he left.

Soon came the night. The moon rose and took the place of the sun. The glorious flame colors of sunset faded to the violet tints of dusk, then true darkness. The howl of the wolves carried on the chill night air, and the two women shivered in terror and cold. The millions of tiny stars that twinkled fiercely above seemed to mock the two poor creatures lying bound and helpless far below.

It grew colder still as the night drew on, and the wolves they had heard in the distance ringed them, golden eyes like the satin eyes of demons, shining through the darkness. "Oh, dear God!" Carol cried brokenly. "Look at them—they're waiting for us to die!"

As she said the words, one of the wolves threw back its head and gave a long, eerie howl. Promise turned her face

478

toward Carol. "It sure sounds like it!" she agreed. "I don't know about you, Carol, but I mean to give them a long wait!" She began singing at the top of her lungs, not caring if what she sang made sense, so long as it was good and loud and fearless sounding.

"Have you gone mad!" Carol cried. "Promise, answer me!"

"Look! They're leaving!" Promise cried, almost sobbing with relief as, one by one, the glowing amber eyes disappeared like candle flames extinguished by a draft. The relief that had filled her as the wolves loped silently away lasted only briefly. If they could survive the cold of the night, they would do so only to face a far crueler enemy with the rising of the sun. Staked out as they were, without clothing to protect them, they would be literally burned alive! As she gazed bleakly up at a glittering night sky, a choking sob caught in the back of her throat, and swallowing became an agony. "Oh, Pa," she cried silently, "if ever I needed a star to wish upon, it's now!"

The stars pulsed hotly. The night wind sighed across the empty plains. Tears trickled down her cheeks and glistened in the light of a pale, silvery moon. But there was no answer, no sudden trail of shimmering light arcing downward through the dark vault above to give her hope. None at all.

Chapter Twenty-Eight

By high noon of the next day, the two women were burned a deep, angry red from brow to ankles, and their eyelids and the tender flesh of their breasts was covered with blisters. The rawhide with which Fights-Wolf had lashed them to the stakes had been soaked by their blood and perspiration, and as the sun dried the thongs they tightened excruciatingly. Their cheeks and foreheads were raw, their lips cracked. If it were not for the relative mildness of the September sun, they would have been dead many hours ago, Promise knew.

Looking sideways through eyes that she could open no wider than slits, Promise saw Carol's head suddenly loll sideways and wondered if she were dead. All night they had talked, trying to hang on to consciousness, but with the approach of day and the danger the sun brought with its rising, they had grown more and more silent.

"Caa-rrol?" she croaked, swallowing in an effort to bring moisture into her mouth. There was no answer. She closed her eyes, wondering how much longer she'd be able to hang on; wondering why she was fighting the inevitable so hard? It would be so easy just to let go and die . . . No one knew where they were. No one was looking for them. Even if Cay had come back from scouting and followed the tracks of the Comanches and their captives away from the smoking remains of the wagon train, he'd never be able to track which way they had been taken, since the war party had split up for the return ride to the Indian village. She wanted to cry, but there was no moisture left in her body for it to form tears, and her sobs came out as strange, croaking sounds. She'd never be able to tell Luke that he'd been right about her father, and that Patrick O'Rourke had stolen the gold all those years ago as he had believed. Would she have admitted that to him, that the father she had loved so had been a thief? Could she have brought herself to tell him, after what he'd put her through? Probably not. But Lord, it sure would have been nice to have been around to make that choice. . . . She strained one last time against the rawhide thongs, muscles screaming, sweat bleeding from her brow and trickling down her body, but it was no use. As Carol's had done earlier, her head lolled to one side and unconsciousness claimed her.

How long she remained that way, she never knew. She remembered later only waking and hearing suddenly a peculiar sound—one that was ridiculously familiar to a girl reared in the Rockies: the braying of a "Rocky Mountain canary"—a burro! The braying continued, then a shadow fell across her body, shielding it from the fierce glare of the sun. She sensed the bulk of some enormous creature crouching beside her and smelled its musk, a peculiar combination of animal furs, sweat, tobacco—and whiskey. She tried to open her eyes but could not. They were swollen shut.

"Water! Please, water!" she rasped.

A wheezy grunt that could have meant yes or no came

from the creature. The burro brayed again and stamped its hooves. Harness rings jingled on other mounts, and Promise realized dimly that there must be more than one rider. Could Fights-Wolf have returned, or other Comanches? No, Indian ponies wore no bridles with rings that jingled that way! Maybe that vast bulk belonged to a *bandito*? She was simply to weak to care. The shadow moved away from her then, and the blazing sun bore down on her face and bared breasts once again. The tiny flicker of hope that had flared up within her dimmed and went out. Whoever it was meant to leave them to their fate.

A deafening shot sounded then, the bullet whining past so close to Promise she felt the heat of its passage on her bare arm. Her ears rang with the explosion, then suddenly she realized that one hand was free of the rawhide thong. A second shot followed immediately in the wake of the first, and both hands were loosened.

"Mighty sorry if I scared you, little leddy," wheezed a voice. "But I'd have had to near break your wrists to cut that rawhide off of you! Hold still now, just a spell, while I get your feet loose." She held her breath as two more shots followed, and she felt her feet fall free. She was too weak and stiff to move, however.

"Thanks, mister! Oh, thanks!" she managed, hearing the dry croak of her own voice as she spoke.

"Christian duty, little leddy, nothin' to make no to-do about!" He clicked his teeth and she heard him move toward Carol. "Well, I'll be!" he exclaimed. "I'd figured little Miss Red here fer a goner!" She heard several clicks and the roll of a gun barrel as the old fellow reloaded, and then four shots sounded in rapid succession.

"Now, young ladies, if that don't bring every goldarned Injun within five miles hot-footin' it here, I'd say we're in business! Mountain Jack Webster at your service, little gals! How's about that water?"

It was the next morning before the blisters on Promise's eyelids had gone down enough that she could open her eyes to see their rescuer, and when she did, she was struck speechless.

Mountain Jack Webster was a giant of a man, close to six-and-a-half-feet tall, she guessed. His massive body appeared even larger in the heavy coat of animal furs that he wore. It reached almost to his ankles and was belted with a length of rope about the middle. A floppy-brimmed black hat that boasted squirrel tails about the crown topped a wild mane of scraggly yellow-gray hair and a full, grizzled beard with drooping mustache. What little remained to be seen of his features revealed a pair of twinkling gray eyes set under beetling white brows and a ruddy nose that appeared to have actively participated in several brawls. She judged him about sixty years old, or thereabouts, but he easily could have been anywhere from fifty to ninety! He reminded her of a great old woolly mammoth bull as he lumbered about the little camp he'd made, seeing to his two pack mules named—he'd solemnly told her earlier—after his two wives, Emily and Jane, now both dead, thanks be! He introduced his little burro as Nugget, and his mangy brown traveling horse as simply Hoss. He spoke to his animals with the affection and intimacy of a man who had spent much time alone with only his beasts for companionship. As he left the pack animals and squatted by the fire to pour coffee, she saw that his gnarled old hands shook on the handle of the kettle, and she blanched. It appeared she had the Lord to thank that his shots had not gone wild when he'd let her and Carol loose!

"That was some fancy shooting you did yesterday, Mister Webster," she told him. "We're much obliged to you."

Mountain Jack slapped his thigh and a wheezing rumble of laughter shook his bulk. "It were, weren't it? Heh! Heh!" He winked. "Tell the truth, ma'am, I didn't know as how I could still do it 'til after the second bullet. Then I figured ole Jack was on a winning streak and kept right on!" He seemed unaware of Promise's strange lack of reassurance as he continued, "Miss Red over there come to yet?"

"A few minutes ago. She drank a little water and went back to sleep. I think she'll make it."

Jack nodded. "Good t'hear it. Mighty good." He cocked a bushy eyebrow in Promise's direction. "Mind telling me now you're rested up how it was you happened to be out here?"

Briefly, Promise told him, and when she was done, Mountain Jack heaved a sigh. It was like air being forced through a pair of cracked bellows. "Schooner was the wagon master, y'say? Goldarned fool! He should've known better than to try t'move a train through *Comanchería* the way things are right now! Still, Joel Schooner weren't never one to think 'bout anything, so long as the price was right. I reckon he learned his mistake the permanent way. Coffee?"

"Please."

"Ain't got no more than the one cup, but I'd say you wouldn't mind sharing, would ye?" He wiped the mug's rim vigorously on the hairy cuff of his coat, filled it, and passed it over to Promise.

She smiled her thanks and took a sip, glancing over at Carol as she did so. Mountain Jack had shown uncommon wisdom in caring for the two of them, she thought. Realizing that any movement would cause agony in their sun-burned condition, he had, as he termed it, "pitched his tipi" over them. His "tipi" was only a blanket lashed to two poles, stretched out, and weighted with rocks to form an awning, but it served admirably to shade them. When it proved a mite airy after nightfall, Jack had solved that problem with still more blankets and furs taken from his voluminous packs. Salves of cactus pulp had done wonders to soothe their burns, and the bloody cuts on their wrists and ankles had been similarly doctored and bandaged—at great sacrifice on Jack's part—with strips torn from the tails of his Sunday shirt. Promise now wore the remainder of that garment as she sat beside Carol under the awning.

"Lucky fer you I spotted them buzzards," Jack said, smacking his lips and wiping his mouth on the back of his fist. Cracker crumbs were caught in his whiskers. "Don't reckon you'd have lasted past nightfall if I hadn't come along. I'm headed for Will Bent's tradin' post. Chances are we'll run into some of them soldier boys from Fort Lyon afore then, and they'll see you two ladies taken care of."

"I sure hope we don't run into any more of the Comanches along the way!" Promise said fervently.

Mountain Jack snorted. "If we do, I don't reckon they'll bother ole Jack!" He tapped his head. "They reckon I'm crazy as a coot—and I'm not about t'talk 'em into thinking otherwise! Scared of crazy folks, Injuns is. I've been tradin' with 'em for years now. Every once in a while, I let 'em get the better of me, just to keep 'em guessing. They ain't so bad, once you get to know their ways. Had me a Comanche woman once. Guess you could say we was married, Injun style. One hell of a woman she was, too! Full-blooded Comanche and wilder than a bucking bronco! She said old Jack was a heap big medicine man, on account of all this gray moss hanging down!" He chuckled and stroked his whiskers. "T'tell the truth, Emily and Jane were duller than last week's leftovers, compared to her!" He'd handed Promise a tin plate filled with beans and crackers as he talked, and he watched, smiling, as she scooped up the last mouthful. "Can I get you some more?"

"No, thank you, sir."

"Jack, little gal. Plain ole Jack'll do."

"Thanks, Jack," she amended as she set the plate aside. "How long do you figure it'll take us to reach Fort Lyon?"

"Five, mebbe six days, all goin' well. Was your folks on the train?" She shook her head. "Husband, mebbe?"

"No. I was alone. Carol here and her husband, Larry, let me ride with them. I planned to take a stage east. When the Comanches attacked, Larry was killed trying to save us." Her voice had lowered to only a whisper at the latter. "She's—she's carrying a child, Jack."

Mountain Jack clicked his teeth in sympathy. "Poor little varmint!" His gray eyes suddenly grew serious and piercing. Amidst their hairy fringing, he pursed his lips. "I reckon you won't take too kindly t'hearing this, ma'am, but folks can be a mite two-faced when it comes to *certain* things." He nodded his shaggy head sagely.

Promise frowned, wincing at the soreness caused by screwing up her features. "I don't understand, sir?"

"Things like what you two little gals have been through. Sure, the folks at the fort will say the right things an' do the right things, but I've seen white women what was brung back from the Injuns before—an' there've been times when I figured they would've been

486

better off left where they was!"

"Surely you can't believe that?"

"'Fraid so, missie! The women'll come buzzing around the two of ye, clucking like a bunch of old mother hens and sighing over all the terrible things what them savages done to yer—and asking you to tell 'em just 'xactly *what* them things was. They'll act like you was their own long-lost sisters, but they won't never ask you to afternoon tea, nor t'their sewin' circle meetings and such! The men won't be much better. Far as they're concerned, the two of yer will be ruined. Goldarn it, I've heard of husbands what wouldn't take back their own little wives, once the Injuns had—"

"But I told you, they never touched us, Jack, not in that way! Not once!" Promise cut him off indignantly.

"Now, now, girlie, I ain't sayin' that they did! But I'd wager a season's pelts you won't find many that'll believe it! It don't make no nevermind to me. Seems ter me if a thing ain't a person's fault, they shouldn't be held to blame for it. But ole Jack don't think like other folks. I just wanted fer you to know it ain't going to be like the return of the prodigal son, no, sir!" His gray eyes were filled with pity at the expressions of anger and despair he saw fill Promise's face. "Ain't no animal so cruel to his own kind as folks, little gal."

Promise, remembering Hollander's lies and Cherry Creek's reactions to them, could only nod her head in reluctant and miserable agreement.

Carol awakened soon after that, but it was almost a week before Mountain Jack and Promise pronounced her well enough to travel. Now that they were at last free of the Comanches, grief over Larry's death hit home, and it took both Promise's and Jack's urgings to persuade her to put her grief aside and think of the child instead. "I reckon you're both right," she said sadly one evening around the campfire. "He died trying to save the two of us. I owe it to him to see that his little baby survives. It's—it's a part of him that's still alive!" Though grief still shadowed her wide blue eyes, and her step had lost its bouncy gait, she seemed much improved after coming to this decision, and with relief Promise realized that her will to live had returned.

As they left the camp that Tuesday morning of the second week of October, Promise looked back to where Fights-Wolf had staked them out and shuddered. She'd never forget this place where she'd almost died! Her wrists and ankles would always carry the narrow scars to remind her if she ever began to forget, which wasn't likely.

Digging her heels into the stubborn pack mule, Emily's sides, she urged the animal after Mountain Jack and Carol.

"It's no use, Luke. Why don't you face up to the truth—we're never gonna find her!" Cay said dully, shoulders slumped as he sat his horse. Beyond them were the telltale signs of yet another deserted camp.

"There's no such thing as never," Luke said grimly. "If you think that way, you'd best ride on to Fort Lyon, Cantrell. I won't ride with a man who thinks he's licked."

An angry flush rose up Cay's throat and reddened his face. "I ain't licked! I just reckon we're chasing shadows! Almost three weeks we've been circling around out here. If Promise survived the ride to the first camp, I doubt she's made it this far. Goddamn it, Luke, see reason! You won't give up; you won't accept the fact that she might be dead because inside you're all filled up with guilt. You feel it was on account of what you did that she was with the wagon train and that you're to blame for whatever's happened to her. Admit it, you damned half-breed, stubborn fool!''

Luke's expression remained impassive. ''Maybe that's part of it,'' he admitted. ''But not all. We'll bed down here for the night and rest the horses.''

Cay knew by the determined gleam in his eyes that Luke had no intention of giving up. He cursed under his breath and dismounted wearily, dragging the bedroll from his saddle as Luke gathered brush for a fire.

When he awoke shortly before dawn the next morning, Luke was gone. He'd left extra ammunition and a blanket beside Cay as he slept. ''You damn fool!'' Cay cursed without anger. He looked around him, but there was no sign of Luke in any direction on the flat plains beyond. Still cussing Luke under his breath, he gathered up his things and prepared for another day's hard riding—this time toward Fort Lyon. There was no sense in trying to follow Luke. If he didn't want to be found, he wouldn't be.

Fights-Wolf grinned as he saw the distant rider mounted on a pony the color of a stormy sky. His own beast had been ridden too long and too hard these past suns. Another horse would give the black a chance to rest while he rode the other. In that way he would catch up with his people who had changed camp many times this moon to escape the sickness spirit.

All day he stealthily trailed the rider who moved at a steady, unhurried pace across the plains, following, Fights-Wolf realized, the path his people had taken. At dusk the rider made camp, and Fights-Wolf hung back, waiting for night to fall so that darkness would aid him in overpowering the man.

He left his pony ground-tied and wriggled forward on his belly to peer over the boulders that ringed one side of the place the man had chosen for his campsite. His lips split in an evil grin as he saw the small fire shedding its narrow circle of light and the bundled figure beside it, rolled in a blanket. *Fool! Offal!* he thought. *Have you no cunning?* Only a white-eyes would choose such a place for his camp! None but a white-eyes would sleep so unprotected! Ah, but they were all soft and weak, every one of them, without their fine shooting sticks that could fire many times at one loading! His black eyes brightened with anticipation as he drew a wickedly sharp knife from his breechclout and edged forward slightly. How many such guns would this one have?

Poised above the sleeping man, he raised his hand aloft, firelight glinting on the blade as he brought it down into the bundled figure below. The point thudded against something hard, and Fights-Wolf threw the blanket aside, cursing as he saw the boulders there in the shape of a man. Soft laughter sounded behind him, and he spun around to see the rider standing at his back. He wore fringed buckskins, leggings, and moccasins.

"What kept you so long, friend?" Luke drawled. "I've been waiting for you since sundown!"

Fights-Wolf said nothing, eying him sullenly, but Luke knew he was only biding his time, waiting for a fraction's hesitation on his part to spring. He drew his own knife from the cuff of his knee-high moccasins and weighted the blade in his palm. "Soon you will die, Comanche dog!" Luke said softly, goading the brave.

"Never!" Fights-Wolf hissed, betraying with that single, explosive word his knowledge of the white man's tongue. "It is you who will die, half-breed!" He held his arms out on either side of him for balance, poised on the balls of his feet with his weight slightly forward. The knife gleamed evilly in his fist, as if it reflected the silver fire of Luke's weapon.

"I'm ready when you are, Comanche," Luke said calmly, his eyes never once leaving the Comanche's fierce, dark eyes. "Before the Sun rises from his lodge in the east to ride across the dawn, you will have told me all that there is to know of the white woman with eyes the color of the grass. Prepare your death chant, great war chief of the Comanche! Soon, you will take the star-path!"

Something flickered in the brave's stony countenance, and in that barely perceptible spasm, Luke knew that the brave had recognized Promise's description. He smiled inwardly, feeling the lust for blood singing in his veins. The Comanche would talk, sooner or later. There were ways to see that he did . . .

Chapter Twenty-Nine

The little band of three arrived at Fort Lyon mid-morning, twelve days after Mountain Jack Webster had found them, the old trapper having brought the women every step of the way since they had encountered no military patrols. The fort had little to recommend it on that bleak fall morning of gray sky and feeble sunlight. Buildings of sandstone rectangles roofed with dreary sod jutted up from the barren terrain like patches of blight. Above them rose a spindly flagpole of cottonwood branches lashed together, from which the flag drooped forlornly in the damp, cold air.

As they rode into the compound, Promise saw that there was a sutler's store, a bakehouse, a stage station, and a hospital, as well as several other buildings and officers' quarters and barracks for the men. Huddled in the huge, stone-walled corral were several dejected-looking men, heavily bearded. Others, all wounded men, lay on the hard ground or leaned against the corral wall. Sick or well, despite the cold and damp, they wore only threadbare blankets over their gray uniforms. *Gray uniforms!* It struck Promise suddenly that they must be Confederate prisoners. As if to bring home that fact, one of the soldiers guarding them suddenly barked. "C'mon, you damned Johnny Rebs—you want t'eat, you got t'work fer it!" The haggard men moved listlessly to do the guard's bidding as Mountain Jack led them on, past the sorry scene.

Soldiers were drilling in the compound, moving smartly to the barked commands of the drill sergeant. Promise thought that much of their enthusiasm to do so was probably caused by their desire to get warm, for in the past two weeks the weather had turned decidedly cold. Summer was gone, and fall was moving irrevocably toward winter.

Mountain Jack led the odd cavalcade of mules, burro, and horse to the office of the commanding officer of Fort Lyon, Major Scott Anthony. He helped both Promise and Carol down and took their elbows to lead them inside.

"Here we are, little gals," he wheezed. "We done got here safe and sound!"

Major Anthony rose to greet them as his adjutant ushered them into his office. Other officers and their wives crowded into the small room when word of the arrival of the recaptured women spread through the fort. Question after question was put to them: Did they know where the Comanche camp was located? How many warriors had there been? Were there more captives left behind in the camp? It went on and on until both Carol and Promise were close to tears. They wanted to forget, and the remembering and resurrection of those days of fear and deprivation strained their nerves. Finally, their condition was noticed by a tall, handsome, middle-aged woman named Hannah Morrison. She came across to them and put her arm around them reassuringly.

"There now, Major Anthony, I'm certain that these poor dears must be tired and wanting a nice hot tub after their long journey, and a good hot meal and fresh clothes.

With your permission, sir, I and the other ladies will see to them."

Major Anthony appeared startled. "Why, yes, of course, Mrs. Morrison. I wasn't thinking, I'm afraid! Ladies, please go with Mrs. Morrison here. She'll see you well taken care of. I have a few more questions for you, but they can wait until you're recovered. Welcome back, ladies!"

With polite nods, Carol and Promise left the major and followed Hannah Morrison from the office. The other officers' wives trouped after them like a flock of noisy geese.

"A dear boy but inclined to forget that we are not all soldiers!" Hannah said, raising her eyes in the direction of Major Anthony's office. She came to an abrupt halt before the shaggy bulk of Mountain Jack, who was planted firmly across their path. "Yes?"

"I jest wanted to say so long to these two little gals," Jack mumbled, "seein' as how we've bin trailmates for a spell."

Promise reached up and kissed Jack's weather-beaten cheek. "Thank you, Jack," she murmured softly. "Thank you for everything. You saved our lives, and we'll never forget you, or your kindness."

Jack, for all his great girth, almost seemed to squirm with boyish embarrassment. "Like I told you, Miss Promise, it were my pleasure. It done my heart good t'see you two little gals perk up again and get back t'the business of living." He looked with special intensity upon Promise and waggled his finger at her. "I'd wager you ain't finished with this whole business yet, gal," he said tenderly. "Bein' the strong one ain't easy. Don't be afraid t'cry, gal. God give us tears for a purpose, y'know."

Promise nodded. "I know. Good-bye, Jack. God bless you."

Carol echoed her thanks and her farewells, and then they watched as Jack rearranged his packs of furs to even the burden between all his animals, mounted Hoss, and rode from the fort toward Bent's trading house. Promise felt as if she were bidding farewell to an old and cherished friend and advisor as Mountain Jack rode away.

"Now," Hannah said firmly, "we'll see to that hot bath and good meal that I promised you!"

Still feeling as if she were in a daze, Promise allowed the woman to lead them to her cozy quarters.

The feeling of unreality lingered as the days passed, and Promise wondered what could be wrong with her. While a captive of the Comanches and later, while en route to the fort, she had looked forward to being with her own kind once again. But now that she was here and safe, she felt only a deep melancholy, a depression that she could not seem to shake off. Carol was adjusting, putting the past behind her, and looking to the future with touching optimism. Why couldn't she?

The only times she felt truly at ease were when she went to the fort hospital, relieving the officers' wives who voluntarily helped to nurse the sick and the wounded and assisted with the cooking and cleaning. It was with the wounded Confederate prisoners—lodged in a separate, guarded room apart from the rest that had formerly been a storeroom—that she felt the most needed and able to be herself. She came to the conclusion that this was because they, like her, were outcasts, alienated by their differences and their enemy status in the close-knit community of the fort. The other women would have nothing to do with them and looked askance at her willingness to do so.

The three men—one of whom had lost his arm, another who wore a dressing covering his eyes, and a third who had suffered a belly wound—were all touchingly grateful for what little she was able to do for them and vowed again and again that they would never forget her or her kindness preceding what promised to be a long term in a Union prison camp up north, where they would be taken once they were well enough to travel. Promise enjoyed their company as much as they enjoyed hers. She liked to listen to their Southern drawl, and she elevated their flagging spirits by imitating it, much to the wounded men's delight.

"Why, Corporal Shelby, I do declare you ah the most *chahmin'* maan!" she laughingly told the one-armed corporal after he had paid her a compliment. Her green eyes had not sparkled so since she had left New Mexico.

The man whose eyes were heavily bandaged laughed at their exchange. "I haven't heard a prettier drawl since I left N'Orleans, Miz O'Rourke. Are you quite sure you're not a Southern belle by birth?"

"No, sir," she denied. "The farthest south I've ever been is west, to New Mexico and back!"

The man smiled, and she noticed for the first time that he seemed more reserved, more formal, than the others, and a good deal older. He was tall and slightly built, his hair very fair but graying at the temples. He wore a neatly clipped beard that added to his distinguished air. Rumor had it that he was an officer, and that it had been he who was leading the small party of Confederate soldiers up across the Texas border and into the Colorado Territory when they were ambushed by Union soldiers patrolling the area. Major Anthony had speculated that they had intended to rendezvous with Reynolds' Rebs and collect from them the proceeds of the holdups and robberies they had undertaken, and carry it back down south to aid their cause. But even under duress, he had stuck to his story that he held the rank of sergeant, and that his name was John St. Paul. He would divulge nothing more of himself or his mission. His eyes, he had told her, had been injured when the old muzzle-loading musket he carried had exploded in his hands. The fort physician seemed to have little notion of whether he would regain his sight or not, and neither did he care.

"Your father is an officer here at Fort Lyon?" he inquired as Promise helped him to wash up for supper.

"Oh, no, my father died some time ago. I'm waiting for a stage to take me back east."

"Ah!" The man smiled. "You must have a beau waiting for you there."

"I wish I did! But no, that's not why I'm going there. I aim to look up my mama's family. I have grandparents and an aunt whom I've never even met," she confided as she ladled the thin soup into enamel bowls.

He nodded. "They'll be happy to meet such a lovely young woman as yourself, especially when they learn that she's their granddaughter."

Promise pursed her lips. "Now, how would you know if I'm lovely," she teased, "unless you can see through those bandages?"

"I assure you I cannot," he insisted, "but there are some things you don't need eyes to tell!"

She blushed prettily. "Oh, get along with you and your flattery!" she chided. "Here's your plate, and the spoon's right there—a little more to the left. Yes, that's it. Can you manage your supper now?"

He insisted that he could, and she bade the men and the guard at their door a cheerful good night and left, heading for the room she and Carol shared over the sutler's store. The Whittackers, civilians who ran the store that supplied whiskey, tobacco, and other such items to the military men, were kindly folk, especially the wife, Esther, who treated them both as if they were the daughters she'd never had. Amos Whittacker, on the other hand, seemed to have more difficulty in treating the two women normally. There was a certain wariness in his expression, a hesitation when he spoke with them, that made them feel uncomfortable in his presence.

As Promise had told John St. Paul, she had hoped to be able to borrow or earn enough money to enable her to take a stage east. To her chagrin, she learned that the stage lines had been closed down due to Indian hostilities in past months. It seemed she must remain in limbo here at Fort Lyon indefinitely. Eliza Daniels, whose husband had run the stage station, was also awaiting the reopening of the stage lines with as much impatience as Promise. She seemed to feel that their common frustration to be well away from Fort Lyon gave them a sort of bond, and she attached herself to Promise like a leech. Promise could not stand the woman. Scrawny of build and beady eyed, inquisitive and overly critical of everyone, she reminded Promise of a malicious bird! Coupled with that was Promise's certainty that Eliza was hoping their supposed friendship would lead to girlish trading of confidences, and thence lurid recountings of all she had suffered at the hands of those "red savages." To Eliza's supreme irritation, no such confidences were forthcoming, but this did not deter the woman from trying. It seemed she dogged Promise's footsteps from sunup til sundown.

"I swear, Carol, if she could, she'd follow me up here to bed!" Promise exclaimed one night as they readied themselves for bed in their small room over the sutler's store, exasperated by a day of dodging Eliza. "She's like a dog worrying a bone!"

"And a juicy bone at that, nosy old biddy," Carol agreed. She reached out and squeezed Promise's hand. "We've come so far, honey—don't let her get you down."

"I'll try not to," Promise agreed grimly, "but sometimes I think she's even worse than Fights-Wolf!" Her green eyes gleamed in the lamplight.

Carol shuddered. "No one could be that bad!" she said fervently.

"I'm sorry. I didn't mean to remind you."

"That's all right. I reckon I'm over the worst of it now. The dreams—the nightmares—all have stopped. The Indians that come to the fort don't upset me any more." She paused and frowned. "You're still having bad dreams, aren't you, Promise?"

Promise shrugged as she braided her hair for the night. "Some. But—but mostly I keep dreaming about Luke." She sighed heavily. "Since we were captured, what happened between us seems different, somehow. I know how he felt, how bitter he must have been after what my pa did. I'm not saying he was right to use me to get even for it, but I understand why he did it."

"You still love him, don't you?" Carol asked, blue eyes grave.

"Yes!" Promise whispered, and cried for the first time in many weeks.

The next morning, Cay rode into the fort and was greeted by squeals of delight from the two women. His own delight was obvious, and he repeated over and over in wonderment that he and Luke had feared them both dead.

"Luke?" Promise asked, breath bated. "But Luke wasn't—"

"He came after you, Promise," Cay told her solemnly. "He left Santa Fe a few days after the wagon train. He told me that there wasn't anything going to stop him from getting you back." There was pain in his handsome face as he saw the dawning of joy on her lovely features. "We tracked the Comanches who had taken you for miles. We found their camp, but it had been deserted. I—I was ready to give up. I didn't believe we'd find either of you alive, but Luke did. He's still out there on the plains, Promise, searching for you. If he doesn't come in to the fort in a week or so, I mean to go back out and find him. He'll be real happy to see you safe and well, *caballera*," he added huskily.

Promise nodded. "I'll be real glad to see him, too! I—I have something I must tell him, you see." She smiled up at him. "You seem a little different, Cay, since I saw you last. You've finally given up on me—the two of us—haven't you?" she pressed gently.

Cay grinned. "Yes, ma'am, I reckon I have! See, I may be a mite slow at times, but only a fool keeps on banging his head against a closed door indefinitely! I know now there wasn't a hope for you and me, Promise, honey, not with you feeling the way you do about the darned half-blood! Now that I know he feels the same about you, it seems to me a smart man would step aside and admit he's licked. I mean to take off the blinders I've been wearing when it comes to women and have myself a look at the other pretty little fillies!" He winked roguishly, and both Carol and Promise laughed.

"I hope your intentions are honorable, Mister

Cantrell," Carol demanded sternly. There was, however, a rosy color to her cheeks and a bright sparkle to her blue eyes as she made the statement.

"Indeed they are, Miz Bushley," Cay confirmed thoughtfully, gazing down at her.

Promise slipped away to the long sandstone building that housed the hospital, amused to see that the pair did not even notice her departure.

The wounded prisoners were resting on their cots when she went in to them. They seemed bored and restless with their confinement now that their health was improving and were eager for conversation as she swept and dusted their cramped quarters.

"Has Doctor McDonald been in to see you today?" she asked them, pausing in her work.

"He has," the one named John St. Paul confirmed. "He's decided the bandages are to come off my eyes tomorrow. I'll be able to see our angel of mercy, and to thank her properly for all she's done!"

His tone was so confident, so optimistic, that Promise's heart went out to him. "I'm sure you will," she said gently. "I just hope I don't disappoint you!"

"You won't, ma'am!" Corporal Shelby volunteered with a wink and a grin. "She's as sweet and pretty as a magnolia in full bloom, Colonel—ain't that so, LeRoy?"

The other man agreed, darting a sharp look at Shelby, who colored deeply and looked as if he'd like to kick himself.

Promise pretended she had not noticed the little corporal's slip of the tongue and went about her work. "I suppose you all have families back home?"

"A wife, Lucille, and a fine little baby boy," Private LeRoy Germaine supplied in an effort to cover the few tense seconds of silence. "When I marched out of

N'Orleans, he wasn't even walking. I imagine he's talking and walking and everything by now!"

"How about you, Sergeant?" she asked John St. Paul.

"My wife passed on several years ago," he said quietly. "We never had children."

"I'm sorry," Promise murmured.

The man shook his head. "Don't be. I was a good husband to Danielle while she lived, and her passing was expected. She'd been an invalid for a great many years prior to her death. It was almost a blessing."

"Oh," Promise gasped softly, surprised by his emotionless tone.

"I'm sorry if I shocked you, Miz O'Rourke, but I regret to say I never loved my wife. Nor did she love me, though we were close friends, which is more than can be said for a great many couples. The marriage was one of convenience, arranged by our families, you see." He smiled. "It might surprise you to hear that the true love of my life was a little Yankee girl. Now, isn't that something? A Johnny Reb that lost his heart to a pretty Yankee belle! Her papa was madder than a hornet when he found out about the two of us, and I never saw her again. I never forgot her, though. Never."

His face seemed suddenly older and drawn, and he passed his hand across his bandaged eyes, muttering a curse under his breath. "You take my advice, Miz O'Rourke, and take a firm hold of what little happiness life offers you and hang on tight. If you pass up that chance, it might never come again."

Promise nodded. "I intend to do just that, sir, Lord willing."

She was tending the Fort Lyon sick the following morning when the physician, a blunt Scot named McDonald, called her into the adjoining room to assist him.

"If you would clip away the dressings, Miss O'Rourke, we'll see how this fellow is faring." His tone was cold, as if he were angered that his services should be required for Confederate wounded and would not have seen to their injuries if not bound by his physician's oath to tend all in need.

Biting her lip to control the slight tremor in her hands, Promise carefully clipped the bandages away from John St. Paul's eyes. There were ugly scabs all about his cheekbones, and some raw flesh that needed cleansing on his brow. He kept his eyes tightly shut under the pads of gauze that remained when she was done, and she knew by the sudden tenseness of his body as he sat on the side of his cot that he was apprehensive.

"Thank you, Miss O'Rourke. If you'll step aside, I can manage the rest," Doctor McDonald said.

Promise nodded and walked across to the narrow window, barred since the room had been converted from a storage area to a prison ward, beyond which a guard patrolled, rifle smartly carried across his shoulder.

"Open your eyes slowly, St. Paul," the physician instructed, "and try not to look into the light." The man's eyes fluttered open. He blinked despite the gloom, having been in total darkness for so long. "Well, man?" McDonald demanded. "Can you see me?"

There were tears on St. Paul's cheeks as he nodded, and his voice was husky with emotion and relief when he spoke. "Yes, I can see you, Doctor—but I'd rather see Miss O'Rourke! I warrant she's a prettier sight than you, sir, to a man who's been in darkness for close to a month!"

He stood and walked across the room to where Promise stood, stopping a short distance from her. She saw that he was very handsome with the bandages removed, and with a start she realized that his eyes were as green as her own.

503

"Well, my dear, it appears I was wrong yesterday when I said that I didn't need eyes to know that you were lovely." He smiled, seeing her surprised expression. "You're not lovely at all—you're beautiful! Very beautiful."

She said nothing. She simply stood quite still, staring at him as if she had never seen him before this moment. Her cheeks were burning suddenly, and there was an insistent throbbing in her temple. *No.* It couldn't be. It—it just wasn't possible, she thought incredulously.

"I've offended you, ma'am? Please, accept my sincere apologies! I had not intended to speak so boldly—" he apologized, his expression concerned.

She blinked. "What? Oh, no, Sergeant, it was nothing you said, believe me," she insisted. "I—I really should be going. Good day, gentlemen."

Four pairs of startled eyes watched her as she fled from the hospital building and out into the chilly compound.

She kept herself busy the remainder of that day, helping Esther Whittacker in the sutler's store. She was grimly determined not to think about the Confederate "sergeant," or the fact that he'd loved a Yankee girl, or the fact that he had green eyes—as her mother had said her Courtney Fontaine had green eyes. If he was indeed the man who had fathered her, she didn't want to know of it! He had spoken of love, but surely if he was Courtney Fontaine, he would have found some way to come back to his Mary, instead of leaving like a thrashed hound with its tail tucked between its legs and marrying another woman? The truth lay at her fingertips. She had only to go back to the hospital, to face the man, and ask him straight out if his northern sweetheart had been Mary Haverleigh and if his name was Courtney Fontaine, and she would know . . . She shook her head. No. She didn't want to know! Patrick O'Rourke had loved her dearly, had been all the father she had ever wanted or needed, despite his faults, she told herself firmly and tried to put her suspicions out of her thoughts. But from that morning, she never went back to the hospital quarters again.

Love bloomed between Carol and Cay Cantrell, and to watch it lifted Promise out of the overly pensive, brooding mood she had fallen into since that morning when she had looked into the Confederate soldier's green eyes and had begun to wonder.

In two short weeks, admiring glances had led to stolen kisses and furtive hand holding, and Cay wore a besotted expression on his face that reminded Promise of a love-sick calf. It came as no great surprise to her that the whirlwind courtship should progress rapidly to its logical and romantic conclusion. When Carol came up to their room one night, her face aglow, her eyes like sapphires, Promise knew what had happened long before the words tumbled from her lips in excited torrents.

"Cay's asked me to marry him, Promise!" she cried breathlessly. "And I told him I would!" Her expression grew more sober. "He knows all about that—that Indian, and the baby, but he says it makes no difference to him, that he loves me and that he'll be a good father to Larry's child, that he'll raise it as his own. I know we're rushing into this, but I don't care! Cay has some money saved at the bank up in Denver. He means to buy a small spread at first, then add to it later. Do you think we're a couple of lovesick fools, Promise? Do you? Maybe we should wait awhile? I—I know how Cay felt about you . . ."

Promise hugged her. "Do you love him?"

Carol nodded. "Yes, I believe I do. I'll never forget Larry, or the love we had, but Cay's offering me a new life, a chance at happiness. I reckon we have as much hope of that as anyone else does—maybe more."

"Then I'd say you've answered your own questions, Carol," Promise murmured. "I wish you both all the happiness in the world!"

Carol nodded happily. "Thank you! Maybe—maybe when Luke gets here, things will look up for you, too."

"Maybe," Promise agreed, but there was sadness in her eyes. "Luke and I—well, we came together for all the wrong reasons, Carol. We hurt each other terribly. I'm not sure if that can be mended between us, however badly we want it to."

Carol snorted. "Now who's giving up before she's even given it a try?" she asked pointedly before rolling over and falling asleep.

After a few moments, Promise blew out the lamp and snuggled under the covers, smiling in the shadows. Carol was right. The only battles lost before they were fought were the ones never started!

Chapter Thirty

"I expect you just can't *wait* to see that stage back east, can you, Miss O'Rourke?" Eliza said. "I know Clinton and I are just counting the days 'til they let the stages through again! Where did you say it was your poor mama was from, child?" Her dark eyes were as beady and bright as a predatory bird's as she peered at Promise.

"I don't think I said," Promise murmured absently, wishing Eliza would go away and leave her alone, "but it was New York." She looked beyond Eliza's scrawny figure to the fort gate then swept the compound with a glance, wondering where Cay and Carol could have disappeared to and hoping against hope that they'd return and help her get rid of Eliza Daniels. Her expression softened and her green eyes took on a dreamy, faraway look. She couldn't really blame the two of them for wanting to be alone under the circumstances, bless them! Eliza Daniels chattered on, and Promise nodded in what she hoped were appropriate places, while she turned her attention once more to the fort gate where there were several people coming and going. There were sentries, of course, as well as civilians like the Danielses who held position at the fort, ranchers from outlying homesteads, and a few cavalry men returning from reconnoitering the surrounding territory. When the dust from the cavalry horses had settled, she saw a scout enter the gates on a blue roan horse. He wore a tan buckskin shirt and pants, and the edges of both had long fringes that fluttered in the sharp wind. She couldn't see the face beneath the dark Stetson, but for a second, the way the man rode reminded her of—

"But just exactly where in New York?" Eliza Daniels persisted, stepping in front of Promise and blocking her view. "New York's a big city, honey."

"I'm afraid I couldn't say," Promise murmured, craning her neck to look over Eliza's shoulder. "See, Mama and her family kind of lost touch over the—" *It was him!* she realized suddenly. *It was Luke!* She stepped quickly past Eliza, knocking her with her shoulder as she did so.

"Oh!" Eliza gasped as Promise kept on walking without so much as an apology.

She'd walked halfway across the compound before she realized she had moved. At the flagpole in the center she pulled up short and stood there, holding her hair down about her shoulders in the wind as he rode slowly toward her. The blue roan was caked with trail dust, and it moved as if the effort to lift one hoof after the other required tremendous effort. Her heart skipped a beat, and her tongue felt suddenly tied. Her knees turned to jelly and she felt peculiarly light headed and giddy as she saw him take off his hat and lean forward a little, his slim brown hands resting on the high pommel of his saddle. *He looks awfully tired*, she thought irrationally, hands fidgeting nervously with the folds of her skirt. *The lines from his eyes and about his mouth are deeper.*

She's changed, he thought. *There's pain in her eyes, and new knowledge. She's a woman now, still beautiful, still vulnerable, but not a girl any more.* "Promise," he greeted her, nodding as he dismounted the roan. "I didn't expect to find you here."

She shrugged and gave him a foolishly happy grin. "I know. Cay said that you wouldn't give up looking for me. He planned to go out after you if you didn't come in by the end of the week." She looked down at her hands, toying now with the ends of the knitted shawl and darted an uncertain glance at him. "I—I really do thank you for going to so much trouble on my account."

He nodded and led the roan toward her, running the reins through his hands as he came. "I couldn't give up until I was certain you weren't still out there somewhere," he said huskily. "It's real good to see you." *Words*, he thought wryly. Why was he standing there mumbling polite words when what he really wanted was to take her in his arms?

A tinge of warm color seeped into her cold cheeks at the expression in his eyes. She hugged herself about the arms and shivered.

"Luke, I—"

"Promise, I—"

They both spoke at the same time, and both broke off self-consciously with an embarrassed smile.

"You first!" Promise urged.

He shook his head. "No, go on."

"Perhaps I should," she agreed. "I swore if I ever saw you again, I'd say what I had to say before I backed out of ever saying it!

"I learned something out there, when the Comanches attacked the wagon train. At the time, I decided that should I run into you again, I'd keep what I learned to myself, but I realized later that I *had* to tell you or keep lying to myself." She bit her lip and looked down again at her nervous fingers, twining in the ends of the shawl. "You were right all along about my pa," she began, raising her eyes to look him squarely in the face. "I didn't want to believe it, even after I learned the truth, but it's true! He stole the gold you and Jake Colter worked for together. He hid the nuggets inside the hollow knob of that walking stick he had, the one with the horse's head." Seeing him nod, she continued, "That's why you couldn't find it all these years. It was there all the time, right under my nose!" She shrugged helplessly. "I—I know that nothing can give you back the years you lost on account of what my pa did, but—but I want you to know that I'm real sorry. And another thing—I know my pa fired first that night, and that you shot him in self-defense. I've always known, I guess. I just remembered it the way I wanted to." There. She'd said it. Suddenly, it was like a weight had been lifted from her. A shudder ran through her, for admitting the truth about Pa had hurt more than she'd dreamed. "I guess knowing what I do, I should hate him, but I don't," she added. "Whether he was right or wrong, I'll always remember him with love. See, I guess that's what love is all about, at least in my mind—forgiving someone when he goes wrong, keeping right on loving him despite it, trying to understand and help him through the bad times." She smiled, embarrassed. "Leastways, that's how I see it. Maybe I'm wrong."

For a few moments after she had finished her breathless outpouring, he remained silent. At length he nodded. "No, I'd say you're right," he agreed. "I've done some thinking, too, since I left the ranch to come after you. I don't blame you for hating me, *desperada*. I had no right to take my bitterness out on you. My grandfather warned me it might go sour on me. He warned me that I'd end up losing you, but I guess I was too blind and crazy to see it then."

He took her elbow and led her out of the wind that blew her cornsilk hair across her face in long streamers, to the shelter of the front of the sutler's store. His horse plodded behind him. "After you'd gone, the Shadow S didn't seem to mean much to me any more. I'd always thought of it as my father's dream, anyway—to see it built up and prospering, something to look up to—not my dream. When you left, I realized that all that had changed over the weeks. It had become my dream, too, but once you were gone, something was missing—someone to share that dream with. Someone to share my life with, too.

"Freedom! I'd always figured that meant no ties, having nothing and nobody to tie you down. That's not so. It's being able to feel the way you want to, to think any way you want to. It's something inside a man, wherever he is. Prison walls can't take away a man's freedom, except in the physical sense, unless he lets them. But I reckon the walls a man builds up around himself can."

Heart filled to bursting, she reached out to touch his sleeve, brushing it fleetingly with her fingertips before she self-consciously drew her hand back. She tossed her windblown hair over her shoulders and smiled shyly, aware of the tingling sensation in her body at his closeness. "Sounds to me as if we've both been doing some mighty hard thinking, Mister Steele," she murmured.

He touched her cheek with his fingertip, tracing its downy curve, aware of the sudden rush of heat in her face as he did so. "I'd say you're right, Miz O'Rourke!" he said huskily. She moved quickly back, out of his reach. She seemed shaken by the fleeting caress.

"I—I should be going," she said, breathless. "Eliza Daniels is waiting for me over there." She nodded across the compound to where the woman hovered, impatiently pacing and casting meaningful looks in their direction. "She and the officers' wives have been very kind. They've collected some clothes for me to—to take with me on the stage back east, seeing as how mine were all lost."

His jaw hardened. "Then you still mean to take that stage?"

"I guess so," she said in a quiet voice. She turned to walk away, pausing to look back at him at the firm touch of his hand on her shoulder.

"No," he said roughly, urgently. "We have to talk about that, too. My horse needs seeing to. Can we talk later? After supper, maybe?" His dark eyes roved her pale, lovely face with the passionate intimacy of a caress.

"Yes," she agreed quickly. "I'd like that." She hurried away.

He watched her trim figure cross the compound, cornsilk hair billowing about her shoulders, until she reached the other woman, then he led his horse away as the pair entered one of the officers' quarters on the north side of the fort.

Eliza Daniels said very little as Promise rejoined her, but the malicious curiosity in the dark gleam of her eyes said volumes. She held her silence until they had almost reached the Morrisons' quarters, then asked in a too-casual voice, "I know it's none of my business, I'm sure, Miss O'Rourke, but who was that—that *Indian* you were speaking with?"

Promise pursed her lips, a flush of anger seeping up her throat at Eliza's tone. She was finished being polite to this nosy, small-minded old biddy! "You're right, Miz

512

Daniels—it's none of your business," she rejoined sweetly. "Shall we go in?"

Eliza gave a shocked little snort. "Well, excuse me, I'm sure!" she sniffed, tossing her rigid, mousy ringlets.

Several of the officers' wives were seated about a long, rough-hewn pine table in Hannah Morrison's cozy quarters, working on a large piece of quilting done in colorful triangles of calico scraps. A fire gave a cheerful glow to the women's faces in the gloom of a November afternoon as they bent neatly coiffed heads to their rows of tiny stitches. Next to the hearth stood a large, blue-flowered teapot, and on a low chest was a willow-patterned plate bearing several small cakes. It was a cozy, domestic scene that would have seemed commonplace to anyone else, yet Promise was struck not so much by the ordinary scene, but by the resemblance it had to the gathering of women in Fights-Wolf's village as they helped flesh a buffalo robe. It was a thought she knew the women would not appreciate her sharing!

They all looked up as Promise and Eliza entered, and she saw the women adopt expressions of sympathy and understanding, and yes, pity, too, as easily as she had once slipped on the *kachina* mask. Mountain Jack Webster had known what he was talking about when he'd warned her of how it would be at the fort. The women meant well, they truly did, and they tried hard to be good Christian folk and accept her. But in her heart she knew they hadn't. In their eyes, she was a fallen woman, soiled by her association with the red savages they so hated and feared, even though fascinated by them. She'd always be someone to whom they could piously offer charity and sympathy but never friendship given from the heart. No, she was definitely not the sort of woman they'd want

513

their sisters or their daughters to become friends with, and *certainly* not their brothers or sons!

"Won't you join us, Promise, my dear child?" Hannah Morrison offered. "Julia, honey, pull up a chair for Promise." She patted Promise's hand.

A faint smile playing about her lips, Promise sat in the chair offered her. "Thank you, Mrs. Morrison."

"Hannah, child, Hannah! We're all good friends here, aren't we?" Hannah Morrison corrected, beaming. "My, you look so pretty in my old plaid dress. And I'd say your rest has done you a world of good, honey. You don't look nearly so peaked as you did, does she, girls?" The other women about the table murmured agreement, save for Eliza Daniels, who grimaced and pettishly refused to comment.

"I do so hope you're beginning to put your terrible ordeal behind you," Julia, a fragile blond woman, said, "though no doubt you must still have awful nightmares about it, do you not? Why, the other poor creatures we've seen brought in here after being recaptured from the savages were half-demented by what they'd been through! I do so admire Major Wynkoop for securing their release from that awful Black Kettle. Whatever Major Anthony and the others might say about him being too friendly with the Cheyenne, at least he was able to get the women and little children released before he was relieved of his command! They say," she added, leaning forward and lowering her voice conspiratorially, "that one of them was so badly abused, she hanged herself from a tipi pole rather than live with her shame. Of course, you and Missus Bushley appear to have been able to put such . . . nasty things behind you." She arched her eyebrows hoping—Promise knew only too well—that Promise would offer to share the details of those "nasty" things.

Promise smothered an indignant comment. "I suppose Carol and I were lucky, in a way. After I was able to convince the Comanche that we could heal the little girl, they left us pretty much alone, as I told you before." Six pairs of eyes looked upon her with obvious disbelief.

"Oh, but to be stripped naked and tied up in the sun to be cooked alive!" Julia shuddered. "I think I would rather have died!"

Promise gritted her teeth. "You'd be surprised at how badly you want to live, ma'am, whatever the circumstances, when it comes to a choice between life and death."

"But that poor little Becky!" Hannah cried. She shuddered. "I certainly hope my Charles and his men are able to find her and bring her back before she's ruined for life by those heathens and their savage ways!"

"She was being well taken care of, Hannah," Promise insisted. "Grey Blanket, an Indian woman in the village, had lost her own daughter. She loved little Becky very much. Maybe she's better off with someone who loves her, with her own folks dead."

Those six pairs of horror-rounded eyes gaped at her again as the women digested Promise's shocking statement.

"Being raised by—by Indians little better than animals is better than being raised by your own kind?" Julia exclaimed, clutching her throat in shock at such an idea. "How could you believe such a thing, after all you've been through?"

Promise turned to answer her in time to see Eliza Daniels whisper something behind her hand to Julia. The blond woman's eyes widened still further and she turned a bright pink and gasped, "So! That explains it!" She caught Promise's eyes upon her and quickly looked away.

Promise said nothing, but she had caught Eliza's

whispered comment in part and guessed that the news of her conversation with Luke in the compound—and probably the fact that he'd been seen to touch her cheek—had been spitefully relayed and, no doubt, considerably exaggerated! Silently, she fumed.

"That Mister Cantrell seems such a charming young man," Hannah intervened as the air in the room suddenly crackled with tension. "I do believe he's quite taken with that nice Carol Bushley."

"It does appear so," Eliza agreed. "It is such a shame that she was—well, you know. It'll be so hard on her when he moves on as such young men will do and finds himself a woman that's—that's more his *kind* of woman," she simpered slyly. "After all, she can't expect a decent man to overlook the fact that one of those red-skinned devils actually—well, you know, and treat her like she was just a regular little widow carrying her dead husband's child. Men are very particular about such things. Oh, no insult intended I'm sure, Miss O'Rourke!"

"And none taken, I can assure *you*, Mrs. Daniels!" Promise countered sweetly. "However, I'm afraid you're wrong. I'm certain you'll be the first to congratulate Carol and Mister Cantrell when they share their good news."

"Good news?" Eliza echoed, her creamy smile curdling.

"Why, yes! You see, Cay's decided Mrs. Bushley is *exactly* his kind of woman! They plan on getting married and starting a ranch up near Denver. Didn't you know?"

Promise stood and pushed back her chair. Enough was enough! "If you'll excuse me, I do believe I'll go and lie down for a spell. I must be more tired than I thought." It was no lie. She *was* tired—of them and their narrow minds and attitudes.

"But what about the clothes we've collected? Surely you'll want to try them on in case they need to be altered?" Hannah asked, gesturing to a pile of threadbare castoffs in one corner.

Promise flashed her a sweet smile. Poor Hannah. Of all of them, she was the kindest. "On second thought, Mrs. Morrison, I do believe I'll have to refuse your generous offer, however well intended. My mother was never one to accept charity from anybody, and I've just realized I'm every bit as proud as she was. Good day to you, ladies. And, thank you!"

She swept from the Morrisons' quarters with her head held high like a proud blossom upon a rigidly straight stalk, her back ramrod stiff. She'd wear the clothes she had on her back until Hell froze over before she'd take those old, gossiping, small-minded busybodies' hand-me-downs, she determined!

Though she looked for him as she crossed the compound, she didn't see Luke again until later that evening, when she and Carol made their way back to their bed above the sutler's store after supper. He was standing under a lantern that hung from the corner of the stage station, smoking a cheroot. Lantern light spilled all about him, gleaming upon his blue-black hair and tanned features.

"Carol, do you mind going on alone?" she asked. "I promised Luke that we'd talk."

Carol smiled, her pretty blue eyes lively and filled with happiness. "Go on with you. Cay said he planned to come by the store and visit with the Whittakers for a spell, anyway. I'll be seeing you later." She waved. "Good night, Luke, Promise!" She hurried off across the shadowed compound leaving Luke and Promise alone.

Neither of them spoke for several moments. Then all at once—how they never could quite recall afterward— they were in each other's arms, holding fiercely, kissing hungrily, clinging to each other as if they would never let go. The ardor of Luke's lips evoked a reaction within her body that was tantamount to an explosion! All the bitter pain of their separation, all the unrealized longing she'd carried in her heart since that night in the box canyon was ignited as she felt his arms about her, fanned into raging fire by the rough warmth of his lips. She shook, she quivered, she vibrated with the sheer power of her emotions exploding like sunbursts throughout her being!

His lips trailed down from her sweet mouth and he feverishly kissed her throat, nuzzling his mouth against the soft, vulnerable pulse spot below her ear, interspersing each kiss there with murmured endearments. She arched back her head and closed her eyes, fingers curled about his strong shoulders as she surrendered to his caresses and kisses. Memories of their past passion swept through her like wildfire, brought back by his familiar inflaming touch, his masculine scent, the sight of his handsome face in the lantern's amber glow.

"Oh, Luke, Luke, my dearest!" she sighed against his night-black hair. "We were such fools! Hold me! Never let me go again, never!"

"I won't, my dearest *desperada*! I give you my word, here and now. Never again!" As he said the words, he gazed deeply into her eyes. The smoldering desire in their dark depths stunned her anew, and she swayed under the impact of that scorching gaze.

"I want you, Luke, want you so much!" she cried softly, her small hands balled into fists where they rested against his broad chest.

He held her against him, stroking her hair. "I know, my love, I know! I want you, too. But we can't—not here. There're too many people here who wouldn't understand. I won't give them the chance to hurt you with their ignorance!" He rained tiny kisses over her flushed face.

Her fingers splayed across his upper arms then tightened with the fierce pressure of her need, digging into the hard-muscled flesh through his buckskin shirt. Her body burned like a brand against the length of his. "There must be somewhere we can be alone together? Please, Luke, I can't bear it!"

He hesitated, then nodded, turning away and leading her after him as he strode silently through the shadows to the stables.

"Wait here," he ordered softly, and she nodded without a word, hearing the racing clamor of her pulse singing in her ears.

Minutes later he returned leading his saddled horse, now rested. He lifted her up onto its back and mounted behind her. They were through the massive fort gates scant seconds before the guards closed and barricaded them for the night, riding swiftly across the wintry terrain. Moonlight cast its silver everywhere upon the iced puddles of the rutted track they rode, throwing skeleton trees into sharp, black relief. The blue roan's hooves drummed on the hard, cold earth, their beat matching the racing beats of their hearts. An owl glided overhead, hooting mournfully in the frosty night air as it hunted its prey. For all that Promise wore only a shawl above the heavy plaid dress, Luke's arms about her and his broad chest pressed firmly against her back kept her as warm as if she sat by a fire. And, too, she felt warmed from the inside, filled with the rosy glow of desire . . .

It seemed far too long before they reached their destination, yet for the lovers a minute, a second, would have seemed too long that night! Promise saw that the place Luke had chosen was the camp of his mother's people, the Cheyenne of old chief Black Kettle, now located upon the banks of the Sand Creek. From across the creek's sandy banks, the tipis glowed like giant golden candles from the fires lit within them.

"We can be together here," Luke said softly against her hair. "Unless you'd rather go somewhere else?"

She knew he must be thinking of her capture by the Comanche and quickly murmured, "No, no, as long as we can be together! Flattens-Grass was very kind to me before."

He nodded and urged the horse down the sandy banks and across the creek, its hooves cracking the thin, glinting layer of ice that covered the water.

Minutes later, Flattens-Grass and her husband, Four Winds, were greeting them and bidding them to warm themselves before a fire. Luke drew his uncle aside and they talked quietly for a short while as the women smiled shyly at each other and murmured greetings in their own tongues. Flattens-Grass showed Promise the beadwork she had been doing by the light of the fire when they arrived, a belt with a design of little turtles nose-to-tail all along its length, worked in red and yellow and white. She made signs to demonstrate that it was to ensure the wearer of getting with child, and Promise laughed at her imitation of a heavy-bellied woman and nodded with understanding.

"Four Winds has promised to see that a tipi is prepared for us," Luke said at length as he came to her side. "While it's being seen to, I will take you to meet my grandfather, Yellow Rock. He was angered that I didn't bring you to see him the last time we were in Black Kettle's village. In a little while, we can be alone."

She smiled her agreement, thinking that she would have met the Old Man in the Moon himself had Luke wished it!

To Luke's eyes, the *shaman* seemed frailer than when they had met last. There was the barest tremor in his gnarled old hands now, a tiredness about him. After greeting a sleepy Red Leaf and his cousin, Scarred Hand, who had already retired to their buffalo robes, Luke led Promise to stand by the fire across from the old man. They watched respectfully as he offered his pipe to the heavens and then the earth, then to the direction of the four winds before drawing deeply upon it. The scent of sumac and other herbs filled the tipi.

"My heart is gladdened to see you again, Grandfather," Luke greeted Yellow Rock.

"And mine soars like the eagle to see you here again, Grandson," Yellow Rock rejoined. "You and your woman must warm yourselves. The night is as sharp as the edge of a tomahawk." He smiled faintly as Promise moved to the left and took her place cross-legged before the fire. He approved of her good manners and of her modest behavior. He said nothing as he puffed upon his pipe, waiting for his grandson to recover a little from his journey and begin the conversation when he was ready to do so. Such was the custom, to allow a guest time to collect his thoughts and words, and it was a good one. But it was not long before Tall Shadow found his tongue, and the *shaman* was inwardly amused. The reason for his impatience was obvious, mirrored in the grass-colored eyes of the woman with hair like the sun and in his grandson's dark eyes. Ah, to be young again, to feel the hot fire of youth throbbing in his veins once more! he thought indulgently.

"Grandfather, when last we met, you told me of a vision you had been given, of a dove who had evaded a mighty hawk and fluttered free of its talons, leaving the hawk lying still upon the ground. It was many moons before I understood the meaning of this, and many suns more before I listened to the good council you had given me. But the Wise One Above smiled upon one of his foolish children! He opened my eyes to what lay in my heart before it was too late. The dove indeed fluttered free, Grandfather, but now she has willingly returned to the hawk." He smiled across at Promise, who lowered her radiant green eyes modestly and wondered what it was he had said. "Grandfather, I would have you meet my woman, the one I once gave the name of Mourning Dove. In the tongue of the white man, she is called Promise. It means a vow, given in trust." In English he added, "Promise, this is my grandfather, Yellow Rock."

The *shaman* beckoned her forward. He smiled, and, despite his frailty, his black eyes twinkled. "She is indeed a prize amongst women, my grandson!" he approved softly. "She appears strong and well able to bear you children. For such a modest beauty as she, a brave would hazard much to make her his woman. You are fortunate she is not of our people, Tall Shadow. I fear you would need many, many ponies to gift a father for such a daughter, after our customs!"

Yellow Rock laughed at the rosy blush that stained her cheeks as Luke translated his words and his compliments to her. She thanked him, and he nodded. "Go now, my children, while the Old Woman yet shines in the night sky. Share what is in your hearts after the manner of all men and women who love."

Luke murmured his farewell, rose, and left the tipi,

leading Promise after him. Minutes later, they were in the tipi that Flattens-Grass and others of the village women had quickly erected for them, set apart from the others.

It was large and cozy, made of new hides and without the yellowed hue from the smoke that older tipis bore. Warm buffalo robes had been spread across the flooring of rawhide, and a crackling fire burned in the center, its smoke drawing well through the star-filled smoke hole high above. The herbal scent of dried wildflowers which had been sprinkled upon the fire filled the tipi.

Now that the moment she had longed for was at hand, Promise felt tongue-tied and unaccountably shy, as if she were a virgin maid about to lie with the man she loved for the very first time.

He sensed her shyness and, smiling, moved across the tipi to the heaped buffalo robes. Sitting down, he beckoned to her, murmuring, "Come here, little dove."

She moved as if in a dream to stand before him, then halted, wanting to go to him but unable suddenly to make the move. Doubt swept through her as she recalled with agonizing clarity the pain she had felt on learning how he had sought to use her. Could she open up her heart again? Dare she let Luke become so important to her a second time, and in so doing take the chance that she might be hurt again? God, she felt so naked, so vulnerable now! Her heart swelled with love for him, but she was uncertain if his declarations of love could be trusted!

He saw the uncertainty, the doubt in her eyes, and took her by the hand and tugged her gently down to sit beside him. He cupped her lovely face in his large hands and gazed deeply into her eyes. "You're afraid, aren't you?" he asked tenderly.

"Yes, oh, yes!" she whispered, searching his face for the answers to her unspoken questions.

"Don't be," he implored her, stroking her silky hair. "I love you, Promise O'Rourke! The lies, the pretending, they've been over with for a long, long time—before we ever reached the Shadow S. I—I was afraid that if I told you it was I who killed your father, you'd leave me. I couldn't bear to take that chance! I won't ask you to trust me again, honey. I did that once, and it was a lie. I'm asking only for a second chance, asking you to let me show you just how much I love you, day by day. Just one day at a time." His black eyes were tender as he caressed her face, tilting her chin so that she looked up at him. In the flaring light that danced upon the walls of the tipi, she had never looked more lovely, he thought, her hair gilded with firelight, her eyes luminous with unshed tears.

She drew a deep, shaky breath before answering him. "I may need every one of those days, Luke," she said honestly. "You see, it's the tender betrayals that hurt the most! I—I came close to losing my mind when you told me what you'd set out to do. You can't rebuild that trust overnight." He saw the shadow that flitted across her face as she recalled that time, and it tore at his heart. She smiled tremulously. "But I do know this, Luke, my dearest—I'm willing to take a chance on you again." She clasped his hand to her cheek, then kissed it. "I love you way too much not to. Way too much!"

"I'll never give you reason to doubt my love again, baby," he whispered huskily. "Never . . ." He took her in his arms and gently turned her to face him, lowering his dark head as he kissed her. She parted her lips in willing, joyful surrender as his warm mouth captured hers, and tongues of flame curled through her as their bodies pressed close together. His mouth teased the corners of her own. The tip of his maddening tongue delved tentatively between her lips, and in the fiery rapture of his kiss, desire swept through her and consumed them both.

He paused to draw the damp shawl from about her shoulders and set it carefully aside before facing her once more. As if she were a fragile blossom that he might crush with a firm hand, he lightly stroked her cornsilk hair, loving the way it shone like a heavy curtain of shimmering satin in the firelight. His eyes never left her radiant face as he spilled the gleaming gold through his fingers, thinking as he did so that the gold in his hands far outweighed that which was taken from the earth, both in beauty and value. The breath caught in his throat. "Promise, my golden Promise!" he murmured now as he turned her away from him and swept that shimmering silky curtain aside.

Gooseflesh rose along her arms and a small cry of delight broke from her moistly parted lips as he showered tiny, feather-light kisses over the bared downy column of her neck. She gasped as she sensed his strong hands unfastening the little buttons that closed her dress in back. As the heavy cloth fell away, he continued his delectable kisses down the narrow ridges of her spine. "So soft, like velvet . . ." he murmured huskily, reveling in the smooth satin texture of her flesh. The subtle scent of her body reminded him of fresh wildflowers and tall meadow grasses swaying in the summer sunshine. He nuzzled her warm body and inhaled her perfume as if she were a mountain rose freshly plucked from the briar.

Soon she lay unclothed in his arms, their breath mingling as they kissed sweetly, deeply yet again. His hands cupped and caressed each ivory breast in turn, dwelling leisurely upon each dark-rose nipple until the miniature peaks firmed under his touch, becoming as swollen and unfurled as a flower that opens its tiny buds to the sun's warmth. His hand brushed down, across the sleek expanse of her rib cage, lingering fleetingly there as if to measure the tempo of her racing heart. Still his lips nuzzled the soft hollow where throat met shoulder as he caressed her, and she stirred in his arms as the curling warmth of desire spread heat throughout her body. It was as if fire raced through her veins out of control, making her pulse sing with a giddy, reckless joy, heightening every sense to new and breathtaking acuity.

She arched her head back to return his kisses with kisses of her own, reaching up to clasp his dark head and pressing her lips over his with a fierce passion she had not known she possessed until now. She reveled in the feel of crisp black hair laced between her fingers; in the delicious contrast of hard, male flesh against her own quivering softness; in the masculine roughness of his jaw when she pressed her own burning cheek to his. With a yearning sigh, she leaned from him and drew the damp buckskin shirt from his chest, hanging it carefully from one of the poles of the tipi to dry. His eyes gazed lovingly upon her as she padded gracefully back to his side, her body burnished by the firelight, reflecting its flames in the emerald depths of her eyes. He held out his strong arms and she came into them, molding her body to the hardness of his. Breathing shallowly, he pulled the furry buffalo robes up about them and tenderly lay between her thighs.

Her arms enfolded him, drawing his head down to be pillowed in the valley of her breasts. A joyful gasp escaped her as she felt his hardness fill her, and like a flower parting its petals to the morning sun, she gladly offered her sweet, nectared warmth to him. As he surged into that moist, silken sheath, he felt waves of ecstasy encompass her, and she cried out her rapture to the amber shadows as he branded her flushed face with his kisses.

Like young, vigorous, wild things, they loved again and again that long night through, scaling the heights of passion and floating down to blissful release over and over. Both rejoiced in the dazzling pleasure they gave each other as they moved effortlessly from plateau to plateau, ever upward to the dizzying pinnacle where both would soar free to the zenith on the wings of rapture. Bodies, minds, and hearts overflowing with rainbow-colored emotions of lightning-bolt intensity, they clung fiercely to each other long after the last pinnacle had been reached, as if afraid to let go for fear they might never be together again. He breathed her name over and over against her hair as if it was a powerful chant, with magic in the chanting.

Only in the gray hours shortly before dawn did they sink into exhausted sleep, their limbs entwined, their breath commingled. Their sleeping faces were aglow in the fire's radiant warmth.

Through the smoke hole, the Old Woman, the moon, and her son, the bright Morning Star, smiled down upon the lovers and blessed their union.

Chapter Thirty-One

A watery yellow sun and a bleak gray sky were showing through the smoke hole when Luke and Promise woke the next morning. Her face still wore the glow and softness of the night of love and passion they had shared, and she stretched like a sleepy cat as Luke stirred beneath the buffalo robes and leaned up on one elbow to peer down at her. His face, too, seemed softened and lit from within in some mysterious way. His eyes, as he dipped his dark head to lightly press a kiss to her nose, were filled with love. "Morning, *desperada*," he murmured huskily against her hair, nuzzling beneath it to her sleep-warmed skin and kissing her throat.

"You promised," she accused drowsily. "Last night you promised you'd never call me that again!" She opened wide green eyes to look up at him with mock reproof. "It reminds me of a time I'd rather forget!"

"You'd rather forget the first time that we met?" he asked teasingly, tracing the outline of her rosy lips and drawing his finger away when she pretended to bite. "I don't know if I like the sound of that, honey."

"You know what I mean! I had so much on my mind then—I was almost crazy with worry about Mama and the cabin and all. I guess I must have been desperate to even consider robbing Hollander's bank!" Her eyes narrowed suddenly, and she swept up dark gold lashes and looked at him with sudden suspicion. "Whatever happened to the money sack? You gave me back the clothes and guns, but not that!"

He grinned, teeth flashing white in the gloom of dawn against the copper tan of his skin. "It's safe; don't worry. I made a very generous donation to the San Rafael Mission—in the name of Mister Matthew T. Hollander of Cherry Creek himself! I even added a note to the effect that it was to be used to help widows and orphans. Under the circumstances, it seemed fitting, wouldn't you say?" His dark brows rose inquiringly, and Promise giggled.

"I would indeed, Mister Steele," she agreed. "I'd love to be there when Hollander learns what a generous benefactor he's been!"

"I doubt he ever will," Luke said with certainty. "Hollander didn't strike me as the type of man to visit a mission, unless it was to rob the poor box." He pulled the buffalo robe away from Promise and slapped her bared bottom. "Now, out, woman, and fetch my clothes like a proper Cheyenne wife!"

Promise grabbed for the edge of the robe and jerked it back up to cover her. "If the mighty Tall Shadow wants his clothes, then he'll have to get them himself. It's freezing out there!" Her green eyes sparkled defiantly above the hem of the shaggy robe.

He shrugged. "I can see I'll have to find myself a second wife, one to do all the work. You," he added, a gleam in his dark eyes, "I'll keep only to warm my buffalo robes."

"Mmm," she murmured approvingly, "that sounds wonderful!" She sat up suddenly, pulling the pelt up to cover her breasts. Shoulders bare, cornsilk hair tumbling about them in disarray, she cocked her head to one side as she watched him pad across the tipi to collect his buckskin shirt and pants. "Which of us would take care of the little papooses?" she asked.

Without turning to look at her, he stepped into his pants and pulled them up over his long, wiry legs, before fastening a wide rawhide belt comfortably about his waist. "We'll worry about that when the time comes," he answered over his shoulder.

She grimaced. "Maybe we should worry about it pretty soon," she said casually. "I've a suspicion that in the spring, around April, you're going to be a father."

He spun about to face her, the emotions of surprise and joy chasing each other across his face in quick succession.

"Are you sure, honey?" he breathed, striding quickly to where she sat and kneeling at her side.

"As sure as I can be until I start growing," she confirmed.

He pulled the buffalo robe from her and bared her to his gaze, his eyes lingering on her breasts, fuller than he remembered, and on her belly, still girlishly flat. He leaned over her and gently kissed each breast, then her flat, velvety stomach, and, finally, her lips, drawing out the kiss and holding her so tenderly she felt dizzy with the love and joy flowing between them. When he released her, she murmured, "You're happy then? I was so afraid you wouldn't be! I didn't want to use the baby to force you to stay with me, Luke," she said earnestly, searching his dark eyes. "I wanted you to decide for yourself, of your own free will."

"Wild horses couldn't keep me from you, my love," he whispered, his chin resting on the crown of her head. He held her at arm's length and gazed into her eyes. "I love you, my golden Promise! I love you!" He saw happy tears fill her eyes. "If you'd walked out of my life, carrying my child—" He shook his head. "I think I would have gone *loco*!" They clung to each other again, and then Luke stood and continued dressing. "Are you coming down to the creek to wash up?"

Wrinkling her nose, she nodded. "I guess so. I'll bet it's iced over!" she added with a shudder.

"I reckon you're right," Luke agreed with a smile. "Before we leave, we'll say good-bye to my grandfather. I'll see if Flattens-Grass can find you some warmer clothes to wear on the way to the Shadow S. If we set out today, there's a good chance we can make it back to the ranch before winter sets in. Another week or so, there'll be blizzards and heavy snow, and we'll be forced to stay here until the spring."

"The sooner we reach the Shadow S the better!" she agreed. She frowned, her mind still on what he had said about going *loco* if she had left him, along with their child. "But . . . could we go by the fort on the way? There's—there's someone I have to say good-bye to."

He frowned but nodded. "If it's so important to you, we'll go there, Promise. But . . . folks are likely to shun you when you go back there after spending the night with me. I don't want to see you hurt, *desperada*."

"Do you think I care about what they say, Luke?" she asked huskily, rising from the buffalo robes and padding barefooted to his side. "It's my life, not theirs."

He nodded. "Then we'll go to Fort Lyon first," he agreed. He bent down and ducked through the tipi opening. "Come on, Promise! Last one in is a skunk!" he teased.

She went to the opening and peered out, withdrawing her nose sharply as an eddy of cold air swirled about the tipi. "Any one in is a *frozen* skunk!" she grumbled before reaching for her clothes. Luke's laughter reached her as he strode down to the icy creek.

She rode into Fort Lyon before Luke on his blue roan, dressed in a shift of fringed white buckskin decorated with blue and yellow beads. She wore knee-length fringed moccasins on her feet and was wrapped warmly in a magnificent robe of ermine pelts, black tips left dangling all about the hem. Her hair was braided in two long plaits that reached down past her breasts. She felt—and looked—like an Indian princess, and though she wanted to giggle at the open-mouthed astonishment of the fort's population, she remained serenely poised as they rode across the compound, aware of many eyes upon them.

Before the sutler's store, Luke dismounted and lifted her down to the ground. "Go and find Carol and Cay, and have them come here. I think I'll stay here with the horses."

"But why? Come with me! Who cares what people think?"

He shook his head. "I'll wait. There's something in the air here today that doesn't sit right with me." His dark brows came together in a frown. "Doesn't it seem like there're more men about than usual to you?"

"I guess so. Maybe a patrol just came in?"

"Could be. But somehow I don't think so. Go and find Cay and Carol, then let's get out of here. Whatever it is, I don't like it."

The tone of his voice alarmed her. He wasn't the sort of man to make a fuss over nothing. She nodded and hurried quickly into the sutler's. Amos Whittaker's mouth dropped open when he saw her and her attire. He grabbed a hold of the pipe that always jutted from the corner of his mouth just before it fell.

"Miss O'Rourke?" he muttered incredulously.

"Yes, Mister Whittaker. I came to say good-bye, and to thank you and your wife for your kindness. I really do appreciate all you've done for me! I'd like to say good-bye to Mrs. Bushley, too. Could you tell me where to find her?"

Still dazed, Whittaker nodded. "She and Cay Cantrell took a walk down to the corral. They left a few minutes ago. What in the world are you all dressed up like that for, girl?" He spat into the brass spittoon in one corner. "You look like one of them damn squaws that's always hanging around here. Let me ask Mrs. Whittaker if she ain't got somethin' else you could—"

"There's no need for that," Promise cut in. "I like what I'm wearing just fine!" She tossed her head defiantly and headed for the door. "Thanks for everything, sir!"

Despite what she had told Amos Whittaker, Promise did not go immediately in search of Carol and Cay. Instead, she made her way across the compound toward the hospital quarters and went inside. A guard blocked the door to the room where the Confederate prisoners had been housed.

"I'm sorry, ma'am. I can't let you in. The prisoners are being moved out today. They'll be leaving shortly." He eyed her attire with frank disapproval.

"Leaving? But where are they taking them?"

"Fort Leavenworth, ma'am. From there they'll be moved to a prison camp."

"But I must see Sergeant St. Paul!" she cried.

The guard's expression hardened. "I'm sorry, ma'am. Orders are orders."

She flung about and stormed from the hospital. She was too late! She would never know the truth! She hurried around the corner of the sandstone building and saw the barred window that looked out from the storeroom where the prisoners were being held. Without hesitation, she ran to it and looked inside. All three men were there. Their wrists were shackled, and there were irons about their ankles. They wore their gray coats in preparation for the journey as they sat dispiritedly upon their cots.

"Colonel Fontaine!" she cried loudly through the window and gasped as the man who had called himself John St. Paul turned smartly in her direction. Dear Lord, it *was* him! she realized, shaken to the core.

Quickly, he masked his expectant expression and raised his eyebrows. "Colonel Fontaine? We have no one of that name here, Miss O'Rourke." His green eyes, so like her own, were guarded.

"I think you do, sir," Promise insisted. "You're Courtney Fontaine! I saw the expression on your face when I called your name."

"No, you're mistaken, Miss—"

"You don't have to pretend, not with me!" she whispered fiercely. "I'm not a spy! I don't care what your rank is, or what commanding officer you served under, or about anything like that!" She drew a deep breath. "I—I just wanted to tell you that I'm Mary Haverleigh's daughter."

His face paled. "What? Mary's daughter? My Mary's?"

"That was her name, then—the Yankee girl you lost your heart to?"

"Yes!" he breathed. "But how—"

"She told me all about you, sir. She never stopped loving you, not until the day she died! Her—her very last words were of you."

"Then she's dead?" His shoulders sagged. "When?"

"This last summer, sir," she whispered and saw him nod.

"I went back, you know, to her home, but . . . she'd gone. I loved her, Miss O'Rourke! I wanted her to be my wife. I searched for her, but I never found her, and in the end I went home and married the woman my father had chosen for me." His tone was bitter, and his fingers were clenched around the bars of the window. "I should never have stopped searching!" he added and looked up, into Promise's face. A growl of anguish tore from his lips as he looked into green eyes that were the mirror image of his own. "Dear God! Mary's daughter—and mine?"

She couldn't speak, could only nod her head as the tears streamed down her cheeks. "Yes," she managed at last.

"There's no time," he whispered brokenly. "They'll come for us soon, and I don't even know your name, child."

"Promise," she answered, smiling through her tears. "It's Promise Katherine."

He reached through the bars and took her hand in his. "A child! A sweet, beautiful daughter! I didn't know—I never once imagined—"

"I understand."

"I've so much to make up to you, Promise," Courtney Fontaine said urgently, "and no time to do it. Damn this war! But one day, when it's over, I'm coming to find you, Promise, I swear it! If I live through it, I'll be coming back. Where will you be?"

"New Mexico. I'll send word to the blacksmith, Henry Crowley, in Cherry Creek, north of here, when I'm settled. He'll tell you where to find me!" she promised breathlessly.

Courtney Fontaine nodded. He drew her hand to his

lips and kissed it. "They're coming for us now, my dear. We'll be leaving soon. God bless you, child!"

"And you, sir!" she whispered fervently.

She watched through the window as Union soldiers marched the three men outside to join the ragged, small party of other rebel soldiers who had been billeted in the corral under threadbare tents. All too soon, the order was given to march, and the little formation set off. The cold wind chilled the tears on her cheeks as she watched them go, and she raised her hand to wave when her father saluted her in farewell as he passed. There were tears in his eyes, too, she saw. She turned away, feeling deeply shaken. Another minute, just one, and she would have been too late to tell him! She said a fervent prayer for his safety as she ran back toward the sutler's.

Outside the store again, she saw that Carol and Cay had returned from their walk and were talking to Luke. She hurried across to the three.

"—and the corral's full of horses. Some of them look like they've traveled a few miles, too!" Cay was saying. "Chivington's in command. He and the Colorado Third Regiment have been marching along the Platte River, opening up the trail that was closed there earlier on account of the Indian hostilities. They arrived here from Denver this morning."

"Denver? But there's at least two feet of snow on the trail from there! Only a fool would force his men through that," Luke argued. He paused thoughtfully. "Or someone with very pressing business to tend to?" He raised his eyebrows, and Cay nodded.

"Just what I was thinking, Luke. Can't find out anything for sure. Chivington's ordered his men to keep their mouths shut about whatever it is they're up to. But I will say this: Major Anthony seems mighty glad to see him! I hate to say it, Luke, but I do believe all this has something to do with the winter campaign against the Indians that was rumored earlier this year."

"I think you're right," Luke agreed grimly. "I think I'd best ride back to Black Kettle's village and tell them to be careful."

"I thought your mother's people were under military protection?" Cay queried.

"They are," Luke acknowledged. "But it wouldn't hurt to warn them. Chivington's reputation as a man who's determined to subdue the Indians makes me wonder if he might not overlook the fact that the Cheyenne, and the Arapahoes with them on Sand Creek, are friendlies. They came to Fort Lyon and put themselves under military protection according to Governor Evans's own proclamation!"

"Hell, they'd be sitting ducks!" Cay exclaimed.

"They would." Luke turned to Promise at his side. "Mount up, honey. We have to leave right away!" he ordered. Pale and worried now, she nodded and he lifted her up onto the blue roan's back, grasping the reins and swinging up behind her.

"Good-bye, Carol, Cay! Good luck!" Promise called over her shoulder.

"And to you!" Carol called back, forcing a smile. "Come and look us up next time you're up Denver way!"

"We will! Good-bye!"

Luke kicked the roan into a trot as they crossed the compound, headed for the gates. As they reached them and made to ride on through, the guards there sprang forward, rifles in hand, blocking their exit.

"No one comes in, and no one leaves!" the young corporal yelled. "Now, you an' yer squaw get on down from that horse, else we'll have ter shoot yer! Major

537

Chivington's orders!" He cocked his rifle, and Promise gasped in fright.

"I've got a ranch down by Santa Fe," Luke said calmly. "I'd planned to ride out today, hoping to get there before the winter sets in. Me and my woman aren't looking for any trouble."

"An' you won't find none, if you do as we say." He sniggered. "And nor will that yeller-haired squaw ridin' with you! Now, get on down, damn yer red hide!" He jerked his rifle barrel toward Promise. "If not, she gets it first!"

The other guard suddenly shoved back his cap and grinned nastily up at Promise. "An' if old Sam here misses, *I* won't!" he threatened.

Promise found herself looking down into Todd Plimmer's leering face. She opened her mouth to retort, but Luke nudged her in the ribs to silence her.

"I guess orders are orders," he said and wheeled the roan's head around, urging him back across the compound toward Carol and Cay, who were watching with anxious expressions.

"What in the hell is happening?" Cay growled, grabbing Luke's horse's bridle as it slid to a halt alongside them.

"Seems the guards have orders to stop anyone from leaving or entering the fort," Luke said grimly. "Now I know they're up to no good! Get down, Promise. Cay, look after her for me 'til I get back, will you?" The two men's eyes met in understanding.

"That goes without saying, Luke," Cay said gruffly. "Good luck!"

"No! Take me with you! I'm not afraid! God, Luke, don't go!" Promise cried as Luke firmly lifted her down from his horse's back and into Cay's arms.

"Hush, now, Promise. We don't want those fellows at the gate to suspect anything, do we?" Cay said, his tone urgent. "If you make a fuss, they'll know he's up to something."

Sobbing quietly, she nodded and ceased fighting Cay's hold on her. She watched as Luke swung his horse around to face the gates, then tensed as he lashed the reins cruelly across its hindquarters. The roan whinnied shrilly in terror and pain, and reared up on its hind legs briefly before bolting forward.

"Hiyaah!" Luke yelled, lashing it to even greater speed.

They neared the gate, thundering across the compound, sparks of ice flying as the lightning-swift hooves of the racing horse struck the hard, frosty earth.

Too late, the now relaxed sentries at the gate realized Luke's intent. They sprang to block his path, leaping hurriedly to either side as it dawned on them that he meant to run them down if they didn't get out of his way. Scrambling to their feet, they belatedly raised their rifles to their shoulders and began firing. As he passed them, Luke hung down under his horse's neck, Cheyenne fashion, and the bullets whistled harmlessly overhead. The sentries cursed and roared for the bugler to sound the alarm, firing over Luke's racing horse as he exploded through the gate and out into the barren countryside beyond.

Soldiers came pouring from the barracks like blue-uniformed ants. A massive, bearded, barrel-chested officer came striding from Major Anthony's office and began barking orders in a deep, resonant voice that carried like a bull horn. Confusion reigned as men hurried to the corral for their horses, to the armory for their guns, or merely back into the barracks to finish dressing.

Promise leaned weakly against Cay's chest, dimly hearing Carol's soothing voice telling her not to worry, that Luke had escaped. The sentries' shots still seemed to ring in her ears. Oh, how her heart had leaped with each one as it cracked through the morning air! How she'd gasped in horror, fearing each bullet had found its target in the body of the man she loved! Her relief that he had escaped was swiftly followed by overwhelming despair as a cavalry unit formed ranks and trotted quickly from the fort gates in pursuit of him. How long could he hope to evade so many? she wondered desperately, biting her knuckles in her fear. "*Dear Lord, keep him safe!*" she prayed, eyes squeezed tightly shut. "*You've listened to me before, Lord, so please, hear me now! Bring him back to me!*"

"Miss O'Rourke? Miss Promise Katherine O'Rourke?"

Promise opened her eyes to see a uniformed officer standing before her, two militiamen at his back.

"Yes?" she whispered, still trembling.

"Ma'am, it is my unfortunate duty to inform you that I have been instructed to escort you to the guardhouse, where you will remain until such time as Major Anthony determines you are to be released."

Cay stepped in front of Promise, his blue eyes hard and glinting angrily. "On what charge, Captain Pearce? Miss O'Rourke has done nothing!"

"She was seen in the company of a man who later fled from an area placed under military restriction, sir. I'm afraid I have to follow orders."

"The hell you do!" Cay growled, lunging at the fresh-faced, ginger-haired young officer.

"No!" Promise cried, hurriedly springing between the

two of them before Cay could bring back his fist to strike the captain. "Cay, please," she implored him, "just let me go with him. I'm sure this can all be straightened out real soon. Carol needs you by her side far more than I do. Cay, listen to me!" She grasped the angry man's upper arms and shook him slightly. "She's afraid, Cay, afraid she'll lose you like she lost Larry. Go to her! I'll be fine." She forced a smile.

Cay, jaw working furiously, fists clenching and unclenching at his sides in his anger, looked over his shoulder to where Carol stood, silent and drawn. Her face was pale, and her fingers were pressed to her swollen belly .Tears sparkled in her eyes. "I promised Luke that I'd look after you," he said hoarsely.

"I know. But what harm could possibly come to me in the guardhouse?" She smiled again. "It's probably the safest place in the entire fort! Captain," she murmured, turning to the officer, "shall we go?"

Cay watched as the captain took her elbow and led her across the compound, the two militiamen marching behind them shouldering their rifles. He went to Carol and took her in his arms, soothing her with gentle words, caressing her hair. "It's all right, Carol, honey. She'll be fine," he tried to reassure her.

Carol nodded. "She will be—just as long as Luke comes back all in one piece. If—if not, I don't know what she'll do. She really loves him, Cay!"

"I know it," Cay agreed, slipping his arm about her shoulders and leading her away. "I reckon she loves him about as much as he loves her."

The cavalry detachment that had been sent out after Luke returned an hour and a half later. Promise, standing

541

on tiptoe to peer through the barred window of the guardhouse cell in which she had been locked, searched the body of men for Luke's face but could not find it. Her heart lurched in her breast, and for a second or two she came close to fainting from sheer dread. Her relief was only marginal when she saw Luke's blue roan at the rear of the column. That the animal had been ridden hard was obvious by its dispirited gait and the way it carried its head low, with ears flicked back. The sick feeling jolted through her again as she saw that Luke had been slung across his horse's back, his hands lashed to his feet under its belly. He wasn't moving.

"Halt!" the captain ordered. "Sergeant Lee, cut the prisoner down and see him lashed to the flagpole."

"The *flagpole*, sir?" Sergeant Lee queried, hoping he had not misheard the Captain. He rubbed the purpling bruise on his cheekbone. Hanging would be too bloody good for that half-blood, to his mind. Packed one heck of a punch, he did, as Jed Lee could testify only too well! He'd fought like a pack of damned savages before they'd laid him out cold, he had. "Are you sure you meant the flagpole, sir?" he repeated.

The captain fixed a frosty eye on the sergeant. "You heard what I said, Lee!" he bellowed. "See to it! I mean to make an example of this man, to deter others from attempting to leave the fort. Lieutenant, see that my horse is watered and rubbed down." The captain dismounted and strode into Major Anthony's office.

Promise watched as they cut Luke from his horse and dragged him across the ground to the flagpole of cottonwood poles lashed together that stood in the center of the compound. Even from this distance, she could see the livid bruises on his face. A soldier came with a bucket of water and threw it at the prisoner's face. He gasped and came to, flicking his head to rid it of water. Then he was made to stand. Before he had reached his feet, another soldier wrenched his hands up behind him and pulled him roughly backward, tying him to the flagpole. His ankles were also securely fastened. He raised his battered face and looked without expression toward the fort gates.

Sergeant Lee chuckled. "There, Injun! You don't look so damn fierce now, do you?"

Todd Plimmer, who was still smarting from the severe reprimand he had received for failing to halt Steele when he thundered from the fort, strolled across to the flagpole and grinned at Luke. "I'd say he don't look fierce at all, Jed! Fact is, he looks sort of tame!" He eyed Jed Lee craftily. "Still, I wouldn't take no chances, Jed, not with this one here. Knows all sorts of sneaky Injun tricks, he does. Got himself a taste for white women, and all. That bitch in the guardhouse and me was plannin' to get ourselves wed, when he came along an' ruined her," he lied.

"You don't say!" Lee exclaimed. He gripped Luke tightly by the chin and jerked his head sideways. "That true, redskin?"

Luke said nothing. Todd Plimmer laughed.

"It's true, all right. Don't make no nevermind, though. I found out just in time what kind of a woman Miss High-and-Mighty Promise was—a two-bit tramp who'd been running around with half the men in town!" He walked up to Luke and shoved his face inches in front of his. "Ain't that so, Luke, old pal?"

The nerve in Luke's temple throbbed wildly, and the arrow-shaped white scar there showed silver against the tan and bruises. Muscles in his jaw worked violently with the effort to stay silent. Behind him, his fists strained against the rope until the veins in his neck bulged like taut blue cords with the effort.

Todd brought up his rifle and lodged the barrel under Luke's chin. "Answer me, redskin!" he snarled. "Ain't it true your *squaw* ain't nothing but a two-bit whore? Maybe I'll have me some of that real soon—*ah*! Goddamn you!" He reeled away as Luke spat full in his face.

Luke smiled, yet his eyes were as cold and black as obsidian. "Tell the truth, Plimmer," he said softly. "She saw you for what you were—a no-good yellow belly, with nothing better to do than try to force yourself on women with no men to defend them!"

Todd's lips twisted in an ugly smile. He brought back his rifle butt and slammed it hard into Luke's belly. "Yellow belly, huh?" he jeered. "Let's see how you like talking back with my rifle in your gut!"

"Sergeant Lee! Private Plimmer! You're wanted in Major Anthony's office, on the double!" barked Captain Pearce. "Send a man to guard the prisoner."

"Yessir!" the two men said simultaneously, saluting before they hurried off to do Pearce's bidding.

Promise sank down to the rough pine bunk in the cell, her fingernails gauging the flesh of her palms in her anger and misery. "Oh, Luke, I've got to help you!" she whispered, pressing her burning cheek against the cold sandstone wall of the cell. "But how?"

Chapter Thirty-Two

Yellow Rock's breath poured from his nostrils like twin spirals of smoke as he labored to clamber up the rocks, to the highest point of the sandstone cliffs that looked down across the Smoky Hill and, in the distance, the Sand Creek.

Although the ice gave a slippery coating to the rocks, the old *shaman* climbed with an agility that belied his years and the fragility of his body, silently intoning again and again the sacred words that would bring about a successful conclusion to this vision-seeking quest—his last, he knew, before he took the star-path to the home of the Wise One Above. Despite the cold, he wore no clothing other than a short breechclout and moccasins, no decorations in his hair as it furled in the wind. Instead, he had painted himself with sacred white clay and carried a sacrificial offering of tobacco and his medicine rattles with the bear claws that had always proved powerful on past quests such as this. For two days he had fasted, eating and drinking nothing. Then this morning he had left the camp while it was yet dark, purified himself in a sweat lodge, and then again consecrated his body in the smoke of a fire made of pine needles and sage. Ready at last, he had begun the long walk and the difficult climb to the highest peak for many miles, where he would be closest to the One Above. The place he had chosen was not without risks. Here the great mountain lion lived. Here the mighty bear was known to come, to ask wisdom of the Great Spirit. Yet Yellow Rock was not afraid.

At the highest peak he halted and stood upon a narrow ledge, looking down at the barren, wintry terrain that swept away in all directions below. The gray sky was suffused with pale yellow now, as a feeble sun gave forth wan light and bade his wife, the Old Woman, the moon, return to her lodge. The wind was cold and whistled about the sandstone cliffs like the sounds from a bone flute. Yellow Rock removed his rattles from the medicine bag in which he had carried them and placed them reverently on a natural bed of flat rocks at his feet. Then he filled the pipe he had brought with him with the sacrificial offering of tobacco and offered the sweet-scented smoke to heaven and earth and the four winds. Thus prepared, he stood very still, naked and erect, and began to chant. The chant had no words, was simply a sound repeated over and over, yet by it Yellow Rock would attain the vision state, a oneness with all things and their source, the Wise One Above.

For many hours he stood there, motionless, his moving lips the only indication that he yet lived. But it was not until the sun had ridden across the heavens and had almost reached his lodge beyond the mighty blue water in the west that the vision Yellow Rock had asked for was granted him.

All at once, he felt removed from his mortal body and seemed to be slowly spinning from it, whirling into space. A sound like that of a mighty, roaring wind filled his ears, and the light which was the Wise One Above dazzled his eyes with its brilliance. As if he had exited from a long tunnel, he found himself floating above the beloved Earth Mother, looking down upon her and her children. Like the hawk, he glided through the heavens, riding on the wind. Below, he saw the camp of his people upon the banks of the Sand Creek. Frost silvered the bushes and feathered the grass and the cold, cold earth. He saw the children playing; he saw the young boys racing their ponies; he saw the braves carving bows of willow and fine feathered shafts for the hunt; he saw the women fleshing buffalo robes and at their beadwork. All was good. The People were happy and contented. As he soared above them, Yellow Rock smiled, feeling warmth within and about him to see them so.

But then, he sensed something dark coming toward the camp, something that had the great size of a herd of humpbacks, yet it could not be seen clearly now, for it was almost dark about the camp. Closer it came, this something that could not be named, and from within it Yellow Rock saw a rider separate from the rest, a rider coming slowly toward the camp dressed all in robes of red and black. He was mounted on a pony the color of the night. When this rider lifted his head and looked up to where the soul of Yellow Rock hovered, the old *shaman*'s spirit gave a great shudder, for he found himself looking into a yellowed skull. Behind the rider, Yellow Rock now saw a vast host of spirits, following Death upon his night-black pony like a great war party bearing down upon the camp of the *Tsis-tsis-tas* . . .

A mist obscured the old man's vision then, a mist like the damp gray mist of early morning, yet through it could be heard the crying of little babies, the screams of frightened women, the wailing of lost children. When Yellow Rock looked again, the village lay in ruin! The bodies of the people lay broken on the ground. The icy creek ran red with blood. All about, the bluecoat soldiers of the white men violated and abused those whom Death had marked as his . . .

Yellow Rock returned to his waking state trembling, as though a violent ague gripped his body.

He had been granted a vision, as he had requested of the Wise One Above, yet its revelations had filled him not with the peace and serenity to face his approaching death but with dread and a deep sorrow. He had not seen himself in the ruined village. He knew that his time must be very near now. He had been given a sacred duty to warn the people of Black Kettle's village of what was to befall them, and he must hurry to do so before it was too late!

As he clambered back down the slippery cliffs, the years that before had rested so lightly upon his bony shoulders were now as heavy as the rocks themselves. It was as if a cruel fist had fastened over his heart and squeezed it, and the pain brought tears to his old eyes, tears that numbed like snowflakes on his seamed cheeks in the bitter wind. Knees trembling now with fatigue, he began the long walk back to the Cheyenne village upon the banks of the Sand Creek.

When he reached it, it was almost dark, and all was as he recalled at the start of his vision. The children were playing. The young boys were racing their ponies through the dusk. The women were singing happily as they prepared the evening meal or fleshed the buffalo skins the hunters had provided a few suns before. He stood silently and watched the peaceful scene, loath to disrupt it with portents of death and destruction. At length, he sighed heavily and walked to the tipi of Black Kettle, his chief.

When he left again much later, he was more numb than even the snows of winter could numb a man. Moreover, his numbness was mixed now with a deep shame. He, Yellow Rock, respected *shaman* of the village, had failed! He had betrayed the sacred duty entrusted to him by the Wise One Above to warn the people of what was to be, for they had not believed him. The elders of the village had listened and considered what he said. The few war chiefs and young men of the village had politely asked questions concerning his vision. The younger *shamans* had hidden fond smiles behind their hands, and nodded with their heads while denying in their hearts the truth of what he had told them.

"No, my old friend," Black Kettle had decided at length, after conferring with his advisors and passing a pipe amongst the gathering to aid the wisdom of their decision, "what you have seen cannot come to pass. We have obeyed the orders of the white chiefs. We have promised to help them in fighting other tribes who do not wish peace. We have made our village here, as they demanded, so that all white soldiers will know that we are not for war, but under their protection. What your vision has told you will never be! Go back to your lodge, old friend. Warm yourself by the fire. Eat and rest. This winter will be one of peace and comfort for all of us."

And so, he had left. He had done all that was in his power to do. What would come to pass was now in the hands of the Wise One Above. With all his heart, he prayed that the vision had indeed been false.

"Corporal Smith? I'm Private Plimmer. Captain Pearce sent me to relieve you."

"Not before time, neither," Corporal Smith rejoined

549

with a grin. "I was afraid I was going to miss that game of poker me and the boys had planned for the barracks tonight. Damn if I don't feel lucky!" Corporal Smith put on his cap and shouldered his rifle. "Don't expect much in the way of conversation from her," he added, jerking his head toward the cell where Promise sat. "Silent as a grave, she is!"

"Well, we'll have to see what we can do about that, won't we, honey?" Todd said, winking at Smith. "Say, friend, don't be surprised if you don't get that game of poker tonight. Word has it you're moving out by dusk." He tapped the side of his nose. "Very secret mission, courtesy of old Chivington himself!"

"Christsakes!" Smith cursed. "Can't that old war-horse hang up his boots for one night? It's freezing out there!"

"'Fraid not, friend. He's getting a mite riled up about the Third. Thinks everyone's laughing behind his back on account of the regiment being raised to fight Injuns and hardly drawing blood since it was started. Most of us have almost completed our hundred days in the militia, too." He chuckled. "They're calling us the Bloodless Third!"

"Huh. You don't seem too upset by it," Smith commented, buttoning on his coat.

"I ain't! I only signed on for the hell of it and to shut my father up!" Todd Plimmer rejoined. He sat down and propped his feet up on the desk before him, arms clasped behind his head. "Ah, this is the life!"

Corporal Smith scowled as he went to the door. "Don't get too comfortable, Plimmer. If the Third's moving out tonight, you'll be freezing your backside off with us, 'stead of staying here all warm and cozy!"

"Nope, not me," Plimmer retorted. "See, Captain

550

Pearce was a mite perturbed about that half-breed getting past Lee and me at the gate. He restricted me to the post for forty-eight hours and put Jed Lee on report, seeing as he was ranking officer." He grinned. "Have fun, Smith, old friend."

With a snort, Corporal Smith left the guardhouse.

Todd Plimmer turned to look over his shoulder to where Promise sat silently on the pine bunk in her cell. "You see, honey," he drawled, "I fixed it so we could be all alone, like I knew you'd want!"

Promise tensed after Todd's ominous statement, but to her surprise, he made no move in her direction, and as the dreary hours ticked monotonously by, marked off by the round, wooden clock that hung on the guardhouse wall, the tension eased. She had been silly to fear Todd would try anything, she decided. He wouldn't dare, not in his position as a soldier.

From time to time, she went to the barred window and stood on tiptoe to peer out. Luke still stood lashed to the flagpole, yet he did not appear cowed. He held himself erect, gazing toward the gate as if the sheer force of his will could cause it to fly open. But she knew how it felt to be bound and helpless, understood the futile rage that would be torturing Luke, and her heart went out to him. How many hours had he been forced to stand there that way, without food or water, hands painfully tied behind him, in the bitter cold of the compound? It was almost dusk, so it would have to be at least eight hours! As she watched, she saw uniformed men come pouring from their quarters, horses brought at a run from the corrals. There were hundreds of troops she realized. It appeared almost all of Fort Lyon's hundred or so men were there, not to mention the several hundred Chivington had brought with him. He was striding about barking orders, and even from this distance, she could hear the excited edge to his tone, the anticipation. *He enjoys it; he enjoys the killing and the fighting*, she realized, and she wondered that this man who had once been a minister, could take such pleasure in the slaughter of his fellow man. She shivered. On the few brief occasions she had seen Chivington, she had thought that his eyes burned with a strange, heated glow. She knew now what that glow was: the burning conviction of a fanatic. She watched as he swung stiffly into his saddle—a massive, impressive man in his tailored blue uniform—and gave the order to move out. Shortly after, the troops trotted their horses from the compound, once more leaving Luke a solitary figure beneath the flagpole.

She whirled about at a sharp clanging sound behind her and saw Todd Plimmer hanging onto the cell bars, a club in his hand which he was running along them. The sound set her teeth on edge.

"Well, well, honey! I reckon we're about as alone now as we're ever going to be here, don't you?" he said softly, eyes flickering over her. "Say, you look pretty damn good in that squaw's getup, hon! I'd say it suits you, seeing as how you're now a whore just like they are!" Chuckling, he unclipped a key ring from his belt and selected one, fitting it into the lock of her cell door. She didn't move or indicate that she had heard him or was aware of him in any way, and he liked that. She must be pretty damned scared of him, he decided, and he liked the thought of how much more scared she was going to be when he'd finished with her, yessir! He licked his lips greedily as he crossed the cell toward her, taking his time, drawing out the moment in a way calculated to shred her nerves. She'd been so darned uppity that day in back of the *cantina*. How high and mighty would she be this time, with no Luke Steele to back her up and bolster her courage? How collected would she be, naked beneath him, while he enjoyed what she'd denied him for so long? He rubbed his groin suggestively as he at last stood in front of her, and he saw the disgust in her emerald eyes and in the contemptuous flaring of her nostrils as she turned her head away.

"Still think you're too good for Todd Plimmer, eh, gal? Well, honey, you ain't too good for nobody, not since you took up with that half-blood. Does he let you have it good and hot, honey? Is that how you like it, good and hot?" He grinned. "Well, hell, I can give it to you as good and hot as you like!" He reached out and stroked her fair hair. She'd been the best-looking filly in all of Cherry Creek and, to his knowledge, in the whole territory. Since he'd seen her last, something had been added to that beauty, something that made him grow light-headed at the thought of taking her. She was a woman now, he realized, where before her loveliness had been the innocent loveliness of a young girl. There was a quality of sensuality that had not been there before, and his body recognized that quality and responded urgently.

"Take your hands off me," she said quietly.

"Well, excuse me, *ma'am*!" he jeered. "I didn't realize I was touchin' anyone that mattered! I thought I was just getting to know me a little old Indian gal!"

She stared at the wall, ignoring him, refusing to rise to his taunts and insults as she knew he wanted her to.

Her lack of reaction angered him. He crouched beside her and gripped the hem of her buckskin shift, raising it. "Come on, gal, let Todd have a peek at that pretty little—"

She stood abruptly and walked across the cell away from him, turning with her back toward the wall to face him.

"You just can't get it through your head, can you,

Todd? I feel nothing for you, nothing at all! If you were the last man on this earth, that wouldn't change a thing."

"You'll be feeling plenty real soon, Promise, honey," he vowed, wiping his lips on the back of his fist. "See, I don't give a damn whether you like me or not. The choice ain't yours to make. I mean to have you, Promise O'Rourke, any way I can. Don't make no nevermind to me if it's there on the bunk or on the floor, but I'm going to have you!' He took two quick steps across the cell, arms outstretched to plant a palm on the wall at either side of her head. At the last minute, she ducked under his arm and through the cell door. Laughing, he followed her out into the guardhouse office.

"Nowhere to run to, honey, not this time! It's just you and me, little gal—and the only guns here are right where I can reach them," he finished, tapping his hip. "So, why don't you just give in, gracefully like, and take off that pretty dress so I can see what I'm getting?"

She said nothing, edging back so that the desk was now between them. Todd's eyes were glittering with lust. His breathing came thick and unsteady at her in the chilly guardhouse. He reminded her of an animal, almost drooling at the mouth. That he liked this game of cat and mouse was obvious in his expression.

Suddenly, he leaped up onto the desk and towered there, throwing back his head and roaring with laughter as her green eyes widened in dismay. "Got you now, honey!" he crowed. "Any way you move, I can get you easy as pie! Go on, sugar, make a run for it! Go on, baby!'

"No. Whichever way I run, you can catch me," she said dully, shoulders sagging. "I guess you've won after all, Todd." The resignation in her tone was not lost on him, and it was edged with just the right touch of anger, she could tell by the look of pleasure that replaced his wary expression.

He clambered down and sidled toward her, grinning. "I just knew you'd see it my way in the end, honey," he said triumphantly, reaching for the fringe of her shift and raising it to bare her slender thighs. His other arm coiled about her waist and he jerked her roughly to him, his hand burrowing beneath her buckskin shift and stroking her legs. As it rose higher, he suddenly fastened his hot, wet mouth over hers, kissing her with such bruising force she fought for breath. He ignored her struggles in the fierce, relentless grip of his lust, thrusting his hips against her body, heedless of the slender hand that wormed its way down to the gunbelt at his hips.

Moaning with feigned passion, Promise submitted to Todd's kisses, endured his feverish touch upon her thighs as she brought her hand up, up, and alongside his head. As he made to push her to the dirt floor beneath them, the butt of the gun in her fist came down hard across the back of his head. Todd released her and crumpled to his knees, a curse on his lips even as he lost consciousness and toppled forward.

Promise dropped the gun and rolled him over, breathing heavily with a mixture of relief and fear. She drew his army knife from his belt and hurried to the door of the guardhouse, flinging it open.

A chill gust of wind lifted her cornsilk hair over her head as she looked furtively about her. Across the compound, a sentry patrolled the fort walls, a rifle resting across his shoulder. The red tip of his cigar betrayed his position. He was stomping as he marched to warm himself. In the center of the compound stood the flagpole and Luke, his head bowed on his chest with cold and fatigue now. She waited until the guard had turned away, then ducked low and sprinted across the open ground toward him, silently blessing the frigid weather that had left the usually crowded compound empty.

Chapter Thirty-Three

"Who—"

"It's Promise," she whispered. "Stay very still while I cut you loose!"

"How in the hell—"

"Never mind now. I'll tell you later," she promised, sawing at the ropes bound tightly about his wrists. "There!" She crouched down and quickly did the same to his ankles. "Come on! The guard will be back any minute!"

Keeping low, she padded swiftly from shadow to shadow. After a muffled groan as feeling returned to his hands and feet, Luke followed her, moving silently. They made it just in time, pressing themselves flat against the dark forefront of the stage station as the guard wheeled smartly about to patrol back along the wall toward them. Their luck held. Not once did he turn to look down into the compound. His attention was riveted on the moon-washed, barren countryside beyond the fort.

"Clinton Daniels gave up the post of stage master, but he and his wife sleep upstairs," she whispered. "The new man that came to replace him sleeps with the horses, though. They put Sky in here with the others instead of turning him out into the corral."

Luke nodded. He lifted the door latch and pushed it ajar, then stepped inside and pulled her after him. For a second or two, they stood still until their eyes had adjusted to the pitch black of the stables. The scent of hay and horses filled the darkness.

"Stay right here," Luke ordered, edging between the stalls. He whistled softly and his horse whinnied in greeting. Luke, guided by the sound, found him easily. He untied the hackamore from an iron ring and led the horse from the stall, his hand pressed over the animal's soft nose to keep him silent.

A shadow suddenly loomed up from the hay in one corner of the stable and lumbered toward him.

"What in the hell's going on here—"

Swiftly Luke handed the rope bridle to Promise and spun around to face the new station master as he staggered groggily toward them.

"Heh! You can't take that horse! I've got orders not to let—uh!" The man folded neatly to the straw as Luke clipped him under the jaw. In the darkness, he never knew what hit him.

Luke and Promise quickly made their way out to the front of the stage station and Luke held the wide door open to give his horse room.

"Listen now, *desperada*, there's still the gate and the guard to deal with. You stay with my horse. I'm going to try to open the gate. When I whistle, give Sky here a slap across the rump. When he reaches me, I'll be on him and gone before they know what's happening!"

"But why can't I ride him through the gate to you?" she whispered insistently.

"It's too risky, baby. There might be shooting, and I don't aim to risk you getting hurt." He touched her cheek tenderly.

"But . . . we're going together, aren't we, back to the Shadow S?" she asked, her expression confused in the shadows.

"Sure we are. But first, I have to try to overtake Chivington and his men and get to the Sand Creek before they do."

She shook her head slowly in disbelief. "No! They'll kill you if you try to warn the Cheyenne, and I know it! Or you'll be killed in the fighting! You mustn't go, Luke, you mustn't! We've wasted so much time, the two of us. Let's just ride out of here together. By dawn, we could be well on our way, be starting our future together! That new life we talked about would be beginning!"

Anguish in his eyes, he shook his head. "Not until after I do what I have to do, *desperada*. They're my mother's people, and they're in terrible danger. They're my people, too. I couldn't live with myself if I didn't try to warn them. Chivington means to see them dead—all of them! I'll come back for you just as soon as I can, I swear it. Wait for me, baby!"

"No, no," she moaned softly, grasping his buckskin shirt. "You won't come back, I know it! You'll be killed! What about us, Luke? What about our child if you die out there? If anything happened to you, I couldn't bear it! If you truly love me, don't go!" She reached up on tiptoe and kissed his face again and again. "Please, Luke, take me away with you tonight. Don't go to the Sand Creek!"

He untangled her arms from about his neck and shook her slightly. "Try to understand, Promise, I *have* to go." He clutched her fiercely and kissed her lips, his mouth hard and bruising. "Don't let me down, baby!"

With that caution, he moved past her, glancing up to where the guard paced the fort walls, and he waited.

"Don't worry, I won't let you down," she said bitterly. "Go on then. Go and get yourself killed out there—and don't bother coming back for me, because I won't be here!"

Her words fell heavily on the silence as he sprang forward, and though the instant she had said them she bitterly regretted having done so, it was too late to take them back, to say she didn't mean it, for Luke had made it to the gate undetected.

He moved from inky shadow to inky shadow. She held her breath and crossed her fingers as he lifted the heavy wooden bar that held the gate shut. It fell to the ground with a dull thud. He flung one half of the gate wide open and whistled softly.

Sky pricked his ears back and Promise let go of the hackamore and slapped the horse sharply across its rump. Sky lit out toward his master and the gate in the same moment that the guard realized something was awry and ordered Luke to halt.

As the horse drew alongside Luke, he grasped its mane and flung himself lithely astride its bare back. Before even a shot was fired, Luke was half a mile from Fort Lyon, riding like the wind toward the Sand Creek. Fear for his people gripped him as he glanced up at the sky. It was dark yet, but a faint lightning in the east foretold the coming of dawn. He had a feeling of dread inside him as he kicked his horse to even faster speed; dread that he might be too late . . .

Heavy of heart, Promise stirred herself enough to retrace her steps back to the guardhouse. She didn't know where else to go. In the uproar following Luke's escape, she went unnoticed.

In the guardhouse she stepped over Todd Plimmer, still sprawled upon the floor, and picked up the ring of keys that lay beside him. Inside the cell again, she locked

PENELOPE NERI

herself in and tossed the keys to the ground beside Todd.
When a soldier came to relieve Private Plimmer one hour
later, he found the usually talkative guard unusually
silent and the prisoner fast asleep on her bunk.

But despite appearances, Promise was far from sleep.
Her heart ached within her breast, as if she'd suffered
some physical wound there. Her eyes burned from her
silent crying. How could she have let him go with those
words? she asked herself time and time again. Oh, what
she would give to be able to change them, to tell him that
she loved him so, to come back safely to her, and that she
would wait for as long as it took him to do what he had to
do! *I didn't mean it, Luke, my dearest!* she cried silently. *I
didn't mean it!*

Morning found her huddled in the ermine robe on the
edge of the rough, wooden bunk. She was pale and drawn,
and there were dark circles of exhaustion ringing her sad,
green eyes. Despite the luxurious softness and warmth of
the furs in which she was wrapped, she felt chilled to the
bone with misery, not the bitter cold of that bleak
winter's morning. It was November 29th, she realized.
Clinton Daniels had mentioned that, Indians and
weather permitting, the stages would begin running again
on the first of December. Would Luke come back after
what she had said, or would she be on one of those stages?

The guardhouse door opened and Cay and Carol came
in, bringing a gust of cold, damp wind with them. The
guard rose to his feet.

"Good morning, ma'am." He nodded at Cay. "Mister
Cantrell."

"Morning, Corporal. We've come for Miss O'Rourke,"
Cay said. "She's to be released right away. Major
Anthony left these orders to that effect." He handed the
guard the necessary papers, which the corporal scanned.

"Everything seems to be in order, sir," the corporal acknowledged. "I'll have Miss O'Rourke out of there in two shakes." He took his keys and unlocked the cell. "There you go, miss."

"Thank you, Corporal," Promise murmured, flashing a grateful smile at Cay and Carol. As they left the guardhouse, she whispered, "Oh, I'm so glad to be out of there!"

"We thought you might be!" Carol said, smiling. "Did you hear the news? Luke escaped last night! They're saying someone cut him loose right under the guard's nose!"

Promise grimaced. "I'll give two guesses who that someone was!" she said wryly.

Carol's blue eyes widened. "Not . . . you? But you were locked up!"

Promise quickly told them both how Todd and his lust for her had unwittingly helped her to free Luke, finishing, ". . . and after he'd ridden away, I went back inside and locked myself in again!"

Cay and Carol laughed, then Cay said soberly, "I'm real glad Luke was able to get away, but I don't reckon he'll be able to overtake Chivington and the regiments with the start they had!" He shook his head, his blue eyes grave. "It sure didn't look as if they had any intention of trying to talk peace with the Cheyenne when they got there, either. They took howitzers, Promise, and there were over six hundred men with Chivington—the entire Colorado Third and First Regiments as well as the Fort Lyon First!"

"So many men?" Promise said, blanching. "But there can't be more than a hundred lodges on the creek banks, and they're mostly filled with women and children!"

"If that's the case, they'll be sitting ducks," Cay said

ominously, and Carol gripped his hand and squeezed it tightly, biting her lip.

It was only then that Promise became aware that they were being watched. They'd stopped before the sutler's to talk, and she noticed now that Hannah Morrison, Julia Oliver, Eliza Daniels, and some of the other officers' wives and a few civilian women were standing there in a tight little knot, staring at her. Some of them quickly looked away when they realized that she had noticed them, but Eliza Daniels showed no such tact.

"So, you hussy! It wasn't enough that you had to ride off to spend the night with that—that redskin! You had to come back here dressed like one of their squaws!" Eliza's eyes gleamed maliciously. "I knew all along just what sort of woman you were. I just knew it!" Hannah Morrison, kindly as ever, tried to hush her up, but Eliza would have none of it. "If you hadn't been locked up all night, I wouldn't have put it past you to let that half-blood escape, no sir! *Indian lover!* You aren't fit to associate with decent women! But those Indians will get what's coming to them this morning, you'll see! Remember what happened on Platte—all those innocent women and their menfolk and children murdered by those red savages. And Minnesota, too! Seven hundred or more good, white people butchered by those red trash! I hope Major Chivington kills every last one of them, and your . . . *lover* with them!" She spat the words, each one like acid dropping into the cold morning air with a sizzle.

Promise flinched. She had grown even paler with Eliza's outburst, but now her jaw came up defiantly and her slanted green eyes flashed. "I'm sorry you feel that way, Miz Daniels, but then, I don't expect you're the only one that does. See, I expect there are plenty of *Indians* who feel as you do about the white men! We've taken their land, we've run off or killed their food supply, we've brought our sicknesses to their villages. Wouldn't we retaliate with bloodshed if the same thing were to happen to us? They're people too, Eliza! They feel hunger and fear, they feel pain and despair, they love their homes and their families as we do. But in numbers we are many, and they are few. We'll defeat those red savages, as you call them. We'll kill and kill and crowd them out 'til there's nowhere left for them to go. Those we don't kill outright, the sickness will take care of. We'll have all the land we want, whatever the cost, whoever is hurt by our greed!" She laughed harshly. "I ask you, Miz Daniels, are we *really* the civilized ones?" With that she turned and walked away with great dignity, head held high, lips a straight, thin line as she kept a firm grip on her feelings.

Only Carol and Cay guessed at the agony inside her, the wounds Eliza Daniels's words must have caused, the pain at the woman's hopes for Luke's death.

After a few seconds of shocked silence, the women hung their heads and quickly found other business to attend to, unable to meet either Cay's or Carol's eyes.

The Whittakers agreed to let Promise stay with them until she had decided what to do, but their reception and attitude toward her was now decidedly chilly. By that evening, Promise had come to a decision. If Luke hadn't returned by the day the stages began running again, she would leave Fort Lyon and head east, as she had planned. Without him, without his love, there was nothing to keep her there. Nothing.

Chapter Thirty-Four

It was bitterly cold in that hour before dawn. The Cheyenne lay rolled in their blankets in the warmth of their tipis, sleeping the deep sleep that such cold induces. Only Yellow Rock was yet awake, sitting cross-legged before his fire, smoking his long-stemmed pipe.

There was a heaviness in his heart, for he had warned his people of the destruction to come, and they had not listened to his words. He knew that the horror his vision had foretold was close at hand. Death was riding through the shadows to visit the tipis of the *Tsis-tsis-tas*, the Cheyenne, even now, and like an unwelcome guest, He would not leave.

Yellow Rock set aside his pipe and folded his arms across his bony chest. He had dressed in his finest garments. He had prepared his spirit to take the star-path that hung in the sky to the land of the Wise One Above. He had said his farewells to his loved ones. Only one thing more remained to be done: the singing of his death song. Even as he cleared his throat to begin the chant that would carry him from this world into that other, he heard the shrill cry of a woman on the silent, cold darkness, and knew that it had started. The hand that gripped his heart and made it heavy squeezed still tighter, and there were tears in his old eyes as he began:

> Only the land may last forever,
> Only the mountains need not count
> The passing of the moons.
> The time of man is short upon
> The face of the Earth Mother.
> Soon it is over.

Flattens-Grass shivered as she stepped through the frost-painted grass to the creek, and she pulled her blanket more closely about her. There was a thin layer of ice upon the water this morning, and she took up a rock and broke that layer before dipping her kettle into the frigid water and drawing enough with which to cook the morning meal.

The sun had barely risen and only a wan yellow haze broke through the black sky of night, shining weakly on the tipis ranged upon the Big Bend of the Sand Creek, where the Cheyenne and the Arapahoe had camped at Wynkoop's orders. Other women were stirring, their teeth chattering as they left their lodges to relieve themselves. Then they, too, took up cooking kettles and headed for the icy trickle of the creek to draw water as Flattens-Grass had. The light was as gray as the pelt of the timber wolf, and the air cut like the sharp edge of a skinning knife. Flattens-Grass called out in greeting as she recognized Red Leaf coming toward her.

"You are well, wife of my husband's nephew?" she greeted.

"I am well, Flattens-Grass. The child grows strong within my belly. He kicks and demands to be born this morning, but I have told him he has two moons more before he may become his father's good friend!" Red Leaf proudly patted her swollen belly.

Flattens-Grass smiled fondly. Such was the custom. If a woman was delivered of a male child, his arrival was announced to his father as the coming of a close friend. If it were a female child, a simple "It is a girl child" was all that was said. Red Leaf seemed certain the child would be male and appeared well and strong in both body and spirit. Flattens-Grass was glad, for she would need strength in both. Though she had long ago realized that she was barren and had been filled with shame and sorrow that she could give her husband no sons or daughters, she had helped at the birthing of many babies. A woman needed great strength at such a time, she knew. Red Leaf would surely be well able to deal with it when her time came.

"What is that?" Red Leaf asked, lifting her head to look beyond Flattens-Grass.

Flattens-Grass turned to look, and something cold touched her heart. "Buffalo?" she asked. "Surely not."

In the dim light, something moved beyond the camp, something big that could not be given a name. Other women around them on the sandy banks of the creek saw it then, and cries of alarm spread through the women. The whispered single word, "*Bluecoats!*" was suddenly on every woman's tongue.

Women ran from the creek, back to their tipis and their sleeping husbands and children. Flattens-Grass and Red Leaf ran, too, to waken Four Winds and Scarred Hand and Yellow Rock, the aged *shaman*. Dogs began yapping as the village was jerked to life, and across the creek the horse herd began milling about and snorting as fear rode the wind.

Four Winds sprang from his robes, pausing only to fasten on his breechclout and leggings and pull a shirt over his head as he quickly left the tipi. Outside, he saw at once that Flattens-Grass had spoken truly. There were two bodies of bluecoat soldiers stealing upon them, one from each side of the creek! Barefoot, he ran with other men to the tipi of Black Kettle, their chief.

The old chief's voice quavered as he bade the braves be calm, not to give in to panic or the urge to fight. "Were we not promised the protection of the bluecoats?" he asked them. "Then why should we fear? Why should we fight? Perhaps these bluecoats do not know that we are friends of the one called Evans, or that we are good Indians." He drew a large American flag from a *parfleche* that hung at the rear of his tipi and carefully unfolded it. "By this, given to me by the white-eyes chiefs as a symbol of peace and friendship, they will all know that this village is not for war." He called for a lodge pole to be brought to him, and when it had been, he fastened the flag to it and gave orders for it to be placed outside his tipi. Then he stepped outside.

Many men, women, and children had run to Black Kettle's tipi when they heard of the soldiers' advance upon their camp. Shivering with cold and the belly-churnings of fear, they surged about the old chief and demanded of him what should be done.

Four Winds exchanged glances with his nephew, Scarred Hand, and saw him shake his head. He nodded almost imperceptibly in the gray light, and the two braves melted away from the crowd, other braves following.

At the perimeter of the throng, Four Winds paused and embraced his wife. Though she had borne him no children, he loved her dearly. In all ways, she had proved the best of women. "Go back to our tipi, beloved one. Gather up blankets and what food can be quickly taken. Go then to the lodge of Scarred Hand, and take his woman and the old one with you. Head for the Smoky

Hill. I will come to you there."

Tears in her frightened eyes, Flattens-Grass nodded. "I will wait for you there, my husband!" she promised before moving quickly away as he had bidden, toward their lodge.

Meanwhile, Black Kettle tried to calm his frightened people. He stood beneath the flag, raised his hands, and bade them listen.

"There is nothing to fear, my people! When the bluecoats see their flag above this lodge, they will know that Black Kettle and his people are their friends. They will not harm us!"

Aged White Antelope, that great warrior of the Cheyenne, went to stand in the icy waters of the creek. He crossed his arms over his chest in a stance that could only be interpreted as peaceful. He raised his face to the oncoming soldiers and waited until they were close enough to hear him. Calmly but strongly, he asked them not to fire. A shot whined through the gray dawn light, and old White Antelope fell.

The women and little children screamed and tried to flee. The braves realized too late that Black Kettle's confidence had been misplaced and dashed to their tipis to take up bow and arrow, lance or rifle against the soldiers. They had waited too long! The soldiers opened fire upon the milling women and children, shooting into the mass before they had time to scatter and run. Still Black Kettle, his wife beside him, held his ground, even as the bodies of his people toppled around him, even as the soldiers surged forward, still repeating that they were friends to the white man . . . Above him, the flag fluttered in the sharp wind.

Four Winds, Scarred Hand, and other braves headed for the vast pony herds and their war horses across the creek, yet they saw that even here the bluecoats were ready for them. Shots rang out, and Four Winds and his companions dived for cover, using what few weapons some had with them to defend themselves from under the tall, sandy banks of the creek that offered a little protection. Women and little ones fleeing for their lives poured, shrieking, down the creek banks to huddle alongside them, yet even their presence did not deter the soldiers. They began raking the creek beds with heavy fire, turning the air blue with smoke and the stench of cordite. Under the hail of bullets, the Cheyenne were slaughtered like fish in a barrel.

Four Winds felt a great despair sweep through him as he saw the women die, the children killed. He snatched up the bow from a fallen brave and nocked an arrow against the bowstring. Then he stood erect and chose his target from the wild-eyed, yelling bluecoats and let it fly. As the shaft sped from his bow, he thought it much like his soul that would soon take soaring flight from his body. His last thoughts were for his beloved woman, Flattens-Grass. His last prayers to the Wise One were for her safety. There was no time now for the chanting of his death song. As a bullet exploded white fire through his brain, he dropped to the earth like a stone.

Flattens-Grass raced like the wind for her tipi as her husband had commanded, snatched up a gray blanket and a *parfleche* of pemmican, and ran from it, down the rows of tipis to that of Scarred Hand and his woman.

She ducked quickly inside to find Red Leaf crouched upon the ground beside the body of Yellow Rock, weeping.

"He is with the spirits, little mother," Flattens-Grass said firmly. "There is nothing more we can do for him now. Quickly, fetch blankets and food!"

As if dazed, Red Leaf did as Flattens-Grass had said. Together they ran from the tipi and along the creek banks

569

in a path traveled by other women, some hefting little ones along in their cradle boards, others struggling with small children clasped shivering to their breasts or pulling older children along behind them. Their rasping breath made great plumes like smoke in the frosty morning air as they stumbled and ran, dark eyes wide with terror, mouths open in silent screams, the whimpering of the little ones spurring them faster, ever faster, over the crunching, frosty ground, slipping and sliding in their frantic haste.

Red Leaf, weighted down by her swollen belly and the blankets she carried, tripped and fell heavily. With a sob, she bade Flattens-Grass leave her and go on, her eyes enormous and liquid with tears as she murmured, "There is pain here, and I cannot keep up. Go without me, Flattens-Grass! Save yourself!"

Flattens-Grass shook her head and grasped Red Leaf by the elbow, dragging her after her. The blankets tumbled from the women's hands and were left behind. The *parfleches* filled with pemmican dropped unnoticed to the hard, dark earth as, hanging onto each other they fled, turning from the trickle of ice-encrusted water of the creek to the west, toward the Smoky Hill.

Still Black Kettle and his woman stood before their tipi. The village was empty now. All within it had taken flight. Only the dead and the dying remained. The camp had become a charnel house. The smell of blood lay sweet and coppery on the air, and red spattered the frosty ground.

"It is no use, wife," Black Kettle cried brokenly. "To stay here is to die! My words of peace have fallen on deaf ears. The white man has answered them with bullets instead of frienship." The lines in his old face were etched as deep as tomahawk wounds, and his mouth was a twisted, bitter slash against its grayed hue. He took his old wife by the hand, and together they tried to run from the soldiers on horseback, the soldiers on foot, the soldiers manning the guns that overran the Cheyenne village.

But the old ones were not spared by the savage Third. Soldiers bore down on them, whooping with the lust to kill, firing at anything that moved. Black Kettle gave a great cry as his woman was shot then hit again and again. She flew backward to the ground, jerking as nine bullets ripped into her old body and stained her buckskin dress with rusty gore. Weeping, the old chief reluctantly left her for dead, vowing silently that he would return to carry her body away for proper burial.

Nor were the little children spared the horror of that day. A small child toddling naked in the sand and wailing for his mother, dark eyes dilated with terror, was shot at and missed. Crazed with fear, he tried to run. Laughing, another militia man declared that he could finish the "little red bastard," and took a potshot at him, cursing foully as he also missed his target. The child, dropped by the bullet of a third man, gave a tiny whimper and lay dead.

The village emptied now, Chivington's Third pursued the Cheyenne and Arapahoe fugitives on foot up the creek beds, gunning down the terrified little parties of Indians who had dug into the sandy banks for refuge. The majority of these were defenseless women and children, for there had been few braves in the village despite Chivington's belief to the contrary. The men had been well disciplined. As instructed, they showed no mercy, took no prisoners.

At about noon, a strange hush settled over the Big Bend of the Sand Creek. The firing stopped. The wan winter sun hung low over the stark land like a bleary eye. Smoke from the gunfire wreathed the creek banks and mingled with the damp, cold air. All the Cheyenne had gone. All the Arapahoe had gone. Most lay dead. Others had managed to flee and were even now being relentlessly pursued into the hills as they tried to drag their bleeding wounded and their old ones and their children after them.

Luke whipped his horse into a gallop and careened down the frosty trail that led from Fort Lyon to the Smoky Hill by way of the Sand Creek Big Bend. He could hear gunfire in the distance and once heard a scream carried to him on the cold, biting wind. He gave no thought to the lathered pony beneath him as he lashed the rope across its back. His thoughts were only for Yellow Rock, Scarred Hand and his woman, Four Winds and his; for all of his people. The camp had not been filled with warring braves as the soldiers had said, but with women and little children for the greater part. They believed themselves safe. *The white chiefs had promised.*

His mouth twisted in a curse as he hauled on the reins and pulled his horse up on the banks of the Sand Creek. He was too late! The lodges had been torn down and ransacked. Bodies lay upon the frosty earth where they had fallen. Soldiers in blue uniforms were moving about, their laughter carrying across the creek to where he sat. There was no sign, anywhere, of any living red man, woman, or child.

A great sob tore at his throat, and he let loose a loud, wailing cry that floated heavenward on the frosty air. His hand clenched over the hilt of the knife Promise had given him, and in his blinding grief he drew it forth and bared his chest, weeping as he raked the knife point down in a sweeping curve across his torso. Another anguished cry, and he slashed again, numb to the pain, for it was as

572

nothing compared to the agony of his heart and soul. Blood trickled down to pool at his belt, but he did not notice it as he kicked the blue roan forward. The horse's hindquarters worked furiously as Sky scrambled down the steep, sandy banks of the creek, fighting gamely for footing.

On the opposite bank, Luke rode slowly between the soldiers. They paused in their mutilating to watch him, growing silent as they saw the expression on his face. Not one made a move to stop him. Not one dared.

He rode between the toppled and broken tipis to the one that had sheltered his grandfather. The lodge poles had been wrenched apart, and the skin covering lay blood-spattered on the ground. Beaded shifts and shirts, moccasins and a cradle board lay broken and trampled a short distance from the tipi, along with Scarred Hand's bow and his quiver of arrows and Red Leaf's little sewing case of needles and beads and quills.

He dismounted and threw the lodge cover aside. Beneath it, the body of Yellow Rock lay undisturbed. Looking about him, Luke saw a gray army blanket bundled to one side, the initials U.S. stamped upon it in black. He gritted his teeth and instead found another more fitting covering for the old man's body, a buffalo robe undiscovered by looters. He spread it on the ground and lay the old man's body upon it. In death, the old *shaman* weighed no more than a child. He fastened the body securely with a length of buffalo-hair rope and lifted it across his horse's back. Leading Sky, he went in search of the others.

It was over an hour before he found Four Winds. His uncle had not escaped the soldiers' mutilation. Fingerless, earless, scalpless, nevertheless he recognized his mother's brother's face and lifted him, bound also in a blanket, onto his horse. Though he searched for much

573

longer, he found no bodies that resembled those of Flattens-Grass or Red Leaf, or even Scarred Hand. Still leading his horse, he walked from the destroyed village toward the Smoky Hill, looking straight ahead and seemingly unaware of the bloody bodies that lay to either side of his path.

"Halt! Where in the hell y'think you're going, you damned half-breed!" one of the soldiers called out. "Bring them bodies back here!" He stepped forward, blocking Luke's path, his rifle in his hand.

Luke halted. "No." He spoke softly, but the look in his eyes paled the soldier.

Sergeant Lee wetted his lips and dared a glance over his shoulder to where his commanding officer sat beneath a cottonwood hiding his head in his hands. "Let him pass, Sergeant," the shaken lieutenant commanded. "Let him pass, I say!"

The soldier fell back and Luke walked on. Others on horseback passed him as they rode back toward the Sand Creek, having killed all the Cheyenne fugitives they could find. But there was something about the tall half-blood's straight back, the glint of something dark and terrible in his eyes, that prevented them from challenging him. As if he wore the magic Ghost Dance shirt and could not be harmed by the white-eyes because of its magic powers, he moved unchallenged and unharmed between them all.

It was dusk before he reached the Smoky Hill. Stars were coming out like fireflies in the murky, gray-violet sky. Pines stood like dark giants atop the crest. All of the Cheyenne that had been able had fled there, and they were camped in the cold night without blankets or food, without medicine for their wounded, without flint with which to start a fire. They lay upon the hard, cold ground, with only brush piled upon their bodies to prevent them from freezing to death in the November night.

As Luke strode into their pitiful camp, Scarred Hand came forth to welcome him, and with him Red Leaf and his uncle's wife, Flattens-Grass. She asked eagerly if Luke had seen Four Winds, the hope that had flared in her eyes with his arrival dying as she followed his gaze to the weary horse and the two ominous bundles upon its back.

"He is dead, my aunt," Luke said gently. "He died with great courage, defending the village with his bow in his hand." He lifted Four Winds's body down and lay it at her feet. She darted forward, a great sob issuing from her, and made to uncover the body of her beloved husband. But Luke caught her about the arms and held her back, for he would not let her look upon her husband's disfigured face. Scarred Hand took her elbow and led her away, but before he could prevent her, she snatched the knife from his belt and hacked off her braids, then the top joints of her two little fingers. Her wails of grief and pain were joined by the laments of Red Leaf as they mourned Four Winds and old Yellow Rock.

They were not the only ones that night who sang the death song, the song of mourning for lost loved ones. As the moon rose high into the night sky, countless shrieks and wails rang out over the Smoky Hill like the sounds of souls in torment. The coyotes tucked tails between their legs and trotted off into the shadows, yelping softly. The wolves raised their noses to the moon and bayed. It was as if the whole world mourned for the more than seventy people—most of them women and little children—who had been massacred that day on the banks of the Sand Creek.

Chapter Thirty-Five

Luke rose early the next morning. He took himself off to a place a little apart from the others of his people and found there a tall tree. Working silently and with reverence, he raised his grandfather's body between two forks high in that tree, far above where human hands could reach it or predators could disturb its resting place. Yellow Rock's feet were turned toward the rising sun, after the custom of the People, and then Luke lashed the robe-bound body securely in place. Here the elements could absorb the mortal shell which had been Yellow Rock; here, close to the sky, without earth or covering to keep it from the creator, Yellow Rock would lie until his body was returned to the spirit form from whence it had come. There were none of the great *shaman*'s medicine rattles to place with his body, that he might have use of them in the Other Side World; nor was there the medicine bag with amulets which he used to heal, or the bonnet of buffalo horns which he had worn to dance away the evil spirits. Not even a bow or a single horse would go with him on the star-path. He was leaving this world almost as naked as he had entered it. But Luke knew that his grandfather had known that this was to come. He had known, and he had accepted it.

He returned then to the little camp. The few remaining Cheyenne were moving like living-dead, their eyes still dull with shock as they tended the wounded who had survived the bitter cold of the night as well as their wounds. Among them, he saw Black Kettle bent over his wife's fragile body, and he marveled with the rest of them as he heard how Black Kettle had gone back for his fallen wife, believing her dead, and had found that despite nine bullet wounds in her body, she yet lived. He had carried her up the stream bed amidst the gunfire, until he had met with a mounted brave preparing to flee. Together, they had brought her here. But few of the great ones, the chiefs and the warriors, had survived. Gone now was White Antelope, who had stood with his arms crossed upon his chest and asked the soldiers not to fire; gone, too, were Yellow Coyote, Yellow Shield, Spotted Crow, and countless others.

"Where will you go now, my cousin?" Luke asked. "You are welcome to come with me, you and as many as wish to come with you."

Scarred Hand shook his head. "No, Tall Shadow, we will not run and hide," he said bitterly.

"Even our brother, the wolf, pauses to lick his wounds before carrying on. Are we so different from our brother?"

"Do the whites kill the mates and the cubs of our wolf brother? Do they destroy his lodges, mutilate his body so that his soul can find no peace? No, Tall Shadow, it is time now, while the women still wail for their fallen warriors, for the children who will never again suckle from their mothers' breasts, to unite and rise up against the white man in a great war and sweep him and his women and children from our land! We will send a pipe to the Sioux and to the Northern Arapahoe and smoke with

577

them in a council and speak of war against the whites!"
Scarred Hand's eyes glowed with bitter hatred. "And, we
shall win!" He clasped Luke by the upper arms, his
fingers digging into them. "Join us, cousin! Join your
mother's people when we take the warpath!"

"I should join my mother's people to make war on the
people of my father?" Luke asked him softly.

Scarred Hand released him. "Ah! Then so be it, Tall
Shadow. I do not envy you the two bloods within you, or
your heart and your spirit which must always be divided.
It is not an easy path to walk."

"It is not," Luke agreed. "But then, no man's path
through this life is easy. We all have burdens which we
must bear. A man must ask himself if the path he chooses
is the right one for him, and if the answer is yes, then he
must follow that path all his days, without swerving.
Farewell, cousin! May the Wise One Above watch over
you in the path *you* have chosen, and over all of the *Tsis-
tsis-tas.*"

Scarred Hand nodded solemnly and Luke left, riding
back down the hill through the bitter cold of early
morning. A single star shone above, hard and brilliant.
The sun revealed itself as a lemon-colored wedge through
a rent in the charcoal sky and the wind was sharp, as if
given teeth to rend the clothing and tear at the body
beneath. Luke was aware of none of this. He hunched
over his horse's neck and urged him back in the direction
of the fort, making a wide circle around the Big Bend of
the Sand Creek. Sorrow filled his heart and made of it a
weight too heavy to bear. He knew that for now he must
be alone, must spend a day or two with grief as his
constant companion . . .

As he rode, another thought filled his mind, and a
single word formed on his lips. It was not a thought of

578

those who had died. It was not a word of hatred or revenge for those who had killed. It was a word, a name, that offered life and love. It was a thought that warmed. "Promise!" he whispered through pale, chilled lips as he rode on. "Promise, my love . . ."

Promise stood before the stables, clad warmly in the clothing she had reluctantly accepted from Hannah Morrison, waiting for the stage that would carry her east. Frost lay sparkling and thick upon the ground, and there was a threat of snow in the pallor of the sky above. Yet even had the sun blazed and scorched the green grasses yellow or shone so fiercely it dried the rivers and the creek beds, it would not have melted the ice within her breast that was her heart. Only one thing could do that; only one man. And he had gone without her. For two days she had waited for him to return to her after she learned that he had not been killed, that he had been seen riding away from the Smoky Hill the day after the massacre. Those two days had been torment. Now, she had forced herself to accept the truth. Luke had taken her words to heart. He was never coming back.

"Ready, Miss?" the stage driver asked, rubbing his hands together and blowing upon them to warm them.

"Yes, I'm ready," she said at length, hugging herself.

"No baggage? Nothin' at all?"

"No. Nothing."

The driver shrugged. "Go on, then, up with yer. We'll be stopping to change horses at Booneville. You'll be able to get down then and have a bite to eat and stretch your legs some." He grinned. "Ain't no fear of us being attacked by redskins, I don't reckon. Not today! The Third wiped 'em out real good."

He turned away without seeing the expression on her face.

Promise accepted his arm and swung herself into the coach. She sat down and settled her skirts across the seat, clasping her hands primly in her lap. Across from her sat Eliza Daniels and her husband, Clinton. Eliza gave a little sniff of distaste and drew her skirts away from where they touched the hem of Promise's skirts.

"What's the matter, Missus Daniels?" she couldn't resist asking. "Being an Indian-lover isn't catching—or at least, I didn't think it was!"

"Jezebel!" Eliza hissed. "Have you no shame, you hussy?"

"None whatsoever, Missus Daniels," Promise said firmly. "See, I don't have a thing to be ashamed about!" She set her jaw firmly and leaned back to look out of the window as the stage got under way.

Eliza Daniels gave another shocked little sniff and turned her head to look in the opposite direction.

The stage traveled west toward Booneville, passing the ranch of William Bent, who kept the trading house on the Arkansas River. The rumbling wheels and the wintry terrain soon became monotonous. Promise retreated into her thoughts, hoping that in doing so the awful numbness inside her would go away.

She had no idea whether she would be able to find Mama's family back East, or if she managed to do so, how she would be received by them. Since Mary Haverleigh had disgraced herself by running off with her father's Irish groom, it was very likely they would want nothing to do with their granddaughter, Promise. What, she wondered, would she do then? How would she support herself and the baby even now growing inside her? She sighed heavily, and the Daniels seated opposite her

580

exchanged smug little smirks at what they obviously considered to be signs of repentance from her.

Angry color bloomed in Promise's cheeks. She jerked her chin up and looked haughtily from the window of the stagecoach, her expression changing to one of disbelief and joy. Her heart skipped a beat, for riding along the side of the trail, heading toward Fort Lyon, she saw Luke. The joyous feeling soared inside her, swelling until it seemed her heart would burst clear from her breast. He had been coming back to her! He hadn't gone without her!

"Stop the stage!" she cried, standing up and leaning dangerously far from the window. "Stop it right now, do you hear me?" She banged her fist loudly on the side of the coach, ignoring the Danielses' indignant pleas for her to sit down and behave like a decent woman. At last, the coach rolled to a halt.

Hands trembling, heart galloping, she unfastened the door and sprang down to the hard, rutted road, still rimmed with frost. Barely had her feet touched the ground when she picked up her skirts and began running, petticoats flying as she raced back the way they had come, after Luke.

"Wait for me!" she screamed. "I'm coming! I love you, Luke. Wait!" Her prim, shabby hat blew away unnoticed as her hair unfurled and streamed behind her like a cornsilk banner waving a signal to him.

Luke heard her wild cries and turned to see her. His heart gave a great leap in his breast. His black eyes glowed with the love he felt for this woman. He swung Sky's head around and galloped the roan back down the trail to meet her, reaching low from the horse's back to scoop her up into his arms even as she ran.

His arms held her close. His lips sought and found hers. They were swiftly locked in an embrace, a kiss, that spoke of all the time they had lost, all the yesterdays that had been denied them. At length, Luke set her before him upon Sky, his arms circling her waist as he held the reins. She looked up and his voice caught in his throat as he saw the love for him there, shining in her radiant green eyes. "I didn't mean it!" she said fiercely. "I didn't mean what I said! I love you, Luke! I do!"

He nodded. "And I love you, little one," he murmured, his voice husky with the emotion that filled him. "Shall we go home, *desperada*? Back to the Shadow S?"

She cradled her head against his broad chest and leaned into his arms with a sigh of utter contentment, hearing the joyful racing of Luke's heart beneath her ear. "The Shadow S or a tipi on the plains—I don't care where we go, just as long as we can be together, always!"

"Always!" he echoed, losing his lips against the windswept fall of her cornsilk hair. "Always. . . ."

Epilogue

Promise snuggled under the colorful patchwork quilt, watching drowsily as Luke left their bed and went across the cabin to get dressed. She admired his lean, well-muscled body with possessive pride. *My husband*, she thought a little smugly. *My Luke*. And she smiled, still not accustomed to the idea that they were really man and wife, even though they had been so for five months now.

Their bid to make it back to the Shadow S had failed. The Cold Maker had come to the Colorado Territory in strength, riding his white pony far and wide and spreading his white robes across the mountains and plains to cloak the land in snow. Luke and Promise had awakened in their camp the morning after their joyful reunion to find a mantle of feathery flakes coating their blankets and hair. Ruefully, Luke had decided they must winter in Colorado and postpone their return to his ranch until the spring. The blizzards that shrieked across the plains in winter months were lethal to men and beasts alike.

It had been his idea for them to return to the cabin beside the Cherry Creek and renew the lease for a few months. He had swept aside her arguments that Hollander would cause trouble for them with a firm promise that he would take care of the banker himself if it became necessary. And take care of him he had. When Luke and Promise had walked into the bank, Hollander's face had lit up—but not in a pleasant way.

"Well, well, girlie! If it ain't my little bank robber and her half-breed! What can I do for you folks today?" he had sneered.

Those had been the last coherent words he had uttered. Before the pasty-faced bank clerk's bulging eyes, Luke had lifted Hollander up by his collar and carried him into his office before releasing him none too gently. Luke had grinned at the clerk as he went to close the door. "I'd appreciate it if you'd tell anyone that asks that Mister Hollander is conducting a real important business meeting and doesn't want to be disturbed," he'd drawled, and the clerk had gulped and nodded vigorously.

Back inside Hollander's office, Luke had raised his dark eyebrows in the fleshy banker's direction. "Now, Hollander, what was it you were saying back there?" He jerked his head in the direction of the bank proper.

Hollander had wetted his lips nervously, eyes traveling from Promise to Luke and then back to Promise again. "I . . . Well, I—"

"Like I thought," Luke had cut in. "You don't have a thing to say!" He'd paused. "In case you decide after we leave here that you do, I'd recommend you think about it for a spell. And while you're thinking, do you recollect a certain deal made with a little widow-woman for her land? Up by Denver that would be."

Hollander paled and nodded.

"I was figuring you might," Luke said, smiling. "Well, listen up, Hollander!" He grasped the banker by his collar again and slammed him up against the clapboard wall. The clock upon it clattered, then whirred and chimed a time or two and fell silent. Hollander's eyes bulged from his head, and his face turned a mottled shade of purple from Luke's grip. "Miss O'Rourke here is going to become my wife. *My* wife, you hear me?" The banker nodded. "Now, I'm a real bad-tempered son-of-a-gun, and I don't take too kindly to folk badmouthing my woman. One wrong word about her from you—just one—and your shady dealings with that little widow are going to be spread out before the sheriff like they were his Sunday supper, *comprende?* Your ugly face will be on wanted posters from here to tomorrow, my word on it! And if you think a half-breed's promise isn't worth a plugged nickle, try me!" He released the banker and the man slithered down the wall to the floor like a dead snake. "When you get up, we'd like the lease to the cabin down by the creek," he'd said then, and that had been that. They'd left with it and hadn't seen Hollander since!

Sarah and Henry Crowley had been delighted by their return once Sarah had recovered from her initial shock that Promise was carrying Luke's child without benefit of wedlock. The blacksmith's wife had launched into wedding plans, and the service and an intimate but lively wedding breakfast had taken place on Christmas Day. Luke and Promise became man and wife in Cherry Creek's small, white-framed church. Henry had acted in her father's place and given the bride away, while the Crowley girls had been her attendants. Sarah had cried noisily throughout the service as if it were one of her own daughters being married. Promise's thoughts had naturally turned with sadness to her mother. Her disappointment that Mary O'Rourke would not be there to play the piano as they had once laughingly vowed she would do was dispelled by Henry's enthusiastic sawing of a merry polka on a battered fiddle while his sons, Hal and

Mike, joined in with a guitar and harmonica. Somehow, Mama could see her now, could see how radiantly happy she was, she was certain. *"I love him, Mama! I love him just the way you loved your Courtney Fontaine!"* she'd whispered as she lay beside Luke on the morning after their wedding night.

Carol and Cay, also married now, had come down from the small spread Cay had purchased to be there at their wedding, and she and Luke had received a letter from them only last week with the news that Carol had given birth to a healthy boy, on whom Cay doted. There had been tears in Promise's eyes as she read that their son had been named Larry after his natural father, and Charles after Cay. She'd smiled at that. Long ago, one night on the wagon train, Cay had teasingly vowed that she'd never learn his given name unless she married him. But she had!

"Are you awake, honey?" Luke asked, coming to stand at her bedside.

"Mmmm, yes," she murmured, rolling onto her back to gaze up into his handsome face. He bent down and kissed her good morning, stroking the outline of her rounded belly beneath the quilt and blankets. She smiled as the baby kicked, and she saw the expression of delight on his face. He wanted their child as much as she did.

"I'll be leaving soon."

She wrinkled her nose in displeasure, curling her arm about his neck and ruffling the dark hair at his collar. "Do you have to go?"

He nodded. "It'll just be for a few days. I should be back by Sunday at the latest."

"Won't you at least tell me where it is you're going?"

"Nope," he refused with a grin. "I've asked Sarah and Henry to come by and look in on you. Don't go having that baby until I get back."

"I'll try not to," she promised with a smile. She tossed aside the covers and rose from the bed, cornsilk hair tumbling about her shoulders.

As she crossed the cabin, Luke thought how lovely she was in the mornings, her face soft and dreamy with sleep, her flesh rosy with warmth. If anything, he found her even more beautiful with her breasts and belly full and rounded from their child. Despite the imminent birth, she moved with grace and took down a warm woolen robe from the hook, pulling it on over her bare loveliness.

"I'll fix you some breakfast before you leave," she murmured, smiling at the familiar expression in his dark eyes. She had feared his desire for her would lessen as she grew heavier with the baby, but he had rid her mind of such doubts in no uncertain terms.

She cooked them flapjacks and ham and a pot of scalding black coffee, and they sat side by side at the scrubbed wooden table, eating and talking. When they were finished, Luke rose and took the rifle and hat from the pegs and left the cabin. She leaned against the porch railing and waved until he had vanished from her sight, then she paused for a moment before going back inside.

Though it was a brisk, invigorating morning, spring sunshine filled the yard and the meadow beyond. The singing of the birds in the apple tree by the steps was as sure a sign of spring just around the corner as were the pink and white buds bursting from its gnarled branches. From here, she could hear the rushing of the creek, swollen with the thaw of the winter snows higher up in the mountains, yet the Rockies still wore glistening white caps in this month of April. She pressed her fingers to her belly as the babe turned, feeling the thrust of a small hand or foot against her hand. "Soon, sweetheart, soon!"

she murmured. It would not be long now, she sensed. Some inner clock that ticked off the days until the baby's birth was winding down. She looked forward to holding their child so much! She had Luke and his love, and soon she would have his son or daughter. It seemed wicked that one woman could have so much; could be so happy! When the child was weaned, Luke had agreed that she could return to her place as one of his *caballeros*, too, and his promise had been the perfect crowning touch to a future that seemed to stretch ahead of them like a trail paved with purest gold.

She was asleep when Luke returned four days later. The evening before she had been filled with a sudden urge to clean the cabin, and despite the late hour she had swept and scrubbed by lamplight until satisfied all was in order. Her surprising zeal for housewifely duties had startled her on reflection, but she had put it down to missing Luke and wanting something to take her mind off his absence. She awoke to the sound of his boots on the plank floor and his calling of her name. A thrill of pleasure rippled through her to see him standing over her, his height and form, his very presence, filling the room. "I've missed you, darling," she greeted him.

"I've missed you, too," he admitted, a mysterious glint in his night-black eyes, a smile of mischief tugging at his lips.

"Come on, out of bed," he urged. "I have a surprise for you." When she was up, he took her hand and led her out of the cabin, onto the porch.

Her green eyes widened with amazement as she saw that the yard enclosed by the white rail fence was filled with mustangs—beautiful, spirited, wild horses! There

588

were paints and buckskins, white ones and black ones and brown—every color imaginable! They were milling about, snorting and stamping, tossing their heads and whinnying in fury at their capture.

"What on earth . . . ?" she managed, looking with amazement into Luke's grinning face.

"They're all yours, woman," he told her teasingly.

"Mine? I don't understand!" she cried, laughing.

"Yours," he repeated. "It's the custom with my people to gift a bride's father with horses when a man wants a woman for his own. Since your father's not here, I'm giving these to you." He held her by the waist and pulled her as close to him as her swollen belly would allow. "If I had my way, there would have been a thousand horses!" he added huskily. "As it was, I guessed you'd rather have me home sooner than later, so I thought these would be enough. There are close to a hundred mustangs here— my proposal to you, in the way of my mother's people. Will you be my woman?"

"You wonderful, crazy fool!" she cried, tears of laughter spilling down her cheeks. Her tone was very tender despite her words. She flung her arms around his neck and kissed him. "I'm already your woman—your wife!"

"Only in the eyes of the white man's law." He grinned. "I don't want to take any chances of losing you again, *desperada*! This way you're mine in the eyes of my people *and* yours. Well? Do you accept the gift of Tall Shadow?" he demanded arrogantly.

Eyes shining happily, she nodded.

They left the cabin two months later. Promise rode upon Luke's blue roan, Sky, with their tiny daughter,

Katie Star Dreamer Steele, tucked snugly in a cradle board hanging safely from the pommel of her saddle. The babe slept as soundly as if she were rocked in a wooden cradle, rosebud lips pursed as if suckling, thick, dark lashes quivering on her cheeks. The jet-black curls that capped her little head were her father's gift to her; her complexion of downy pale gold, her mother's. Both Luke and Promise were certain that no babe born before could compare with their little Katie, whom her father had delivered the morning after his return to the cabin that day in late April.

Before them stretched the endless plains, amber and brown, dotted now with brilliant red, white, and yellow wildflowers. The sky was a vaulting, brilliant blue, unmarred by even a solitary cloud save for where snowy banks huddled like sheep upon the distant mountain peaks. Promise took a deep breath and inhaled the clear, sweet air. They were headed for the Shadow S, headed down a golden trail into the future. "You were right, Pa," she murmured softly to herself. "When you wish upon a falling star, your wishes do come true!"

She swept her Stetson from her head and flung it high into the air with a wild whoop of sheer happiness.

MORE CAPTIVATING HISTORICAL ROMANCES!

THE BEST IN ROMANCE FROM ZEBRA